"Okay then. So, what's your favorite thing to do to relax?"

Oh, I knew the answer to that. I glanced out the window, away from Jess. It'd been too long since I'd had the kind of physical relief I really wanted. If I was going to catch a break, that's the one I'd choose if I was being honest with myself. My thoughts drifted back to a happy memory— Los Angeles and the company I'd ordered there for a night while passing through. It had been the highlight of the trip, by far.

But, I had to ask myself, would I have to keep using paid escort services to make it through? The thought made me feel guilty, but the temptation was already there. It was so much easier to call a service and pay someone for exactly what I wanted, someone who didn't care a lick who I was or what I wanted them to do as long as the money was good, than to be honest with the people I worked and lived with. Their judgment was something I couldn't face.

"Just sleep, I suppose," I told Jess. It was a lie, but one I knew he'd believe. Like most of my band, Jess was aware that insomnia kept me awake most nights. "Need to get me some of that, for once."

Also recommended...

You may also enjoy these other ForbiddenFiction works:

Don't... by Jack L. Pyke
"Don't... open me." Three simple words that tease Jack, taking him places from his dark past. For Jack, BDSM is a way to resist his worst impulses. Yet, the stranger calling himself The Unknown seeks to use that to seduce him. As Jack slips further down into the abyss, two men hold the power to save him. Will it be Gray, the Master who knows Jack's every secret? Or Jan, the first man to give Jack a reason to hope? With deadly ghosts coming out to play, Jack may lose everything, even his life. (M/M)
http://forbiddenfiction.com/library/story/JP2-1.000134

House Breaking by P. L. Ripley
When brothers Kevin and Jesse break into the old Victorian during a blizzard to steal whatever treasure they can find, they never thought someone would be home. Or that the owner would have a fully functional dungeon in the basement. The owner decides it's time Kevin and Jesse learned a lesson about good boundaries — and bondage. (M/M)
http://forbiddenfiction.com/library/story/PLR-1.000169

Song of the Lonesome Cowboy

Lynn Kelling

ForbiddenFiction
www.forbiddenfiction.com

an imprint of

Fantastic Fiction Publishing
www.fantasticfictionpublishing.com

SONG OF THE LONESOME COWBOY
A Forbidden Fiction book

Fantastic Fiction Publishing
Hayward, California

© Lynn Kelling, 2015

CREDITS

Editors: Rylan Hunter
Cover Design: Siolnatine
Cover art: Photos by Patrick at Dreamstime, Alex_Arta and PublicDomainPictures at Pixabay
Production Editor: Erika L Firanc
Proofreading: Kailin Morgan

SKU: LK1-000185-02 FFP
ISBN: 978-1-62234-214-3

Published in the United States of America

DISCLAIMER

This book is a work of fiction which contains explicit erotic content; it is intended for mature readers. Do not read this if it's not legal for you.

All the characters, locations and events herein are fictional. While elements of existing locations or historical characters or events may be used fictitiously, any resemblance to actual people, places or events is coincidental.

This book depicts depicts fictional BDSM; it is not intended to be used as an instruction manual. It contains descriptions of erotic acts that may be immoral, illegal, or unsafe. The characters are not models for the Safe, Sane and Consensual forms embraced by most current practitioners of BDSM. The authors take license with the use of BDSM for dramatic effect. Do not take the events in this story as proof of the plausibility or safety of any particular practice.

For those who live in the dark,
but are fighting their way to the light.

Contents

Chapter 1

Congratulations and Celebrations

"Oh, y'all have got to be kidding me with this. Really? Really, dude? For fuck's sake."

Two people were sprawled over a small couch in the backstage dressing room of Houston, Texas's Arena Theater. You could still hear the roar beyond that cramped, windowless room as the audience scattered. It was a riot of thousands of overlapping voices as they made their way out into the night, or hung around, hoping to get lucky in one way or another. But we were inside, hidden away behind the scenes. The walls around us promised privacy they never seemed to deliver. The sounds of moaning and flesh moving against flesh from over on the couch made me want to get the hell out, too. I'd come into that green room to celebrate the end of a long, good tour with the most important people in my life. Trouble was my best friend had started celebrating without me in ways that did nothing to trip my trigger. It left me out in the cold, alone.

The pair on that couch were so tangled up around each other's bodies, they looked more like a beached octopus than human. Appendages wiggled, reached and grabbed. One of them — the guy — was my best friend and lead guitar player. The other was some poor, topless, random girl plucked from the horde of concertgoers to be taken advantage of for a while. Instinct told me to save her somehow, even if she didn't want to be saved. Mags, my lead guitarist, had his hand wrapping her huge, pale breast, the flesh spilling over his fingers as he squeezed. His careful mess of black hair and opened black shirt in the dim light helped smudge detail, all of that darkness moving over her like shadows. He rutted between her spread thighs, both of them

1

still with their pants on. At least Mags had been kind enough to spare me that much.

I wanted to cover her or draw her away from him, send her home where, hopefully, no one was waiting to prey upon her like Mags planned to. Mags grunted like a greedy hog at the trough come supper time. He gave me a sideways glance and Cheshire cat grin before taking a drawn-out lick over the tip of his date's tit. A jeweled piercing, spearing her nipple, gleamed. His lips pursed in a kiss around the stud embedded in dark flesh and she gave a breathy sigh of pleasure.

"Do you even know her damn *name*?" I asked. "Do you have any idea how disrespectful it is to treat someone like you're treating her right now?"

"I know her name. Name's Sugartits," Mags murmured, fumbling between their bodies, trying to pull his cock out.

"Yeah," Sugartits cried, making me even more uncomfortable. "Do me! Fuck me! Come on, yeah."

Out in the hall, a girl shrieked, "*I love you, Tucker Reynolds!*" My gaze caught on a bouquet of flowers left on my side of the room. It sat on the dressing table. My name was printed on the card. Security would hold the fans back, but it looked like someone else, with clearance, had already gotten through. Would the sentiment in that card be as harmless and heartwarming as that profession of love I'd just heard? Lord, I hoped so.

Mags kept taking advantage of the woman beneath him as I walked over to the table and the flowers. I plucked out the card, slipped it from the envelope and read, '*Congratulations, Tucker.*' It was signed *N. Briant*.

Just a harmless gift from a fan, right? Except it wasn't.

My hand started to shake while the bottom dropped out of my stomach. The entire dressing room — hell, the whole building — had fallen away. All that was left was that damned card, those words, and that name. I could practically hear his calm sing-song of a voice. A wave of nausea swept over me, followed by fear that had claws, scratching at my skin.

I tore the card into little pieces, hearing moaning and my own suddenly-labored breaths. It wasn't supposed to go this way. It should have been a proud moment — our little triumph after a lot of hard work. Our crew, our fans—they were the ones who'd been there with us for the ride. They were the ones I thanked my lucky stars for every damned day. It didn't seem like too much to ask for the band to take a moment together to reflect and appreciate. What good was all of this anyway, if we couldn't step back, see where we were, and be glad? Maybe I should have known that at the end it would always just be me, alone, being eaten alive by the gut-churning, shameful knowledge of what I'd done to get us there.

The pieces of the card tumbled into the trash can, but I couldn't let go of that name. It was a poisonous whisper that stayed in my head. He always found me. He always knew just when to reach out, knock me off my high horse and make me feel dirty again. His little reminders were like the ground falling away, and being left with nothing but thin air.

I knew it couldn't keep going on this way. It had been a long show that evening, more than three hours, figuring in some technical snafus. The whole time, I'd been crying it all out into the mic under hot lights, blistering under their glare which thankfully washed out my unnerving view of the sea of captive onlookers. Usually it was too intense up there to allow any inner reflection. There was no choice but to act, to sing from the heart, to shake your ass and put on the best damn show possible. I'd been performing for enough years to have some practice at bypassing the threat of choking under pressure. But pressure needed to vent eventually. You couldn't just keep letting it build and build 'til you burst. Sharing a moment of quiet moment with my friends was supposed to be the reward before exhaustion and too many sleepless nights made me collapse. But the combined effect of that card and the sight of Mags taking advantage of a stranger instead of sharing in our triumph—it was too much.

Mr. Briant preferred my hair tied back. Always had. With a clumsy hand that was still shaking, I yanked the leather tie from my hair with enough force to rip some right out, while the rest tumbled down my back, nearly reaching my hips. The damn tie had been tight enough to give me a headache, anyway. Blood pounded behind my eyes. My temples throbbed, and with my voice raspy from singing hard all night, I hollered, "I can't do this anymore, Mags! What's wrong with you? We just came off stage, man, can't you just let us have this one

3

moment to be happy?"

"What's wrong with you?" Mags threw back at me, climbing off of Sugartits, his pants hanging open.

"What's wrong with *you*?!" I repeated, then gestured at the noise barely blocked by our closed dressing room door. "Doesn't any of this mean anything to you? Because it does to me. Do you even care? We're not here to get laid, you asshole! We're here to do a job, as professionals, not take advantage of people who look up to us!"

I tipped my Stetson forward to hide more of my eyes when Mags started staring at me harder, puzzled by the outburst.

That's when one of our other band members walked in. From the look on his face, I knew he'd heard the yelling.

"Calm down, cowboy," Mags said to me, then to the other man, "Gray, I've got this."

"Got what?" Gray replied. He only gave Mags a brief glance before settling for just watching me like I might do something crazy. Maybe I *was* crazy.

"It's just a little fun," Mags said defensively, with an uneven grin. "Two consenting adults and all. No need to take offense. It's got nothing to do with the show or whether I care or not. Of course I care!"

I didn't like how they were all watching me, not with how that card was still making me tremble and want to go hide and be alone with my guilt.

"I can't do this." There was a bare plea in my voice, too raw and worn down. The pressure of holding it all together and pretending everything was fine for so long was too much, too heavy. There was a lot the rest of my band could never know about, but protecting them from the truth was destroying me. Jabbing a finger of accusation at Mags, I switched gears and yelled, "He doesn't even *realize*... He just *takes* and he doesn't stop to see or —"

"Hey, let's get out of here, okay?" Gray told me. He came close, laid a hand on my shoulder and stooped down a little to look me in the eye, peering under the brim of my hat. "You're exhausted and you don't need this right now. Let's walk to the car. It's right out back."

I didn't reply. The pressure was still crushing me, feeling like a thousand pounds I couldn't ever shift. But it was easy enough to let Gray, whose real name was Jess, move me, guiding me toward the door and escape.

Mags huffed, sounding a little perturbed, "Look, I'm sorry, okay? Where you goin', partner?"

Again, I shifted the hat on my head and slung a jacket over my shoulder.

"Where do you think I'm goin'?" I countered.

From over my shoulder, I saw he had that look on his face — the one that first started showing up when we were in high school and I'd catch him grabbing the ass of some perky cheerleader. That look said a lot of things, quietly enough for me to interpret as pity and judgment without ever really knowing for sure. Maybe he thought he was braver than me for being able to approach girls and ease across a few lines along the way. Heaven knows I was never able to follow his lead. "Stick around and I'll make it up to you. Promise." He said it like he was doing me a favor.

"Oh yeah?" We locked eyes for a fleeting, horrible second and it made me hate myself a little more — add it to the heap — because part of me *did* want to stay, especially because he wanted me to stay. I hated how beautiful his brown eyes were, his kissed-dark lips, even while he was pawing at some unfortunate woman in desperate need of self-esteem. Mags wore his beauty on the outside, always had. It was his gift and curse. Though I'd seen it all before, so many times, I still wanted to see it again — his cock, how fired up he got during sex, the particular expressions that came across his face — just so that I could put myself in her place in my imagination, erasing her like she'd never been there at all.

Pathetic. Absolutely pathetic.

Pushing out through the door, Jess and I stepped into the hall. I left the door open rather than pull it shut behind me. The people crowding the hall shrieked and surged for us, and for the dressing room.

"Sweet Jesus, he's beautiful," one girl cried. "Tucker! Tucker, over here! Marry me, Tucker! I'll give you lots of babies!"

"Just a quick picture!" yelled another. "Come on, please? Tucker, please?!"

"We love you, Tucker! Your voice is almost as pretty as you are!"

No matter how many times I heard things like that, I was never

quite able to believe them. Such sweet sentiments made me feel bashful. Disbelieving the kindness didn't keep me from wanting to lose
myself in them at the same time. The love of those who saw value in
my music was what kept me going. It was my safety and refuge in the
dark.

But, that night there was nothing left in me to give. The crowd
could have torn me apart and I would've happily surrendered to it,
looking for some peace in the ending. The venue's security team kept
the fans back, making a human wall with outstretched arms. I waved,
smiled, and blew them all a kiss. There was nothing I'd have liked
better than to dive into the throng, dissolving into those people who
cared about me for some reason or other like I was music instead of a
sorry excuse for a man.

There was a collective scream of delight that washed over me
without really touching me at all. The truth about what a terrible person I was kept it back, pushing hope out of reach.

Two girls broke free. Security ran after them, but the girls—
younger and limber—were faster. Never underestimate the power of
hormones on the rampage.

Since my escort kept the girls from getting to us, they took the only
other route available to them. They burst into the dressing room.

I almost smiled, hearing Mags' yell, as well as a stream of colorful
curses from Sugartits. One towering security guy, whom I didn't par-
ticularly recognize, was valiantly trying to pull the girls off of the half-
naked, recently re-entangled duo of Mags and his date. Surrounded
by some more hulking security, I felt Jess put his hand on my lower
back. He ushered me safely through the hall, toward the exit and the
car waiting in the night.

Chapter 2

Handlers, the What-Ifs, and the Real Problem

Country singer/songwriter, too short, too quiet, too filled-to-the-brim with guilt over doing and desiring things I shouldn't — it was the story of my life. Plenty of people made it clear to me that it wasn't an option to be openly gay and be a country music artist. That'd be going against rules that had been in play since that particular music genre had been created. The suits writing the checks couldn't see how a respectable Southern gentlemen who just happened to be queer could charm the ladies and make them swoon. If that wasn't enough, I had to sell the country boys on the idea that my voice was the one worth spending some of their hard-earned money on so it could fill up the cab of their trucks. That's just the way it was. In order to be successful, you had to play by the traditional rules. On the bad days and nights, the isolation and constant fear of being found out was enough to drag my ass down to places darker than the Tennessee swamps on a moonless night. On the good days, you knew how lucky you were and counted your blessings for the chance to do what you love for a living, to perform and be successful at it, and to do so with your best friends in the world.

Magnusson "Mags" Palmer had been my closest friend since high school. Dark hair, dark eyes, tan skin, tall, hard body, square jaw and the epitome of "bad boy", he got all the girls he wanted. He was the youngest of five boys and the Palmers were one of the poorest families around, so being deprived of attention at home meant he acted out with friends and at school to fill the void. In our town, just like in so many others, you could bet everybody knew all the gossip about everyone else. When they saw Mags, they'd just shake their heads saying there goes another one of those Palmer boys strutting around like God's gift when everyone with eyes to see could tell he was nothing but trouble and good for even less. But, underneath that cocky attitude was a boy who just wanted folks to think he was worth something in a world that kept trying to beat him and his family down. Once I understood who he really was — a fighter for all the disadvantaged, and a pure-hearted soul — I learned quickly how to forgive his chronic bad behavior.

We were damn near inseparable from the start, but we made an uneven pairing. I was shorter in comparison. My hair was a lighter shade of brown, my skin slightly paler thanks to my tendency to stick to the shade with a guitar in my lap rather than always being out in the sun chasing chances to get in trouble. It made me the barely-there sidekick with as much ego as a piss-ant. I didn't think much of my looks in high school along with everyone else, but by the time I was gigging, my long, wavy hair and pretty face weren't things I got bullied for anymore and the girls started to come around. Problem was — and it was a big damn problem — I didn't want girls. I wanted Mags.

My voice was my best feature, more so even than my too-long eyelashes or my well-worn-denim blue eyes, though my momma might disagree. It got me booked with an agent, signed to a record label at age twenty one, and enough fans to keep me working and on the road. I brought Mags with me. I knew of no one more talented at wringing emotion out of nothing but strings and wood.

For a long time, life was all about the music. It was bigger than me or my troubles. It reached people, spoke to them, moved them, and that drove me on, the rest of it be damned. To see all sorts of people, from all walks of life, relating to my lyrics and my melodies, was magical. The music connected all of us. It made the tough times seem less lonesome.

But loneliness wasn't the real problem. Mags wasn't really the problem, either, as mad as he made me sometimes. The secret threat in those little gifts I kept getting, like the congratulatory flowers delivered to me that evening, were the problem — one I couldn't ever share with my band.

"This way, Mr. Reynolds, Mr. North," one of the venue's handlers said, walking me and Jess out of the Arena Theater. A few security guys cleared the way. "This car will take y'all back to the hotel."

"Thank you so much," Jess told the handler with a smile.

Most people turned their head at Mags' fondness for sex with the fans. It was far from unheard of, after all, for a musician to want to get laid, especially when out on the road. At least Jess seemed to be as bothered by it as I was. Sometimes that was a source of relief, proof that my annoyance wasn't just a product of jealousy. Other times it stuck me in the awkward position of having to defend Mags' behavior to Jess.

Jess was a studio musician we'd begun working with on a regular basis. We got teamed up with him, saw how well he worked with us and our vibe, and asked him to stick around for good. Gray North was his stage name. For the first couple of years, I didn't know his real name was Jess Grayville. Mags and I both had thick Southern drawls, but Jess was a Northerner who spoke with an ambiguous American accent. With his thick, short beard, impressive build and the confident way he carried himself, he looked more like security than someone blessed with talent at playing the violin and piano. He was just trying to sell the tough guy act, roughing up his image just enough to appeal to the blue-collar country crowd and fit in with a band rather than get stuck in a studio somewhere.

Jess wore a wedding band on the third finger of his left hand, but I never met nor heard much about his wife, even when my band became a regular thing for him and some of that surface glamour faded away. After dealing for so long with Mags waving everyone he fooled around with in my face, it was kind of nice to have someone around who was more like me. That ring did catch my eye on a regular basis, though, shining there like proof of how pure and normal Jess was. It set him above the likes of me and my slutty guitarist, who seemed to be constantly down in the dirt doing shameful things while Jess was a good, loyal, humble husband.

Jess was more than a few inches taller than me, broader, too, with a strong jaw, buzzed short brown hair and a kind face. The only part of him that gave away the fact that he had the soul of an artist was his green eyes. There wasn't anything at all mean about them, and they

9

could look right through you into the shadowy places others might miss. When Jess gave you his patient, curious attention, he was really seeing you, and in ways most people didn't.

The last night of the tour, in Houston, by the time Jess and security pushed me into the car, I was already feeling guilty about my outburst with Mags. Still, I was glad Jess had been there to give me an out when I needed one. We were chauffeured to our hotel from the venue, racing away into the night while Mags and Sugartits probably tried to get back to business in the dressing room.

The streets blurred past, streaks of gold and red lights from other cars and trucks. The streetlamps shone down from above, chasing away small circles of the night. Though the car was warm, the air outside had a bite that felt like winter was trying to crowd out fall and get down to business. The tour had spanned the months of August, September, and October across several states in the deep South where a gust of hot air was a blessing you were thankful for under a big yellow sun that tried to cook you alive.

Rubbing a hand over his short hair, Jess said with a crooked grin, "I hope you know how jealous I am of your hair. It looks good loose like that. I don't know why you'd ever tie it up. On me though, with the beard and all, it'd just make me look like a shaggy mountain man."

With a grin, I said, "Is that your way of telling me I need a haircut?"

"No, that's my way of saying if you see me trying to yank at these itty bitty strands on my head to make them grow faster, don't look at me funny." It made me laugh.

"I tie it up for the heat, mainly."

"Well, if I've learned anything from women, it's that sometimes discomfort is worth the price of beauty."

"Oh, man," I said, shaking my head at him with a faint chuckle. "Now I *know* you've been under the stage lights too long. You better grab a cold drink from that little fridge before the heat stroke gets the better of you. Y'all having a beauty crisis or something over there?"

"Yep," Jess nodded. "I'm about as beautiful as the wrong end of an alley cat."

"You are too much," I said with an amused smile. My mood shifted on me, though, so I told him, apologetically, "I'm real sorry you got stuck in the middle of all of that back there."

"Oh, don't worry about it. Were you just frustrated with him, or what?" Jess asked, adding, "Not that I blame you."

"It's not just him," I sighed, "but it's mainly him. He really knows how to push my buttons. Old friends are the best at that, aren't they? It's just... we all put a lot into this tour, and this being the last night... I was hoping it would be special. We could toast to our success and recognize all of the hard work together, as a band. Then I walked in there and...." I shook my head.

"And he was trying to get into someone's pants," Jess finished.

"Mags just lives in the moment in a different way than I do, is all," I explained.

"You're cerebral, he's physical."

With a grateful smile, I told him, "And you're just a sweetheart, watching out for me. I appreciate you getting me out of there before I could say something I'd regret. There's something about Mags that just greases the tongue. Anything at all could come flying out."

Bypassing the compliment, Jess gazed out the window and said, "Mags has been in rare form lately, never giving you space. Maybe you should try talking to him now, before we leave. Tell him he needs to knock it off, get his own place, his own rooms."

"Mags get his own room?" I grinned. "You really think that's ever gonna happen? You know how long this has been going on, right?"

Jess looked my way and shook his head. His hands clasped between his knees, his golden wedding band catching the passing, flashing lights.

"More years than I can count," I told him. "He was pulling this public spectacle hook-up shit in high school with the cheerleaders. Always a show-off. Always got his arm around some girl he should have respected more than he did, trying to bring her along even as he stuck by me. Then again, he was always the one watching my back, pulling bullies off of me, saving me from all of those kids who loved to pick on me for being small and quiet. He's been loyal as hell, really, once you get past the Casanova nonsense. He's not the thing keeping me up at night, anyhow, and we need him around if we're gonna knock this album out. No way around it."

"That doesn't mean he can't have his own place. Don't you think

it might help you decompress at the end of the day if *that*," he nodded back at the direction we came from, the Arena Theater, "is kept
separate from his job? I agree with you about the lack of respect, and
that is a problem. It would be the same thing if he was an addict or
something. You do that shit on your own time if you don't want to
ruin everything else."

"Yeah. Maybe."

What Jess couldn't know was that I got off on it. I enabled the
habit. Being in the room with Mags when he got it on was as close to
the action as I'd ever get.

Jess wouldn't understand anyway. Once you had a spouse, someone who had promised to love you, no matter what, you forgot what
it was like to be alone and without any decent options.

"If you'd like to talk about the other thing keeping you up at night,
I'd be happy to listen, you know," Jess told me.

He'd caught that, huh? I gave him a small smile but tried not to
give anything away. It was for his sake that I covered up the pain, not
mine. As long as my problem remained mine, if wouldn't endanger
those who mattered.

"Good to know. Thanks. It's kind of you to offer," I replied. "Don't
want to ruin your night with my problems, though."

"You wouldn't be," Jess urged.

"Yeah, maybe. Maybe not. How about we just focus on the
positive? It was a fuckin' good show. Y'all kicked plenty of ass out
there."

Trying to let it go, to leave the creepy nervousness behind with
the scraps of paper in the trashcan, I blew out a breath and stretched a
little to try and relax. Then I saw Jess was cracking open a small bottle
of champagne that had been sitting in an ice bucket at our side.

Laughing a little as he poured some into a pair of glasses, I felt
more of my dread float away.

He passed me a glass and held his up. I touched the edge with
mine, making a light clinking sound.

"To a fuckin' good show, plenty of ass-kicking, and a damn good
tour in general. Tucker Reynolds, thank you from the bottom of my
heart for all that you do," Jess said sincerely.

"You're too damn nice, you know," I grinned, chuckling a little as

I blushed. "Hell, I'm just the singer. I couldn't do any of this without you, the band, the crew, the *fans*. It's a great big joint effort. I'm just happy to share the ride with such good people. Thank *you*, Jess, for everything."

We sipped the champagne. The car sped onward.

Jess cleared his throat and gave me a sly little look. "Admit it; you're looking forward to some good home cooking, aren't you? Come on, what's the first thing you're going to have when we get back? Creole jambalaya? Ribs with collard greens? Fried chicken with gravy?"

"*Oh*, that sounds so good. You're killin' me," I laughed, clutching my empty stomach. After a thoughtful pause, I admitted, "Well, okay, maybe some apple julep sangria with shrimp gumbo."

"See," Jess smiled, laughing with me. "You've thought about it."

"Okay, yeah, I have," I confessed. "We've all been grabbing whatever we can for so many months. There is nothing — *nothing* — like some *real* Southern home cooking. Does that mean you're gonna let me tempt you to indulge with me? We can share the guilt from eating 'til we want to bust?"

"Absolutely I will. You have nothing to worry about anyway. Always have been the skinniest of all of us. But even if you weren't, who cares? You've gotta do what makes you happy. And some of that apple julep sangria you mentioned would make me *really* happy right now."

Sighing a little, I sank back into my seat. I was relieved to be on the way to some sorely needed rest, but unable to shake a nagging sense that trouble was riding me down. Part of me wanted to use some of those wee morning hours, when I should be sleeping but wouldn't be, to get back to writing music. That's when I felt most alive and hopeful, and *man* did I need some hope. Another part of me was just terrified of what that congratulatory card might imply. I prayed it was nothing, that next time it wouldn't be a request for a meeting or an unannounced visit. The champagne sloshed sickeningly in my empty stomach just thinking about it.

"You've earned a rest," Jess said when I fell quiet and started to drift deeper into the dread, enough for it to show. There was a softness to the way he said those words that tried to slip under my defenses. "You're too hard on yourself, man. We've accomplished amazing things. Sales are up. Shows were sold out. The press loves you. Critics rave about you. Fans adore you. It's okay to step back and take some time for yourself now. The rest will come when it comes."

"Yeah," I murmured. I nudged his leg and gave him a half-smile. "You're a wise man, Mr. Grayville. I'm already thinking ahead, more than I should. Better to remember where I am."

"Okay then. So, what's your favorite thing to do to relax?"

Oh, I knew the answer to that. I glanced out the window, away from Jess. It'd been too long since I'd had the kind of physical relief I really wanted. If I was going to catch a break, that's the one I'd choose if I was being honest with myself. My thoughts drifted back to a happy memory — Los Angeles and the company I'd ordered there for a night while passing through. It had been the highlight of the trip, by far.

But, I had to ask myself, would I have to keep using paid escort services to make it through? The thought made me feel guilty, but the temptation was already there. It was so much easier to call a service and pay someone for exactly what I wanted, someone who didn't care a lick who I was or what I wanted them to do as long as the money was good, than to be honest with the people I worked and lived with. Their judgment was something I couldn't face.

"Just sleep, I suppose," I told Jess. It was a lie, but one I knew he'd believe. Like most of my band, Jess was aware that insomnia kept me awake most nights. "Need to get me some of that, for once."

"So, what is it that keeps you up, if it's not Mags?"

I shrugged. "Hard to say. You ever have trouble sleeping?"

"Sure. I'll lay there, thinking about things I wish I'd done a little differently, wishing I'd said things I didn't have the balls to say in the moment."

"The what-ifs," I agreed. "I know those."

We drove on. He was looking at me; I sensed it while fiddling nervously with the cuff of my sleeve. Could he tell? Could everyone tell? I'd always been afraid to ask and wouldn't dare to guess. Maybe they all knew I was queer, closeted, and secretly lusted after my band mate. Maybe they all just played along for my benefit because they felt sorry for me.

"But you're okay, right?" Jess asked gently.

"Yeah, I'm okay," I murmured, without looking up. I didn't want him to see what a huge lie that was. "Thanks for asking. The music is more important than personality quirks or stress. It's fine. I'll do what I need to rest up. If Mags gets out of hand, I can handle it. I know the bastard better than anyone."

"Are you disappointed it's over? The tour?"

"Maybe. Are *you*? I mean, hell. I'm worn right out, but I don't know. Maybe I'm not ready to walk away from it all yet. Anyway, we had a good time, didn't we?"

"Yeah, we did."

I chanced witnessing Jess's pity and glanced over, meeting his gaze. There wasn't any sort of judgment in his eyes, but I wasn't quite sure what was there instead, other than his worry for me, which I didn't know how to process. It felt like he would have been willing to sit there all night, driving around Houston, watching the lights and talking quietly about whatever came to mind. There was no one else around who would have done something like that, just savored the moment without needing there to be an end goal. There was something so patient and present about Jess. It was unsettling, but almost irresistible. There were few good listeners in the world. It was crucial to hang on to one if you could grab hold. Yet, at the same time, I knew he was a good man with a kind heart, and I didn't want to expose him to the danger that was constantly present in my life, the shame that kept me up at night. Jess had no idea that I wasn't a good man, like him. I'd only wind up being a bad influence, or give him reason to hate me. Still....

"Are you available to hang out for a few weeks? I've got some ideas to run by y'all. We could jam, see what happens."

"Absolutely." Jess smiled behind his beard. He looked genuinely happy to be asked. "I'll be there. You can buy me an apple julep sangria, show me around a little."

"Consider it done," I chuckled.

"And you know, I'm always here to talk if you've got something on your mind, no matter what it is. You don't need to try to impress me, Tucker. I'm already impressed, but I could be a friend, too. We're all human. Sometimes just venting a little can help a lot."

"Thanks, Jess," I replied as the lights streamed by. "I appreciate that, and I do consider you a friend."

"I've never spent more than a few days in Nashville, you know. Going in and out for gigs, I never really stayed long enough to enjoy the atmosphere. It'll be cool. Hey, maybe Jovie can join us to work on some harmonies. Could sweeten up the sound and she's easy to get along with. No ego."

Jovie was a vocalist that had stepped in on the tour to sing the female parts of some songs. She was strawberry blonde and Hollywood pretty, like so many girls trying to make it in the business. But Jovie had true vocal talent and the soul to back it up. It helped her rise above the rest. And, like Jess said, she was a sweetheart.

Wondering if Jess was asking about Jovie for his own reasons, like maybe he was sweet on her and looking for more ways to enjoy his time in Nashville, I commented, "Yeah, she fit in pretty nicely, didn't she?"

"Might be a great collaboration. Your voices work amazingly well together. You should give her a call."

"Get some new blood in the group."

"Exactly," he grinned. "Keep things fresh and interesting."

"You're not trying to set me up, here, are ya?"

He laughed, bit his lip and ducked his head a little, avoiding eye contact like I had been. "Of course not. My intentions are pure."

"Yeah, right. And Mags is lookin' to take a vow of celibacy."

Chapter 3
The Next Best Thing

"Howdy. How's it goin'?"

That was the hesitant, cautious greeting I heard after answering the phone. It was like someone poking a venomous snake with a long stick, only I was the rattler and Mags was the one about to get a bite taken out of his ass.

"Oh, y'know. What's up?"

Mags paused as he considered his phrasing before replying. My tone made it plain that I wasn't in the mood for any more of his shit, and maybe it threw him off a little.

He asked, "You, uh, you want me to get my own room?"

Had Jess called and said something to Mags? Jess and I had each retreated to our own rooms when we'd gotten back to the hotel. It was possible that Jess had given Mags a warning if he suspected I'd let Mags off the hook again. Or was Mags just finally getting a clue? Of course, it could be neither, and that wary tone only meant same old, same old.

I sighed. "She's still with you, isn't she?"

"Would I be calling if she wasn't?"

"God damn, man."

"Hey, no problem," he said, backing off. "Just thought I'd ask. Didn't want to assume, have you miss out if you wanted in. You're my boy, right?"

Oh, I was his boy, all right. Sitting on the couch in our suite, there was a glass three-quarters full of whiskey in my hand. I tried to give it my full attention. The smell of it got in my head, tickled my brain. Wondering what the hell was wrong with me, I tried not to immediately give in. Maybe the whiskey could be enough. It could lead me down to the bar, out of that damned room and farther from temptation.

In the past, I'd relied on addictive substances to get me through sexual situations I didn't want to think about too clearly. Realizing I was doing the same thing with Mags only made me feel small and beaten. I told myself I had to be capable of making a better choice, instead of putting myself through hell again. According to my track record of making bad decisions, getting high or drunk before sex typically led to suffering. *My* suffering. And here I was, firing off the same chain reaction with someone who was supposed to be on my side. What the hell was wrong with me?

I'd crushed on Mags for so long, and all it had ever gotten me — all it would ever get me — was that damned uncomfortable, unsatisfying, inappropriate place I was in. Threesomes, watching him, imagining some of our places swapped around, and it wasn't enough. But it was all I would get. I never grew out of getting hot over other men. The music industry told me I couldn't be what I was. The church said god wanted me burning in hellfire, and any bad things that happened were punishment for being gay. And here was my best friend in the world, simultaneously getting me close to my dearest dream, yet holding it just out of reach. If I lunged, and grabbed for it anyway, I'd lose him, too.

I couldn't face the thought of losing him. We were far too tangled up in each other for that. So, something was better than nothing, wasn't it?

"I'll call the front desk, be by to get my shit later," he muttered, sounding like he was giving up. Much to my surprise, it sounded like he was really going to go through with it, for my sake. He wasn't even trying to make a big deal out of it, either. Maybe I should have been relieved, but I wasn't. Not at all. Because if I let him go now, how far might he stray?

There were a few things that were certain. There was no fucking with them; they were simply the facts I had to work around. One of them was that Mags had no idea what I'd suffered through — what I was *still* suffering through. The danger was still out there, watching, lurking, waiting. So far I'd kept Mags safe from harm, but would it last? Was it better to keep him close, keep an eye on the bastard, or get him as far away as possible? It was hard to tell. And on the other hand, I knew letting Mags talk me into another threesome would only leave me feeling like I'd made yet another terrible decision worth feeling shitty about. But I also knew this might be the beginning of the end of my friendship with Mags. We were fighting all the time and avoiding each other more and more because there were just too many damned lies between us, and I was too angry over how much I'd suffered so he didn't have to at all.

Mags was bad for me, plain and simple. Didn't matter. I still wanted him. Hell, I loved the guy.

"This isn't going to be an all-night thing. And if I get even a whiff of a suspicion that you're pressuring her to go through with this, it doesn't happen and she goes home. You got me, Mags?"

The cool glass pressed against the skin of my temple, a small, real sensation to anchor to while insanity ran rampant over my conversation and decisions.

"Oh yeah, I got you. No problem, darlin'," he replied, sounding happy as could be. "I'm glad to hear you're interested. Be up in a few."

I hung up.

"God, you asshole. You're such an asshole!" I ranted at myself, futilely, "What are you doing?"

The thing to do was to leave, to get my good ol' Stetson hat and my jacket, and hit the bar downstairs. It would kill time, as well as put some space between me and the devil with the girl on his arm. That's why I kept sitting there, drinking my whiskey, telling myself I was about to get up, about to leave and make a better choice.

Ten minutes later, Mags walked in, laughing with Sugartits, who gave me a blushing smile and a kiss on the cheek before heading off to the bedroom, hurried along by Mags' firm slap to her ass. Mags shut the suite's door and locked it. He set his black hat beside my tan one, shrugged off his leather duster, and twisted the shirt up over his head. Bare-chested, wearing only boots and jeans, he walked over to me in the kitchenette.

His dark eyes were on me, measuring me, trying to figure me out. It was sexy as hell. I loved to let him look, even if I couldn't meet his

19

gaze, or even get close.

Why did he care, I wondered, and not for the first time or five hundredth? Was it just the money and fame our associations brought him? Was I the one thing keeping him from being a penniless no-body? It didn't seem possible he was so insecure about his ability to make a living on his own, but maybe it was true. It seemed to be his biggest fear, winding up like his parents, or his brothers. Mags would have done anything to keep from ending up with nothing. His dad lost his job a long time ago, and was too proud to keep looking very long for work when he constantly got turned away for being too old. That left his mama paying all the bills on a teacher's meager salary. And Mags' brothers, older and more favored, more skilled at sports and school, never made it out of our old hometown. Stuck there, with limited prospects, they seemed to be on the same path they'd been trying to step off of since birth. It had to terrify Mags. What if the fame didn't last? He had nothing else to fall back on, no other talents or skills. It was music or nothing, which left him feeling one bad turn away from becoming his father.

Did that make me his meal ticket? Was that all I was? Even worse, would I do anything different if I was?

I was leaning forward a little against the counter's edge. It ground against my thick belt buckle, which dug painfully into my abdomen. I leaned a little more so the hurt notched up. The rim of the glass, held in my hand, hovered by my lower lip. It trembled only slightly as Mags pressed up against my side. The heat of him hypnotized me. The welcome, velvety softness of his skin brushed my arm. My senses all focused on him, and the details of how he felt while right against me, with nothing in between. The hard, lean muscle of his body con-tinued to rub against my arm and hip as his lips sought my ear. He whispered, "Come on, partner. She wants you to have her mouth while I take her ass. You saw that ass, right?"

He smelled of gin, cigarettes, and sweat. The low, familiar whis-per of his voice made me hard, right away. I loved the sound of it, and the way it vibrated against the shell of my ear. How many times had we done this and found ourselves in similar situations, given in, while my conscience paid the price?

God, why did those flowers have to come today? I couldn't stop seeing them, knowing what they meant. The thought of them kept making my skin crawl, as if there were fingers touching me in places they had no right to touch me, lingering there just to make me that much more uncomfortable and aware of what a fucked-up person I was.

I took a sip to distract from the trembling of my hand, put the glass down and tried to face Mags.

There he was—trouble dancing in his big, warm brown eyes and crooked smile. He was hidden under the sweat, the exhaustion, and the fine wrinkles by his eyes, brought of a lifetime of laughter. The boy I fell in love with, long ago, was right there telling me he couldn't wait to get down and dirty just for the hell of it. It was in his energy and every fiber of his body. There was nothing he liked better than having a good time and getting away with something. Damn, but it had been so long. Too long.

Sometimes I forgot how well he knew me. This was one of those times.

He smiled a different sort of smile, held out an opened hand. I clasped his arm with mine, by the inside of his elbow. Our forearms were flush as he clapped me once on the shoulder. "Look, I'm sorry if I pissed you off earlier. I didn't mean to hurt you, you know. I'd *never* want to hurt you. And I do want to celebrate. That's what you were looking forward to, right? Let's celebrate. We'll do it *our* way. It was a good tour, man. You know it?"

It was the way he said it that got me. They were just words, but, coming from Mags, with that particular inflection... It meant something else entirely. The whole seductive act was gone for the moment. He was just proud of me, of *us*, and the sweet music we'd played, the time put in and the sacrifices made. I needed that. I needed it bad, and he knew, of course. He could tell.

"Yeah it was, wasn't it? We survived at least. No close calls."

Suddenly, there was a look on his face like fear had trailed a cold finger down his spine. He held my gaze with eyes just a little too wide, the hairs on his arms standing on end. Mags didn't let go of me. The hand he had on my shoulder gripped harder as his expression changed again. He was reliving it—the close call we'd had, together. It felt like it had been yesterday.

21

"You still think about that night, huh?" he asked with a self-conscious bow of his head, finally letting me go.

"Sure do. It was... what? Five years ago? We'd been leaving the venue. Middle of the night. We didn't have the kind of security then that we can afford now. If we had, it probably never would have happened, but you never know. If the crazies want in, they'll likely find a way."

It had just been us, walking out to an old van.

"I don't believe that," Mags argued. "That's fuckin' pessimistic, man."

"Yeah, well...."

"I'd left my damn guitar case in the van," he remembered.

"You always had that guitar strapped on your shoulder, no matter what," I smiled.

"Course! You kiddin' me?" he scoffed. "I'd feel naked without it."

The building where we'd played the gig and the surrounding areas had been mostly deserted.

"I never saw it coming, with how dark it had been and how tired I was, but you did," I told Mags.

The guy had been older, with wiry gray hair and a mean look. There was a knife in his hand and eagerness in his eyes to use it.

"What do you think he wanted?" I asked Mags.

"The cash in our pockets, or something of ours he could hock," Mags replied with a brief look into my eyes that sent butterflies knocking around in my stomach. "Or maybe he just wanted to use that knife."

They'd acted at the same time—Mags and the attacker—with me in the middle. The old guy in tattered clothes, mumbling to himself, lunged. He tried to plunge the knife into my back just as Mags swung the only weapon he had with a throat-tearing yell of rage and fear.

"Smashed that gorgeous thing over the side of the guy's head," Mags sighed, likely remembering his old guitar, a favorite of his he'd had for years.

The pieces of the instrument had fallen at our feet.

Mags had grabbed me, yanked me out of the way and wouldn't let go, couldn't let go even as the attacker lay bleeding on the ground.

Mags had been panting, his eyes wild with the could-have-beens.

"Thank god you did. You saved me, Mags. Wasn't the first time, or the last."

Mags had a knack for saving me, putting himself between me and harm's way, whether it was as dire as it was that night, or just a random, overexcited fan, bolting past security, looking for a hug or a scrap of clothing to take with them. Mags would be there, every time, telling me to get behind him, using himself as a shield the world could throw themselves against. Even when we were kids, he'd always stuck up for me, being bigger and meaner than I was, putting any bullies off before they could get any ideas. I think he liked being the tougher one for once, after being picked on himself by all of those big brothers of his. Compared with me, Mags was the badass, and it suited him, gave him some confidence.

"I know you were always the little brother, but you've been one hell of a good big brother to me," I told him softly.

"Yeah, well..." he murmured, blushing and sweet as sin.

So many memories. The past was rushing in. I wanted to shut it all out, both the good and bad, and just enjoy the moment with my friend. I wasn't sure how to, though. Tension crept into my body when the memories lingered and I was reminded how, with the tour over, every day would be like this now. Too much reflection on things I hated to see. Not enough activity to keep me moving and busy, lots of opportunity for cruel people to show up on my doorstep for more trips down memory lane.

When I crawled out of my head a little, I noticed Mags had a proud, sentimental look in his gorgeous eyes. He looked around the suite, at where we were, together, against all odds. "We really did it, didn't we?" Mags said. "Hell of a ride. Hell of a ride. Wouldn't wanna take it with anyone but you, you know."

He grabbed my whiskey, sniffed it, then downed the rest like he was saving me from the booze. I blessed him for it. The empty glass clinked on the counter as he set it down with a heavy exhale.

He glanced to the bedroom, to me, looking impatient to do some dirty deeds.

"What are we doin', man?" I asked with some exasperation. "We're too old for this shit."

He scoffed, waving the suggestion away. "Are you kidding me? No one's ever too old for this! We'll be a pair of geezers popping Viagra, hunting out a prime piece of ass down at the local bingo joint."

"Dear Lord," I groaned. "Heaven forbid."

"You're a superstar!" Mags exclaimed, grasping onto the chance to use sex to move past the sappy moment as fast as he could. "You need to get *laid.*"

His eyes twinkled and his eyebrows both jumped. With an incline of his head toward our waiting conquest and a light slap of my cheek, he coaxed me on. Hell, but he was cute.

"Come on, Tuck," Mags whispered, seducing me all over again. "*Come on.* You know you want it. *I* know you want it."

He placed his hat back atop his head. His fingers nimbly unfastened his belt and opened his fly without hesitation or modesty, since I'd seen it all before, many times. His jeans hung on his hips, with nothing underneath but firm, tan skin. As his hand gripped my bicep, ready to drag me to bed if need be, I held him up by asking, even demanding, "What's her fuckin' name, Mags?"

Without missing a beat, he answered, "Karen Andrews. Y'all want her number, too? I memorized it. Wanna call her momma and ask permission first? Maybe ask momma to come join in? *Stop thinkin' about it and take your fuckin' pants off.*"

I sighed and let him lead, because, really, how could I resist?

It was dark because he knew I liked it better that way. We fucked her on Mags' bed, so mine wouldn't get dirty. That had been Mags' concern, not mine, but I appreciated the courtesy. All of those little ways he looked out for me only spurred me on, made it harder to say no for my own sake.

"Tuck, come on. Get on the bed. Stop hiding."

He had two lube-slicked fingers stuffed through her asshole, pumping and twisting, while his other hand stroked his cock, his butt clenched tight. He knelt behind Sugartits, aka Karen, on the bed. Karen was on her hands and knees, naked except for her boots and Mags' Stetson on her head. She was moaning softly, rocking slightly back and forward on his fingers, her big, pierced breasts bouncing. It was him I watched, though, the way he knew just how to thrust his fingers inside her, and the way his bare ass clenched up with each downward stroke of his dark, thick shaft. He'd always had the prettiest cock I'd ever seen.

"Tuck!"

"Yeah. Fine. Christ."

I didn't want to go closer. There was nothing for me there, no spark to lure me in, only reminders of every way I was screwed up.

Mags took one brief glance my way as I stood from the chair I'd been sitting on, palming my stiff dick through my boxers, and he rolled his eyes with exasperation that I was still wearing any clothes.

I cursed, angry at myself again, like usual, knowing there was no saying no to Mags even though it'd be better if I did. Using an elastic band around my wrist, worn there with my usual assortment of bracelets and leather cuffs, I tied my hair back in a knot. I climbed on the bed without taking the boxers off, mainly just to piss off Mags. He pulled his fingers out of her, wiped them off and ripped open the condom wrapper. While he rolled it on himself, I shifted over in front of Karen, who opened her mouth wide and pushed the hat back on her head.

I had to ask myself, who was this girl, Karen Andrews, being used by people who knew nothing about her, and never would? The whole scene made me sad. She was somebody's daughter, for Christ's sake. Maybe she was also a sister or a mother. How big were her dreams? Lord, but I hoped they were bigger than that room, and that moment.

Mags cursed and took the hat off of her completely, probably because it was blocking his view of the action. He tossed me a rubber of my own and fit the head of his dick at her hole. With one hand planted on her hips, he pushed inside with an open-mouth soundless gasp and look of concentration. I closed my eyes after I'd gotten the rubber on and held the latex sheath by the root of my dick. Karen took it into her mouth. She hummed happily and I thrust, pushing farther back over her tongue, into her throat, my hands hanging by my sides.

When I realized I was still only paying attention to Mags' grunts and growls, I tried to stop, to give Karen my attention instead of him.

It wasn't fair to her, to be ignored when she was the one trying so hard to make me feel good. But the more I thought about her, the more I wanted to get the fuck out of there entirely, and fast. I was betraying all of us by being there and taking part. It would have been so much better if I could have simply gotten off on the things I was supposed to.

Mags moaned, "*Yeah,* give it to her. Fuck her mouth." So I did. I couldn't help it. Having him watch, spurring me on, it made my balls ache, put steel in my cock. She sucked passionately, her mouth wet, hot and snug as a glove. I barely had to move or do anything at all. As Mags worked his way deeper into her ass, he pushed her forward onto me. When I opened my eyes, he was balls deep. What if there was a way to keep pushing toward each other and have Karen fade away, leaving only the two of us, and we'd meet in the middle? Hating myself for the fantasy, I pushed it out of my mind.

He tugged back a little. I could see his flushed, thick shaft on the withdrawal, the shine of the latex and lube on it. Oh, how I wanted to feel him like that, riding me instead of her. If he stuffed me full of him, I knew I could make him moan. He tugged an inch or two out from her before plunging back in, knocking her forward and onto my cock. It lodged in her throat, made her grunt. She choked on it before he pulled her back again, and let her gasp through her nose for air.

I tried not to watch, but he liked when I watched. He was trying to impress, and my attention was his reward, telling him he was everything he hoped he was, and not the wannabe trailer trash he feared he was under a thin gloss of fame.

If I resisted, and didn't look, he would demand it of me outright. There was always something uncomfortable about that, so I didn't try to hide that I had my eyes on him as much as her, if not more.

"Pull out for a sec."

"Who put you in charge?" I asked.

"Just do it, fucker."

I saw him stare at my dick as it slipped from between her lips and curved up, ready for more. His pretty lips drew back slightly as he gritted his teeth, hissing as he pounded her ass, really giving it to her as he chased his orgasm. With a rough gasp, he came, twitching against her round, jiggling cheeks. He shivered, his hands wound around her to cup her huge breasts. Karen hummed and sighed, arching into Mags' touch.

I asked, "Y'all done with me now?" It was meant as a joke, but he gave me a look I'd seen before in answer. I groaned. "Jesus, what?"

"Fuck her ass. I wanna watch."

A laugh was surprised out of me while a tickle of unease stirred in my belly. "No! And, you know, maybe you should ask Karen what she wants instead of just assuming."

"Come on, Tuck. It's better than porn. Humor me."

"Are you even hearing me right now? And what about what *I* want?"

"You get to fuck her ass. It's a nice one. Plus, she wants it, don't ya, Sugartits?"

"Yeah, fuck me, Tucker," she begged, breathless, drunk on booze and lust. At least her interest sounded sincere. That helped me feel less like I was taking advantage. "Please, Tucker? It'll be so good. I'll make you come so hard."

For some reason, I gave in. I moved around behind her, pretending I was getting behind him, instead. Mags took my spot, cupping a hand under her chin to tilt her face up as I entered her, breaching her fucked-loose outer ring.

His eyes were on her face, not me. He smoothed her hair back as she gasped. I gave it to her fast and hard, wanting to be done, to finish before my nerves and rational thought could wilt my hard-on. I focused on the fact that he had just been in her, that he wanted me to do it. Maybe it meant that way, way down deep Mags was fantasizing about letting me fuck him like this, too. I kept my eyes closed, not wanting to know anymore who was who or where I was.

I came with a growl, the old anger at myself returning. No sooner had I filled the rubber than I pulled out, holding the sheath on me. Before he could say anything, do anything, see anything, I went into the bathroom and slammed the door closed.

Standing there in the dark, the lights off, I tried not to scream with rage at being so fucking worthless and damaged, hating the tears on my face, the hurt in my heart, and the shame, most of all.

It was a long time before I came out of there. When I did, Mags was in bed. Karen was gone.

"I got rid of her," Mags said hesitantly, sounding like he was hoping to appease my bad mood and make me happy with him again. Might be that was the tone he'd used to speak to his father whenever Mr. Palmer was pissed off again, yelling at everybody, stuck with a house full of kids and no escape, no way to pay for all the bills. And there'd be little Mags, smallest of the bunch, knowing he'd fucked up again somehow but not understanding why or what he'd done, just knowing Daddy was upset and that was bad for everyone. "I was real nice about it, too. Just sent her home, told her to get some sleep and said I hoped she'd had a good time. Tuck, you mad at me again? I did what you wanted, right?" he asked.

He was just so blind to everything I needed him to see, and didn't have the strength to show him outright. That's what kept us at odds with each other, and always would.

"Whatever," I sighed, slipping under the covers, my back to him, knowing he was still watching, wondering what he saw.

Chapter 4

Company

"Morning." Jess smiled, holding a suspicious looking bag in the crook of his arm. He was wearing a Seattle Seahawks baseball hat along with a pair of jeans and a well-worn grey t-shirt to fit his stage name. Gray North, through and through.

"Good morning to you, Mr. Grayville. What is that?" I squinted, chuckling as he brought a pitcher of liquid out from behind his back, being careful not to spill any. "Jesus, that's not—"

"Apple julep sangria," he said proudly as I laughed, doubling over in my seat at the little table in my hotel suite. "Swear to god."

My hair tumbled forward, over my right shoulder. Remembering what he'd said the night before, I'd forgone the hair tie that morning.

"How in the hell did you get that? That's *amazing*, man. You're a goddamned miracle worker," I said, shaking my head and unable to keep from smiling.

"Down at the bar, I might have bribed some people, bought my own ingredients, too. There's a farmer's market nearby. I know you said you were sick of fast food and missing that good home cooking, so...."

He set down the pitcher and the hemp bag, then began unloading its contents. There were fruits, vegetables all carefully wrapped, and fresh-baked pastries.

"You brought breakfast?" I asked, eyebrows raised, stubborn smile on my lips. "And what'd I do to deserve that, besides adding too much drama and grief to your night a few hours back?"

"You're the only one I'd want to share breakfast with, and it's no fun to indulge alone," he replied, taking a seat across from me and wiping his hands on a paper towel. A pair of cups emerged from his bag as well and he began pouring out the sangria.

"Sangria instead of coffee?"

"Absolutely," he insisted, looking eager to give it a try. "Unless you want to go ahead and mix some of this *into* the coffee, but I don't think I'd recommend that." He sipped some and made a moan of delight. "It's damn good. Here." He handed me my cup.

"Thank you, sir." I tipped my hat to him and took a sip of my own. "Son of a bitch," I remarked with delight. "You nailed it, man. I'll be goddamned."

"You know I'm hardly ever recognized, so I thought I'd take advantage, go scout out the area and see what I could bring back. The neighborhood's nice, once you get away from the over-developed section right off the highway. How was your night? Restful?"

"Not as much as I wish it was," I admitted.

"How come?"

I shrugged, unwilling to bring up the note from Mr. Briant that I couldn't get out of my mind, or Mags and how we passed the time with Karen. Jess started to make a salad while I picked at a pastry, breaking off pieces to chew on.

"Anything on your mind, keeping you up?"

"Eh, just the usual. Running it all over in my head once things quiet down. Best way to avoid sleep, I guess. Frustrated with the things I did *and* the things I didn't do. Lying in bed always makes me feel like I'm fuckin' everything up in one way or other."

"Mm," he hummed, trying to hold my gaze. He seemed to wait for me to say more, showing me he was willing to listen. It made me anxious. The desire to shake off his attention somehow was strong. I scratched at the inside of my left wrist, under the cuffs and bracelets where the skin was scarred and uneven. "If you want my two cents, which might not be worth much, I think you're just way too hard on yourself."

"You used to doing this?" I asked him instead. "Taking care of people? Going out of your way and all? You seem to have a knack for it, I must say."

Maybe he'd finally mention the wife and tell a tale or two about her so I wouldn't have to answer questions. It would have been nice to vent a little about my true worries, just to try to get them off my chest so I could breathe easier, but that was just a fantasy. Jess would never understand why I kept giving in to Mags despite knowing better, and saying a single word about Mr. Briant would have been way too dangerous. The whole point of keeping quiet was to spare those I cared about from pain. I'd been coping on my own this long. I'd just have to figure out a way to keep going, even if it felt way too big to manage anymore.

"I don't know," he answered good-naturedly, thinking it over with a tilt of his head. "For my family back home, sure. Guess you're my family now, though."

With a smirk, Jess grabbed his cup for another drink.

"Is that so?"

"For now." Though I kept trying to throw up walls to keep him at a safe distance, his friendliness kept allowing him to find doors I didn't even know were there. He was easing closer faster than anyone else around. "You're stuck with me for a little while longer, at least. Me and my celebratory, drunken breakfasts."

"With salad," I added in a little tease.

"With salad," he agreed, as he handed me a bowl. "Here, have some. You sure you're okay?"

The room was quiet. Mags was asleep in the bedroom. There was no one else around. It would have been the perfect chance to have a quiet, intimate chat and get to know each other better, without interruption. It was like he knew how much I had to confess.

So, I filled my mouth with a big bite of fruit and murmured around my mouthful, "Yep, sure am."

In Los Angeles, I had learned about a discreet group of folks known as The Company. The name fit, since they provided a physical sort of company for lonely folks like me. It turned out they had affiliates in many major cities, like Boston, Chicago, and even Houston. They had a long damn reach, like a short tree poking out of the earth, with roots that ran on and on through the dirt, touching... searching out dark, hidden places and wriggling their way in.

I made some calls, got some recommendations, and made an appointment. It was to take place just a few hours after my late breakfast with Jess. Because Mags had pushed me into participating in sex with Karen, I needed something that was only mine—my desire, my choice—to take me out of that bedroom and those circumstances, having the wrong kind of sex with the wrong people for the wrong reasons. Since there was no way I could bring anyone back to the suite, I booked a room at another hotel across town. No one but my bodyguards and my manager knew where I was going, and even they didn't know why. I'd just told them I needed a break and turned my phone off to avoid interruption.

As soon as I got to the door of the temporary hotel room, with my security guard at my side while I fiddled with the key card lock, the nerves set in. The bodyguard would stay in the hall, watching the door until his shift was over. Then a new guy would take the next shift in a seamless transition. It was a system I liked, mainly because that meant the guards wouldn't be able to compare and contrast what they observed before and after my company visited.

Finally, the door's lock turned green and allowed me to enter. I gave the guard an awkward grin and closed the door on him once I'd slipped inside. Gazing in a slow circle around the room, my attention caught quickly on a bucket of ice sitting on a table. Inside was a bottle of champagne.

I hadn't ordered champagne.

It didn't make sense and I didn't want to understand what it meant, or why it was there. But, right away, I knew. A while back, I stopped trying to figure out if it was the bodyguards passing information through the label, or if my phone was being tracked, or if Mr. Briant had an in with The Company. No matter which pieces I tried to cut out, the end result was always the same. So, I suspected all of them and everyone, accepting my fate like the pessimist I'd become.

I didn't want the champagne in the room. I hurried over to the table, intending to get rid of it, and saw another little card, just like the one that had come with the flowers the night before.

No part of me wanted to open that card and read its contents, but what if I just threw it out and it contained a warning I should have heeded? There were always little warning signs with Mr. Briant. If ignored, the consequences would be torturous, to say the least.

So, my heart pounding, breaking out in sweat, my knees feeling weak, and a moan held in behind my sealed lips, I opened the card.

Enjoy yourself tonight! N. Briant

"No. Fuck you. *Fuck you!*"

The card shook as my hand shook. Revelations I didn't want crept in anyway.

He knew about my company. He knew I'd hired a prostitute for sex. He even knew what fucking *room* I was using.

And he wanted me to enjoy myself.

Sure he did. He was always glad to see me enjoying myself.

But after I'd gotten my rocks off? That's when the horrors began.

"*No.*"

I pushed the thought into the dark with all of the other things I kept there, refusing to study. It didn't have to mean anything. It was just a card and some champagne. It didn't have to imply he'd be looking for me soon. It was harmless. It had to be.

A broken whimper slipped through my defenses.

Get rid of the champagne, instinct told me. I couldn't have it in the room. I'd have tossed it from the window if the damn thing wasn't sealed shut and we weren't ten stories above the ground.

Bottle in hand, I went to the room's door. My bodyguard gave me a quizzical look, but I ignored it. A couple of women were walking down the hall, talking quietly and dolled up in little cocktail dresses.

"Hey, want some free champagne? Someone sent it to my room by mistake," I said, offering the unopened bottle.

"Sure, thanks," one of the women replied, giving me a bigger smile once she'd gotten a better look at me. She took the offered bottle but hesitated in continuing on her way. "Hey, you look familiar..."

"Yeah, I've got one of those faces. Have a great night, ladies."

I ducked back into my room quickly, letting the bodyguard handle the rest.

The card was lying on the carpet near where I'd found it. I ran to it, tore it up into pieces and took the shreds into the bathroom where I flushed them away.

Sitting in the middle of the bathroom floor on the cold, white tile, I drew my knees up to my chest, held my head in both hands and tried to calm the hell down. Soon, I'd be faced with someone looking to cut right to the evening's down and dirty goal. There wouldn't be a slow lead-up; I'd just be thrown right in. It was something I was used to, and had experienced many times before, but somehow it was never easy. I had to get myself ready for it, mentally.

Mr. Briant wasn't there. I kept reminding myself of that. He wasn't coming. Someone else was. Someone kinder.

I wouldn't let him ruin this for me. He'd already ruined too much.

The memories were trying to come back, though. I shook my head to pry them loose, squeezed my eyes shut and forced my thoughts somewhere else.

It had always been that way. If sex was involved and Mags wasn't around, if it was just me, waiting on a stranger, my thoughts went to the worst places. It took real effort to get myself back on track, whether there had been a creepy gift left for me by my personal devil or not.

I made myself get to my feet and get out of the damned bathroom. That helped. The room was free of contamination now. My terror eased.

That's when the other sort of panic set in. It always hit when I knew I was about to be alone and having sex with another man. Then, I wasn't someone with a modest degree of fame or success, or an adult who'd survived some awful things and come out the other side mostly intact. I wasn't a man at all, but a weakling, a coward, and a damned liar not fit to lick the boots of my scheduled guest.

He got there right on time, nine p.m.

I opened the door and tried to form words, but my tongue was thick and dry in my mouth. My thoughts were clouded by fear. My stomach was in knots. My skin felt too tight—both too hot and too cool. Glad for the leather strip that secured my hair back, and how it helped me feel more controlled, I continued to fidget while taking a good look at the stranger waiting to be let in.

He was real damn cute, which was, of course, both a good and bad thing.

"Hey. You're Ken? I mean, you look like a Ken. It, uh, suits you. Anyway. Come in. Sorry."

"Nervous?" Ken smiled, with pearly white teeth. He was adorable, with light brown hair that was blond at the end of each tight curl, cut fairly close to his head. Tan, toned and sporting an All-American vibe with his coral-colored polo shirt and tailored gray pants, he looked like a living, breathing Ken doll.

I was about to fuck a Ken doll.

A hysterical laugh chased up my throat. Bottling that up as tightly as I could, I stepped aside. Ken walked in. He was an inch or so shorter than me.

"Yeah, you could say that. I'm Tucker. Pleased to meet you. Welcome to my, uh, hotel room. Can I get you a drink?"

Not champagne, though, I thought. *We're fresh out of that, thank god.*

"No thanks, Tucker," Ken said. There was a friendly look to him. It was pretty dimly lit in that small room, with only a single bedside lamp on and the curtains closed. Ken walked right up to me, standing too close, and slipped a hand around one side of my waist like there was no such thing as personal space.

My knees almost gave out. My legs felt weak, the muscles tingling uncomfortably. He was so close; I could smell his aftershave and the mint he must have eaten on his way to the hotel. It wasn't just the reminder of Mr. Briant's attentions that had me rattled, though it had left me feeling like he was over there in the corner, watching all of this go down with a patronizing smile on his face. No, it was the way all of the people I'd been around day in, day out, for months, hovered at the edges of everything. Mags, Jess, Jovie, the rest of the band and crew, my manager, agent, and publicist... the whole team of them seemed ready to bust down the door at any moment, just to prove their suspicions right and show me once and for all that there's no such luck but bad luck.

Yet, Ken felt so good, smelled so nice. And, most of all, I was just sick and fucking tired of being so alone all the time. I had to try to let someone in, even if it was the wrong someone. Anyone other than that awful fucking man seemed a better choice.

"Um," I murmured, looking down, then off to the side, then closing my eyes altogether. "Sorry. Just..."

"Nervous."

"Right. Yeah. Exactly. I can't believe your name is Ken. Well, I mean it's probably not your actual name. I get that. So, good choice, I guess. I'm a nervous talker, if you couldn't tell."

"Maybe you could tell me why you're nervous," Ken suggested gently. His hand on my waist slipped under the fabric. Skin-on-skin, he rubbed around to my back. His hands were really soft, warm, and dry. "Touch me. It's okay. I want you to."

"Well, that's the thing, actually, that makes me nervous. Always has. I'm used to other guys seeing me naked and actually performing sex, but the touching throws me off. Especially if the guy touching me is as good looking as you are. I've only recently started experimenting with touching all y'all. I mean, this isn't my first time or anything like that, but it's still new. Sorry."

"You don't have to apologize. You're cute. Sweet. It's a turn-on. I like it. Here." He took his hand back, pulled his shirt off, and dropped it to the floor. His chest was free of tan lines, his nipples dark and small. They got hard when my hand brushed his abs. "Good. Keep going," he said encouragingly. "Go on. Feels nice."

Giving in, my opened right hand moved up over his chest. The stiff tip of his nipple dragged under the pad of my thumb, the skin around it silky soft. While I was distracted, he took hold of my jaw and leaned in for a kiss. I made a soft sound of surprise as his lips lightly brushed mine, then with a little more intent. My mouth opened slightly with a silent gasp of surprise as he cupped my crotch and squeezed it a little. The tip of his tongue teased at the center of my lower lip. It slipped inside my mouth as his head angled to the side. Ken drew me in, easy as you please.

The kissing was a great distraction. His lips were full and soft, but the best part was how he wasn't greedy. He was more of a tease—give a little, pull back, take a little more, and lure you in. I didn't even feel him open my fly, so when he used both hands to pull my pants down a few inches, I moaned, "Fuck," and pinched his nipple, which made him breathe out a small chuckle. Those white teeth and the smile in his eyes held me there. It kept me calm as his palm stroked up my cock, lifting it, pressing it upward as I got hard.

"What do you want? Name it," he tempted.

His hand on my dick rotated, grabbed it by the root from above instead, and tugged. It brought me close to him again, chest to chest. He kissed my answer away, swallowing it right down.

I knew what I wanted, always did. The trouble was asking for it, and being ready for it, too.

The nervousness came back, hard. He must have sensed it after a moment, from my expression or the way the sounds I was making as he stroked me got an edge to them as the fear grew.

"You all right? Don't think about it. Just say it." He looked me in the eye. "I'm ready however you want me. You wanna let me suck on this?" His fingers brushed my shaft and his eyes pushed me to give in. He was impatient, eager. "Wanna fuck me with it? Or do you wanna see how hard *I* am, let me do something about that?"

The easiest thing would have been to fuck him, get off, and get done. I could. I'd done it before. But part of me didn't want to take the easy way out anymore, ignoring my instincts and desires just to cut through the fear that much more quickly. Trouble was, the rest of me was still terrified.

"I-I don't know. I'm not sure," I stuttered, close to tears, the shame coming back, the frustration and anger with it. Those emotions were old buddies, after all. They always came together.

"Here," he suggested, reading me. "Let's try something else."

He turned me around, pulled me back against him, the two of us almost the same size. I heard him unfastening his pants, detected movement behind me as he took them off. A second later, he was right back there, standing against me, pushing my pants lower, too.

"How's this feel?"

His fingers curled in a loose fist around my shaft, pumping. His free hand stroked over my hip, down the inside of my thigh, and up over my balls. He played with them, rolling them. Gently, Ken kneaded the skin of my sac and tested my boundaries. His soft lips peppered kisses down over my neck and shoulder. He stroked up my shaft. His thumb rubbed firmly over the head of my dick.

"G-good. Feels good," I admitted, the words choked out, almost grunted.

"How about this? This feel good, too?"

The long, hot, hard line of his bare cock brushed between my butt cheeks. He pressed against me from behind and fit his dick there. It nestled snugly. He used his hands to keep my body pressed tightly against him. It was like he knew I needed to be given more, fast, instead of eased in any slower. Slower would have only given me time to question things.

I shuddered, hugely aroused. My cock jumped in his hand, slick with pre-come.

"*Fuck.*"

Reading my signs and seeing how what he was doing was working, Ken started rocking against me, just a little, riding the crease. He hummed with pleasure.

God, it felt good. I clenched around him, made him moan. It was so damn wrong it came full circle to being right again. He tugged me faster since he could tell I liked it. In my head, in a flash, it all played out in vivid color, sound, and sensation. I'd move forward two steps and let him bend me over the bed, stick his fingers inside me, get me wet, make me loose. Then we'd fuck in that random, tiny hotel room in the middle of Houston, Texas, at the end of the most successful tour of my life. I should have been so happy, living it up with the select few of my inner circle and riding high over how much we'd achieved. Instead, I was alone, scared, and tormented, with no one but this random hooker named Ken who was about to fuck me for the first time.

"Hey, um, can we," I started, turning in his grasp, prying him off, pulling free. Averting my eyes, I tugged my pants back up. "Can we get on the bed? Try something else?"

It would have been so easy to keep going, to come, to let nature take its course. That's what spurred me to action.

Not like this. Not today. Not with this man, who I didn't even know. I would come to regret it. It would only make the shame worse.

I realized from the look on his face that Ken was judging me. Ken the hooker, with the pearly smile. Or maybe that was just the paranoia talking.

I tried to remind myself of all of the people Ken must have fucked, the things he'd done countless times. There was no reason to be shy. You'd think after my history of musical and sexual performances I'd have been a little more confident.

"Like what?" he asked, biting the edge of his lip. He looked so damn sexy.

Staring at his bitten lip, I said, "Sixty-nine."

"Any chance I can get inside you, after? Virgins are my biggest fetish."

The serious, eager nature of the request caught me off guard. Ken's expression had shifted just a little but the effect was profound. It was in the air around him, pulsing with his heartbeat. His warmth and scent were filled with it—how much more experience he had, how easy it was for him to do anything he wanted to his conquests, and how I'd become one of them.

There was no inner debate happening with Ken like there was with me. He saw me, he wanted me, and he would do whatever he could to get me. It was as simple as that. Damn, but I admired him for it.

The argument usually came easy, but this time I tripped on it. "I-I'm not a v—"

"*Please?*"

Ken's eyes lit up, sparkling with the filthy ideas flickering in his brain, no doubt. He came close and gave me a passionate, dirty kiss. Reaching inside my drawn-up pants to grab my bare ass, he thrust in a hard grind against my dick with his.

With a rough groan I kissed him back. We shifted slowly toward the bed. With both hands, he groped at my ass. His dick nudged mine as he got more turned on. I realized I had to get this going before he could tempt me.

"Please? You'll love it."

"Maybe," I relented. "Maybe later. How long can you stay?"

"Long as it takes. What are you afraid of, anyway?"

"Loving it," I replied honestly. Maybe too honestly.

He stopped, blinked, his expression blank. Then he laughed happily. It was a great sound, deep and powerful in its sincerity, almost musical. It made me wonder how he sounded when he sang.

"If you did, you'd be in damn good company." Ken gave me a sinful grin as he dragged me down to bed.

Chapter 5
The Virgin Fucks a Ken Doll

"Wow, you really don't have any tan lines at all. Is this just your natural skin color?"

"Still nervous?" Ken asked me.

Oh, if he only knew. They said pain couldn't be remembered, that the mind wiped it away in memory. Somehow, though, mine lingered like a scar. Intimate touches—hell, intimate *moments*—had direct associations for me with agony, humiliation, and the purest forms of discomfort. That was the part of my identity I'd never shared with anyone. Usually, when I battled instinctive negative reactions to being touched, it came across as innocent nervousness, and I let it. It was easier that way. No explanations needed.

The truth was a lot darker.

"You can tell?"

Ken replied by acting instead of trying to talk me through it. My moan was almost shouted as he deep-throated my dick in one swallow. I clamped my jaws shut, fighting my usual tendency to be a loud lay. I was on top, straddling his body, my face in his crotch.

"Fuck! It's too good," I panted. "Fuck. Oh *fuck*." Despite my mental and emotional trials, the reality was that Ken was real damn skilled at his profession. I was a goner. I'd be coming in seconds.

The only thing to do was let my leash on the panic slip a bit more. I had some guy's dick in my face, a guy whose name really wasn't Ken and whose throat I was currently buried in. That was good. That was very fucking worrisome, so I held on to that.

The condom was already rolled on. Ken was ready to go. When I warned him, "I may not be any good at this," it came out whimpered.

I quivered as he sucked me tighter than I'd ever experienced before. Helplessly, I thrust against his soft lips. He pulled my cheeks apart and began to rub repeatedly over my hole with a single fingertip. Instantly more aware of the area, it made me self-conscious, but I was horrified at how good it felt. Guilt always came with surrender and pleasure.

"Please," I begged, mainly because I didn't want to come yet, but also because I wanted out of my head, out of my life and the inescapable, private ways my past was haunting me.

Desperately needing distraction, I guided Ken's prick to my lips. Opening wide, I set the head of his cock on my tongue, fed it back and closed my lips around him. The constant sucking and rubbing made me hum and groan around him, but I focused on trying to make *him* come so it wasn't an option to fuck me once I was spent. Then it would be done. I could stop worrying about the what-ifs and let it be done so I could run away yet again like the coward I knew I was.

Ken had tossed a small bottle of lube onto the bed. He was working some of it onto and around my hole, the fluid warmed by the friction. Taking deeper, longer pulls of Ken's warm, swollen dick, I tasted latex instead of flesh.

Since I was staring at them, I started playing with his balls, fondling, tugging. Ken retaliated by grinding a knuckle into my asshole. The muscle parted around the bent finger and inner alarms started to blare inside my head. My dick slipped free of his mouth. He shifted a little under me on the bed and dread pushed my orgasm back, farther from my reach, which was good and bad. I forgot to keep blowing him, so his long, gorgeous cock fell from my lips, too.

"Oh yeah, so sweet," he moaned, pulling at my rim, opening my hole. The tip of a finger touched there, slick with the lube, went right in to the first knuckle, rubbed in and out, in and out. He was staring right at my ass, watching me take the finger.

He drew a startled shout from me when he fed the digit deeper, to the second knuckle, twisting it around in there, pulling down as he drew it out. Then he was pumping it, fucking me with it, giving me more with each thrust. I couldn't stop picturing myself on that bed and what he was doing to me, seeing the whole scene like I was hovering above it, or standing apart with a camera in hand and watching through its lens. Doubt as well as pleasure made me breathe hard, my blood pounding under my skin. My whole body was quaking slightly, from head to toe, even as I fought against the growing urge to push back against the finger, and ride it.

My straining cock was being neglected; he was using one hand to pull my cheeks apart, the other working in my ass. Voices whispered in my head that it was because he was forcing me to display what a shameless bottom boy I was, and how much I was getting off on the ass play.

"Still nervous?" he asked, teasingly. Right after he said it, he inserted a second finger; spread the two apart in a V, prying at the outer muscle.

"Yes," I whined breathlessly, caught in a tangle of conflicting reflexes.

"Keep using your mouth. Concentrate on that, okay? Don't think about it too much. Just feel it. Love watching you take my fingers. Haven't felt anyone tight as you in a long time. I can barely move in here."

Both fingers pushed in to the hilt and I cried out, blowing out each shallow breath in sharp exhales. I was pumping him with my hand, but decided to follow his suggestion and swallowed him back down instead.

"*Yeah*, feels so good," he praised. I couldn't tell if it was sincere or not. He really did seem to be enjoying himself, which made me feel relieved. It helped me keep going.

Two fingers were hooked in my ass from the side. He left them there, rubbing around in small movements while he went back to sucking me off. There was nothing for it. I had him stuffed down my throat, filling my mouth, sliding on my tongue while he gave me the most skilled, effective blowjob possible and fingered my ass. I came a few seconds later, my yell muffled by his flesh, thrusting desperately against his lips. Shuddering, whimpering like the bitch I was, I slowly came down.

Gradually, I came back to myself. Ken was still hard. I was panting like a dog against his thickly muscled thigh, covered in silky blond hair.

The fingers pulled out. Like the expert he was, he pulled himself out through my legs, freeing himself quickly.

"Wait," I blurted, before I could think to pull the word back and force myself to go through with this silently. That would only compound the nightmare I was already caught in. "I just need to...."

"Need to what? You okay?" Ken asked, maybe noticing the strange tone my voice had taken.

How to say it? Was there even a way? He had to understand. Sex was his life. If there was anyone least likely to judge, it had to be Ken, or so I told myself to push past the unease trying to strangle me senseless. "I just never...." I took a deep breath, blew it slowly out. "The nerves aren't from being a virgin." The confession hung there. Ken's hand was on my back, caressing gently. "I was, uh, *fuck*. I was abused. Not in a traditional sense, if there is a traditional sense. It was different. And terrible. And it screwed me up on many levels. So that's why I-I'm scared, but I don't want to be scared, especially because of *him*."

"I'm sorry you went through that, Tucker," Ken told me gently. It sounded sincere. There was an echo in his voice hinting that maybe he knew others like me who were trying to get past it and keep living, somehow.

"All of this scares me," I told him. "All of it. But I *want this*, you know? Maybe you could help me get through it? I just want to get through it. Please?"

"How about we go slowly and you tell me how you're feeling? Whether to back off or keep going?"

"Yeah, okay," I nodded, feeling a little better — a little lighter — for having told him at least that much.

He placed two pillows under me.

"Let's get you comfortable, okay? Lie down on these," he said, guiding me so they were raising my hips. "We good so far?"

"Yeah. Yeah, I think so." The position felt dangerous, but only because I liked it. My body was tensed up, bracing for anything, trying to resist what was going to happen. When Ken seemed to notice my tension, he began massaging me, using long strokes of his hands over my back, down my arms, down the backs of my legs. The calming, non-threatening nature of the touches helped. My breathing evened out and my muscles began to unclench.

"Can you spread your legs for me, so I can get closer?"

He'd been sitting by my side rather than behind me. I knew the whole idea was for him to be behind me, so I complied.

When he settled between my legs, they were nudged farther apart than I was comfortable with. As soon as I tensed up again, he resumed the massage. "I'm not going to hurt you," Ken promised. "I want you to feel good. You believe me?"

"I do. It's just... difficult to relax and just let it happen. Everything feels kind of wrong."

"You want to stop?"

"No. No, I really don't. That feels good. I just need a moment to get used to this."

"No problem," Ken said easily.

I tried to catch my breath. The bed was comfortable, pressed against my face and chest. Ken's talented hands slid over my skin firmly enough to coax me to give in to him. He was damned persuasive, even when he wasn't saying a word.

Soon his massaging touches began to slip lower. He rubbed over my ass, through my crack, then outward again. It just felt like another part of the massage, which helped me calm down and go with it. His patience set me at ease, making it feel like he understood just what I needed.

"You ready to try this?" Ken asked, sounding hopeful. "I'd like to prep you a little more, if that's okay."

"Okay," I answered, feeling braver. "Let's give it a shot."

"Good," Ken said warmly. I heard the squirt of lube. With a single finger, he pushed some of the slick into my ass. I groaned, but with pleasure rather than protest. He pressed in deeply, spreading the fluid around. He did it again, making sure I was really wet. The sounds grew more obscene, but he was moving easily. There wasn't any discomfort.

He gave me another finger. Then, when I just kept moaning and surrendering to it, a third.

"I think you're ready. *Are* you ready?"

"As I'll ever be, and that's the truth."

I felt him lay down on my back—his lean, hot, naked body—and he kissed over my back, up my neck. It gave me goosebumps and I smiled.

"This okay?" he asked, as he lined up his cock, applying just enough pressure to tell me what was happening. "I want you so much, Tucker, but if you need me to back off, I will."

The sounds I was making gained a fearful edge. I hummed a little and tried to anchor myself to reality instead of the doubt and memories in my head. I'd spent so many years denying myself because of that damned man. He'd stolen so much of my life, robbing me of experiences and maybe even love. It was enough. It was time to fight back, even if I was scared.

There was no going back from this, ever. If I didn't say stop, I was saying yes. Was I really saying yes to this?

"Hey," Ken insisted. "This okay? Want me to back off?"

"It's okay. I want this. Do it." I was choosing to go forward. It was the only decision left to me. I'd been going backward so long. There was nothing good left for me that way.

He breached me as I cried out. His crown popped through my rim. With gentle pressure, he went a little farther before tugging back, then pushed right back in, building a rhythm. The movement eased the slightly uncomfortable stretch and feeling of fullness. All of my attention focused on him, and the way it felt to have him inside, claiming me. It was a beautifully new, wonderful sensation — one I'd been dreading for what felt like forever. I was delighted to discover it wasn't anything like I worried it would be.

Ken moved carefully, went slowly. I was breathing hard and just letting it happen. That was more than enough. I remembered how long his cock was as he kept sinking farther into me, like he'd never stop, like he'd just keep going forever. It was strange how being connected to him in such a way was comforting, like maybe I didn't have to be so afraid anymore. I really wanted that.

Amazing. It had really happened.

Ken was in me, fucking me. We kissed as I gasped and he moaned, but he did most of the kissing. I was so delirious; I could only try to kiss him back. My fingers pushed through his tight, golden curls. He undulated on top of me, and the noise of my inner dialogue was so much quieter. Trying to hold on to what was real and happening, I pushed back the nagging doubts and just felt Ken feeling me. The insane length of him worked in and out of my ass in long, slow strokes that made me shout and beg him.

It was intense, but that was okay. There was no pain, not even when I looked for it.

He stopped a few times, like he was trying not to come, then kept going, even though I pleaded nonsensically. It was all overwhelming and my natural way to express myself was with words and notes, so it couldn't be helped. His hips slapped my ass, beating against it. It was so strange to be so full of him. When he came, he was buried completely, kissing my neck with trembling lips.

Softly, he asked, "How was it? You all right?"

"It was real nice," I grinned, chuckling with my relief. "And I am. Thank you for understanding and, you know, helping. You go on and take the shower."

I was still catching my breath and slowly growing accustomed to my bold choice to finally, *finally* have sex.

"We done?" He sounded surprised, disappointed.

"Hell no. I just need a minute or two to rest."

"Good," he grinned, kissing my cheek as he climbed off.

Hours later, following a nap, things got heated again. It was two in the morning. We'd been kissing in the dark, lying under the covers in bed for a long time.

"I'm up for it if you are," I told him when he didn't pressure me to go farther. I felt a little shocked at the plain, bold truth of those words. The smile on my face didn't fade, either. Maybe I was learning a little about myself after all. If so, it was about damned time.

"Is that a trick question?" Ken retorted with a wicked grin. "Well, what're you in the mood for? We can stay here, stay cozy, or try something *fun*."

"*Fun*, huh?"

"Yeah, are you intrigued?" He asked it like he hoped I was. The whole conversation made me feel like I was just a kid again, and getting away with something wild behind everyone's back.

"I am, actually." Fun tempted me more than a more intimate arrangement did, anyhow. As long as I was having a good time, the night would be a huge success. "What do you have in mind?"

"Well, I can show you," Ken offered. "And if you don't like it, call me crazy and do whatever you like to me."

Still smiling, leaving my baggage behind with my popped cherry, I let Ken lead me out of bed and over to the couch. After some arranging, I was on my back, legs in the air, each one clutched in his hands. My ass was hanging over the arm of the couch.

"Okay, I do think you're crazy but let's try this anyway," I told him. With how open I was, given round one, and the position he'd put me in, Ken slid right into me like he belonged there. He got even deeper and it felt like dying, but only the best kind. I'd conquered enough of my fear to keep going and trust myself a little. Feeling proud of myself, and freer, I cried out without holding back. When I saw him enjoying my noise, I thought of the neighboring rooms around us, and also my bodyguard in the hall, so I bit down on my own arm to muffle the volume. The last way I wanted to end the night was with complaints or reasons to feel bad about the things I'd done. Ken just held my legs open and did what he does best.

I masturbated to relieve pressure, but when he started to rock against my gland, I came suddenly. The whole thing was like a dream I kept expecting to wake up from, but I'm happy to say I never did. Damn, but he was good at his work.

When he left in the middle of the night, I slipped a few hundred bucks into his palm, even though his fee was already paid.

He made me promise to call him again, anytime.

Chapter 6
Hiding the Ache

Exhaustion persuaded me to stay in the temporary hotel room for the rest of the night, even though that hadn't been the plan going in. There was a steady hum of paranoia from knowing Mr. Briant was aware of exactly which room I was in, but it's not like I could escape him anyway. He'd find me if he wanted to, one way or another. That had been the case for years. At least being with Ken was enough of a distraction to keep my mind off of it. Later, though, I thought I might think it over some more—how I might try to slip away and avoid Mr. Briant's gifts, just for a little while at least.

Part of me wanted to go back to the suite and to Mags, who was probably still wondering what he'd done to get on my bad side. I hadn't told him my intentions to leave or where I was going. I'd slipped out when he was with the rest of the band and road crew, having dinner at a restaurant downtown that they'd rented out for the evening. After Ken left, I turned my phone back on and saw how many messages I'd gotten, of both the text and voice varieties. Well, that was a kettle of worms.

Without checking any and silencing the phone, I flopped down onto the bed and promptly passed out.

Come morning, I was sore in all kinds of new places and simply could not stop grinning like I'd gotten away with something. For most of my adult life, powerful forces seemed determined to keep me from acting upon my sexual desires. It wasn't just the actual hell I'd been through in my younger days, it was everything that had come after and how screwed up my head and heart had been. Despite all of it, even the fact that a monster had left me a little reminder immediately before the act and in the damned room, I'd been able to go through with it. It seemed like a miracle. Every time I thought of how I paid a living Ken doll to take my virginity, it brought a huge, happy smile to my face. I knew it made me look suspicious, so I had to get that under control before talking to the band. They were likely the ones who'd left all of those messages, wondering what hole I'd fallen into to account for my absence.

Following a long shower during which I couldn't stop fingering my own ass with fascination, I tied my towel-dried hair up at the base of my neck rather than wasting time trying to dry it. I put on the one clean shirt I'd brought with me—a button-down light blue one with the top three buttons left undone—my favorite pair of jeans, worn in all the right places, and my favorite pair of boots which had been handcrafted just for me by a friend and fan of my music. Spying my face in the mirror over the sink, it was clear that my blue eyes looked slightly shell-shocked. I also was in dire need of a shave. Other than that, I looked pretty normal. It was possible no one would notice how drastically things had changed.

It was like I'd had a necktie too tight around my throat for years and had just managed to take it off.

I could breathe. There had been so much fear in my heart, centered right around that one act of submitting sexually to another man. I'd been conditioned to react in certain ways, to think less of myself than I probably should for wanting to be on the receiving end of anal sex. Maybe it had taken several years, but I'd found some courage after all to do what seemed impossible. I'd done something terrifying, and survived. If I'd known it would be like this, I would have done it a long time ago.

Hopefully the relief would stand up to the crushing weight of shame and the depression that seemed to always be waiting, dangling above my head, just waiting to drop. If I thought too much about the flowers and the champagne, it *would* drop, and I'd be unable to function.

That was a road I'd been down, many times. Each time I stepped onto it, I went a little farther, and I knew what waited at the end. It was better to try to set my feet onto a different path altogether.

My security guy drove me to get some breakfast and coffee. Then, we headed back to the hotel where the label had put all of us up. The tour bus was parked around the side of the building, with people loading things and milling around. We were all due to fly home that day.

As we pulled up to a back entrance, I resolved to stay a few more days in Houston, and maybe even skip the flight altogether. I could rent a car, drive back home on my own, taking back roads and gathering inspiration for new music. The farther off the grid, the better. Already, I had ideas for songs. I kept thinking about William, the guy I'd hired to sleep with me in L.A. He was blond, beautiful and seductive. He'd been nice to me when I'd needed some kindness. It had been so heartwarming to hear how he'd found love and was trying to get free of what must have been one of the toughest sorts of lives to lead.

If William could find love and escape oppressors, find his own kind of happiness, maybe there was hope for all of us — myself included. I wanted to write a song about that — the struggle to own your dreams, to chase them and hold on no matter who tried to kick you down. Sometimes it was like love and happiness was a big bucking bull, trying to knock you off, to bolt free or throw you into the dirt, and all you could do was hold on and pray.

I tried to hold on to my resolve to listen to instinct rather than let the beast made of my doubts toss me off his back, then kick me over the cliff of depression. All that waited at the bottom was an early grave.

Following my muse wasn't the only reason for wanting to get away. Exhaustion had been my cure for insomnia. Responsibility and unavoidable distraction were my way of dealing with anxiety. If things were settling down — and they were, without a doubt — a storm of negative thoughts and emotions would settle on me, too. There'd be more questions I couldn't answer, explanations I wouldn't give. Maybe if I went off on my own, where no one could reach me or find me, there would be no more little gifts warning what was to come, sooner or later. I'd be able to hide away somewhere to rest and heal myself rather than let the dark tempt me into taking an action I'd been resisting for years. There was one sure way out of the pain, but would it mean peace for me or victory for those who'd hurt me? Uncertainty about the answer was what kept me trying, in small ways, to circle closer to a healthier mindset.

We went up a service elevator to avoid crowds. Mags and Jess were both there when I got up to the right floor and over to the suite. From the looks of them, they were ready to let me have it. Dreading the confrontation that seemed unavoidable, I drank my coffee, walking past them and into the room. They were both waiting in the entryway, mouths tight with displeasure.

"Need anything else, Mr. Reynolds?" my morning escort asked.

"Nah, man. Thanks though," I told him. He nodded and closed the door behind him as he left to stand in the hall.

"The fuckin' hell have you been, asshole?" Mags sounded shriller than I expected him to. The reaction made me a little angry. He had no fucking idea what I'd gone through to spare him torment and misery. He had no clue how much effort it was taking to stay positive and not give in to the awful truth behind the lies. Yet there he was, yelling at me for daring to try to find a little happiness without him.

"Calm down. I was out. Y'all go out. Y'all don't ask me permission first."

"You were out all night!"

Avoiding eye contact, I sipped my coffee. There was an itch under my skin. Setting down my cup for a second, I removed a few bracelets and scratched. That was the guilt, tempting me to try to dig it out and bleed it over the carpet. In my mind's eye, behind the stew of negative emotions, there played an endless loop of Ken. He was standing between my drawn-up legs, with his tan, chiseled body and his long, pretty dick, sliding into my ass, his golden curls catching the lamplight. I couldn't believe it had really happened. Detaching a little from the present, I wanted to draw inside myself and relive the new, pleasant memory, ignoring everything else that threatened to bring me down.

I sank down onto the couch, and restlessly rolled up the sleeves of my shirt to expose my itchy wrists. The room was suddenly too full, too warm.

Jess was watching me, following my fidgeting. When I realized he could see the scars on my arms, which were usually covered with sleeves or thick bracelets, my heart jumped. Mags had never cared enough to notice those, but Jess was looking right at them. I paled and quickly rolled the sleeves back down.

Trying to deflect the attention, I said, "Well, I'm back now, aren't I? The world didn't end, praise Jesus. Y'all flying out?"

Mags huffed, arms folded, looking more put-out the longer I avoided tumbling into another yelling match with him.

"*I* am," Jess said, his deeper voice resonating in the air. "But you said you wanted me in Nashville, right? What time frame?"

"You can head down whenever's convenient for you, really. It'll be a process. I'm not even sure when I'll get there. Might take a little road trip for a few days, clear my head before setting to work. You know how it goes. If you wanted to spend time with family first or whatever, then you should do that."

"Nah, I'm ready when you are," Jess assured me. "I'll stay as long as you want me to, but I promise not to crowd you or anything. If you need a break, then take the break."

"Magnusson!" I yelled as the man in question's raging bitch fit continued to silently consume all the air in the suite. "The fuck, man?" He was scowling, angrier than ever.

"We were all waiting for you! You were so upset with me when I wasn't ready to celebrate the other night. Now, when I go out of my way to set something up for us, you bail?! What good is a party to wrap a tour if the lead singer ain't even there? You knew we were going. It wouldn't have killed you to get in touch and say you were ditching us. And now you're not even going home yet? What's this road trip shit?"

He was upset I hadn't invited him along. I could get what he was saying about the party, but his attempts to make good lately only felt like too little, too late. He was reverting to the little boy again; hurt he was being left out the way his brothers had always left him out. You could see it in his defensive glare and bruised pride. Truth be told, I hated to have him thinking poorly of me, but there was nothing left in me to give him. My well had run dry. He could yell into the void all he liked, but it wouldn't fill it up again. Only time and space would do that.

"I don't know," I admitted tiredly. "Seems like a good idea. I'm stickin' around here for another day or so to unwind a bit. Then I'll decide. No one's forcing y'all to leave, but I'm sure you must be sick of hanging around me. We've been under each other's feet for a long damn time, sharing a bus or a stage or a room or a meal. You should take a break, too, change your scenery for a while before we kill each other."

But he was looking at me like that was the opposite of what he wanted, and that he knew I knew it. He'd never come out and admit it, though.

I'd been his guide, showing him the way like his parents had never been able to do. Trouble was, I was a shitty guide on a bad path in the middle of a nightmare. And Mags didn't have a clue, bless his heart. The only reason why he didn't have a clue was due to how long I'd fought to keep him in the dark and spare him facts. I was the very last person he should have been following. It tore me up inside, seeing him so damn mad at me for basically keeping him out of harm's way.

Mags ran his tongue over the front of his teeth, thinking it through, staring me down. Jess glanced between us, probably trying to figure out whether to mediate, and if so, how. He really was a peacemaker. I was grateful for it. It had to have been nice to have such a sunny outlook on everything, so much so that you tried to shine light on other people's troubles, too. It was more than I'd ever been capable of, by a long shot.

"Fine," Mags relented. "I'm leaving tomorrow. Me, Gray, Jovie and whoever else can meet up and get the house in order before y'all get there — we'll start playing around with new sounds and ideas. You have a direction you want us to go in?"

"Yeah," I said, sitting forward. "Actually, I do."

The last album had been a party. It was borne of frustration and wildness, cravings for dangerous things, and reckless abandon. It was loud and fun to play live. One reason we'd all grown so skinny was how every damn day we were dancing around the stage, sweating it out, giving it our all, trying to sincerely reflect the emotion behind each song. The record sold really well and the radio stations loved the tracks.

But I was exhausted in every possible way — physically, psychologically — and it was time to dial it down. We'd gotten the world's attention, now we could soften our tone, and whisper some truths to shake them up and make them think. It was time to do something that would resonate and linger.

"I want to go more acoustic and toned down. Bringing Jovie in for more vocals, we could do more melodies. The main theme that's been sticking in my head is release and letting go. That's what I want to work around. Do something more seductive and introspective. How's that work for y'all? Less percussion, more piano and strings. Harmonies."

"Sounds fantastic, actually," Jess said, latching onto the idea. "I love it. I've got your back on both piano and violin. Could be a great way to follow up what we've got going on."

Mags looked like he still needed some convincing, and was suspicious of my intent. More likely than not, he wanted me to clarify what kind of release I was talking about, if it was sexual or practical. We'd been drifting apart, so maybe he thought I was letting go of him or the whole damn band.

Maybe I was. Things needed to change and there was a lot I needed to let go of for good. I wanted to try to release only the bad, but if it turned out I needed to let it all slip from my fingers just to make the pain end, I was ready to do that.

But Mags couldn't know.

So, I told him, "You've got to miss just getting out the guitar, no complications or distractions, and finding a tune that connects. Try it. See where it takes you. You know I believe in you, Mags."

He took a deep breath, then blew it out. "Yeah, okay. That'll get us started. Make sure you include us if you get any specific ideas for anything. How long you gonna be? Not too long, right?"

"Nope, not long. Just want to get my head straightened out. Need some fresh air and quiet."

Mags seemed content enough with that. He walked away, into the bedroom, digging out his phone. I was relieved.

Jess lingered.

I felt him watching me, looking at my hair wound tight behind my neck, and just kind of wished he would go too, rather than draw this out anymore. I was split in two, half of me stuck back there with Mr. Briant, the other fighting tooth and nail to get the hell away from who I'd been in whatever way I could.

Jess wandered closer, lowering his volume and easing some notes of familiarity into his voice as he asked, "You okay, cowboy? Rough night?"

"Nah, pretty good night for once, actually. It helped me figure some stuff out."

Despite my assurances, he kept looking at me like something was broken. When he eased down onto the arm of the couch, letting the relative quiet wrap around us, comfortable to leave it there if that's what I needed, it made my skin prickle a little bit. There was something about the way he slipped in, getting closer to the heart of things than Mags ever could, then stayed there, waiting.

While he sat with me, hoping I'd elaborate on the 'stuff' I'd referenced, I wondered what his wife looked like, how young she was, and how short she wore her skirts. Mags would have asked if he'd cared at all. That wasn't the kind of guy I was looking to be, though. Private lives were meant to be private. If Jess didn't want to make that part of himself public knowledge, it wasn't my place to pry it from him.

"Never noticed your scars before," he said quietly.

Exhaling heavily, I let the comment sink in before answering. "Yeah, I don't like to see 'em."

"Accident or intentional?"

I just looked at him in answer, not wanting to lie but unable to admit the truth. Whatever he saw in my expression seemed to cause him a moment of pain, so I quickly said, "They're old, okay? I'm fine."

"They don't all look old," he countered. There was a subtle note of fear in his voice, which only made me feel bad for causing him to worry.

Head bowed, I rolled up my sleeve and ran my hand over the roadmap of lines, the flesh too marred to ever smooth out again.

Jess was quiet, staring at my arm, wearing that anguished look on his face. There was a noise in the bedroom, like a suitcase landing heavily on a bed, temporarily breaking the stillness.

"He's never noticed them," I told Jess. "Not in all of these long years. Not very observant, I guess."

"I've got some experience with self-harm," Jess told me under his breath. "Not personal, but... Will you promise me that if you feel the urge to do it again, you'll call me first to talk things out? Please?"

"Like I said, they're old. Really," I reassured him, glancing briefly up at his concern. "I'm okay."

"Are you saying that just to pacify me? There's been a difference in you lately. When there aren't many people around and you let your guard drop, you just seem... upset, or unhappy, or worried. I don't know. But I'm here for you, man. Honest."

Those damned flowers. The awful champagne. The certainty that it was starting again....

My whole body tensed up. Tears threatened, but I blinked them back and cleared my throat. After a pause, I tried on an appreciative grin and said, "I know you are, Jess. Thanks. It's nice to know you see me clearer than Mags does. There's just a lot catching up to me lately. The less busy I get, the more I think about things I shouldn't, because they're all things I can't change. I just have to figure out how to live with them, somehow. How are you? You've gotta be sick of some of this band drama shit by now."

He followed my glance in the direction of the bedroom where Mags seemed to be gathering his things. "Yeah, it's wearing on me just a little. Might stop home first, like you said, before diving in. That was a good suggestion. My family lives right on the coast, on the out-skirts of Seattle. Being away from them and the ocean for so long al-ways makes me feel like I'm going crazy. It'd be good to get back, get lost in the wilderness for a while."

My coffee cup was empty. I stood to toss it and had to grit my teeth against a deep-seated, low ache that flared when I moved. Once I started to walk, I fought the urge to take wide-legged steps to the trash can. I was getting off a cushion, after all, not a damned horse.

"Stop back, then. Reconnect," I told him. "I'd love to see that part of the world sometime—the Northern West Coast. It's someplace I don't get to a whole lot, but I remember the vibe up there. It's unique. Everything I've heard about what I haven't seen sounds great, though. And I'm sure they miss you back there. Hell, we've been hogging you for months."

He replied with a shrug and a grunt, going toe to toe with me on the whole clamming up tactic. His thumbs were hooked in his belt-loops, his eyes tracking me like a hunter. I could imagine him with a shotgun, wearing camouflage, and hiding in the brush.

"You absolutely sure you're okay? You look a little stiff."

"Slept in a weird position, I think. Threw out my back or something," I lied.

"Mmm," he hummed, like he understood but maybe didn't believe me. Or maybe I was just paranoid. "Look, I appreciate you keeping us in the loop when you need to take off and where you'll be. It was a little scary how you just vanished last night without a word. I know Mags was getting on you, but that wasn't really fair after the way he'd acted the other night."

"Maybe. It's always so hard to tell with him. The more I give, the more he takes, but when I stop giving or hold back at all, he gets so damned offended. I don't even know what to say to him anymore. We're too different lately. I don't mind making the extra effort to keep in touch with you, since you don't rag on me like he does. I just need a break from trying to pacify him when I'm barely keeping it together. But, you know, that's probably just the exhaustion talking. If you caught me scratching," I sighed, fighting the urge to scratch again, and settling for rubbing my arm instead. "It's just 'cause it's become a nervous tic. I'm all right, Jess. I'm looking forward to the road trip. Getting away from stress usually helps me remember what's important and stop worrying so much."

There was enough honesty in that that he seemed contented with the response. There was a heck of a lot I was holding back on, though, and it weighed on my heart. But Jess was too nice for his own good. The last thing he needed was to be burdened with my problems. "Good," he said, rubbing a hand over the back of his neck and looking kind of sideways at me. "Okay. If you're sure. If you want some company, let me know. Otherwise, I'll go on and pack, and work on getting out of here."

"Yeah, go ahead. I'll catch up with you in a bit, before you go."

"Keep me posted on everything while you're gone. Or if you just want to vent to someone who knows how it goes, you can call me for that, too."

"I'll remember that. If I haven't said it already, you should know you've been an incredible addition, and not just musically. Having you around has made it a lot easier on me, in a lot of ways I had no cause to expect. I really don't know what I'd do without you."

He took my extended hand, shook it with a firm grip. The wedding band sparkled as he overlaid our joined hands with his left. He was golden, like that band; just good and decent all the way around. It suited him. I couldn't help but see it separating us, though. We were in different leagues. Even if there was some way to tell him what was really on my mind, someone like Jess would never understand. Sure, he could say he wouldn't judge, but my secrets were things everyone judged, whether they admitted it or not. And I couldn't bear to have him look at me, knowing the disgusting things I'd done.

Jess gave me a handsome smile, full of friendliness, and told me, "I'm really looking forward to the new music."

"Me too," I replied, looking up at him. "Safe travels. I'll be in touch. Probably so often you'll be turning your phone off to avoid me."

Chapter 7

Lying Prick

Audiences could tell when you were trying to bullshit them. The honesty and emotion were either there, in your heart, your voice, your performance, or they weren't. There was no faking it. It was always clear to everyone if a singer was feeling the song or not. Intuition prickled through the senses of everyone listening in, a sort of magic there was no way to measure. So, you had to own it, wring it from your veins, bleed reality, splattering everyone with the gore of your essence.

I gave them the truth they craved. With every lyric, every verse, it was there, always. I tapped into my experiences, made those personal connections to infuse the music with pieces of truth. There was so much out there to listen to that if you wanted folks to hear what you had to say, and stop them for a moment from changing the dial or switching tracks, it was crucial to only put out raw, unfiltered humanity. Granted, I was highly selective about which emotions and experiences I wrote about, choosing mainly the good, relatable ones, especially with the last album. It was nice to go onstage and force myself to tap into my joy or hope for a few minutes for the sake of a song. It helped remind me I had the ability to feel that way.

Of course, my honesty of expression only applied to the music. Everything I couldn't tell friends and family I was craving or lacking went to the public in the form of marketable product. In a very literal sense, I sold my soul. The hope, the love, the struggle to rise above or fight back against unsavory circumstances — with precision it was cut from me by my own hand. Chopped into pieces, raw and pulsing, it was diced and rearranged by professionals and sifted through microphones to flow along wires and circuits.

I left it there and walked away.

I guess that made me a coward. There was no fight to keep what was left of goodness sacred. My heart was consumed by the masses and, at the end of the day, nothing was left. When the filter of the music wasn't there, I couldn't look honesty in the eye. It slipped away, frightened off by the fear.

When it really counted, I was a lying prick just like everyone else.

It seemed impossible that I could ever meet someone. To approach a man I was attracted to, talk to him, seduce him, date, and work up to intimacy at a normal pace — there was nothing more farfetched. The courage it would have taken to put it all out there, and see if it was good enough for someone else to want me, was nothing but a song.

There were easier ways to fight loneliness. If you could manage a phone call, you could have a night's company with someone good looking, who knew you expected sex and was willing to accommodate that. There were no explanations needed. You listed your preferences and paid the fee. It was as simple as that. Get what you want while they get what they need. The oldest business in the world had persevered for obvious reasons.

Thinking about how well my evening with Ken had gone, I went into the bathroom and got undressed. There was a Jacuzzi tub. I filled it with hot water, turned on my mp3 player, and got in.

No one was around. I let my thoughts float free, remembering how Ken had touched me. First, I focused on when he'd sucked and fingered me while I sucked him. Picking and choosing some details to switch around, I imagined being able to taste his cock without the rubber in the way. I also fantasized about giving him more power to act and touch me however he wanted, without any of my doubts to trip him up. Now that I knew he was kind and respectful, it seemed possible to indulge a little more. Thinking of that, making it real in my mind, I stroked myself hard under the bubbling water. Music tickled my ears, along with the hum of the tub's jets. The air was hot and steamy, thick enough to press on my chest, open my pores and cause sweat to bead on my skin.

My hand kept tugging and I thought of getting fucked by Ken on

Mags' bed. Maybe I'd let him come in my ass. Maybe I'd fuck him, too, and see how he sounded when he was the one taking a cock.

I was getting closer. My balls drew up tight. The pressure built up more and more.

Toys were new to me, too. That was a whole uncharted world to explore. Was I brave enough to let someone like Ken use them with me? If so, what would he want to try? The possibilities were endless.

The more real it became in my mind; the more I needed to keep shifting it around for my own comfort. If I did do something like ask Ken for another date, after telling him as much as I had already, I needed to feel more in control of what was going on and take it farther away from the dangerous coziness of a one-on-one scenario. Taking on two guys at once would have been terrifying, but maybe if there was a woman there who understood my preferences and wanted to be the one doing the fucking, I could actually enjoy it for once. For the sake of all of the women Mags and I had taken advantage of together, she could take advantage of me. Perhaps some of that guilt I always carried around on my back could be purged, leaving me lighter. Women didn't scare me like some men could, so a female presence would absolutely take the pressure off. There wouldn't be any danger of having Ken expect another heart-to-heart confession if there was a new third party involved.

Granted, none of it was ideal, but it was the best of bad options. Without wanting to but needing to, I was still playing by old rules I had no choice but to follow. Instinct drove me to test the boundaries but breaking out of them entirely would have been too dangerous by far. Being with Ken and an understanding female, turning the tables a bit, might help me find new ways to test my independence one little step at a time. If this worked, maybe next time I could go farther.

Worry fell away in the safety of the dream. I could almost feel it, getting fucked with a long, thick dildo while Ken's bare cock fucked my mouth, the taste of him dragging over my tongue.

Breathing heavily, eyes closed, mouth open, I sank lower in the water and moaned a little as my balls drew up tighter, getting ready to shoot.

"Here you are," Mags laughed loudly. He was obnoxious as only a drunk person could be. The bathroom door slammed open, banging against the counter like a shot as he came into the room.

"Get the fuck out, dude!" I cursed, hurrying to try to cover my-self.

He glanced into the water, saw everything and laughed even louder.

Perching his ass on the counter by the sink, he tipped his beer at me and said, "So, date night, huh? Gettin' lucky I see."

"Will you get the fuck out?!"

I drew my knees up, used the anger and panic to push my orgasm back.

Trying to catch my breath, to block his line of sight by draping a washcloth over my dick, I groaned, "Fuck, Mags."

"Don't let me interrupt, Casanova. You've got her right where you want her!" He mimed jerking off briefly before chuckling into the mouth of his beer. Turning his head slightly, he checked his hair in the mirror, carefully arranging the tousled, dark spikes. "Nothin' special downstairs tonight. You want me to make some calls? Or we could go out and find some company. Celebrate our last night with a *real* bang."

I peeled the washcloth off of my crotch, lifted it from the water soaking wet and flung it at him.

"Shit, dude! Don't throw your jerk cloth at me!" He swatted it away. With a splat, it landed on the floor. He took another swig and walked out. As he went, he called back, "I think it's your turn anyway. Why don't you call up whoever you were with last night and share for once?"

"Not your type, trust me, asshole," I growled. "Shut the fuckin' door!"

I saw the reflection of his arm reach in and pull the door quietly shut. It was a relief.

For a minute or two I tried to calm down, to slow my racing heart-beat and remember where I'd left off. It wasn't too late to finish. My sense memory of Ken was still fresh. I could remember the ways he'd gotten me hard and rode my ass. After a few tugs, I was done.

My lips were sealed tight, but I was always loud when I came, so it couldn't be helped. It was more of a muffled, groaning cry. I pumped harder through the aftershocks. Then I started to climb out and grabbed my towel. I gave my body a pat-dry and squeezed water from my long hair. After pulling the drain-plug out of the tub and turning off the jets, I headed out of the bathroom.

That fucker was sitting right there, on the bed, drinking his beer with a devil's grin on his face.

"You're pretty determined, I see," he chuckled. "Thought it'd take you longer than that."

He started to mime jerking off again and mimicked my swallowed groan.

"Jesus Christ." My face was beet-red. I found some clean boxers and pulled them on as fast as I could. "You know, Mags, I'm really gonna miss this—all of this quality time together. You're really making me regret my decision to get the fuck away for a while. And you know what? You're always so hot for threesomes. Well, guess what? I've got my own planned and you're not getting an invitation to participate, asshole."

He looked hurt at that.

"There's something wrong with you," he said angrily, standing up. He turned his back on me and stormed from the room.

"Yeah, you're right about that," I agreed.

The phone was in my hand. As soon as I was certain I was alone in the suite, I'd picked it up. The only thing to do was make my plan a reality before I could chicken out. I wanted to keep acting on my own desires instead of being the one always led along and taken advantage of. It would be empowering and set me on a better path, or so I told myself.

It was a persuasive enough thought to convince me to dial a number I'd called recently. "Yeah, is Ken available tomorrow night? I'd want him to stay 'til morning."

Tapping my boot on the tile floor, I waited in the relative dark of the bedroom. There were people moving and talking out in the hall. I kept the phone pressed to my ear.

Having sex with Ken had been nerve-wracking, but the victory of going through with it had helped me feel like I was facing an obstacle directly in my path and getting to a better place. Deciding to see him again in the type of situation I'd fantasized about felt like the best, safest way to move forward and keep being proud of myself.

"Yes," an unknown voice told me with supreme politeness. "I see that he is available. Any special requests? We'd like your experience to be tailored to your particular needs."

I hesitated, but having done this before helped soothe my unease. Biting the edge of my thumbnail, I thought of that champagne and the note that had been with it, telling me to enjoy myself. If Mr. Briant had found me and Ken once, he could again. But I'd come too far not to take the next step.

"He needs to show up wearing a suit, looking professional so no one suspects. That's important. I'd like him to wear something more, uh... unprofessional... underneath."

"No problem. The more specific you can be, the better we can serve you."

The stage and performing had been my life. I was always surrounded by hot guys like Mags, looking their best and wearing things meant to show off their bodies or the beauty of their faces. It wasn't a matter of wanting to *be* them, but to get fucked by them. Those were private moments of desire, which I'd never followed through on before.

"Okay. How about something silk or leather, then? And tight. His face made up a bit. He could, uh, bring some toys. And no condoms. Is that do-able?"

"Yes, we can accommodate that. Is there anything else?"

Sure there was. Facing Ken and having to look him in the eye was the toughest prospect of all. Not only would he know what I felt like on the inside, and the ways I reacted when I was fucked and powerless, but he'd know I'd been abused. And not only that, he was coming to fuck me again, expecting me to give away even more. He'd have so much power over me. I had to take some back and shift the dynamics a bit. With my fist balled up, I ground the knuckles against the wall, liking the pain as a distraction to my inner riot of panic.

As much as I wanted it to just be him, it would be better if it wasn't. It would take some of the pressure off and maybe it would be just as good. It would be one blessed step closer to acceptability —

just another threesome like I always had with Mags — instead of me alone with another man, asking to be his bottom boy, begging to suck his cock before doing whatever I could to get him to fuck me with it. No, it was better this way. Maybe I'd like it just as much, even with a woman there.

"Yeah, I'd like Ken to bring someone with him. A pretty lady who's got some experience doing the pitching as opposed to the catching, if you know what I mean. Kind of ties in with the toys request, I suppose."

"Of course. No problem at all. I've noted all of your requests. We'll need an address and to have you complete a health screening. I can provide you with information for the closest medical professional we work with in your area to accomplish that efficiently for both of us."

Lord, my face was hot. It was hard to breathe. I couldn't believe I'd actually said all of that. After taking some notes and passing along the details they needed about the hotel, it was done.

Chapter 8
Surrender

It was tough to have to stand by and see people who had been with us for endless weeks on tour slowly disappear. It was true, it really was over. Then again, everything good always seemed to come to an end. The music still rang in my ears. The crowds were still going wild before my eyes, begging for more. People danced and sang along. Mags was at my side, strumming, and everything was all right.

But now it was done.

There were no more crowds. There would be no more safety in numbers. There were just cars, pulling away from the hotel with people I cared about sitting inside, driving away. I watched them go from the window, wondering if I'd ever see them again.

Goodbyes were said, some temporary, some not. There were hopeful undertones that it wouldn't be the last time we would all be together. You just never knew in this industry when your time was up. This might be the top of the hill — the best it would ever be, for any of us. It was vitally important to celebrate now and not look too far ahead.

So many times, I gave a handshake or a hug, looking my musical partners in the eye and letting them see how proud I was of them, of us. They'd each come through for me in their own ways on our journey together and I needed them to know how much it was appreciated, no matter what form the ending might take.

Jess stood before me, tall as could be with a bag slung over his shoulder, that Seattle Seahawks hat on his head and the beard on his chin. He wore a smile and shook my hand.

"You still doing all right?"

I'd left the hair ties behind and my hair fell around my shoulders, loose and wild like I was trying to be, instead of bound and trapped.

"I am," I said, feeling better than I had, or maybe that was just because he was near, being kind and attentive in ways I had no right to expect. "It means a lot that you always ask. Truth be told, I'm going to miss you."

He ducked his head a little, his smile growing, while I wondered if saying that was inappropriate. He was married, after all. He wasn't a potential mate, but just another person I'd never get to share love with like it seemed part of me wanted.

"Tucker, I'm missing you already," Jess said adorably. "But I'll see you soon and talk to you even sooner. Take it easy on yourself in the meantime, okay? Get some rest. Go for a massage or something." I couldn't stop grinning, and was a little embarrassed by how good he made me feel just by listening as well as he did and trying to see the real me. "And remember what I said. I'm just a phone call away, no matter what you want to talk about or what time it is."

"Thank you, Jess. I hope you get a little break, too. Take some pictures of the ocean for me, while you're there. Maybe some of that fresh mountain air'll come through with them. You never know."

He clapped me gently on the shoulder, looked a little reluctant to go, but did. I stood there, watching him walk away. When he got in the elevator, I went to the window to try to see his car, feeling better when I found him again and could see where he was headed.

Mags was one of the last to go. He was with me until the end, like always. I was barely hanging on to the end of my rope with him at that point. We hadn't spoken since I'd yelled at him after my bath and I couldn't wait for him to be gone. It had gotten to be exhausting to be around him. He didn't know my secrets or how they involved him. All he knew was how to party and coast along on the fame and attention. He'd never noticed how bad off I was, underneath it all. For too many years, I had bottled up my feelings about it. The pressure had become so extreme that cracks were forming. At any moment I might explode and kill the son of a bitch.

Standing by the door in our suite, he looked at me like he wasn't sure what to do or say.

While I chewed on everything I'd never told him, but probably should have, he realized I wasn't going to be the one to break the ice.

"Don't be too long," he warned in a timid murmur. "Or I'll come find you and drag your ass back."

He wasn't kidding, either. He really was that crazy and obsessed with me for his own reasons. I was the source of his livelihood and his support system. In some ways, he was more dependent on me than I was on him.

I stood there, rubbing my arm, feeling far away and beaten down. He came over and hugged me, which only made it worse, reminding me of the love that was still there, between us.

"Bye Mags," I said with a hoarse, emotion-thick voice he probably mistook for simple regret over our fighting.

"Bye *for now*," he corrected.

I said nothing and let him go.

Once he was out of the hotel, and in a car being driven to the airport, finally the air became breathable.

My most urgent need was to find somewhere Mr. Briant wouldn't be able to track me down. Escaping into the wilderness for a few weeks was the solution. In solitude, out of range of the threat I lived with every day, it would be easier to remember what it was like to be myself. It would be a luxury to be able to hear my own inner voice, to feel connected to the world instead of pursued by it. That was the goal, to feel more centered, more certain of myself, and be more forward-thinking. Anything else led to the dark. But maybe I'd decided in time to make my escape, and it wasn't too late. It was my last hope.

If the threesome didn't make me feel better, if being alone and rested didn't give me the strength to keep going, well....

The goodbyes I'd just said might have been more final than anyone else suspected.

I pushed it out of my mind.

The next album couldn't happen until the clamor echoing in my head faded back. After being on the road, living out of hotels and luxury buses, thoughts of camping under the stars and hiking through lesser-known trails was intensely appealing. All I wanted was to be out there, unencumbered, with my guitar, some paper, and nature all around me. No phone, no connections, no people.

For exactly two hours I was nothing but relieved and hopeful.

Then the gears of life continued their motions. There were things that needed to be done. My bodyguards were still there. I'd have to warn them I was expecting company. Company from The Company, but they didn't need to know that much. Rules would need to be laid down that my guests and I were not to be disturbed, no matter what, though I'd never liked a locked door. It was something I'd need to bear one more time.

That got me thinking about the evening. The nerves began to crank up. If it had been nerve-wracking to have sex with Ken the first time, it was at least as much the second because things were going to another level in so many ways. My limits were being tested, but that was the only way I'd find out more about myself.

After the necessary, but blessedly brief trip to a local health clinic for my screening, I used the gym to expend some of that churning energy. Then I went for a swim to cool off. By the time I was back in my suite, and instructions laid out for security, I was a wreck. I showered, shaved, and nursed a bottle of rum.

A few times, my phone rang. Once it was my manager. Another time it was Jess checking in. I started laughing right after I'd answered, and he called me on it right away.

"You're drunk as fuck, aren't you?" he commented, with amazement and humor.

"No," I scoffed good-naturedly. "Just havin' a good time."

"I'm glad to hear it, but you're not drinking alone, are you?" There was his concern again, and the eerie reading between my lines.

"Not for long." I quickly changed the subject. Though the timing was bad, it was so good just to hear his voice and have his company for a while that I kept him on the line longer than I expected.

It was funny, after time had dragged out all afternoon — stretched like taffy — once my guests knocked on the door, the pace of it all really kicked up.

I answered the door with my hair deliberately untied and a blue bandana in my hand, balled up.

Ken was a familiar sight. His perfectly tailored suit and sexy, confident calm made butterflies begin to swoop around in my stomach as I welcomed them into the room.

Holding out the bandana, I murmured to the beautiful lady who followed Ken inside, "Howdy. I'm Tucker."

"Hey, Tucker. I'm Jade," she smiled warmly and moved to kiss my cheek.

"Here," I told her, left with the soft touch of her lips on my skin, "that's for me. A, uh, blindfold. If you could help me get it on, I'd appreciate it. I'm really fuckin' nervous, so, you know. Anything that might help, I'm going for here."

Jade took the bandana from my hand and assured me, "No reason to be nervous. We're just here to make you feel good. It's *all* about you tonight."

I couldn't stop looking at her. Looking at her also meant I didn't have to look at Ken, wondering what he wore beneath that suit and what he wanted to do to me.

Jade had aquamarine eyes, dark hair and was almost unnaturally pretty. It was the type of beauty you couldn't buy from a plastic surgeon, or earn at the gym. You were either blessed with it by God, or you weren't. And there was nothing off-putting or aloof about her. She seemed all Southern sweetness with a wicked little twist. She was also slim and a little shorter than Ken who was a little shorter than me. You could almost line us up like those Russian nesting dolls. We'd fit inside each other perfectly.

"It's funny you say that," I admitted, closing the suite's door. "Because it's usually *never* about me. For years I've been the sidekick when it comes to sex. I guess that's a warning for y'all, not that Ken needs it, that you might have to help me relax a little. I was nervous the other night, and I'm *really* nervous now."

There had been no gift waiting in the room, nothing delivered with a disturbing little note. In a way, it was almost just as bad to be met with nothing because it left me waiting in anticipation of something that might be headed my way.

At least talking to Jade felt easy instead of wrong. Without Mags there to direct our collective attention to the female of the group, I found myself not feeling any jealousy toward Jade at all. I was just curious and even a little excited to see what would happen now that she'd been given the job of helping Ken take care of *me*. The dynamics between me and the women Mags and I had threesomes with had been a burden, I realized. Now, it felt lifted. I could just try things out and not be trapped in a situation that could never work.

Jade had arrived wearing a suit as well, but quickly slipped off her jacket and draped it over a chair. Underneath, she was wearing a blue silk camisole that showed off her breasts, which were big for such a small girl and no bra to encumber them. Ken wasn't watching her undress, I noticed, but was keeping a close eye on *me*. Ken took off his grey jacket, placing it with Jade's, his fingers nimbly unbuttoning his black shirt. After instinctively looking away from the sight of him taking his clothes off, intending to give him privacy, baser needs kicked in fast, so I let my gaze return to him.

Under the shirt, leather straps crisscrossed his chest like a harness. One ran under his pectoral muscles, one across his chest just under his armpits and a few inches above his nipples. In a V, a strap came down from one side of his neck, ran under the horizontal bands, then doubled back up over them to complete the circuit and run back up the other side of his neck to hook again in back. While he slipped off the shirt, moving and turning to set it down, I saw everything, and stared. Bands circled his upper arms. His whole body glistened like he was slicked with some kind of oil. His eyes were lined with charcoal colored makeup and they stared at me with no emotion, no intention to indulge in polite conversation first, just the promise that I was about to get fucked.

"Damn, I need more rum," I moaned as my heart pounded, racing away with itself.

Jade slipped off her A-line skirt, which cupped her heart-shaped ass. It occurred to me that Mags' tongue might literally fall out of his head if he saw her ass. He'd be blubbering like a baby, on his knees, begging for a chance to get inside that. Thinking of him and how cute he was when he was hot for it made me smile.

The blue camisole matched her silk thong. Her black high-heeled shoes stayed on.

Ken was behind me. He gathered my hair, trapping it in his hand. Shifting it out of the way, he nipped at my ear and raised goosebumps over my entire body. The blindfold had been passed from Jade to him and was in his free hand. As he reached around to secure it, he said, soft and low, "We can help with those nerves, for sure. You ready for this? Feeling all right about it?"

I knew he was talking about my confession about the abuse, but was phrasing it in a way that wouldn't betray my trust. Nodding, I said, "I am."

"Tell us a little more. It'll help me figure out how to get us started. What do you mean, you were the sidekick?"

I tried to explain, talking through my nerves. Jade stepped up close, caressing over my chest through my fitted, button-down shirt, her nails scratching lightly.

"Well, it's become a regular thing for me and my best friend to share a woman. He's straight, but he likes it when people are watching him perform, sexually and otherwise. Usually, with threesomes, that job gets passed to me. I'm only there to be close to him, and he just kind of tells me what he wants me to do. Doesn't really matter what I want or how I'm feeling about it all, as long as I'm paying proper attention to him. But, the problem is, I'm in love with him. He has no idea. When we do... that... it's always about the woman, fucking *her*. And it makes me feel left out and awful, because he has no clue that what I *really* want is him. And I don't even know if I want him anymore. Now, I want...."

When I couldn't finish, Jade prodded me to go on. Her silky soft lips dragged over my collarbone as she unbuttoned my shirt. Ken tied the bandana, the fabric drawing tightly over my eyes. Blinded, my other senses cranked up to make up for the loss. Everything was magnified.

"Keep going," Jade coaxed. "Sounds like it's good for you to get this all off your chest. No one should have to stifle their wants like that all the time. We're here for *you* and want to know *exactly* what you want so we can give it to you."

"*I* want to be the one who gets fucked," I confessed quietly. They were both more than close enough to hear. "Not *her*. Not, you know, *you*."

"We can share you?"

Ken began to suck a spot at the base of my neck and cupped my groin, squeezing lightly as I started to get hard. He was pressed up snugly behind me, so that I could feel his chest and the straps winding around it. His cock pressed against the seat of my jeans, between my cheeks.

"Yeah," I agreed. "And I want Ken to take charge of it."

"Mmm, I like the sound of that," Ken said quietly, right by my ear.

Chapter 9

Seduced

They'd brought a bag with them, and I was glad I couldn't see it anymore. I didn't want to know what was inside, to be tempted to worry about it before I was feeling what was happening.

Once my shirt was off, that left me wearing only jeans. They led me to the bedroom by the hand.

Music was playing loudly through the built-in stereo system, to help disguise any sounds that might be overheard next door or in the hall. It made conversation a little difficult, but I was fine with that.

Jade peppered soft kisses over my chest, making me shiver a little. I liked how the feel of her lips moving over my skin kept me from over-thinking what Ken was up to, though I knew he was working my belt open. Once he got my fly unzipped, he pulled the jeans down.

I wasn't wearing underwear. As Ken guided my legs free, Jade kept distracting me from what Ken was doing with her feather-light kisses and it kept my heart from pounding too hard.

"Go ahead and lie down," Ken said. "You two get comfortable while I take a second to get what we need."

"Come on, I've got you," Jade promised, pulling me down with her. She was lying on her back, and the camisole was gone now. I straddled her slim, smooth legs when they slipped between mine, prying my thighs apart as I knelt above her, my hands braced on the bed at her sides.

"That's perfect, Tucker," Ken said. "Can't wait to get my hands on you, too. Just hold on one more moment, okay?" I could hear him rustling through things and couldn't feel him anymore. Feeling self-conscious about him watching me, I distracted myself with Jade, who seemed like she wanted to be kissed. Her lips were sweet, her small gasps intoxicating as I covered her left breast with my right hand, fondling it. It was heavy, warm, and natural. I bent to lick the nipple. As soon as my lips touched her, her nails scratched lightly, wonderfully, over my scalp and my upper back.

"Hey," Ken said, rejoining us. He caressed my lower back to let me know he was there.

"Jade, I want you to hold him, get his sweet ass really spread open for me," Ken said. "Tucker, let me know if you want to slow down or take a break, all right?"

"Yeah, all right. Thanks."

"Here, lover," Jade beckoned, drawing me back up. My hand went back to fondle her breast as she guided me. Her hands wrapped my hips as I shifted up the bed, then reached lower to grab under my ass. She palmed my cheeks with both hands and pulled, spreading me for Ken. My hole was presented for him.

"Oh fuck," I moaned, lowering my head to rest against the bedding at the crook of her neck. In that moment, I really needed her there, as comfort. I'd never felt that before, how having a third person present during sex could make you feel so attended to. It was wonderful to discover. Holding onto her helped ease my fret about how much power I was giving them over me.

"That's it. Just relax. Let us take care of you."

Warmed lube was smeared through my crack. I waited for fingers, blushed fiercely at the feeling of her dainty hands spreading my ass for Ken to do god-knows-what. I tried to clench up, toes curling, but she held firm. A moment later, something cool and hard touched my hole. I held my breath, then grunted against the feeling of whatever it was entering me. It slid right into my ass. The object was narrow, but seemed to flare outward, because the farther Ken pushed it, the more it filled me, stretching the muscle.

"Gonna loosen you up first," Ken explained. "How's that feel?"

He worked it gently, feeding it to me a little at a time. A good four inches of it were being moved in and out at a steady pace.

I tried to answer, but all that came out was a hard moan. Shuddering, trying to clench up every single muscle in my body to make my trembling stop, I fought to get past the anxiety and calm down.

Jade was still spreading me, kissing my shoulder, too. Ken caressed my back.

The toy twisted, inserted deeper, was pushed at a different angle, and I cried out roughly as it was rubbed over my prostate. He worked it there, steadily. Ass out, hands clawing at the bed, I felt him milking my gland and tried to be quiet but the sensation was like electricity jolting me. I sealed my lips against Jade's shoulder as more rough yells threatened, then ripped free.

"How about that? That feel good?"

"*God*, yes," I cried, voice wavering, climbing a few octaves before breaking.

The toy pressed in, filling my ass. Ken left it there. Jade's hands came away and they rolled me over to lie on my back.

I was flat on the bed, then, my ass hanging off the end. Jade must have been kneeling by my head. She had my legs bent back, folding me in half, with one in each of her hands. Holding them behind my knees, she pulled me open wide and held me like that. I was breathing hard. After only a moment's wait, I felt hands manipulating me. My balls were gently massaged. My cock was steadied in a hand. A mouth lowered onto it. At the sound of a low hum, I knew it was Ken sucking me. The feel of his tongue, his lips, the inside of his cheeks tight around my dick – it was heaven on earth. Everything felt so intense, and knew he could taste me. He kept humming and moaning like he loved it. After sucking me down to the root once, he pulled off and licked, base to tip, over and over again. I groaned behind gritted teeth and grabbed fistfuls of the bedding at my sides.

"Love getting to taste you," Ken told me.

The tip of his tongue traced up the underside of my dick. His lips closed around the head. He sucked and my knees twitched, trying to close as it all overwhelmed me.

"Relax," Jade coaxed. "Just relax."

"Fuck, that feels good," I groaned.

I blew out a breath, fought not to come. My hips chased up. I needed to get farther into his mouth. Pushing against his lips, I tried to go deeper, but he didn't let me. His hand lightly worked my shaft as he tongued the head, licking at my slit.

"Oh, Jesus," I growled, thrusting futilely again.

"Can't forget about this, though," Ken said.

Jade pulled my legs wider. Ken's fingers found the base of the flared toy in my ass and began to work it out of me, slowly. Sweating, panting, quivering, I felt my body expel the object. My cock was so hard it hurt.

Once the toy was out, I was a little sore, but wet and looser.

"Gonna get him started," Ken said to Jade in a sex-roughened voice. It was like you could hear the effect of my cock on his mouth.

"You sure?" Jade questioned. "I thought—"

"I'm sure," Ken said, cutting her off. The bed shifted like someone was leaning against it.

My breath caught when I felt his cock against my hole, ready to push through.

"Tucker, you want it?" Ken asked me.

"Yes. I want it," I confessed. "Fuck me."

He entered me with a hard push, sliding through my rim. Taking me with a rough exhale and an eager thrust, I felt him bottom out fast.

"Fuck yeah," he sighed, tugging back a little, then sliding in again.

I couldn't shut up, my natural inclination to express myself vocally kicking in strong. The only way to get through everything I was feeling was to cry it out. He leaned down and kissed me, drinking down the sounds.

It didn't last long. He pulled out before he came, muttering to Jade, "Switch with me."

The bed shifted again, even more than before. Bigger hands than Jade's took hold of my knees. Someone who had to be Ken was kneeling by my head again. "I've got you," Ken's distinctly male voice said from close by.

I was glad for the feel of him, because the image I conjured of Jade putting on a strap-on made my heart race a little, wondering just what in the hell I'd agreed to anyhow.

"Hold your legs back like this," Ken told me, waiting until I had them in my grip before letting go. He caressed down my chest to my stomach, then even lower, leaning down over me so I could feel the heat of him in the air, right above where I laid. He moved like someone who'd never heard the word shy and couldn't be bothered to care about anything but instinct, palming my balls, drawn up tight enough to make me moan. My dick jumped, begging him please.

Then Ken was sucking me, upside-down this time, while we waited for Jade. She was pretty damn quick, though. I liked having Ken covering me like that, shielding me a little from whatever might happen next. I'd only really started to relax and get into it, since the blowjob was something familiar to focus on, when I felt something that wasn't fingers touch my hole, pressing there.

A cool, thick object entered me, making me shudder around a heavy exhale, my fingers clawing at my thighs. It was bigger than I'd expected and felt different than Ken had.

She knew how to use it, too. I was shouting in seconds.

Ken pulled off and asked, "You want the blindfold off yet? Really think you should get to see this."

"Yeah. Okay. Take it off," I gasped. Maybe it would help me take back control a little to look.

When the first thing my gaze fixed on was Jade's wicked smirk as she thrust deeper into me, I moaned and closed my eyes fast. Ken chuckled. I opened my eyes again just a little to peek down through my open, drawn-up legs, past my dark, swollen, shiny wet cock to the long, flesh-colored dick harnessed to Jade's pelvis. Straps wound around her hips, between her legs.

"I can go all night," she smiled.

"Oh, fuck, that's true, isn't it?" I grunted as she ground against my gland.

"Best thing about being fucked by a girl is our awesome staying power," she bragged, drawing back and giving it to me again. To Ken, she said, "Keep sucking, babe. He loves it."

I was grateful when my view of Jade joyously riding my ass was blocked by Ken as his mouth lowered back onto me. Tilting my head back, I saw his dick was close. It was stiff, barely hidden and stuffed inside a silk thong. Another pair of those leather straps wound around his upper thighs, which looked good enough to make my mouth water. I freed his dick and guided it between my lips.

Ken moaned and cursed around his mouthful. His hands rubbed over my body as he sucked me and I sucked him. They were all over my ass, feeling where that fake cock was fucking me like he wanted to be the one using it instead of her. Ken must have wiped himself off, because all I tasted was skin. I sucked away his pre-come, savoring the thick, salty taste before going for more.

I had let go of my knees in order to steady Ken's dick, but tried to keep still nonetheless. Jade was giving me long, slow, deep strokes, and it felt so good I wanted to cry. I was filled at both ends and buried balls deep in a gorgeous man's throat. Jade was giving it to me good for all of those women I'd felt bad about having sex with for the wrong reasons. I bucked against Ken's mouth as I came and unloaded down his throat. Jade didn't miss a beat and kept right on going. I sobbed with delight. It couldn't be helped. It was amazing.

It didn't matter that they were strangers to me. I was used to not knowing anything about the people I had sex with, with Mags or otherwise. That's the way it had always been, from the very beginning. It was just sex, no emotional involvement needed, but it was *spectacular* sex. The sound of Ken egging Jade on, telling her to give it to me harder, holding me down, spreading me out, I burned it in my brain.

Sure, I knew I was only enjoying Jade's participation because of Ken being there, touching me, sucking me, and telling Jade what to do to me. But it was something, and something was a lot more than I'd had before.

Jade bit her lip in concentration, an eager smile constantly playing at her mouth while she gave it to me good. She loved her job, and, hell, I loved it too. There wasn't any pain at all, just the wet, easy slide of that thick toy up my ass. It felt like she fucked me for hours and all the while Ken caressed and kissed me, keeping me lubed and opening me wider so she could go deeper. Once it was clear that I was getting worn out, Ken asked how I wanted him.

"Let me see you come," I murmured. Craning my neck to see, I saw him straddle me. He stroked himself and came over my cock and balls, smearing it around my hole as Jade rocked in and out.

She pulled out. Together, they wiped me clean as consciousness slipped from my grasp.

When I woke, Jade was gone, but Ken remained, lying by my side and smiling happily. He whispered, "Sleep," and I did.

Chapter 10

Revealed by Morning's Light

Come dawn, regret hadn't found me out yet and I was still glad I'd done it. There was Ken, a living doll, lying in my arms. But as the morning sunlight grew, filling the room and shining on some truths I'd avoided seeing, I began to notice other things, subtler details. Like the puffiness around Ken's eyes, caused by what looked like exhaustion. He had a scar, too, just under his jaw on the left side, and I wondered why. This man had his own story. It hit me then, that I had no idea what it was. With country music, songwriting and singing were all about telling the story, so just looking at Ken made me try to guess what his could be.

Maybe he hated his job. Maybe he wanted to get out, to be free, like William. He could be the exact opposite too, living for pleasure and the thrill of meeting someone new, never getting enough to make the need for more go away. What if he loved someone, but lived with the pain of selling himself to strangers, rather than letting those moments be sacred, shared only with someone he loved and who loved him back, just as much? Or, looking at that scar—a twisted line of raised skin, a bit paler and pinker than the rest of his tan complexion—it was possible that life was mostly cruel to Ken.

I'd lost count of how many sex workers I'd hired in the past few years, but I'd never really stopped to consider how life could be on the other side of the door. Usually, my guests were sent away as soon as the deed was done. I wasn't used to facing the morning with my company. In that quiet moment, looking at Ken sleeping peacefully, I made myself turn it all around to see it from the other side. When you were the one knocking, sent to an address to please or else, it was a much different view than it was when you were the one asking them in, unable for whatever reason to arrange a date that wasn't charging by the hour or menu item.

I wondered where William was, if he'd truly gotten out. I hoped so. Fear for him blossomed in my gut, knowing what sort of penance must be paid when you disobeyed powerful masters like The Company. How long had I been pinned down under the thumb of Mr. Briant, and everyone who worked for him? He was the master I'd been required to serve, and he was cruel. I knew the chance of getting free from him was so slim; you could barely pass a sewing needle through the gap. Maybe more than anyone, I understood how likely it was that William had been tracked down and tortured for trying.

Disgusted with myself for using people like William, Ken, and Jade for my own selfish purposes and temporary pleasures when they had enough to deal with otherwise, I sat up, swung my legs over the side of the bed and rubbed awareness into my face. There was a man in my bed, with whom I'd shared more than I had with my closest friends, and I didn't know a thing about him. It wasn't fair to Ken.

What was I doing?

I was fucking strangers who had no say in it, who had to do as they were told so that I could get off.

How selfish and ignorant I'd been, but then I guess I had learned from the best.

Realization was a horror that made me itch. I scratched at my arm, digging in. I'd been hiring these people to fuck me, then paying them to be quiet. More than that, I'd been so wrapped up in the act of sex and all of the emotions tied to it, it never even occurred to me until that moment that maybe I deserved better and much more than one-night stands.

Craving a shower and an exit even more—a knee-jerk reaction to discovering the ways I'd been cruel without even seeing it—I looked around. It turned out that we'd fucked and slept in Mags' bed. That made me feel nauseous instead of triumphant. The instinct to go, to run, was strong. The bathroom was a few feet away, offering a pathetic kind of refuge. It was my suite, with my stuff in it, scattered all around the various rooms. I couldn't leave entirely. There was nowhere to go. There was no way out.

Ken's suit was folded up and set on a table. The tangled web of straps Ken had worn underneath the suit lay strewn on the floor. The bag of gear and toys was set against the wall. You couldn't have made me look inside for all the money in the world.

I was staring blankly at that damned bag, and everything it reminded me of, when I heard behind me, "Hey, handsome. Going somewhere?"

With a glance over my shoulder, I saw Ken and his adorably drowsy smile. It looked honest, but that scar, tucked under his jaw and more real than any words, mocked me and my pride.

"I'm sorry," I sighed, wanting to ask forgiveness and searching for the words. That regret I'd avoided for a few hours slammed into me then, like a closed-fist punch. It made me wince. "Look, if you want to get out of here... get back to your own home and bed... I mean, you had no say. Probably didn't even want to come here. I'm such a jackass."

The apology tumbled from my lips. The yearning to make Ken understand how clearly I saw things now, was strong. I'd been in his place, told to show up and serve, or else. It was my duty to set him free.

"Hey," Ken hushed. He clasped my arm, up by the elbow, and pulled me back down to the bed. "C'mere."

"You don't have to," I said, fighting it. I hadn't earned his kindness. "We don't even know each other. I feel like I've taken advantage of you."

He kept hold of me, like he was as determined to make me stay as I was to run. Other ways I could try to make amends started to come to mind. Maybe, after being sexually taken advantage of so often, Ken would like to have someone show him some care and make sure he was all right. After all, that was what I'd try to do with William, giving him some time to make his escape on what was supposed to have been our second date. William had needed some cover as he'd driven off with his lover, escaping The Company for good. If I could, I'd give Ken the same kind of gift in a heartbeat. That's what I would have wanted, anyway—someone kind, looking out for me.

Ken, or whatever his name truly was, had more willpower than I did. He kept drawing me in until I was lying beside him again, in the rumpled mess of bed sheets. Gathering up my long, wavy hair in a hand, he brought it forward over my shoulder, then smoothed it out and tucked some of it back over my ear. His voice was quiet, but confident. "I had a hell of a fuckin' good time last night. Look in my eyes and tell me I'm lying. I dare you."

Maybe it wasn't the ideal situation, and maybe Ken's kindness was more business than personal, but hell, it was something at least. For that day, and that morning, I'd take it and be grateful for it.

"You really want to be here? There has to be somewhere else you'd prefer instead."

"Why would I want to be somewhere else?" Ken chuckled. "You're quite a handsome sight to wake up to, you know. I'm counting my blessings right now."

It didn't seem like bullshit. He must have seen my confusion because he began caressing my arm, soothingly, as I said, "I'd just like to do right by you. I don't know your circumstances, if you're safe or happy or if I could help you out at all...."

"Are you kidding? I'm in a beautiful suite with a gorgeous man on a glorious day. It doesn't get much better than this." In response to the expression on my face, he added, "I'm not shy about doing everything I can to get what I want and speaking my mind when I need to, Tucker. Trust me, ain't no reason you need to worry. I'm fine. I'm great, actually. How about *you*? Are you asking me these things because no one's bothered to ask them of you? I'd like to do right by you, too, you know. I'm glad it's just you and me this morning, to be honest, and I have you all to myself. I was jealous of Jade getting to have you so long."

I felt suffocated by my ignorance. Only very reluctantly did I meet the gaze of the man in whose arms I lay. He was still smiling. The scar was there. So were the bags under his eyes, but behind his gaze was absolutely no sign of the torment I felt. He was relaxed, completely at ease and yes, happy in a way that only came after good sex and with only hopeful, exciting things waiting on the horizon. Could it be that Ken had a clearer conscience than I did?

"I don't know how I am," I admitted. "A lot of times I'm mainly scared, or lost. I've been trying to untangle some of the mess I've gotten myself into, but I'm too close to see the knots, if that makes any sense. I've been wanting to get away from it all, get some perspective to see if that'll help me clear it up. You're part of that, I think. You've been helping me figure out what works and what I want from sex."

"How about right now? What is it I can give you that you've been missing and that'll help you not feel so scared?"

As soon as he asked, I knew in my heart what the answer was. It had been there for a long time. "I guess, just some comfort from someone I trust, someone who isn't going to hurt me. I've had my guard up for so many years, I'm not sure I even know how to drop it anymore."

"Hell, I'd love to give you some comfort," Ken said with an eager sigh, drawing me closer. He kissed my breath away, rolling on top of me. There he stayed and we just kept on kissing. The longer it went on, the more I stopped trying so hard and let go, let him lead. Trailing my fingers over his soft, tan skin and firm back, I lay there as he kissed my lips, then my neck, nudging my hair aside with the tip of his nose. He wove his fingers into my long hair, combing gently through it, sending little tingling fireworks through my scalp and down the rest of my body. Eventually, once in a while as we both got hard, he would grind lightly against me.

He propped himself up on one arm, gazing down at me with a cute grin. Rubbing up and down my arm, he seemed to be watching every reaction. My nipples got hard and my blood was really pumping. I felt a little breathless and writhed with lust in response to his touches.

It seemed to go on and on, like time had stopped and we'd slipped into another world where nothing else existed but how much I could feel him wanting me, and feel myself wanting him back even more.

"What do *you* want?" I asked. "Name it. Anything. Anything you want, you can have."

"Already told you what I like, haven't I?" he said. He was breathing harder now, too, and his eyes slipped closed. "I want to feel you again, just you against me. Get inside you for a while."

Feeling braver thanks to his request, I let Ken roll me over onto my side as he eased down behind me. He took a moment to spread some lube on his dick. He was propped up a little on his arm, watching me. His dick nudged my ass, gently at first. Then he thrust with some more intent, working it between my cheeks. I lifted my leg to let him get as close as he wanted and he started kissing me again, moaning a little. I got off so hard on knowing I was turning him on. It didn't seem possible I could be making him so happy while he was making me feel so good.

"Okay, come on. I'm ready. I want it."

"God, I want it too," Ken moaned, making me laugh.

All it took was a push. He slowly worked into me and there was no soreness or discomfort. I wanted to press down onto him, because I needed more and for him to keep going. I didn't want it to ever end.

I held his gaze and loved the rapt expression on his face. There was a fire in his eyes, the heat of it washing over my body, trailing over my skin like tongues of flame. When I started stroking myself, Ken chewed on his bottom lip and growled a little, which made me grin.

He kissed my breathless chuckle away and effortlessly slid the rest of his length into me.

"Mmm," Ken groaned, frowning, holding where he was. I felt so full; there wasn't any room for loneliness or doubt between us. He carded through my hair, then caressed the side of my face with the backs of his fingers. "This is a damn good place to be."

All I could do was hold on to his thigh and rock against his slow, steady movements as he worked himself in and out with long strokes. There was no fear. He made me feel safe in a manner I'd given up hope of ever having.

Ken took his time, working my cock with his hand. I came first, with a shudder and an enthusiastic, disbelieving cry. He wrung the orgasm from me and kept dragging his gorgeous cock right against my gland on each push.

By my ear, he whispered, "Gonna shoot so deep inside you, you ain't never gonna get me out." The promise in the words made a shiver of pure desire race down my back.

"I believe that," I groaned. It was true. I'd be stuck with him, a memory to carry with me, for the rest of my days.

We said goodbye with a hug. It reminded me of how I parted with

William, who'd been trying so hard to break free from a helpless, scary situation. The circle had turned, and maybe I was on the other side of it this time. Ken wasn't trying to escape anything, but he'd been like William in the way he'd been kinder than he'd had any right to be. Each of them had shown a glimmer of understanding and, despite whatever they might be going through in their own lives, they'd spared a moment to bring me some comfort.

Who knew what was waiting for Ken or William today or tomorrow? Nothing past the present moment was certain and I felt protective of them, wishing there was a way I could give something back besides money. There was no way to explain the tears that fell from my eyes as I silently begged all of heaven to watch out for both of them — Ken and William.

Ken touched my face, smiling sweetly. He looked so comfortable in his own skin. It was mesmerizing.

"Thanks, for everything."

"No, thank *you*, Tucker."

"Take care of yourself. Please. I mean it," I told him. "If you ever need anything, you have my number. Don't hesitate to call."

After a soft kiss, he said, "See you later, sweetheart," and went on his way with a wave.

Then he was gone. I'd shared something important with a man I knew I'd likely never see again, and I was alone in a hurtful, profound way. But at least, for a little while, I'd had him. Bless him for proving that it was still possible to trust and surrender, and feel nothing but grateful after.

Some of the guilt was gone, too, though. Ken had convinced me that I couldn't assume anything about his life. Not so surprising really. Everyone had secrets. People wanted to fit you into a neat little box, but life wasn't like that. We were all more complicated than we appeared to be on the outside. It was a good thing, something to be thankful for. All of those unexpected details were what gave people and circumstances their beauty.

So, Ken wasn't as bad off as stereotypes wanted him to be. I was glad, but it left me with a conundrum. My heart was a bit lighter, that was for sure. But it was going to be a lot harder to resist the urge to hire company again once the loneliness demanded it.

Chapter 11
Whore

The trip from Houston, Texas, to Nashville, Tennessee, could have been made in one long day of driving. Instead, I detoured into the Appalachian Mountains and called it the scenic route. There were trees forever, stretching from earth up to heaven and paths carved between, snaking deep into the wild. Civilization fell behind. As the buildings fell back into the forest and the untamed staked its territory, I was lured in. That place, those mountains and winding roads begged you to bask in the glory of nature and get the hell away from just about everything else. Nothing was clever enough to reach through the thicket, except air and shafts of sunbeams. There were no wires or inside sources from which my pursuer could divine my location, as long as I was careful about it.

All I brought with me was a tent, some camping gear, my guitar, and my conflicted thoughts. My phone was the only connection to the greater world, and that was left powered off and locked in the rental car. Paranoia told me he might be able to track the phone's signal somehow, so I hiked away from the dirt road where I'd parked, just in case. The woods would be my camouflage.

At a remote, little-used campsite far away from any sign of humanity, I made my way to a clearing overlooking a stream and settled in for an extended stay.

Daytime was wonderful. To help me sleep better through the night, I'd stay active, gathering firewood or exploring the area on foot. For hours at a stretch, I'd walk and walk. The sounds of the forest were the only music needed — the wind stirring millions of leaves with each gust, the soaring birdsong and steady hum of insects. It was so easy to get lost in it all as the woods pressed in close.

As far as food was concerned, the nearby stream was stocked with fish. As often as possible, I caught my meals, making good use of what was all around me, feeling thankful for the modest bounty right at my fingertips. There was a primal sense of power in being able to survive when so much was stripped away. Whatever I could catch, I cooked over a small fire. The crackling of the wood, the savory smell of the meat and the simplicity of it all was soothing after living every day for so long with so many complications.

I hiked and hunted from morning until night until my legs and feet ached. Then I hiked some more, teaching my body to deal with the pain and conquer it. There was so much to see, so many hidden valleys and grand hilltops to discover. The wilder my surroundings became, the safer I felt. And the harder I pushed myself, the more I'd convinced I became that I'd be sleeping soundly, soon.

It was a whole other story once night fell. Even if I was exhausted, I'd still hear things out there, moving around. The flimsy walls of the tent weren't nearly enough protection from the nocturnal activities of the creatures surrounding the campsite when everything was pitch black. There was no way to tell what was stalking through the area, snapping twigs with steady footsteps or rustling the leaves. The harder I listened, the more indistinguishable the sounds became, sounding less like insects or small creatures such as squirrels or raccoons, and more like something larger, maybe man-sized and equipped with a night-vision device. A spider would scurry over the back of my hand and I'd flinch, thinking it was the unwanted brush of fingers instead. The less I could see, the more paranoid I became. Even if I'd had a light to turn on, it wouldn't have helped; it would have only made me that much easier to find.

The memories were inescapable at night. There was no activity to take my mind off of things, no friends or co-workers to chat with about safe, normal topics. My campfire and flashlight brought no comfort when there was so much beyond the range of their light I couldn't make out.

Each evening, after the sun had fully set, I'd seriously question the logic of going out there to stew in my thoughts and the ramifications of terrible decisions. There was no hope there, only certainty about everything I knew I couldn't avoid. The depression would settle on me like a thick, wet blanket, smothering.

I'd take off the bracelets I wore as the tickling of gnats and mosquitoes made me itch, and I'd scratch at my arms. Sometimes scratching wasn't enough. I'd start to hear my tormentor's unforgettable sing-song of a voice, or tumble backwards into a nightmarish memory. My imagination would paint the night with familiar colors and I'd think of how often he'd been sending me his little gifts. It had to mean something. At night, I became certain it was leading somewhere bad — *really* bad — and there was no way to avoid it other than ending it all. Then, visions of what might be waiting for me once Mr. Briant finally caught up with me would play out for hours, like I was trying to convince myself to go ahead and off myself already.

On one of those bad nights, after thirteen days' worth of camping, I did turn my phone back on. That night had been worse than all the rest. The crunch and scurry of the forest had me panicking enough to venture back to the rental car just in case my cowardice had me deciding to get out of there. Running felt like a better choice than some of the others I'd considered. Instead of leaving, I just sat there, in the car, staring at the glow of my phone. Right away, an avalanche of emails, messages, and texts began to pour in. Seeing it happen made me want to turn the damn thing back off again. But, before I could decide what to do, staring at my one connection to the rest of my life, the phone rang in my hand.

"You've gotta be kidding me," I sighed.

Ready to ignore it, instead I found myself answering after seeing who it was. He was probably the only one I could have talked to, and I'd missed the way he could always anticipate what I needed when things felt awful.

"You okay?" was the first thing I heard. Not hello, just that little question about my wellbeing.

"Course I'm okay," I answered. My skin pebbled with a wave of relief at getting to talk to him. For the first time in a while, I felt a strong need for some company. Not sex, mind you, just a friend at my side, seeing and hearing me. And not just any friend either. It was easier to connect to Jess than anyone else. Sure, it made me feel guilty and a little ashamed, because he was yet another straight guy in my life that I'd grown fond of in complicated ways.

Wondering if he was with his wife, I played with the scruff covering my jaw, scratching through it. I hadn't shaved since Houston, chalking it up to part of a not-so-clever disguise in an attempt to blend in with the rest of the mountainfolk.

I asked, "How are you?"

"Holding down the fort and worrying about you, mostly. It's good to hear your voice. I'd gotten kind of scared we'd never hear from you again. You know how long it's been, right? I don't suppose you'd tell me where you are?"

"Hmm. I'm not sure where I am. All I see is trees and stars. Where are you? Listening to the ocean, hopefully."

"Nah," said Jess. He paused a moment and I thought about his name. Funny how the rest of the band respected his stage name and always used it. I was the only one who could help but call him Jess. He hadn't seemed to mind, and I was glad. I loved his real name. It was so soft on the tongue, unlike my own name which was hard and ugly, like a kick in the ear. "I'm at your house, actually."

I could picture him there, in my rooms, wandering around my things. To everyone around him, he was Gray. But, with me, and in that conversation, he was only Jess. In a strange way, it made him seem closer all of a sudden.

"Jess?"

"Yeah?"

"Is Mags with you?"

There was a long pause and I knew he was yelling at me silently for giving a shit. I deserved it, so I endured the wordless, formless berating.

"No," Jess finally answered. I could hear the hardness to his voice. "He's out for the day, making the rounds. He's been using the gym a lot during the days and god knows where he goes at night. I'm sure he'll be back later. He's claimed your room, by the way. I think he's trying to piss you off from afar in order to lure you back here to kick his ass out."

"Jesus H," I sighed. "He's not bringing people in there, is he?"

"You'll have to ask him," was my roundabout confirmation of the fact.

"Shit." The phone beeped as another call tried to come through. "That's probably him right now, isn't it?" I told myself more than Jess.

"Hmm?"

"Oh, call waiting on the phone. Never mind. There no chance I'd answer, anyway. I've got no clue what I'd say to him and I'd rather keep talking to you. Hey, did you go to Washington at all? Please tell me you did."

"Yeah, for a week. It's been two, you know."

"I had a vague idea. It's hard to care what day it is out here. It's nice to not have to live by a schedule for once."

"Bet you smell nice," he said.

I laughed. "Hey, I'll have you know that I've been skinny dipping regularly. That counts as a bath. Ask anyone."

In my mind's eye, I tracked him, trying to guess which part of the house he was in. He came to life in my imagination, and I could see him standing there, in that place I'd left behind. Maybe the secrets waiting in the walls like phantoms would start talking. The lies I'd told would begin to wander around in the form of specters, rattling chains, moaning and demanding attention. That vision made me want to save him, and spare him. He was too good to be dragged into any of my shit.

I thought of those gifts and notes, and of Mr. Briant. What if he showed up at my house, looking for me but found Jess instead. It made me queasy, terrified for Jess's safety. I scratched at my wrist and wished for my guitar pick. There had to be a way to warn Jess to get out of there, but the only ideas I had sounded too crazy in my head to voice.

Hushed, Jess asked, "You're not drinking alone or thinking of hurting yourself, right? Don't give me nightmares about you passed out next to an open fire with no one to put it out if it spreads."

If I ended up never going home, I wanted to have no regrets when it came to Jess. So, I countered, cutting right to it, "Why do you give a damn about me, Jess?"

"Oh," he said in that deep, full voice of his, "you know. Obvious reasons. You're important to me and you should know you have people worrying about you. I know it's selfish, but we need you. If no one else is telling you that, then I'm happy to."

"Every time I see you or talk to you, right away I'm just so damned happy about it, but at the same time I know it's not good for you to be around me. You're such a good guy and I'm *not* a good guy. So what if I can sing? Lots of people can. There's some... really shitty people out there and I feel like being near me puts you in harm's way."

"What are you talking about? I *know* you're a good guy, Tucker. And this isn't about how well you sing. You, as a person, are so damned important to us. We love you, man. You know that, right?"

"I've done some bad things."

"You think you're the only one? Everybody does bad things. Whatever it is you feel bad about, believe me when I say, without even knowing what it is, that I've heard worse. You want to talk about it? Tell me what's bothering you?"

"I can't talk about it," I murmured, looking around at all of that thick, shifting pitch-blackness surrounding the car. Talking about the devil might lure him out. "Why didn't you stay longer in Washington? You deserve the time off."

"Maybe I do, but my life is here."

"What about that ring on your finger?" I asked, before I could catch myself. Immediately, I tried to take it back, but all that came out was sputtering.

"That's, uh, not something I talk about either," he told me.

"I'm sorry. I didn't mean it like that. It's your own business. I just don't want to have you waiting on me when I don't even know what I'm doing. You're dealing with Mags day in and day out and I don't know the state of things at the house. Y'all don't need anything, do you? No packages have come for me there, right?"

"We're fine, Tucker. The house is fine. There's mail, but nothing urgent. Look, if it's Mags that's the problem, tell me where you are. If anything happened to you, if you got sick, or fell and hurt yourself out there, all alone... It's fucking scary, okay? I know you like to go off on your own, but at least let me be your back-up plan in case of an emergency. I won't tell anyone else if you don't want me to. I could drive out and check on you, see that you're alive and not the hostage of an overgrown grizzly and I'll be on my way, let you have as much time as you need. It'd be really good to see you, too. I wouldn't bother you, you could still have your space but at least you wouldn't have to be so alone."

Part of me wanted to say yes, and to have him there. He would be that friendly presence to keep me anchored, especially when the daylight ran out. It would be nice. Jess didn't get in your face like Mags did. In fact, Jess wasn't like Mags at all, in any way.

But there was still the problem of what to do about the lies and dependency. If I invited Jess in, I'd be letting that part of my life — my band — shatter my solitude, and it would rain chaos on my peace. There was still a lot I was lying to Jess about. It wasn't just Mags. If Jess came to me, I'd have to start lying again. In the woods, by myself, maybe I could learn to live with what I'd done with William, Ken, and Jade — not to mention Mr. Briant, my own personal boogeyman. I had to try. It would eat me alive, otherwise. The guilt and shame were out of control. They were right on the surface, for anyone to see.

I didn't feel strong enough to cope anymore. It was impossible to keep pretending everything was fine, like I could keep going on with things as they were. I couldn't. The lies and the truth had been eating me up inside for so long, there was nothing left but hollow emptiness. I was a shell of a man, ready to crack under the slightest pressure.

Pushing Mr. Briant out of my head, I tried to force my thoughts elsewhere, to my temporary lovers. They'd each been so kind. They were safer memories to visit.

When my eyes closed, I heard them, their moans, the way it felt to be fucking each of them, in all of the different ways that I had. If I concentrated on it, I could still feel myself inside William — hot, snug, and seductive. Jade was there, too, with her dark hair and aqua eyes, joyously taking my ass for a ride that lasted halfway through the night. And Ken, my smiling doll, who knew and loved himself so well and had been so blessedly sweet to me....

Those secret moments, connections with people that had burned so hot and went out as quickly as a candle flame after a single breath — they were lost to me now, and it choked me up. Or maybe that was just the old pain bleeding out. If there was anything time had taught me, it was that the bad would keep on bleeding as long as the wound was still open and festering.

I kept losing the good people in my life, but the bad seemed to stick around forever.

I made an awful sort of noise into the phone, a choked sob that Jess had to hear. Too late, I twisted the phone away from my mouth and squeezed my eyes closed.

"What's wrong?" Jess demanded. "Tucker?! Please talk to me, man. I'm honestly trying my best here."

"God, what have I done," I moaned softly. "What am I *doing*? What's wrong with me? Hell...."

"Hey," Jess said, sounding shaken. "You're freaking me out. Please just tell me what's wrong? Are you okay? Are you hurt?"

"I'm sorry. This isn't... it's not your problem. You shouldn't have to deal with it. It's nothing. It's me. My life. My fucking decisions. I've been pushing myself, hiking and trying to wear myself out so I can sleep, but it's not working. I just sit here, thinking about bad shit. I'm so *tired*, man. I'm tired all the way through of being something I'm not. I mean, I *loved* the tour. I love our band. You know that. These past few months have been my dream come true but it was like it happened to someone else. I was too worried to even enjoy it."

It felt like drawing poison from a wound — painful but necessary — so I kept going. "I'm sick of lying, and the fucking *game* of it all. I dragged Mags into this and now you're stuck here, too, when you could be anywhere else. *Anywhere else* would be safer than here, Jess. Can't you just go back to Washington? I can't tell anymore if I'm putting y'all in harm's way or sacrificing myself for the money.

"Am I a whore, Jess? Is that what I am? Selling myself, my body, my voice, for... what? Trouble's still out there. Am I doing it for money? What good is money, anyway? It doesn't make you happy. It doesn't make it worth it. I'm still completely alone with memories of the shit I've done at the end of the day, no matter how much fucking cash is in my accounts. I'm still messed up on the inside, putting on this act like I'm perfect. You've been so kind to me, Jess, but I'm just dragging you down."

"Listen. Listen to me," he begged. "I know how it is. I know *exactly* how that feels, okay? Someone important to me struggled with the same types of issues and I can tell you, man, you have to fucking forgive yourself, please! No matter what you think you've done, you're not seeing it clearly. You're too close. You *are* important and you're not hurting us, okay? Don't listen to those voices in your head telling you otherwise. What they tell you isn't true. You're not alone, Tucker. I'm with you, even if I'm not there in person. Mags is with you. You have people who love you and would do anything for you. What you bring to the world with your music — that *means* something. You don't always get to see it, because you're kept safe by the people whose job it is to watch out for you. When you're at a distance like that, you don't see how you bring joy to your fans. But, believe me, people need that. Life is a *bitch*. The things we go through, every day, how hard we make things on ourselves when we don't need to, the doubt and the fear... It's hard, and it's shitty, and it's a struggle, every day, just to survive. For some, the only thing that gets them through is a beautiful song. It's company during the bad times. It's inspiring. It touches the soul.

"Tucker, I've spoken to so many veterans who have seen and lived things that *no one* should have to endure. They've had pieces of themselves taken away by war and circumstance. They see their friends die and think it should have been them instead. You know what lifts them up at the bad times? Anything that makes the loneliness ease back. Music. Connection. Compassion. That's what *I* live for — spreading hope, or just a smile. I'll do *anything*, go *anywhere*, as long as I know that I can make music that matters, and that will live on, long after I die. I may not be a soldier, but I'd like to think I give something back, too, in my own way. Music is one of the most powerful things in the world, and you're part of that. Be proud of it."

His voice echoed in my head, and my heart, breaking through some old walls. He pulled me up, out of my fog.

"You want to know the truth, Tucker? No one is perfect. We all feel like we're failing sometimes, in one way or another. But you're perfect to me, and you're perfect to Mags. Whatever it is you're going through right now, man, you will survive it. You're strong, and you're brave. I've seen you stand up there on those stages, exuding this powerful energy. You have that in you. Take time to take care of yourself, but don't ever doubt that what you do is important, or that you aren't needed, desperately."

Slowly, I caught my breath and dried my eyes. I wouldn't have hung up on him for the world. Feeling him there with me, in spirit, was what kept me going.

"You still there?" he asked after a while.

"Yeah. I am. Thanks for hanging on. There's been so much noise in my head, you wouldn't believe it. I think you got through, though. Don't know what I'd do without you, man. Thanks for saying all of that."

"Tell me where you are. Give me an idea."

"I'll come home soon. I promise." After a moment, I asked, hopefully, "You'll be there, right?"

"I will. I'll wait. I'll wait easier if you'd call once in a while, though."

"Noted. Thanks, Jess. You're one of the good ones, you know."

"You too," he answered with feeling. The call ended, and I thought on it for a long time.

Chapter 12

Saved

For two weeks, I avoided them and kept trying to push them down again but, slowly, the memories came back. With so much quiet around me, of course I knew what would rise to the surface to disturb the calm.

Grade school had been a bumpy journey. I'd been a short, skinny, sandy haired, blue-eyed kid who liked to sing and kept to himself, ordinary in every way. I wasn't interested in girls or being popular, sports or doing well in school. None of that won me any friends. Since I was never book smart, my grades sucked, so teachers didn't favor me either. Once they'd tried to get me to try harder, and failed, they mostly left me alone, too. The only thing I loved was sitting under trees, pouring my heart out when I thought no one was listening.

There was one boy my age, named Angel Rivera, who was quiet like me, and didn't fit in as much as he'd have liked to. His family had recently moved to the states from Puerto Rico. They'd spent time up in New York, too, before settling in southern Tennessee. The cultural whiplash had done a number on him. We met when we were only nine or ten. He'd sit near me during lunch or before the day began. Outsiders always found each other, and that's what we'd done.

He'd told me he liked my singing, after sneaking up quietly enough to catch me at it, and asked to see the songs I was writing. Once in a while, he'd bring over an old guitar that had belonged to his father. I'd sing and he'd play, and it was almost magic.

That lasted a few years before Angel grew tall and strong. Then, the football coaches began going after him, and the more popular kids gave him more attention. Even when he was cooler than me, Angel would always stop to give me a smile and talk for a minute or two. He stopped playing guitar, though, and football eventually led to a career in law enforcement.

Mags and I met in high school after I'd really started to miss my friendship with Angel. By then, there'd been no doubt that I was a nobody. Over the years, after we'd left our school days behind and success with music had made me someone people noticed, I got a lot of questions about why I put up with all of Mags' bullshit for so long, and why I'd kept him around. Those early high school years were why. The things that came later, like the sleeping around, the ways he didn't give a shit about my privacy, the hanging on—it was all nothing to me. Those little annoying things hadn't mattered when the guy had saved my hide so many times I'd lost count before I was even out of my teens. So what if he could be an asshole? So what if he took advantage, and overstepped more often than not?

All Mags had ever done was try to do the right thing. His family troubles left him looking for a safer place where he'd get some respect. He'd never tried to feel like a bigger man by beating someone else down, and he'd always stood up for people who'd been picked on.

I honestly didn't know why he stood up for me that first time, or why he cared. He hadn't known me. I was a stranger to him. But, he went out of his way, for no reason at all. I couldn't puzzle it out. Whenever I tried to—late at night, early in the morning, or out on stage with thousands of people staring at us—it scared me to death that all I could come up with were only vague guesses.

Once, I asked him, flat out, why. Why had stepped in to defend a stranger? Why had he put himself on the line? What was it he'd seen in me that was worth fighting for? It was during one of the darkest times in my life when I'd asked, and, ironically, right after I'd gotten my recording contract.

That was something I had needed to know before we could begin that next leg of our journey. We'd been sitting in my little apartment, with dreams of stardom in the country music industry finally getting some traction. More real than those dreams was a handgun I'd kept under my bed, given to me by my dad for protection. That morning, I'd loaded it, set the barrel in my mouth, and waited to see if I was going to pull the trigger. When I hadn't, a few hours later, I had Mags sitting beside me. He didn't know about the gun I'd put away again, or that I'd wanted to use it. I asked him, "Why, man? Why did you bother with me? We didn't run in the same circles. You were so much cooler than I was. But you stepped up for me anyway. I can't figure out why."

"You're asking now?" he chuckled. "Little late for that, isn't it? You're stuck with me."

He'd looked so handsome and sure of himself, sitting in the dusty light on a cloudy day in my crappy little apartment, which I hadn't cleaned in a while, or decorated much. He wasn't that poor kid dressed in old clothes from the Goodwill and without the smarts to go far in school. No, all of a sudden he was more successful than anyone else in his entire family, just because of a piece of paper—a recording contract with a big name music label. He was so proud and happy about it, Mags glowed with inner light. I couldn't take my eyes off of him.

But my body and heart were bruised in ways that felt like they'd never heal. I'd been dressed in some old drawstring pants and a t-shirt. My hair wasn't brushed. I'd needed a shower and a shave, among many other things. He thought I was tired, maybe sick to my stomach, but it went so much deeper. The reasons to die were bigger than the reasons to keep fighting and getting out of bed. Mags didn't know about any of that. He was in a world apart from me. Success had carved a gulf between us, and I knew I'd never get across to him again.

Mags was full of plans and felt like he had the world by the balls. I loved to see how strong and happy it made him. Mags was my hope. He was my everything.

Even if the numbness and the gun won out in the end, at least I'd helped my friend. It was something, anyway.

"Just tell me why. There must have been a reason," I pressed.

If I knew what he saw in me—because it sure as shit wasn't my voice—it would have given me something to hold on to. I needed a solid reason to keep going, and it had to be something that had nothing to do with singing or the contract with both our names on it. I was standing on the edge of a cliff, and relied on Mags to save me, and pull me back.

"Who else would've, if not me?" Mags said softly. "That's why."

"That's not a reason," I argued.

"You needed me, kid," he said. It was quiet, but sincere. He was looking down at his hands, then only briefly glanced up at my eyes. "It was enough reason then. It was nice to be needed. Still is."

Maybe it did boil down to relying on each other in unhealthy ways. God damn, that was an awful notion.

The event that changed everything and gave me my best friend happened between classes. It was a situation that had become pretty common. Someone yanked my pack from my back, then tripped me so I went sprawling on the linoleum floor.

Other kids were laughing behind me. I knew to stay down, so I did, expecting the swift kick to my gut that always came a second later, along with more mocking laughter of boys bigger and more respected than me.

They did kick and kicked again, knocking the wind completely out of me. My gut and my ribs ached. I wrapped my hands around my head to shield it as I gasped for air which my lungs didn't want to accept.

Coughing and wheezing, I tried to crawl away in search of safety. Really, I didn't expect to actually find it. They'd chase me, keep kicking until I started crying or a teacher yelled for them to stop. That's what always happened. My afternoon would be spent alternately with the nurse, the guidance counselor, and the principal, relaying my story of ignorance, not giving names, just trying to fade away.

That wasn't what happened that afternoon in the October of my sophomore year.

They didn't come after me when I tried to get away.

Instead, behind me, there was the sound of a punch connecting, a grunt and a struggle. Glancing back, I saw Mags, who I didn't know well, yet. He had only been a face in the crowd.

Mags punched that kid right in the mouth. When the kid fell backward over his own feet and his friends scattered, Mags kept throwing blows all the way down to the floor, then pounded him into the ground.

It was beautiful, even if it did scare the hell out of me.

"Stop! You'll kill 'im!" I screamed, when Mags didn't quit. His fist slammed down into flesh even after the kid was clearly out cold, blood seeping from his lip. There was a fire in Mags' eyes, which I only understood later. It had been ignited by the chance to hit back for once. He'd always been picked on by his big brothers, who thought it was easy and fun to let Mags be the butt of all their jokes and pranks. But, when faced with a fight with people his own age, boys his own size or smaller, he had the advantage. He was mad and ready to hit first if it meant the bullies would get a taste of the pain they liked to dish out to others.

"Teach you to pick on people!" he growled at my attacker.

I pulled him off, or tried to at least. That was it. That's all it took.

From that moment on, Mags was my hero.

He got months of detention and started being nice to me, saying hi, and sitting with me at lunch.

I knew early on that I'd never be able to repay him for what he'd done, ever. It wasn't just that he'd stood up for me; it was the friendship that came as a result of that, which was priceless. There wasn't enough money in the world to manage a proper thank you.

We grew up, became men, and still I tried. I paid him back with love, then, and loyalty. There was money eventually, but it was the love that Mags needed even more, and took greedily. He fed off of it like a hopeless addict, and I let him. I had to.

They said that once you'd saved someone, you became responsible for their life from that point on.

I'd argue the weight of responsibility was just as big for the one who had been saved, blessed by chance bravery and unexpected kindness.

The guitar lay on a blanket that I had spread out over millions of pine needles carpeting the forest floor, in the clearing where I'd spent the past two weeks. My phone was off again. My goodbyes had been said. My favorite guitar pick was in my hand. The edge of it was very thin and slightly pointed.

Part of me understood that the view was beautiful, and the weather pleasant. It didn't touch me. The numbness was so heavy, nothing could get through. That was all I was trying to do—cut through that heavy feeling—but it took work. It always had. But I was patient. It wasn't really complicated, just a slight, sawing, back and forth motion, over and over again following the same path across my wrist until the skin slowly gave way. I never knew when my heart would lodge in my throat and the spiral into darkness would begin. A strange grief would begin to pull me down and even though I never knew how far I would fall, I did know who was behind it. There was nothing I could do to make him stop or take back what he'd already done. But if I kept going and didn't care how it felt, maybe I'd carve my way deep enough this time to save myself from ever having to see him again.

Biting my lip in concentration, just trying to tear through everything to something real, I sawed horizontally at my wrist. I'd been doing it for a while. Had it been an hour? Longer than that? The gouged line of flesh was near the faint scars from when I'd done the same thing in the past and hadn't gotten very far with it. There was nothing to stop me now, though. All I needed was to keep going. There was some pain, but it wasn't enough to make me want to stop.

Crimson dripped down my hand, along my fingers, and it was the color of shame. No more lying. The blood was proof of what I'd done. There was no hiding it. It was too dark, slick, and vital to be denied. Relieved, I held out my bloody hand so the drops would spatter the pine needles, red on bluish green.

It was a cop-out. The silence of the forest cocooned me. This was what I'd come there for, I'd realized when I woke up that morning. Not to rest or find myself. I'd come for this. That sawed red line through my flesh. The quiet. The lack of people trying to stop me or step in. The pick which had made so much music, and had kept me trapped, might just set me free.

Sitting beside my guitar with one knee curled up to my chest, I strummed the strings with the bloody pick.

Nature seemed to swallow the sound rather than let it carry.

There were so many memories to sift through. Thinking of Mags was miserable, and worse than the numbness, or the relief of how the pick kept getting me closer to the edge. I was trying to find a way to begin to break free of our friendship. After all he'd done for me, I was planning to betray him. In a way, hurting him would be revenge, because I'd sacrificed myself for him and he didn't even know it. Shouldn't your best friend know when you were falling apart? Pieces of me were missing now, and Mags just kept partying, unable or unwilling to see I was dying. That's why I'd been so angry with him, but I felt guilty about abandoning him, too. Even when I told myself that by finally accomplishing the end of me, I might help Mags grow up and move on, it didn't ring true. So, I left it behind.

Mags wasn't my only problem anyway, or my biggest.

With a deep sigh, I glanced up through the trees' branches and the overlapping leaves, shimmering in the wind. Beyond, clouds floated, weightless, through the atmosphere. Puffy white on blue, it was an ideal view of a toxic world.

I turned on my phone, retrieved from the car. At that point, I didn't care if someone tracked the signal or not. I was fucked anyway. The casing got smeared with more of the warm, sticky red that slicked my fingers. Jess picked up after three rings.

"How are you, cowboy?" he asked softly. There was an ache in his tone.

"What are you thinking about, right now?" I pressed, matching his mellow vibe. The pain in my wrist only made me want to go back to carving into it, but I didn't want to do it while talking to Jess, so I held off.

"My dad," he said. "It's his birthday." I heard Jess breathe out a sad little laugh. "He was really young when he had me, you know. *Really* young. When I was little, he was the best person I knew. He had such a good heart which he wore on his sleeve and just always had this happy, sunny outlook every day, even though he was a teenager with a kid to take care of. He was hopeful and never let it get him down. I feel like the world has it out for guys like him sometimes, because everything that's happened to him since... God, he's gone through *so much shit*. And he just... stopped being sunny... always cloudy and dark instead. It changed him so much and I miss that guy he used to be. Especially on days like today." He took a deep breath, blew it out, and apologized. "Sorry, I didn't mean to unload that on you."

"No problem," I said, letting his voice fill my mind and erase some of that hollow feeling.

"You remind me of him sometimes."

"How so?"

"When you sing, you wear your heart on your sleeve, like he did, and help people connect to emotions and dreams, giving back some goodness to the world. But, you aren't as sunny as you used to be, Tucker," he said with far too much tenderness not to be terrifying, "and it scares me to death. I've tried, you know, to not give a shit and to get you to open up to me like I tried to over and over again with him, and I don't know what else to do for you, except be here. I know something's wrong, and if you'd just *let me in* a little bit...."

"You can't save me, Jess," I told him, thinking of Mags, and how many times he'd tried to save me, too.

"I don't believe that!" Jess growled, his emotions bleeding into mine. "I *have to believe* that people can be saved, that maybe if I'd kept trying with Dad, I could have, and *I will not lose you*, Tucker. Just fucking *talk to me. Please.*"

I got choked up and made an anxious, fearful sound. There was blood everywhere, on everything. It was too much, so I hung up, muttering something about having to go and promising to call back in a minute. I turned the phone off again, wanting the blankness of nothingness back, disliking the heartache.

But it was too late. At least I was feeling something. After a little while, to fill the air with music instead of worries, I set my fingers back to the guitar strings and found a pretty chord.

Look to the future, I told myself. My voice was my biggest weapon. I should use it, I knew, as a way to fight back. If the new album was going to be acoustic and melodic, ballads to tug at the heartstrings, I knew where to begin when looking for inspiration.

It made sense, too, that my thoughts would go there next, after leaving Angel, Mags, and, finally, Jess behind. Because there was one day, one important moment in my life when I'd needed help, and no one was there to save me. Though he was years too late, Jess was still trying to save me, sensing my emotional state in ways Mags never had, even though Mags had always tried to be there in his own ways. Mags never suspected how bad it really was. He had always thought he'd been able to spare me harm from the bullies and from every random act of cruelty, like that old man in the alley with the knife. I never told Mags he'd failed, but it was true. Letting my best friend believe in

his success at protecting me was a gift I gave him.
The truth would have driven him mad.

Chapter 13
Meeting Mr. Briant

My first big meeting with a record company executive happened when I was twenty one. For four years I'd been playing clubs, fairs, festivals and whatever gigs I could get. A talent scout caught one of my festival shows. The demo I gave him got me the interest of the company he represented. The interest got me a meeting with the man in charge. It was much later, *years* later, when I realized they must have done their homework, way back when. Someone had been watching me, making observations, fitting me into slots that had already been there and happened to be just my size.

They were the game players, the ones writing the rules. I was a piece they moved around a board. Move two spaces forward, collect a hundred dollars — that sort of thing. But, back in the beginning, I was oblivious. All that mattered was that they noticed me, wanted me, and I was happy to play along.

His name was Nathan Briant. He was somewhere around forty years old. Maybe he was younger. I was never quite sure.

He was good looking in a corporate kind of way. Fit. Well-dressed. Broad-shouldered and usually wearing a smile so sharp you could cut yourself on it if you weren't careful.

Every time I met him in person, he was all decked out in expensive suits that fit him like a glove. I had no doubt, either, that his haircut alone cost more than my entire outfit, boots included.

Nathan Briant was made of power. It dripped from every gesture, every word. That man made and broke careers with ease and you could feel it was true just being near him. He wielded his sizable power in ways I'd never witnessed before. Just to be invited to meet with him was the biggest thing to ever happen to me, as a musician and as a man. I knew it. I had no notions of self-importance, arrogance, or pride. All I did was sing my songs with a heart full of gratitude for those who appreciated what they heard.

Nothing had prepared me for the lion's den I was walking in to, or warned me that I was lunch.

The first time we met, it wasn't in his office. It was in a sitting room that was used as an informal meeting area. When you walked in, you knew what it was. Even without a long table flanked with chairs, or a big, imposing desk, it was clear the room was designed to make newcomers feel small and out of their league.

The expensive-looking couches and armchairs, the walls lined with gold and platinum records, the view of the city, as pretty as a postcard, from the massive window stretching from floor to ceiling on one of the four walls — it added up to a great big, intimidating impression.

My mom had bought me some new clothes to help me look my best. My dad gave me a ride in, wanting to be there to wish me luck on my big day. He waited downstairs, by the car, until I was done. A modest man at heart, he'd felt his outfit wasn't nice enough for him to come up the elevator along with me, which is why he stayed below. It was the first and last time I ever let him near that place.

The secretary was a remarkably sweet girl named Leigh. She showed me in. I liked her instantly, with her honest, cute grin and curly cloud of brown hair. Everything about her was approachable and genuine. She was bizarrely out of place.

Mr. Briant was seated on the couch when I entered, sprawled out with his arms resting on the couch's back. His feet were planted widely like he was taking up the whole room all by himself. That left me choosing a chair rather than presuming I could sit nearer to him.

I was so nervous — trembling and stammering — and wanting to impress that confident man in any way possible. While we spoke about my music, the label, and possibilities, I sat on the edge of the seat, hands folded, eyes wide.

Time felt like it drew out, but it was probably no more than five minutes of initial conversation before he cut right to the point.

"There's a heck of a lot I can do for you, Mr. Reynolds." He smiled with a shark's cold grin, full of teeth and hunger, his fingers drumming on the top of the couch. "Question is, what are you willing to do for *me* to win *my* favor?"

God, I was stupid. Sitting at my campsite in the mountains, with the comforting sound of Jess's voice faded away and blood dripping down my hand, I recalled that part of my past. It physically hurt to remember how foolish I had been. My guitar pick, splattered red—just as all of the music I'd produced with the label was polluted with mangled shreds of my innocence—moved over the strings of my guitar. The leaves rustled overhead. Trees bent and groaned in the wind. My tears, mourning the sweet kid I used to be before that damned day, fell without any sound at all, dampening the polished wood. I pulled the instrument closer, onto my lap, in order to have something I cared about close by to soothe me as I drifted back in time again.

"Please," I'd said, "Call me Tucker. I'd do absolutely anything, sir. I'll work as hard as you need me to, to make this happen. It would mean so much to me to be able to work with you and your company."

"I believe that," he nodded, cool as could be. "I do, I do. I could change your *life*, son. Your whole life."

My heart was pounding. His eyes were focused tightly on me, and I felt it, waiting and anticipating whatever was to come. As his gaze roamed down my body, I became self-conscious of my outfit and appearance, fearing it wasn't good enough for him. My mouth was dry, so I sipped the glass of water that had been provided. All of my attention was focused on him, his words and every little thing he did. The rest of the world fell away.

"If this is going to happen," he said, sipping his drink, which wasn't clear like my water, but something dark amber in color. "You need to *demonstrate* how hard you'd work for me. Right now."

I had no idea what he meant.

Scrambling for something to say, trying to understand so I didn't seem as big of an idiot as I felt, I sputtered out a few rambling words. Countless teachers, mentors, and other adults in my life had tried and failed to get me to learn my lessons. I could never quite wrap my head around things like they wanted. This was the same thing again. Here was a man wiser and more capable than me, trying to set me on a better path in life, and I was too fucking stupid to know how to follow.

"C'mere, son." After watching me hesitate, he motioned with a hand for me to come closer.

Slowly, I stood. Sunlight flooded in through the window to my right. There were no lamps on, and no overhead lights, just the sun. It cast dark shadows where it didn't touch.

The door was shut tight, with sweet Leigh beyond it. There were no other windows or glass, other than the one which revealed the wide world at our feet.

I headed over to the couch, without knowing whether to sit or linger there, standing. I wiped my hands dry on my new pants from my momma, meant to make me look nice for that meeting. I tucked my hair behind my ears and cleared my throat as my gaze skittered around.

"Come here," he said, spreading his feet wider, thighs fallen open as he pointed to the patch of carpet right in front of the couch, between his parted legs. "Right here."

I walked to the spot, my heartbeat racing away with my panic and desperate confusion.

"On your knees," he smiled, laughing silently at me, like I was the biggest moron on the planet. I was never able to get his sing-songy voice out of my head. He spoke down to me, like I was a silly child and he pitied me for it. There was no meanness, though, no threat in the way he spoke. He always sounded kind, patient, and as if he was willing to humor me and explain, just this once.

As soon as my kneecaps were touching the thin, dark floor covering, he opened his fly and pulled out his cock. It was dark and uncut, the first uncircumcised penis I'd ever seen.

I glanced at it and quickly away, at a spot on the painted-dark wall behind the couch. He wrapped a hand behind my neck, pulling me in firmly, just in case I got any ideas of trying to get free. Where would I go, anyhow? What would I say? I was a young, deeply closeted gay man who had no goddamned clue how the world worked. No one knew about my orientation. I'd always buried my feelings, knowing in my heart that they were wrong. The rules of the world I lived in were crystal clear. You couldn't be gay *and* be a star in the country music industry. At least, you couldn't be both openly. Privately, in closed-door meetings with people expecting you to do them a favor?

Well, that was a whole other story.

With a grunted sound of frightened shock, I felt myself being moved. My hands went to his thighs, automatically. A moment later, his dick was flush against my closed mouth and cheek.

He held me there with both hands until I realized I wasn't getting up or going anywhere. Breathing hard through my nostrils as my pulse raced, he gave me some time to let my position sink in. That was something that held true about Mr. Briant—he wasn't ever in a hurry and he never doubted himself or his ability to get what he wanted.

"That's it," he said gently, like a concerned father figure. "It's not gonna bite you, see? Take your time. Get used to it. You ever give head before, son?"

"No," I whimpered. I'd never touched another man like that. It had always just been fantasy, nothing close to reality. Now that reality had me in its clutches, I instantly regretted ever secretly wanting it at all.

"That's okay. I'm gonna teach you. If you try hard to do it well, there's a good chance I can work something out, contract-wise. We'll bring you on board, make you part of the team, make you *famous*."

He eased up on his grip. One hand came off the back of my head. Then the other did, too. I stayed where I was, my face pressed between his legs, and he was pleased. Breathing against his balls, nuzzling his bare flesh, my nose pushed against his warm, waxed-smooth skin, I tried to calm down before I passed right out. My heart had never beaten so hard in my life.

"Why, you're trembling like a leaf!" he *tsk*ed. "You nervous?"

My voice failed me, so I grunted my answer. He stroked through my hair, gathering it up.

"Nothing to be nervous about. It's just you and me here. We're going to come to an understanding, and I'm going to make you a successful, rich, popular musician. You want that?"

"Yessir," I murmured. My voice was uneven and muffled by flesh. The smell of him filled my head. He was getting hard, twitching against my cheek.

"Give me that elastic on your wrist. We need to get this hair out of the way so you can use your mouth properly."

I backed off an inch or two, tugged the band off my wrist and handed it over. He wound it around his handful of my hair, tying it back securely.

"Now we're ready. That's much better." His thumb rubbed along my bottom lip. I shut my eyes as he pushed the thumb into my mouth and used it to pry my jaw open. The thumb trapped my tongue, and his strong grip demanded that I open up as wide as I could. Breathing shallowly and my hands gripping his thighs again, I whimpered sharply as he lifted his dick and fed it to me.

My soft, small gasps and grunts puffed against his dick, set against my tongue, between my widely-parted lips. Both of his hands clamped down around my skull as he thrust forward. His sheath pulled back as his dick slid over my tongue to fill my throat.

I gagged harshly as the reflex was triggered and my body tried to dislodge the thing stuffed down my throat. Coughing, eyes streaming, I pushed back with my hands against his legs. He just slid himself farther inside, as far as he could go and watched me choke on it, holding me down. My terror was instant. I tried to retch, couldn't inhale, and convulsed in his hands.

The taste of him, the musky smell lingering in my nostrils, the thickness of his swollen cock fitted snugly between my tongue and the tissues of my throat—it was obscene.

"Yeah, I can tell you don't like that one bit, do ya?" he chuckled amiably, renewing his double-handed grip on my head. "This is an important lesson, though, boy. You need to learn your *place.*"

He sounded like he was going to break me the bad news, not riled at all, calm as could be. With a one-handed, iron grip on the back of my skull, the fingers of his other hand moved to pinch my nose shut, cutting off my ability to inhale through my nostrils. He eased me back a little, let me draw the briefest, most desperate inhale of my life down my throat and then thrust back into my windpipe, making me choke on him again, letting me gag violently and fight. Saliva filled my mouth, spilling over my lip. Tears leaked from my eyes and nose.

I thought he was going to suffocate me to death like that.

"We're here to talk about this mouth of yours, aren't we? The only way you're going to get anywhere is if you use it properly. That's my job, see? To show you just how to use it to make us both a lot of money."

He pulled out of my throat and settled for only filling my mouth. He let go of my nose.

"Close your lips," he instructed. I obeyed, breathing desperately through my nose, my lips stretched in a wide O around his shaft. He petted my hair. "Now, suck on that a while. Show me how talented that tongue of yours really is."

Trembling, caring only about breathing, my eyes opened but unfocused, my face covered in tears and saliva, I suckled that man's cock like it was candy, since I had no idea what else to do with it. Scared whines and moans colored every breath I made. He tasted bitter and strange and it felt unnatural to have my mouth so open and so full.

After a while, with him watching closely, he guided my head up a little. His dick sprung free, huge and hard, jutting upright. The end of his cock dragged a wet trail from my lips to my cheek and back to touch my nose.

"Want you to lick that, now. Long licks." He was holding himself with a hand, tugging that sheath back so that his slick, pink crown was revealed.

Not thinking, just reacting, I did it, licking him up to the tip over and over again, pressing the flesh upright with my tongue, and just trying to keep him happy so he wouldn't choke me again. I couldn't shut up though. My noises were constant and terrified.

Strangely, though, the novelty began to wear off. I became less afraid that he was going to kill me. It was just a blowjob he was after, I realized. It wasn't the end of the world. It was giving head.

The more I calmed down, the more he praised me and petted the top of my head. Wanting more of that type of reassurance, I did whatever I could to get it, trying to keep doing whatever things that Mr. Briant liked. If he was pleased, I was pleased. And the sooner I learned my lesson, the quicker it would be over.

"Kiss the tip," he said next, guiding it to my lips. I did, pressing my mouth to it, reverently. "Lick that slit. You like that?"

I groaned and, without waiting to be asked, opened wide to let him enter me again.

"That's it, son. It's not so difficult, now, is it? If you want us to put that mouth to work for us, you've just gotta show me how hard you'll work to use it."

At first, he moved me, pulling my head down onto him, then guiding me back so my lips slipped along his shaft, which was sliding against my tongue. After a moment, I got the hang of it and repeated the motion on my own.

It seemed like forever, like I was bobbing on his cock for hours. There was no goal in my mind, no intent to finish and escape. The only thing I wanted was for Mr. Briant to keep praising me rather than be displeased.

When he unloaded, it caught me by surprise, like I didn't know that's what happened when men got off.

My eyes went wide. I tried to escape but he held me fast.

"You swallow that," he ordered, like he was giving me my penance for being a willful brat. "All of it. Every bit. Suck it all out. Let it go down your throat."

I wanted to gag again as thick, hot, bitter fluid slid back along my tongue and down my throat, but knew to do as he said.

When he was spent, he let me pull off and brought my head down to rest against his damp, softening cock. Gasping for air, I tried to calm myself. Slowly, I did. With every fiber of my being, I knew where I was, and what, suddenly, my place had become.

I'd figured out my lesson.

He wasn't holding me anymore, just stroking my hair.

"When you're ready," he said sweetly, "You come up here and sit with me. I'll get you your water and a towel."

It took quite a few minutes for me to disengage from him. Part of the reason for that was not knowing how to move on to the next moment, afraid to look him in the eye and bear his judgment. Another part of it was something else entirely — something dark and twisted, which felt more comfortable soiled, helpless, and on my knees for him rather than sitting as equals, side-by-side. I didn't have any fear left. There was plenty of shame, but it was mostly shame that I didn't hate what he'd had me do. I'd enjoyed it all in some sick way. That was the idea, though. They'd known somehow that I was their perfect candidate. The shame was the leash they used to rein me in, keep me loyal, and keep me quiet. It was damn effective, too.

But I did get up off the floor. I climbed up onto the couch, shakily. He stood, pants hanging open, his dick still presented to me like he was thinking about using it again. In another perverted way, I was quite glad he hadn't zipped up yet. That would have been much worse, to wipe snot and semen from my chin while he stood there, immaculate.

He stood in front of me as I took his towel and cleaned myself up. I drank the whole glass of water in two gulps and couldn't look him in the eye or even get close.

"Take care of those pants for me, son. Be gentle."

He drank his scotch and waited as I fumbled with his zipper, shifting his flesh with a hand to keep it out of the way.

"Now, how'd you enjoy your first performance? Did you like that?"

"Yessir."

"Good. I'm glad to hear it. Should only be a couple of weeks to get the paperwork in order. I'll give you a ring when I know when you can come back to see me again."

Head bowed, still trying to close his button, I asked with disbelief, "I'm getting the contract?"

"Yes indeed!" He laughed happily. "This is just the start of things for you. I can feel it. You've got a lot of potential. We'll work out the specifics and figure out through some trial and error where your particular *skills* lie. I am *really* looking forward to our next meeting."

I looked up at his eyes, then. Swallowing hard around the sour taste in my mouth, feeling sweaty, flustered, and generally a mess, I wondered what he meant by that.

He touched my lips and hummed thoughtfully, perhaps deciding what that meeting would entail.

"On your feet, now. I have another appointment soon."

Somehow, I was able to stand before him.

"Thank you, sir," I said, more honestly than I ever should have.

He smiled wider with a hand cupped deliberately under my balls. Then, he squeezed, slowly and firmly, up my erection, weighing it, measuring my length and my rigidity.

"I appreciate it. I won't let you down," I told him, my voice quivering.

"Oh, I can tell," he said with happy surprise.

Chapter 14

Indebted

When I was safely at home, alone in my apartment with the door shut tight behind me and after my dad had driven away, I wept like a baby. Later that night, after a long shower, I jerked off, thinking about what had happened. That's how conflicted I was about it, right from the start.

Whoever was responsible for what had happened to me—and I sensed it went beyond just one deviant man in a high level job—barely had to do anything. They already had me. I couldn't confess what had happened with Mr. Briant. I couldn't I walk away from the only real opportunity in my life to be someone. Even if there was some way to prove what he'd done, I would never come forward publicly to admit to sucking off another man just to get a contract. That was a good way to make sure I'd never have a music career. And the label had all the money in the world to hire a team of the best lawyers in the world to snuff out my case in a heartbeat.

It was indeed true that I always secretly fantasized about men, but never dared approach them the way I could, and did, approach girls. There had always been a level of safety in flirting with girls, because I knew I'd never follow through on it. They didn't unsettle me the way attractive men did. I'd looked and imagined what I wanted to do with them, but that's as far as it went. I was almost asexual for my teenage years, doomed to love my best friend, who couldn't love me back in the right ways. Since I couldn't figure out exactly what I wanted or how to get it, I didn't even try. Nathan Briant was the first man I was ever sexually involved with. He broke down that wall for me. After that first meeting, I couldn't stop thinking about his cock.

At the time, and in the weird days following, most of my nerves were due to being out of my element, being confused, being shy, and overwhelmed. I didn't even resent the son of a bitch for what he'd done. Sure, I was scared of him. That was part of the appeal. He was fucking out of his mind, but it made him attractive in the same way it had always attracted me to Mags. Whereas Mags would never in a million years demand I kneel at his feet to suck him off, Nathan Briant had done so right away and, stupidly, I appreciated that about him.

Nathan Briant accepted the fact that I liked cock. It seemed that shameful quality of mine had finally done some good in landing me an in with the record label.

And it wasn't just talk. The label followed through on all of their promises, then laid on more. An uncle of mine had been serving as my manager at that point, and he was in way over his head. There was no one of substance standing between me and the beast with its teeth freshly sunk into me.

At the end of phone calls, Mr. Briant or one of the people working for him would ask me about things like my favorite guitar, or my shoe size. Gifts began showing up at the doorstep to my shitty little apartment.

A Martin D-45 crafted out of East Indian Rosewood was hand-delivered. It probably cost more than my first three beat-up old cars, combined. A pair of ostrich skin boots was shipped from the Nashville Boot Co. They fit like a glove and made me feel like someone important when I was wearing them. One day it was a gold watch. I seriously considered pawning it in order to pay off my utility bill debt, but the label paid it off for me first. Then it was a new mobile phone, so they could always reach me.

It all made my head spin. After living my whole life in other people's shadows, I was finally becoming someone in my own right. I was wanted and appreciated. It was amazing.

They intended to pair me up with some guitarists that were already signed to the label, people who they promised were professional and super talented. That was how Jess and Jovie later came on board, but when it came to who'd be on lead guitar, there was only one person I wanted next to me, and that was Mags.

On the phone, Mr. Briant asked me, privately, how much I wanted Mags to be signed with me, and what I was willing to do to make it happen.

"Anything," I told him, even though I had a better idea at that point exactly what that word could mean. "I'd do anything."

With what sounded like suspicion that I had no idea what I had just said, he asked, "You mean that, son?"

"Yeah, I do."

"Good. I guess we'll see if you really do, shortly, now won't we? Must say, I'm looking forward to that."

As much as that threat made me an anxious wreck, I had meant that I would do anything. I'd wised up a little since that first meeting. When the date was set to finalize the documents at Mr. Briant's offices, with his lawyer, I had solid notions of what I was walking into. Payment would be expected for those favors, and for Mags most of all. It wouldn't just be oral. Mr. Briant would likely want to get his hands on *me*.

All I needed to know was when to be there.

They'd given me more than enough already that I felt Mr. Briant's expectations were warranted. I was willing. I would endure whatever I had to, to make my dreams — and Mags' dreams — come true. It was really no different than letting those high school bullies steal my bag and kick me, then choosing to lie to everyone else to protect them. In fact, the arrangement with Mr. Briant was much better. The rewards were huge, and whatever might happen to me physically, temporarily, didn't matter in the long run, or so I figured.

Of course, I was terrified. Luckily, everyone else who noticed my mood chalked it up to nerves about it being such a grand moment. Wondering what Mr. Briant would expect, what I'd find myself doing with him in secret, stirred all sorts of feelings in me. There was as much lust and excitement as there was dread. After pretending for so long that my dream of being desired by another man would never come to pass, it was good to know there was one person, at least, who liked me in such a taboo way, and was willing to act on it. He was also willing to keep quiet about it. In some ways, servicing Mr. Briant was beneficial to me sexually as much as it was financially and professionally.

The day of the next meeting, for almost an hour, I sat in the reception area with Leigh, Mr. Briant's personal assistant. She tried to set me at ease with some conversation, tales of all of the famous recording artists that had been in the building over the past week and giving some insights into what they were each *really* like. She was adorable in an innocent, pure-hearted way. There wasn't a corrupt bone in her body. She was dimples, giggles, and happiness. That was probably why she had the job, knowing Mr. Briant the ways that I did. He was a lion surrounding himself with lambs for when he got hungry.

The formalities didn't take long at all. Past Leigh's desk was a room outfitted with a conference table and chairs. The lawyer was there, with Mr. Briant. I looked over the document, though my own lawyer and my manager had already seen a copy and approved it. I signed with a shiny, sleek, silver pen that Mr. Briant handed me. It had a bullet-shaped tip and the cap screwed on so tightly that you could barely see the seam until you gave it a twist. It was heavier and thicker in the hand than normal pens and I much preferred looking at it to looking at the other men there with me.

As soon as my signature was inked onto the bottom of each page, the pen was tucked back into Mr. Briant's pocket. The lawyer disappeared, his function satisfied.

I didn't even see him go; I was too distracted by watching what the other, remaining man in the room was doing.

Mr. Briant had the contract in hand. With it, he turned and walked to yet another room, calling back for Leigh as he went.

"Follow me, Tucker. Come on into my office."

"Yessir," I nodded, hooking my thumbs in my belt loops just to have something to do with my hands. The apprehension was cranking up, fast.

Leigh came up behind me. Mr. Briant had walked around an enormous, gleaming, mahogany desk that held a leather blotter but had hardly anything else on it. From a wet bar behind him, he pulled two glasses and a decanter. The contract was at his side, on the desk.

"Hey, darlin'," he said to Leigh, "We're just finishing up here. You take yourself a nice long lunch on me. Go to that new place on Maribel Lane. Give 'em my name, they'll let you use my table."

"Oh, thank you so much, Mr. Briant," she said with glad surprise. "I appreciate that."

"If you can just drop those suits off at the cleaner, you can head on home afterward. If I need ya, I'll ring."

"Yes, sir. Absolutely."

She walked out, closed the door behind her.

He had gotten rid of her. I realized it instantly. In my mind, I saw her eating her fancy lunch, oblivious. I hoped she had not, and would not, have to buy that favor in a way similar to the way I'd had to buy mine. Thinking about that scared me, so I closed the door tightly on that suspicion, the way she had just as tightly closed me in with a man-eater in a well-tailored suit.

"Lock that door for me, Tucker," he said as soon as she was gone, pouring two drinks from the decanter.

I'd been alert on my way in. The building was enormous, a narrow glass high-rise that stretched up into the sky like a great big middle finger pointing up at god, and made up of everything man had to be ashamed about. His office was on one of the upper floors and, as I'd crossed from the elevator to Leigh's desk, I had not heard or seen any other human beings.

There was no one there but us, on the entire floor of the damn building.

Glancing around, afraid to look directly at the predator I was caged with, not wanting to provoke him, I noted, too, the elegantly padded walls, and figured the office to be soundproofed.

I nearly pissed myself as pure terror settled on me.

I walked to the door on unsteady legs and locked it as my mouth went dry and my hands shook.

"We have a lot to celebrate, you and me," he told me. "And there's the matter of your guitarist, Magnusson."

He opened a drawer, pulled out a plastic medicine bottle. Unscrewing the top, he shook out a small pill and dropped it into one of the glasses.

"I-I know I'm indebted to you, s-sir," I stammered.

"Good. That's good," he said serenely, like a doctor trying to put his patient at ease. "This Magnusson is also indebted to me. I assume you would rather settle his debt for him, as well as yours?"

He had dark, unreadable eyes and a mouth that always gave the impression of cold amusement. His hair was graying at his temples and he wore one of those flawless suits that must have cost thousands of dollars.

I was still just a stupid, twenty-one-year-old kid.

"Yessir. Th-that's what I want. Please."

With one hand set upon the contract, swirling the glass with the pill in the other, he said, "This isn't final just yet, you know. I could undo it with one call. It would all go away. No one else in Nashville would give you or Magnusson the time of day if I didn't want them to."

Maybe that was a lie intended to scare me. Anyway, it worked. I was scared.

He continued, saying, "It's not just about what your mouth can do anymore. Now, it's about *you*—every inch of you—being a commodity of ours to do with as we see fit. Now it's time to see if you're ready to put in the hard work that's going to be necessary to make your future as bright as it could be."

I grunted in panic. He looked at me steadily, smiling a little.

"Take them off," he told me, the words slow and low.

"W-what?"

"Your clothes, son," he said with pity. "All of them. Every last bit."

Chapter 15

Bound to Please

It was happening. All of my internal alarms started blaring. While I undressed, clumsily, awkwardly, he sipped from the glass that didn't have a pill rapidly dissolving in it. Not once did his gaze stray from me as my trembling fingers undid each button of my shirt. I peeled it off and dropped it to the floor, since there was no furniture handy to set it on. The space was easily a thousand square feet but the only furniture was that massive desk and the wet bar behind it. The only chair was the one Mr. Briant sat on.

My undershirt came up over my head and fell to the floor, too. Bare-chested and chilly, I toed off my new boots. I pulled off my socks and stuck them inside the boots. The carpet was tightly woven and hard under my feet, not comforting at all.

His smile grew as I tried to unfasten my belt buckle. That grin was an uncomfortable sight, so my gaze stayed lowered. It took a few tries before the belt came free. After pushing my pants down, I stepped out of the legs.

My boxers were next, and I hesitated. It was too intense. I wanted to cry. Not *leave*—just cry. Many times, I thought on that with wonder. It seemed there were basic instincts of survival I'd simply been born without.

"You don't have to pretend you're not nervous. It's as plain as the nose on your face," he chuckled, ice clinking in his glass. "And I happen to enjoy it," he added with a darker tone. "I have something to help you relax, so take those off and get on over here. We have all the time in the world, but I'm *impatient*."

I bent to tug down the boxers. When straightening back up, my hands cupped my crotch to hide it. He laughed softly.

With small steps, I made it, bare-assed, across the room to the desk, feeling woozy from being so damned scared.

The air in the room was much cooler than was comfortable. He must have had the air conditioning set to full blast. My nipples stiffened. All of my body hair stood on end and my balls drew up as my shivering started.

He turned his chair to the side to face me as I came around the desk. The glass was set down, out of the way. He drew that odd silver pen from a pocket inside his jacket and set it on the contract.

I stared at the pen as he leaned forward, drawing me closer with a warm, dry hand on my bare leg.

"No hiding, now. Move your hands."

It was the way he said it more than what he said that affected me most. It was a cheerful threat.

There were only a few inches of space between us as I stood between where his feet, in well-polished black shoes, were planted. My hands reluctantly fell to my sides. Immediately, without hesitation, he took my flaccid dick in his right hand and weighed it. His brazen touch there made my knees feel weak and my stomach churn. Wrapping his hand around my dick from above, he held on firmly, warming it with skin-to-skin contact. Lightly, he fondled me and began to stroke, watching his hand work.

"The shy act for my benefit or is it genuine, I wonder?"

I made a frightened whimper, not knowing what to do, other than stand there, letting him manipulate me.

"Oh, now, that was sweet," he grinned. "I like that. Maybe it *is* genuine. It's my lucky day!"

He didn't let go or stop stroking me, coaxing me stiff with the determination of an old pro. His palm brushed up and down my shaft, his fingers played over my tip. Once the touching started, it never stopped. It felt intensely perverse, dirty, and wrong to be standing in that vast, spotless corporate space, completely naked, being groped by someone who had no right to touch me, and allowing him to do so. Now and then, I'd give a little jerk or twitch of fright, which he'd follow with a slow, long squeeze of the head of my dick, as if to remind me I wasn't going anywhere.

Mr. Briant pushed the glass in which the pill had dissolved over to me, sliding it over the polished, dark wood of the desk.

"Drink that up. Every drop."

I didn't care what the fucking pill was. I just wanted to get it over with.

Liquor was a stranger to me. I'd avoided it, so it was the scotch more than the mystery drug that affected me first. It burned and made me cough, because I tried to drink it fast. It was a good eight ounces, though, without any ice to water it down.

While I gulped the drink, he rubbed over my stomach with his left hand — the right was still busy toying with my dick — going all the way up to my chest and sternum, then down again to grasp my hip. I tried to block it out. The gentleness felt nice. It didn't seem threatening or dangerous. The more the alcohol took effect, the more I was unable to deny how good the touching felt.

His right hand stayed loose, guiding my steadily swelling dick upright, letting it ride through the junction of his thumb and index finger. After a moment of two of that, he pulled it down — straight down — instead and tugged, making me grunt. Next, he took the head in the circle made of his index finger and thumb, squeezing around it. Holding it just so, he stared at the slit, examining the tiny hole. First, he rubbed a fingertip repeatedly over it in small circles to tease it. Then he used two fingers to try spreading it open as much as he could. The intimacy of that made me begin to writhe, but as soon as I did, he said, "Stay nice and still now while I get a look at you. That's it. You know how to obey direct orders, don't you, son?"

"Yessir," I replied as he stared into the little hole he was trying so hard to open up. It was uncomfortable in all sorts of ways. While keeping it spread, he touched another finger there, rubbing.

"How's that? That doesn't hurt at all, now, does it?"

I grunted, then whimpered again. His lips twitched in a faint grin. "I asked you a question," he warned.

"No, sir, I, uh.... It tickles. Feels funny."

"Oh, I bet," he smiled.

My face felt both cold and hot, my skin too tight, my thoughts scattered. I was halfway through the drink when his left hand grabbed me by the balls. Watching my face, he gathered them up in a fist and *pulled*. The pressure increased more and more until I gasped.

"How's that feel, son?"

I couldn't answer. Wincing, bending my knees to relieve the ache and tension, I sputtered, "I, uh...."

"Just some pressure, is all. Straighten up those legs. You can do it."

Biting down on my lower lip to stay as quiet as possible, I squeezed my eyes shut. Hand splayed at my side, I fought to bear it without moving, but my hips tilted toward him. It was very uncomfortable verging into painful, so I made a hard, humiliating grunt or two, breathing heavily.

"Widen your stance a bit, there. Good."

He took each of my testicles in a hand, pulling them apart and down, stretching the skin of my scrotum all the way out. My unease and the cold of the room made my balls keep trying to draw upward, but that seemed to only make him more determined to test the give in my sac, as well as my tolerance level. His thumbs stroked the pulled-smooth skin over my balls and my cock twitched in delight. I was half hard and swelling thicker. My breath came in shaky inhales and sharp exhales, mixed in with low groans.

I took another sip as he gathered my balls in one hand and pulled upward instead, squeezing in pulses.

"Not so bad, huh? See how your pecker is swelling right up? Tells us a lot, doesn't it? Means not only do you not mind the way this all feels, but that you're enjoying it quite a lot. You ever let a man play between your legs like this before, boy?"

"No. No, sir."

"Well, now we know. We've both learned something already, haven't we? It's okay with me that you like it. Might as well, right?"

When he'd squeeze too tight, my stomach would cramp up a little and I'd wince. He caught my eye for a moment but all it seemed I could look at for long was my balls closed up in his fist. I couldn't tear my gaze away.

"You know how very many young men are out there are looking to get signed to our label, don't you, son? Boys that might even be more talented than you are? One phone call is all it would take to get them in here instead of you. Just one. That's important to remember."

He gave my balls a tug.

"Gotta be careful with these, huh?" he asked as his hand squeezed and released. "These are real sensitive. Give 'em a little hurt, like this," he squeezed harder and I moaned with pain, wanting to double over, gritting my teeth, "and it does all kinds of funny things to your insides. You keep drinking, now. That's the best way to please me. Just do as you're told, son. I like you staying nice and still, being as quiet as you can, and doing exactly as you're told."

I downed the rest of the drink.

My head swam. The room tilted and spun. He took the empty glass from my hand.

I wanted to cover myself, but there was no way to — he had me held in hand. He was leaning forward to get a close look at everything he was doing. There was no hiding, but I didn't know what to do with my hands. That seemed the biggest problem — not stopping it, just finding a way to not feel so painfully awkward.

"Now, where were we? Oh yeah." Gesturing to the contract, possessively gathering up my balls and my dick in the fingers of his right hand, he said, "You want this to happen, right?"

"Yes," I managed, close to tears again.

"And you want me to make this as easy on you as possible? Make you feel more comfortable?"

Nodding, I bit my cheek so I wouldn't cry.

"Nervous?" he asked with that same smile which said that underneath the pretend concern, he was quite happy I was nervous. He was encouraging the nervousness.

I nodded again.

"Well, here. This'll help."

He finally let go in order to reach for something. The drug-laced alcohol made me dizzy, heavy, and tired. I stood there as he got up from the chair with two scarves pulled from a desk drawer. There were other things in that drawer that I tried to see, but couldn't. He was too fast. His dark eyes were on me, taking everything in like a mountain lion deciding just how to tear into the rabbit caught in its paws.

Mr. Briant tied the first scarf over my eyes. I didn't mind. At least I wouldn't have to see that look on his face any longer.

He tied my hair back tightly, then said, "Open up for me."

I felt something—cloth maybe, probably the other scarf—touch my lips and press firmly between them, then get pulled backward between my jaws. There it stayed as it was tied in place, the fabric wrapping my head as I bit down on it. I tried to close my lips around it as the fabric quickly grew damp in my mouth.

It wasn't a gag meant to silence me entirely, I realized, just to keep me from talking clearly. He had no interest in what I had to say, just in the types of noises I might make.

I started breathing harder, like I'd been running. My body was jittery, my thoughts getting fuzzy.

"That's better, isn't it?" he asked.

I nodded.

He led me a few steps forward with his hands on my shoulder and the small of my back. He turned me around.

"Climb up on there." My hands were placed on the wooden surface of the desk. He guided my knees so that I didn't smack them on the hard edge. As I got into place, he gave my bottom a pat. I felt something softer than wood under my lower legs and knees, and remembered the blotter. Like he could read my mind, Mr. Briant said, "The leather there should help keep you comfy for a while."

It was good to not be standing. The hands-and-knees pose would keep my hands occupied, which was also good, but the room was still far too cold and most of my lower legs hung off the back of the desk. When I tried to shift farther forward, he halted my progress with a hand hooked around the top of my thigh and said, "Right there is fine."

He nudged my legs farther apart, more than was comfortable. I heard the chair squeak as he sat in it and adjusted its position. Sensing him back there, behind me, made my shivering increase quite a lot. I tried to remember the height of his seat and figured he was probably eye level with my ass. Soft grunted moans slipped through my defenses as I bit down on the scarf.

I heard the sound of wood sliding against wood, like a drawer being opened. I tried to keep track of what was happening with my ears as much as possible.

It was bright in there. Light peeked in at the edges of my vision, around the blindfold. Between the morning sunlight and all of the overheads I knew were above us, I couldn't pretend he couldn't see absolutely everything.

Things clattered softly on the desk as he set them down. I'd never been more scared in my life. My heart was beating so hard, pounding away, that I felt on the edge of passing out. A dizzy spell hit and I got choked up on all of my unease, so I bent forward and let my head come down to touch the wood between my hands, needing to feel steadier.

"If that makes you feel better," he said from directly behind my ass, so close it only scared me more, "you can stay like that too. That's fine with me. No moving those legs, though. That's very important. You move those legs and the paperwork next to you goes in the shredder. But, don't think about that," he added quickly when I made a sobbing noise behind my gag. The tears were falling, wetting the fabric holding my eyes shut. It felt good to cry.

He carried on like he didn't notice or care if I was upset. "We're gonna have fun, you and me," he said excitedly. Something touched between the cheeks of my ass and I flinched. Hands wrapped my thighs, caressing up and down them. I heard him inhale deeply and I guessed it was his nose I felt pressed in my crack.

With a whine, I clenched up back there. He just pressed against me harder and breathed in again.

"You smell nice and clean. I like that. Did you shower before you came here?"

I was panting, but grunted in reply to his question. His hands brushed all the way up my legs to palm my ass. His fingers shifted over to my crease from both sides, pulling my cheeks apart, tugging at the skin around my rim. He stretched the area out, making the skin as tight as he could, prying at the ring of muscle in the center. Something brushed directly over the center of my tightly-spread hole and I quivered violently, moaned loudly.

"Oh, that's sweet," he praised, doing it again. I gasped and he rubbed at the spot, wriggling something there to tease the inside of the rim without entering me. "You've got such a nice, rosy knot, here. It looks almost untouched. Pristine. I'd like you to keep up that shy act. Makes it even more fun for me, and you want to keep me happy, son. You want to do *everything* in your power to keep me just feeling pleased and satisfied."

Something thick and warm rested on top of my hole. There was a plastic snapping sound, then a wet squirt.

"Just need to wet this up a little. There we go," he said, talking to himself. "I saw you admiring my pen, earlier. It is a beauty, isn't it? I had it made just for you. Call it a souvenir. It's even got your name engraved on the inside. Gonna keep that in a special place once we're done. I'll have it with me each time we see one another, so you can go on and look forward to that."

Suddenly, something cold, hard, and thin was shoved up my ass. It went about an inch or two through my hole, twisting like a screw.

I yelled around the gag, my voice rasping as I cried out. My head came up off the desk. I pulled up onto my hands again as I struggled to bear the shock, the proof that this was really happening. It was as much of a fight instinct as it seemed I had, and even so, it wasn't much. I didn't say no or try to get away, even though I wanted to. He'd be angry if I did. That contract kept me where he'd put me. Somehow, I managed not to tuck my hips forward. I didn't want him to do what he was doing, but fought to contain my reactions. Some little voice in my head warned that I'd be even more screwed if I decided to fight back now. Feet flexing, hands splayed, back arched but my knees planted securely, just like he wanted them, I found I couldn't stop crying out my shock and violation. I wondered if he'd be angry, since he told me to be quiet, but I couldn't help it. Those yells were all of my confusion, regret, and horror mixed up together. But there was no one else to hear, so he didn't try to silence me.

Maybe he'd been expecting the reaction, chalking it up to more of the shy act.

"Very nice," he said with an admiring tone as I made gruff, muffled sounds of protest and shuddered. "Thought I'd let you check out my pen a little closer. It's quite a beauty." It twisted deeper. He kept twisting it, constantly twisting as he stuck it farther in there; farther than I thought it could go.

"That's not so bad. Doesn't hurt at all, does it? Just like getting your temperature taken. I just want you to really feel that pen, now, son. That tickly feeling it's giving you in your belly? That's just another way we're signing this contract of yours. Making it nice and official between you and me. In a lot of ways, you belong to me now, you see. We have ourselves an arrangement, so I really want you to pay attention to how that feels."

I couldn't help it, the more he talked about the pen, the more I did focus on it, how thin and hard it was. It felt like he had pushed it in all the way, but was holding the very end with his fingertips, which were touching my rim. The dull, pointed end of the pen was jabbing at my insides, spearing me. His other hand reached under me, then, between my legs, and cupped my erection. It curved up snugly against my belly.

"Well, look how much you're liking that!" He chuckled. "We are gonna have fun together, aren't we, son? You're blushing up really nice, too. I bet you're feeling embarrassed by how stiff this is right now," he said, giving my cock a few tight, squeezing tugs, wringing the pleasure from me whether I wanted him to or not.

Exhaling sharply, over and over again, I quivered, my eyes rolling back. It was the first time someone else had tugged me like that, and he was really going for it, pumping my dick for all it was worth.

"But that's okay. It's okay with me if you like it. Now, I'm going to let go of my special pen. You clench up on it nice and tight. Let me see you do it. Clench your bottom. That's a boy. We don't want it to slide in any farther, because then I'd have to use something special to reach up inside there and pull it back out and I don't think you'd enjoy that at all. I'd like to keep this part enjoyable."

He let go, as promised, but kept hold of my dick, wrenching it down, through my legs, so that it pointed back toward him. His fingers kept it held in that position. I groaned thickly in discomfort. My knees shook. I was afraid they'd slip and he'd be angry.

There were some faint electronic noises from behind me, a series of flashes and clicks.

I knew what those were, but didn't let myself think about it, lest the panic push me over the edge into hysteria. I just stayed nice and still as he took his photographs.

"Beautiful. Just beautiful."

Chapter 16

Good Boy

After Mr. Briant had both of his hands on me again, he began to work the pen in and out of my ass. It had been cold and slick, but the longer he pumped it inside me, the warmer it got. It was so slender that soon I could only feel it because he moved it, but he never stopped moving it.

My initial shock faded the longer he kept me there. In an awful way, I was getting used to it. I was also starting to notice other things, like how damned tired I was and how much effort it took to keep my knees still. There wasn't any pain, but the problem with that was, without it, I couldn't help but get off on what he was doing.

"Gee, look at how wet you are!" He laughed, fucking me with his pen. His fingers pinched uncomfortably around the sides of my cock-head, then rubbed through the fluid dripping from it. "You know, son, God makes some young men bottom boys. It's just their nature. They get off on getting buggered. Can't help it. Now, I can tell by how much you're enjoying what I'm doing with my pen right now that you're one of them. You're going to have to come to terms with the fact that you're a bottom boy, son. All your life you're going to be begging men bigger and better than you to stick their peckers up inside your bottom and take it for a happy little ride. Hey, now. Maybe that's the game we'll play next time, before I give you something like my scarf there, to keep you sweet and silent. I'll let you beg me to play with your bottom's little pink hole, and we'll see what happens. Won't that be fun?"

I grunted hard and growled my protest, gasping for air around my gag and through my flared nostrils. My head spun and spun like a top. When he talked about how things were or what he was going to do next, it only made me more desperate. I'd found myself in a situation where there was no exit, no hope of rescue, and only more terrifying things to come. I couldn't leave and couldn't bear the thought of anything that was happening—especially my pleasure—let alone more happening soon. All I could do was go inward and try to not be aware of any of it. Gripping the wood so I didn't fall off the desk, I soon bowed my head again, laying it against the wood to keep steady. I was ass-up in front of him, with chemicals taking me apart from the inside, fraying my connections to the world. My body felt so heavy. My awareness of what was going on slipped from my grasp with frightening speed. I couldn't even be certain those were the words he was saying. Maybe I'd become delirious already and I was imagining the whole thing.

Pressing my face against the wood, I tried to ignore how good it felt to have him doing what he was with the pen while pulling my dick into its intolerable position. Something told me I needed to stay awake, but I knew I couldn't.

"Gettin' sleepy, I see," he said, *tsk*ing. The pen slipped out entirely, but it left me a little sore inside, with blood pumping just under the skin. I heard the pen get set down beside my left leg with a little tap. The empty space it left in me was filled up a moment later when he stuck a finger in to the hilt and started to rub around inside with it, the other fingers hugging my ass, two on each side. "Okay, you go on and take a nap. It makes me so happy to see you relaxing. You're not trembling like you were before."

The wriggling of his finger, prodding at my insides, made me crazy. It stretched in farther than the pen and rubbed at me in different ways. I wanted to get away from it, and couldn't with how heavy my body had become. I reached out and grasped the front edge of the desk, holding it as I fought to suck air through my nostrils.

I didn't want to take a nap. My head tried to warn me of what could happen if I dozed off. My body told me there was no way around it.

The woozier I got, the more I had to concentrate just to figure out what was happening.

At first, I didn't realize that the whimpered pleading sounds I was hearing were coming from me. He stuck a second finger in me and rotated his hand in there. He reached around, then rubbed against something inside that made me shout hoarsely around the gag, my hips snapping, humping air. My whole body flinched with each touch to that little spot. He yanked on my dick, pulling it even more sharply backward, between my legs, to keep me still. Inside, he fingered that gland, milking me.

He grew silent for a little while as he did that. I convulsed and writhed, making awful kinds of noises that I couldn't stifle. It scared me. All I could hear, between my hard grunts and rough cries, was his breathing.

I heard the chair shift, its wheels squeaking. Something wet, warm, and soft rubbed over the head of my cock. It was his tongue, I realized slowly, licking me clean. After the job was done, lick after lick after lick, he started to suck, pulling the fluid from me. My open hand slammed down on the desk, lashing out, needing to. I was undulating, desperate and restless. He began taking long pulls of my cock, sucking on every inch. A third finger wedged through my rim, prying it open wider than it had ever been.

He stopped milking me, which helped me stop making those horrible, embarrassing sounds. Instead, his three fingers pumped in and out, moving quicker the longer it went on. Soon they jabbed almost violently into my ass, pounding my hole like he was trying to make it hurt as much as he could. Grinding my forehead into the desk, holding on to the front with both hands, my whole body convulsed as I came. He pulled off, slowly stroking me through it with corkscrewing motions. I wished he'd let go and stop holding me at that angle, but I think he enjoyed my discomfort.

"Good boy," he said, "Let's wring that all out. You'll feel better after. In fact, you'll be begging me to do it again, won't you, bottom boy? Go on and make your mess. I've got something here to collect it all with. Gonna save some for myself, put it in my collection with the pen, and the rest I'll use when I fuck this pretty pink hole properly, push that all right back inside where it belongs."

I told myself I heard him wrong. It was all I could do to stay awake. I was losing the battle. My orgasm wore me out and dragged me down, making it impossible to hold on any longer.

I collapsed down onto the desk, folded up with my knees under me. He pushed them up farther up my sides and apart so my abdomen was flat against the desk. I was limp, unable to move. My spread-open ass and genitals hung out over the edge of the desk along with my feet, and that was bad. That was really bad. I didn't want to sleep through the rest. I tried to fight back.

Things were set on the desk with soft *clunks,* one after the other.

"Go on and take a nice nap, son," he told me soothingly. "Sleep for me. Nothing to worry about."

Something cold and hard, like metal, clamped around the base of my sac.

I made a sharp noise.

"Shh, don't worry about that. That's nothing. Go to sleep, now."

I drifted.

Briefly, sometime later, I surfaced.

Something big—*really* big—was sliding into my ass. Deep-seated ache reached all the way up the center of my torso and flared outward like he'd been beating on me from the inside out. My rim felt rubbed raw. It was intensely sore and throbbing. The instinct to reach between my legs and cover myself, to make him stop touching me there through whatever means necessary, was instinctual, but I couldn't move a muscle. My limbs were filled with lead. My head wouldn't budge. Even my eyelids wouldn't lift. A film of something covered my butt cheeks and inner thighs, making the skin feel tight and soiled. The massive object slid farther into my body with one firm stroke, then was left there. It felt like he'd jammed a baseball bat up there and it was agonizingly hurtful. Whatever he'd stuffed me with was too big, the movement too rough and the pain so intense I thought for sure he was going to rupture something and kill me, but I was still paralyzed. The panic swelled when my body didn't respond or even twitch in response to the hurt. I needed to scream and beg and sob as the object somehow went even deeper, hurting even more, but all that came out was a thick, soft grunt. There was nothing I could do to stop him.

Things were pinching the skin around my balls and something sharp was clasped around the head of my cock, which was bizarrely, awfully sore, inside and out, in ways I'd never felt before. It was pain on top of pain and the more I woke up, the more I felt it. From behind me, all I heard was heavy breathing. The huge object pumped slowly inside my ass and I fell asleep again, this time for good.

Chapter 17

No Escape

I woke up in my apartment, in my bed. The view was the same as it had been on every other morning — gray walls, hand-me-down furniture, heap of clothes needing a wash so bad they could stand up all on their own. Dawn was prying its way between my curtains and pointing out how long it had been since I'd vacuumed or dusted. That was normal. Everything else was wrong. I was so confused about how I'd gotten back to my place and all the way into bed; it managed to distract me from how much god-awful pain I was in for a half-second.

Craning my neck, I looked down at myself. I was still dressed in the outfit I'd gone to the meeting in, all the way down to my boots. I was lying on top of the covers instead of under them, belly to the bed and nowhere near the pillows, like someone had just set me there and left.

When I tried to move my legs and roll onto my side instead, it hurt so much, the pain clawed its way up my gut, grabbed hold on my stomach and squeezed. I lunged for the trash can beside my bed and threw up into it. My body was trying to wring out the hurt like you would a soaking wet towel, even though that'd never really work. It took a while for the dry-heaves to stop and for my breathing to get normal again.

Then I just passed out, cold. It was too much to deal with, I guess, so my body turned out the lights on my mind while it tried to work out the problems. I didn't come around again until the blue outside my windows had turned black. I'd slept the whole day away.

It was a little easier to stay awake that time. The hurt faded back enough for me to think instead of just getting to choose between puking or passing out. I needed to pee so badly I wanted to cry, so it was either get up or wet the bed.

I rolled over onto my back with a startled groan, as ache spiraled down all the way through the center of my body. From thighs to stomach, everything in between felt flat-out wrong. Cramps in the lower part of my lower belly made me want to curl up in a ball.

The shirt was easiest to get off, so I did that first, unbuttoning it the way I had in front of Mr. Briant. My hands were just as unsteady but for other reasons.

Sitting up was harder. My mouth hung open around rough cries as I got to my feet. I hobbled into the bathroom with wide-legged steps as if I'd been horseback for a week.

At the toilet, I got my pants opened and stood there, draining my aching bladder for a long, long time. It hurt to pee and it burned as it flowed. That was yet another sign I needed to check myself, but I was scared to. I didn't really want to know, but just go back to sleep to ignore it all a little longer.

When I found some courage, I reached behind myself and gently touched between my cheeks.

"Oh Jesus. Oh *Jesus*," I moaned. The whole area was on fire and swollen up, protesting the prodding like a cat caught in a pricker bush. The pad of my finger felt like a razor sharp claw when I touched and the nerves were screaming their heads off. I tried to remember what Mr. Briant had been doing to me after I fell asleep the first time, because fingers and a pen didn't do that kind of damage, as far as I knew, but those memories had been pushed way down into the dark. It took years for some of them to rise to the surface.

The skin of my balls and my dick were red and chafed as well. Bruises were everywhere. My pee hole was especially sore and red. The inside of my dick ached, too, like he'd stuffed something inside there the same way he had to my ass. I didn't know what could cause that kind of hurt, or if that was even possible. At the time, my knowledge of sadomasochistic devices was relatively slim.

Feeling soiled and slightly sticky from waist to knees, I showered. Afterward, I ate a protein bar, gulped some water from the tap and went back to bed.

The next few days were spent in the dark, in bed, traveling between it and the bathroom. My phone rang but I ignored it as much as I could. If I did answer, it was to my momma's calls. She was wondering how things went. I just told her I'd come down with a bug right after the meeting. Quiet and rest were what would help me most, so if she could let everyone else know not to bother me, I'd be grateful. I told her in particular to ask Mags to stay off my back for a few days, to tell him I had my reasons but was kind of embarrassed so I'd rather he not know to gory details. It was close enough to the truth, anyhow. Very slowly, my body healed. Mentally, I was too shocked to function.

Once or twice, my momma stopped by to drop off some homemade soup. Unable to quite look her in the eye, I said my thanks and took the food, but hurried her out as quick as I could. After that, she'd just leave the Tupperware containers outside my door and give a knock to let me know. That was the start of how I'd pulled away from everyone in my family, and the rest of my childhood friends. It was a sort of closing up, forming a shell to keep them from seeing what was hid inside.

It was maybe a week before I bothered to look out the window at the rest of the world, or go downstairs to check the mail. There was a brand new, shiny black truck parked in my reserved spot. I wasn't too surprised when I found the keys and registration for it in my mailbox, made out in my name. I had a lot of messages from Mags, and my uncle, the manager. A few times, someone pounded on the door, and a man's voice would yell for me to open up. I ignored that, too.

It was dark in my room, the curtains shut, the lights off, but it was even darker inside me. The pain in my body wouldn't give me even a second to forget what I'd agreed to when I signed the contract and everything that happened after; misery was a massive beast sitting on my chest, suffocating me. All I wanted was to stop fighting so hard to breathe and make the hurting end. Nothing else mattered.

A week and half after my meeting, I'd fallen so far down I could only think of one way to fix everything. Nothing was getting better and it never would. That meeting had been a beginning, not an end. All of that pain I was in would go on and on, maybe for years, maybe even longer than that. I hated myself so damn much. My new life was a hell I only had one way out of, so I sat on the edge of my bed, holding the handgun from my dad, meant to protect me from harm. The room was dark, my thoughts black, and my breaths thick with tears. But, maybe, this would make it stop. No more pain. No more meetings. No more need to look my reflection in the eye. I set the barrel in my mouth, where Mr. Briant's cock had been. I closed my lips around it tenderly.

Do it, I told myself. *Get out while you still can. You heard him. This will never be over and you can't live like this. Pull the trigger. It's the only way out you have left.*

My finger rested on the trigger. The safety was off. My breathing was shallow but steady, the numbness strong.

Do it. Do it.

Suddenly, I heard some persistent rattling sounds from the other room, by the door. Mags yelled, "Tucker Reynolds! I don't care what your momma says, I'm not leaving here until I talk to you, so come out or I'm coming in! You think I can't get this door open? Well, I can!"

He'd be the one to find your body. He'd hear the shot. You really gonna do that to him? Are you cruel as well as stupid?

My flimsy courage slipped away.

"Damn it," I moaned. The sounds of Mags trying to pick the lock kept coming, so I stuck the gun back under my bed.

I got up and followed the noises only to find Mags on his knees in the hall outside my apartment with lock picking tools in his hand.

I told him with hollow annoyance, "Cut it the fuck out. Come in if you have to."

"What hole have you fallen into, man?!" he asked wildly, gesturing with his arms. "Don't you know what's happened? What you did? We have to celebrate! This is it, cowboy! We're gonna be superstars! This is huge! *Don't you realize how huge this is?!*"

He bounced on his heels, gave me a big hug and was filled to the brim with pure joy, smiling bigger than I'd ever seen him do.

Then, he seemed to notice the state I was in. It dulled his shine. Wishing he would leave and go be happy somewhere else, I shrunk in on myself, trying to disappear.

"You still sick or something? You look awful," he realized, leaning back to look at me. I was wearing sweatpants and a baggy shirt, barefoot.

"Hey." Bypassing that, I asked him the first thing that came to mind. "You ever try that place on Maribel Lane?"

It felt like an important question. It had been ringing in my head for days, a way I'd pushed things back down when they started to creep up. I tried to trim away everything that had happened since Leigh went to lunch.

Mags asked in reply, "Why, is that what made you sick?"

"Yeah. Something like that," I agreed softly, looking him over, seeing him in different ways, seeing the *world* in different ways.

"Well, hell, kid, let's get you back in bed. What do you need? Soup? Tea? Medicine?"

Right away, he was nothing but concerned. It sucked the rest of the joy out of his face, which made me feel ashamed of yet another way I was fucking things up.

"Love you, Mags." I said the words without really feeling them. Without really feeling anything.

"Me too," he replied with a kind smile, gripping my shoulder.

He put me in bed, covered me up, and went to heat up some soup. It was later on that night when I asked him why he did it, why he bothered to care, back in high school. I needed to know why. There had to be a reason not to shrivel up and stop caring about everything.

There wasn't, though. Not really. Mags was just Mags, a good guy who felt responsible for me the same kind of way I felt likewise for him.

After that, he was there almost every day, checking in on me. He was my dependable link to a world I was trying to tear myself out of.

I kept the truck.

I kept all the gifts. Hell, I'd earned them, fair and square.

Mr. Briant showed up to check on me when I didn't answer or return his calls, either. Something about how he'd bothered to come all the way to my apartment, looking for me, made it impossible to hide or pretend to be out. If I didn't answer, lord knows what he might have done next. So, I did answer, feeling like a shell of a man, and like I belonged to Mr. Briant in every single way I honestly did.

Mags had already been by and left, so there was no chance of us being interrupted by anyone until the next day at least.

There was no hiding anymore.

It was business.

He took what he wanted, and I got compensated for it. Simple as that.

There were two security guys, big as brick walls, on either side of him.

"Hello, there, son!" he grinned, sharp as ever. His dark, hungry eyes roamed over my body, telling me what I already knew. "I've tried calling, but you must have that brand new phone turned off. I was so worried; I knew I had to see how you were doing with my own eyes. May I come in?"

Stepping back, head bowed, eyes wide, I hugged myself and snuffed out every single feeling that sparked inside me. It was better to stay numb and pretend it wasn't real. At the time, I was dressed in drawstring pants and sleeveless shirt. My hair hung down around my face. I used a hair tie around my wrist to pull it back without even thinking about what I was doing or why.

"Wait by the car," he told his security team after he'd seen I wasn't going to fight him.

"Yes, sir," the left one said in a deep voice.

He closed and locked the door behind him, saying, "My guys got you home safe, did they, son?"

"They did, sir. Thank you."

"You're very welcome," he said in the same tone of pleasant surprise he'd had when he fondled my erection for the first time.

I started to tremble. He took my arm and led me back to the bedroom.

I went easily.

"You healing up nice?"

A low moan sounded in my throat, behind lips sealed tight.

"If you check your account," he continued, letting go as I sunk down to sit on the mattress's edge, "you'll find plenty of cash to pay for any medical care necessary. You're young. The young heal up *fast.*"

"Please," I begged, for what, I don't know.

"I came to check on you *myself*. I care about your wellbeing, son," he said softly. One of his hands stroked my hair back.

It fell away and he gave me an expectant look. The only way to play it was to try to keep him happy. It was the only choice I had to avoid more pain.

Lying back on the bed, I scooted up a bit. He sat down beside me. My hands went to my drawstring and untied it. Lifting my hips, I slid the pants down.

I wasn't wearing underwear. He helped remove the pants entirely and gently spread my thighs with his hands until they were as wide as they'd go.

He began to examine me, prodding and poking at my dick and my balls, looking for injury, maybe. Maybe not.

"Legs back, son," he instructed. I drew them up, curling my knees toward my chest but let them fall open. He pulled the pen — *my* pen — from a pocket and set it down on the bed. Then, he bent down and pulled my cheeks apart, taking a close look. "Well, that's not too bad at all! Tightened up nicely, I see. Knew you would. Of course, you'll never be quite as tight as you were, which is a shame, but that doesn't mean we can't still enjoy ourselves."

Looking right into my eyes, he pushed a dry finger up my ass, sliding it past my rim into deeper parts of me which he was well familiar with by then. Then he asked, "Do you want to know what you missed? Should I tell you how wide this little pink hole was stretched open while you had your nap?"

"No," I said instantly, shaking my head. "Don't tell me."

"That's fine. It's probably better that way. Clench on that finger. Clench nice and tight," he urged. "Good. Now, I know exactly what you want and what you're waiting for, so I'll get us going."

The finger drew out, rubbed over my rim, then slid back in to the last knuckle. My knees quivered with pleasure and I grunted. He began to pump in and out shallowly, and lifted my swelling cock to stare at the slit. "You pissing normal? No problems there?"

"N-no," I said breathlessly. I didn't want to let on how good it felt to be touched and looked at by him, but it seemed I couldn't help it. "No problems."

"Feels nice, huh?" he grinned.

"Yeah," I sighed, shuddering, drawing my legs higher as I presented my ass to him.

"Your pecker's thickening up fast. Is that 'cause you like the way my finger feels in your bottom, son?"

God, I didn't want to answer. But I did.

"Yes," I croaked, growling out the sound as he poked around inside of me. "Yes, sir."

"Would you like to have your special pen back for a moment?" he asked expectantly.

"Yes, please."

"Now, you're going to have to be more specific than that," he chuckled, holding the pen up for me to see. "Though I like your manners."

I was breathing hard, getting off on it all and hating myself for getting off on it.

"I-I'd like to have my special pen back, please. I'd like you to...."

"...to what?" he said leadingly.

"To stick it up my ass, sir."

"Why do you want me to do that?" he said, laughing like I was being ridiculous.

My heart was pounding. I had never felt more stupid or cowardly. Every single thing he said only made me feel more humiliated and embarrassed, and I knew it would only get worse. I could barely breathe through the panic and want. It was all mixed up inside me, how scared I was of him, how much I hated that I liked the way he made me feel. "B-because I like how it feels. Please, s-sir."

"Now say it all together at once, just so I'm sure what you mean." He slid his finger out and gave my rim a pinch, which made me twitch, but he just rubbed it between his fingers, then pinched again, even harder.

"I, uh," I gasped, unable to believe it was all happening again, and in my own goddamned bedroom. "I'd like you to please stick my special pen up my ass, Mr. Briant, sir, because I like how it feels when you do that."

"Well, since you asked so very nicely." He grinned, looking like the devil in the flesh. Making sure I was watching what he was doing, he lined up the pen with my hole, then slowly slid it into me. "Now what do we say?"

"Thank you, Mr. Briant. Please fuck me with my special pen."

"I think you're getting a little greedy, but okay." He started to move the pen, pumping it. Quivering, I saw my dick twitch, swelling even harder. "You know it's wrong to enjoy this as much as you do, don't you, son?"

"Yes, sir. I do."

"Are you a pervert, son?"

"Yes, sir. I'm sorry, Mr. Briant."

He let go of the pen, leaving it in me, and fished a plastic baggie out of his pocket. After opening it up, he removed the pen from my body and dropped it into the bag. He zipped it closed again, then set the baggie aside.

I tilted my hips up a little. With a shark's grin, he slid two fingers into me, dry.

"Don't you like that?" he sighed.

"Yes, I do."

"I bet you'd like me to touch your sweet spot again, wouldn't you? Maybe if you ask nicely, I will."

"Please," I begged, not understanding why I was doing it, only that it felt safer, that if I did anything else, it would be wrong and dangerous. The more I played along, the less of a threat there seemed to be in the ways he touched and looked at me. If there was any way at all to be less scared, I was glad to take it. Feeling like a fool was better than suffering. "I want it."

"Of course you do," he grinned.

His head lowered between my thighs. He pulled the finger out, spread me open with both hands and took a wide lick over my rim. Then he stuck his tongue inside there as far as it would go like he'd done it many times before and it wasn't strange at all. His lips sealed against me and sucked. My cock dripped pre-come and I gasped with how good it felt.

Removing his tongue from my ass, he sat upright again. I heard him spit upon his fingers, then felt two push in, reaching around, widening into a V to pry my hole open.

Covering my mouth with a tight palm, I muffled the cry I knew was on its way out. It felt like I was coming apart, and it was awful and wonderful at the same time.

"Now," he said, triggering me with fingers tapping my gland, watching me squirm with too many sensations hitting me all at once, fucking air. "Since I've just done *you* some favors, I think it's time for you to do *me* a few as well. You know I enjoy myself more when you're sleepy, but it's your choice. What do you say, son? Would you rather be awake for this part or sleeping pretty for me?"

In his hand was a pill.

I opened my mouth, stuck out my tongue. He placed it there, smiling.

Chapter 18

Maribel Lane

After that first time in his office, Mr. Briant stayed until I woke up, every time. He would be there as I surfaced, whispering by my ear, explaining how much I'd gotten off on what he'd done, and how I'd shown my desire for him. He told me he'd never seen someone enjoy his attentions as much as I had.

Funny how, as much he insisted I'd loved it all, I woke up, without fail, to nothing but agony. Feeling the effects of it all, I'd question how I was able to feel lust for something that hurt so damned much. He'd explain my reactions, how greedy I'd been for more, how there was no doubt I loved every second of it, and that I should just go on and accept my true nature instead of fighting it.

When I'd imagine myself lying there, unconscious, unmoving, while he fucked and sexually tortured me, I'd realize his fetishes were not just for being in control of sex, but to have me play the part of a corpse. He was a necrophile, getting to do whatever he wanted to my body without having to hear my complaints or protests.

To him, when it really counted, when he was inside of me, I was already dead. The idea of that fucked me up, too.

We met that way a few more times. Once, it happened in his office with two businessmen in the room. Mr. Briant had me undress in front of them and get in a few different poses while they talked. They had strange accents and stayed the whole time, watching my body and sipping drinks, but only got involved and started touching me after the pill had me on the edge of passing out.

Another time was back in my bedroom. I woke up crying hysterically in the middle of it, without knowing why I was crying in the first place. Tape was covering my mouth when I surfaced. My arms were in shackles above my head and stretched out straight. My legs were being held up and spread wide by straps fastened to shackles binding my ankles. The straps were pulled tight, attached to the headboard. There was a complicated metal device clamped around my genitals and a thin silver rod stuck out from the head of my dick. Mr. Briant was concentrating on inserting some sort of metal device into my rectum. It was half inside and the pain of it was the reason for my screams.

He glanced up, frowned at me like I was irritating him and a moment later jabbed a needle into my upper thigh. I was injected with something that knocked me out again in seconds.

Every time, I was drugged and knocked out before it really started. He liked to watch me come first, praising, soothing, threatening a little what was yet to come, with a grin. While I was awake, he never caused me true pain. There were only dirty, addictive pleasures. The pain came in my dreams and afterward, when it was time to try and recover. By then I'd have been paid handsomely and didn't much care to complain about the effects of what we'd done.

The damage to my body was never as bad as it had been that first time, but then again, that was the biggest payment I'd had to make. I had to balance the scales for all of the trouble of signing Mags, for all of their expensive gifts and for the promise of my future in the country music industry.

I was, maybe just a little eagerly, expecting the next call for another of my special 'meetings' with Mr. Briant when I heard the news of his being relocated to an overseas branch of the company.

The in-person meetings stopped right away, without warning. He never explained why he left, though he stayed in contact through phone calls and messages he'd send through the mail. He never said anything specific then, to let on about what he was really telling me. I never got the chance to ask why he'd left and didn't get any answers either. I wondered if the people he worked for had found out what he'd been up to, and felt it would be safer for everyone if he was out of the country. But maybe that wasn't the case at all, and he had simply found a better opportunity somewhere else where he could have his pick of any young men he liked without the interference of a government as nosy as the one in the United States. Either way, physically, he was gone. Our meetings stopped.

The sorrow I felt after he left was awful. Missing him while knowing what he'd done to me was criminal, was almost as bad or worse than what he'd actually done to me. There was relief, too, but it was soon perfectly clear that there would be no one to take his place in my life. I would hear from him, and it would make me feel a complex storm of emotions like dread, shame, grief, and anxiety. I kept expecting to serve and please him like I had. It was pressure that built up inside of me, unable to vent. It didn't feel right to reap the benefits of fame without having to pay it all back with my body.

Sometimes, when we spoke, I would admit my feelings to him in a roundabout way. Basically, I'd say I missed him and the time we'd spent together.

He knew what I meant. In his reply, I'd hear his hunger to get his hands on me again, too, and he'd promise me soon. *Soon.*

I fantasized about him more times than I could count. Crying, screaming with rage at him and at me, it was a battle I fought alone. The hard, unbreakable rules that had made everything I took part in make sense were gone, and I was floundering.

No one knew what I'd done, what had happened. I told *no one.*

Yes, I lied to Ken about being a virgin. I figure if you aren't awake to witness the act, it didn't count.

Mr. Briant made me a better liar. I learned from him how to lie, even to myself.

That was the real reason why I preferred to hire prostitutes when I wanted sex. They knew what it was like to do it because they had no choice, how it was to be both ashamed and excited by the addictive pleasure they got from it. They knew, too, the driving force of how much they could get for it.

I had a hell of a lot in common with whores.

After I'd bandaged my wrist using a small first aid kit from my camping gear, I called Jess back.

"I'm so fucking sorry for hanging up," I said as soon as he answered.

"What the hell, Tucker? Are you okay? Did you shut your phone off again?" he ranted, angry with me but sounding like he was trying not to be.

"Yeah, I did. I can explain. I can. I truly appreciate what you're trying to do for me, Jess, just by giving a shit. I'm just... going through some bad things right now, but I think it's time for me to come home. Will you be there, if I come home? I kind of need something to look forward to and you're the only one who makes me feel better."

There was an ache in my wrist where I'd scraped away the skin. I'd have to hide the bandage under my bracelets and watch, so no one would know it was there.

"Of course. Of course I will," he assured me, blowing out a breath, sounding steadier. "I'd be so happy to see you, man. I can tell you all about my trip, too, and how relaxing it was to be at my cabin on the edge of the woods near the sea. You'd really love it there, I think."

Even just listening to him eased something inside. I breathed easier, and found myself smiling. "I'd really like that. Okay then. See you soon, Jess. Thank you for putting up with me."

Despite his worry, I turned the phone off once we'd hung up. I felt lighter, my thoughts sorted. The numbness had lifted and in its place were all of the feelings I tried to hide.

They were usable, fuel for greater things — useful things. I found a melody that was a mournful echo. The song would start with a riot of noise and passion. The lyrics after were a bruised memory of the clatter.

My voice rose up, melancholy and thick with deep-seated ache, from the dirt of the forest floor to the clear, blue sky above:

> *Every promise was kept,*
> *Though she smiled, and I wept,*
> *The day Leigh had lunch*
> *on Maribel Lane.*
> *Maribel Lane, Maribel Lane.*
> *She'd never*
> *know the truth*
> *of Maribel Lane.*

The Devil came back,
Looky here, son! Gotta act!
The day Leigh had lunch
On Maribel Lane.
Maribel Lane, Maribel Lane.
Lord, I hope she'd never
know the truth
of Maribel Lane.

Then I signed on the line,
Gave up, mute and blind,
The day Leigh had lunch
On Maribel Lane.
Maribel Lane, Maribel Lane.
I'd never know the truth of
Maribel Lane.

Sent, alone, to my fate,
Locked the door, no escape,
The day Leigh had lunch
On Maribel Lane.

My hand gripped the neck of my instrument tightly as I let the old anger roll out into the woods rather than try to draw it back inside again. It felt good to let it out. It was a start. With hardly any effort, I could pour enough soulful emotion into those words to blow them all away. They'd be as breathless as I was, and wouldn't that be some sweet irony? The road that Maribel Lane — my next album — led to was full of inspiration.

Sitting at my campsite, my hideout from the empire I'd built, all of it bought and paid for with lies, pain, humiliation, and filthy sex, I thought of all of that money in the bank, in *my* accounts. I thought of my real estate investments, my cars, my ranch, all of my adoring fans and the way other famous folk tended to smile at me with envy. They were all Mr. Briant's gifts, shameful fruits of my labors while spreading for him like a good, obedient bottom boy. Like the whore that I was, at heart.

The forest was like Mr. Briant. It looked good on the outside, but bad things would happen if I stayed too long. I could hear the music there, and I wondered if the music was all I had left of any true value. Anyway, I meant to use it as my road to salvation and healing. But it wasn't safe for me to be alone, and my time in the wild was coming to an end. As much as I wanted to stay, my music and a man I could never have were pulling me back.

Chapter 19

Stripped Bare

I'd been paying off imagined debts for far too long. It was time to stop. My time alone made it clear that I pretty much had nothing left to give. From here on out, I told myself I didn't owe the label, or Mr. Briant, or even Mags, anything. Mags was in the band because I'd given Mr. Briant free rein to do to me whatever he wanted. Knowing Mags had gotten joy from having a successful career in music because of the price I'd paid for him had been enough to make it seem worth it.

It wasn't worth it anymore.

Now I knew I deserved better. There was too much of who I was at heart that I'd been denying and, though I couldn't imagine how to begin to accept myself, I knew I had to try.

From the wild, I emerged wild. My beard was thick. My hair was even longer than it had been. The first, most important thing I needed to tackle was to take a damn shower, so I stayed overnight at a hotel on my drive back to Nashville, just to clean up for the sake of the people who'd have to smell me.

Meanwhile, memories I'd carefully covered over with years of professional success were raw and bleeding out. More than ever, I was that foolish boy who didn't know any better, standing naked and afraid in a big, intimidating space, in front of a seductively powerful man. He was a part of me who needed to fuse with the rest, instead of being ignored any longer.

At the same time, I was nothing like that boy anymore. I was older, weary, wiser, and clear-eyed about the way the world worked... wasn't I?

Anyway, there was more work to do. Never mind the bandage on the inside of my left wrist and everything tied to the reasons why it was there. The album Maribel Lane was my new goal. I intended there to be more honesty and power in that collection of songs than in all of the rest of my work combined. That's what would keep me going forward instead of being held back.

Thinking about the album, feeling more confident in myself than I had in a long time, I looked through my phone to try to catch up on what I'd missed as a driver shuttled me from the car rental place to my home in Nashville.

A Snapchat message popped up.

It was a photo of the pen — *my* pen. There it was, sleek and shiny, ready to violate me again and make sure I remembered all of the agreements I'd made.

The message, and the photo, vanished like they'd never been there.

My confidence was suddenly gone too.

He was still out there, keeping tabs, watching, waiting. It was only a matter of time before he showed up in person for a private meeting during which he would expect me to make up for all of the years we'd been apart. It would be worse than it had ever been, and I couldn't do it anymore. I couldn't endure that, but how could I stop it? There was no way. Mr. Briant got what he wanted, every time.

Shaken, pale, and filled with new fear, I arrived at my home.

I showed up at my own front door feeling unsure of myself again and looking like a stranger.

It was fitting, because as I searched my pockets for my house keys, a stranger came to the door, as well.

The house itself looked the same as it always had, sitting on a couple of acres, featuring plenty of classic Southern charm. Two-story columns lined the grand front porch and the dramatic entryway. The grounds were beautifully maintained by my staff, who kept the place spotless while I was away. Honestly, I was hardly ever there. It was more an investment than a cozy place to live. The only time I was at my Nashville estate was between tours and when nothing else was going on to distract me, meaning I was usually only there when I was miserable or depressed.

The photo of the pen was big in my mind, so I was pretty distracted. After a quick glance, I thought maybe a new hire on my staff had come to greet me. Then I stopped and looked again. Blinking up at the tall, strikingly handsome, clean-shaven, brown-haired man standing inside my home, I tried and failed to guess at first who it could be.

"Are you okay?" the person asked, while scanning my face for signs of trouble. He didn't say hello, just posed that question and bit his lip uncertainly.

That clarified things fast.

"Jesus!" I exclaimed. "*Jess*? Fuckin' hell, you look different. You look *good*. *Too good*, almost. What happened to your beard?"

"Jumped over onto your chin, by the looks of it," he smiled. "Too good for what?"

"Oh, you know," I murmured, embarrassed and feeling my face get hot. "Recognizing."

"You didn't think I looked good before? You're blushing, by the way."

Pointing a finger at him, I said, "Stop tryin' to get me in trouble."

He just laughed good-naturedly, clapped me on the shoulder and kept on smiling.

It was a damn cute smile, too. I was fascinated by it now that it was finally uncovered. It was sweet as sin and his lips were full and gorgeous. There was no denying it—Jess was unfairly good-looking. It had been hiding all this time behind the facial hair.

The hair on top of his head was a little longer, too, and no longer cut down almost to his scalp with militant precision. In just a few weeks, his hair had come in thicker, just enough to start to lie down against his head. The darkness of the silky strands made his eyes stand out more. And, for the first time, staring at him like a fool, I realized Jess's eyes weren't just green, as I'd always thought they were. They were ringed with a vibrant blue. It seemed he was showing his true colors at long last, both literally and otherwise.

It all just served to shake me up even more.

"It's real good to see you," I admitted. "You're quite a friendly face to come home to."

"It's good to see you too." His smile softened, then faded into a look of concern. "Seriously, though," he said with that lovely baritone. "Are you okay? You look... not okay. And the way you sounded on the phone...."

I started to feel very self-conscious. "Don't worry yourself about how I sounded, all right? I'm here now. Like I said, it was just some bad stuff, but I'm leaving all of that in the woods instead of bringing it home with me. Once I clean myself up a little more and get something to eat, I'm sure I'll look less of a wreck."

"Well, come in," he said, ushering me inside the house and swinging the door shut. Something tightened in my chest, waiting to see if he'd lock it. When he didn't, I found I could breathe again, but I was angry at myself for the reaction. Already, Mr. Briant was affecting me again. That damned photo. That damned man. Why couldn't he let me take my own advice and leave it all behind?

Back in the real world, Jess said, "Give me that bag."

He took it right from my shoulder as I protested, "Why? It's *my* damn bag. I'm not an invalid. I already feel bad enough about making you wait on me for weeks. I don't need the extra guilt for making you act as my bag boy."

"Bag boy?" He gave me a teasing smirk, his brow stubbornly furrowed with that damned concern.

"Hell, I don't know. Just give me the bag."

"What on Earth happened to you?" he asked, searching my face, then my body with his roaming gaze. Right away, I thought of the bandage and fought the urge to check and make sure it was still hidden.

"Went camping?" I said distractedly. "Ate lots of fish? Spent too much time talking to myself? Give me the bag back. There's no reason I can't carry my own bag."

"Yeah, right," he said dismissively. "Why are you avoiding the question? Why were you so evasive and upset on the phone when I talked to you?"

Not wanting to face things while I was still so disturbed by that photo, I brushed off his concern, saying, "Maybe you're just imaging things. Have you been hanging around Mags too long? You know you don't need me in order to do whatever you want, right? You should have taken a longer vacation, gotten out of this damned place."

"That's still avoiding the question."

"Is he still sleeping in *my* goddamned bed? You know he sleeps naked, right? And that his favorite way to drift off is to jerk off? He's been jerking off in *my* bed for a *month*. I'm gonna need to burn it to the ground, because there's no sterilizing that shit."

"Now you're scaring me," Jess said. His expression was tight with worry. He shifted the heavy pack on his shoulder. I'd gone into the entry hall. He was following right after me, and every step farther into my personal space just made me want to back up more.

"You should be scared, with the wide variety of humanity he sleeps with. God knows what kinds of diseases his sperm carries. Why are you standing so close, anyway? You know how long I've gone without brushing my teeth, right?" He didn't say anything, and just kept staring, so my mouth just kept moving, letting things slip that never should have. "I know I already awkwardly commented on this a moment ago, but you really do look... different... without the facial hair." I gestured to my own growth, recognizing the uneasy tickle in my gut for what it was, getting angrier at myself for thinking my married, straight piano player was hot as fuck. Lord, I was hopeless, wasn't I? If it wasn't Mags I was lusting after, it was someone else who was too nice for his own good and absolutely unavailable.

Jess glanced around, but there was no one else in sight in the entry hall. He pulled me farther aside and lowered his voice. With a big hand resting gently on my shoulder, his voice tried to find a way to get to me through all of the other noise and nonsense. "Tucker, please. I can see it in your face. I may not know you as well as some, but I do know how you love to distract curiosity about your wellbeing instead of answering questions directly. I'm not here to judge you, okay? I'm just a worried friend, trying to help somehow. Please talk to me? What happened to you out there?"

I bit down hard on my tongue, my head bowed against his chivalry which was trying to get under my skin and loosen the few ties still holding me together. I took a couple deep breaths. I wished to God to stop thinking about that awful pen and Mr. Briant, and that I could just concentrate on finding a way out from under Jess's pressing at me with his worry. I couldn't, though, because the pen was real, just like that monster was, and as much as Jess wanted to save me, I knew he never could. The memories of being Mr. Briant's plaything were open, festering wounds. Of course Jess could see something was wrong. *Ev-*

erything was wrong. I was uncomfortable in my own skin, with my own thoughts and instincts. I was worried about Jess being around if Mr. Briant was thinking about coming back. Jess was too good inside to be polluted by someone the same way I was. Jess's questions unnerved me even more, proving that nothing was okay. I couldn't even pretend it was. I was failing on every count.

"Nothing would make me feel better than to tell you the whole story, but I can't, okay?" I told him quietly. "I can't go there yet. I'm not as strong as everyone thinks I am. When there's pressure, I just... yield... and there's a lot of goddamned pressure right now. It's all still... They feel really close right now, and they're freaking me the hell out, but they're just old demons. We all have 'em, don't we? Mine came out to play in the dark, but they didn't win. I'm here. I'm rambling but I'm fine. I swear."

His blue-green eyes searched my face. "Is that why you kept your phone off? Demons?"

"Yeah, partly," I replied, thinking of my worry about being tracked, about that photo — here and gone. There was no proof of any of it. All evidence of what Mr. Briant had done and was still doing vanished just the way that picture had. "Don't worry yourself about it. I'm here now. I'm ready to work. That's the whole point of all of this, isn't it? To work? I have ideas, lyrics, hell, I even have a name."

Jess was still standing too close. I could smell his aftershave, and was very glad I'd decided on that detour to a shower and bar of soap. When he licked his sexy, soft lips, which I'd never noticed before, I tried not to stare at them and did anyway. I felt him watching me look at the pink tip of his tongue, and started to get hard for him.

Then he leaned in even closer to whisper in my ear, and my skin pebbled with both fear and want. The heat from his larger, taller body, pressed against mine. His voice was felt as much as heard as it vibrated through the air and into my ear.

"No, that's *not* the whole point. Forget the album and the work, okay? I'd rather you take care of yourself first. We all would. When you're ready to talk, I'm here. Okay? Any time. No matter what it is you'd like to talk about. I don't scare away easily, believe me."

You should be scared, I wanted to say. *There's plenty to be scared of.*

Good god, I was uncomfortable. Sexually attracted to yet another person I could never have and shouldn't want, I had to find a way to push him back and find some air, so I blurted out the question, "How's your wife?"

Shadowy, complicated emotion moved behind his expression. His two-tone eyes bore right into me. But, he didn't back off any, damn him.

"You want to know about that? Okay, I'll make you a deal. When you're ready to talk, I will too. About that and anything else you want to know."

His whispering made me shiver in a strictly pleasant way. I closed my eyes, trying to reason away my desire, to beat it down with cruel truths.

"That's not fair," I hissed.

"Just tell me," he coaxed.

"I can't."

"You *can*."

"Why do you care?"

"Because you're a good guy and my friend and you're clearly in *pain*."

"Can't you just accept the fact that I'm hopelessly fucked up and leave me alone? Please?!"

I hurried past him, leaving behind the damned bag, and raced up the stairs.

My bedroom was empty when I got there, but the bed was unmade, a tangle of soiled sheets. Slamming the door shut behind me, I ripped the dirty sheets off, took them to the window, opened it up and tossed them outside. I closed the window again and sat heavily on the stripped bed to catch my breath.

It was a while later when I was finally ready to come out of the room. As soon as I opened the door, I found my bag sitting there, on the floor. The hall was empty, the house quiet. A handwritten note had been set on the bag. It was just one word, but it was enough to make me hate myself even more.

Sorry.

Chapter 20

Kennedy

For years, the game had been the same—sleepless nights, troubled thoughts, hiding myself from everyone close by and only coming out of my shell onstage. Facing the part of me in the woods that wanted to give up and end the pain for good had helped make me stronger. But I needed to reclaim my life, my bed, and my decisions. I was tired of people pushing me around, telling me what I could and couldn't do, and basing every choice I made on fear of anyone finding out the truth.

Mags had been fucking strangers on my bed for weeks, when that bed was one of the few places I had to feel safe. He'd soiled it, and done it intentionally. But it was my goddamned bedroom. *My* bed. It was time to use it the way I wanted to, and no second-guessing was going to make me change my mind.

Jovie was traveling for the weekend. Jess was nowhere to be found. And I didn't give a shit if Mags saw I had company or not. That meant I was alone in the house, except for a few folks on my cleaning and security team who were hired to be discreet.

It might have been my only chance to get away with inviting someone over, testing the waters of my newfound bravery. It was an opportunity I had to seize, even if my guilt felt bigger than anything else. I couldn't shake that feeling of wrongness, so I just kept trying to go on despite it.

My twisted memories and anger at the world made me want to get fucked and do something perverse. I'd been trying to own the old me who'd allowed sexual torture while I slept in exchange for expensive gifts. It made me want to revert to more wicked ways and act out, if only for one night. My guilt wasn't from hiring hookers. Fuck it; I was a hooker, too.

There was a very good chance someone would show up at the house at some point, though. Some precautions needed to be made.

The compromise I came up with was to specifically request someone transgender with breasts and a cock, who could easily pass for a woman. My imagination conjured up Jade with real flesh instead of plastic harnessed to her crotch. That way, I'd get what I needed, and if anyone saw her, they'd just assume she had a pussy. If I found someone I liked, the way I'd liked Ken with his wholesome appearance, insatiable need, and calming tenderness, it could become a regular thing. It would sate the need just like scratching the persistent itch in my wrist. Maybe it wasn't healthy, but it got the job done.

The part of me that always got hard for Mr. Briant and willingly spread for him wanted someone new to knock me out, or at least get me really high before playing with me, the way Mr. Briant had. It was sick, but I missed it. You couldn't trust a hooker to do that, though. Not even the well-paid, well-cared-for ones. Even with how far gone I was, I knew that was a good way to get killed.

I called my contact with The Company, based out of the Nashville area. A pleasant voice with the Tennessee twang answered and happily processed my request with a thank you, kindly. My guest would be named Kennedy. She would be there in an hour.

I went to shave off my new beard to keep me occupied until she arrived.

I realized my mistake as soon as I was face-to-face with Kennedy. She was pretty enough—Columbian, short, and slender. But what I wanted wasn't someone pretty and too delicate to be able to make me submit the way I craved. It was Mr. Briant's confidence, strength, and power I missed. Sure, he'd damaged me, but he took care of me in his own ways, too. There were echoes of that power in the way Mags was reckless and brave, showing off his talents with sex and being able to have anyone he wanted. The company I'd been hiring got me off, and Ken had even managed to touch my heart, but there was safety in their beauty.

Paying for their time, trying to be nicer to them than they expected, but then taking my pleasure from them anyway — I'd been turning the tables, acting like Mr. Briant had with me. I guess I'd tried to be so kind to those people who were being paid to service me in whatever ways I wanted them to, because Mr. Briant hadn't been kind to me. I'd been trying to do the right thing by them, offering help in whatever ways they needed it, while still taking advantage.

Either way, it was still fucked up and recreating exactly what I'd been trying to get away from.

It wasn't what I wanted, and it definitely wasn't what I needed. In fact, I was horrified at myself.

"Look, I'm sorry. I can't do this." I pushed a wad of bills into Kennedy's hand. "Sorry you came all this way."

We were standing inside the doorway of my bedroom, and I couldn't raise my gaze off the floor. What the hell had I been doing? Had I really been trying to mimic what that damned man had done to me?

"You sure, honey?" Kennedy asked, hesitating.

"Yes. Very. I'm truly sorry."

I knew what it meant. I couldn't pay for sex anymore, not without feeling like I was turning into a monster, too. But where did that leave me, if I was too fucked up to date normal guys? Alone? Forever?

Kennedy receded down the hall to the steps as misery started to open up a gaping pit beneath my feet. I'd tumble down there and never get out again. Her high heels click-clacked on the wooden floorboards on her way out, helping me track her progress audibly. The farther she got, the more I knew I'd done the right thing, even if that left me with nothing and no hope at all.

The front door opened and shut again. With a deep sigh, I realized I needed a strong drink. That required a trip to the kitchen where the booze and ice were kept.

At least I'd had the balls to stop myself from going through with it. Maybe I was learning to know myself after all, even if I didn't like what I found.

Craving only a way to drown my sorrows, I stepped out of the bedroom and into the hall.

"Hey," a deep voice said from right beside me, in the hall.

Seeing that pen in my mind, and visions of Mr. Briant with his massive body guards lurking in the hall, I yelled, "Shit!" and almost jumped right out of my skin.

"Whoa, easy. It's just me," Jess said, hands raised high to show he meant no harm. He looked me in the eyes like he could see more than I wanted him to, like he could see exactly how scared and miserable I felt, but then it got worse, fast. His gaze slid slowly, tellingly down my body, then over to the steps. Lowering his hands, he slipped them into his front pants pockets. "Can I talk to you?"

"No," was my instant, guilty reply. "I mean, I need a drink. Of water. I was going to the kitchen. I'm really thirsty. For water."

"I'll go with you, then. We can talk on the way."

He glanced at my hand holding my bedroom doorknob shut. A motor started up in the driveway. It sounded like my damnation. What had he seen? What did he know? I felt anxiousness twisting like a screw inside my gut, changing my expression and dooming me further.

"I made sure not to block her in," Jess told me, with plenty of inflection and hidden messages. "She's pretty."

I didn't like how he was looking at me, like he had every right to look at me in any way he wanted to, prying open little doors that hid things I'd never wanted him to see. "Don't," I grunted, shaking my head once. It sounded defensive, meek, and pitiful.

He took a step towards me. "She treat you good?" he asked softly. Did he know she was a hooker? He couldn't, could he? Why did I feel so guilty anyway? We hadn't even fucked.

But I'd intended to, so maybe the guilt didn't care if it had happened or not. I'd fucked enough prostitutes other than Kennedy for it not to matter much. I'd used plenty of people, just like Mags had. I had no room to talk.

It was guilt on top of guilt. I was starting to hyperventilate but the strange look on his face caught my attention and distracted me a little. Not only was every little bit of Jess's attention focused on me, my words, my mood, my expression and body language, but Jess looked *angry*.

Why the hell was *he* angry?

"I'm not talking about this with you," I argued.

"Do you talk about it with Mags?" Jess asked, right away.

"No! It's no one's business!"

"Why are you paying for sex?" he growled, looking like he was shocked he'd said it as soon as he did. It was too late to take it back, though, so he plowed on. "You could have *anyone*! Do you realize that? There are *so many people* that want you, that love you and would do *anything* to be with you like she was tonight."

"Yeah, I doubt that," I shot back.

"Why, because she has a dick?"

Everything stopped.

My face went red.

I quit breathing.

When my exhale eventually came out along with a moan, I quickly covered my mouth with a hand, like I could push the sound of it back inside.

"Fuck," he sighed, after he'd seen my reaction. "I'm sorry. *I'm sorry.*"

Instinct told me he didn't seem angry anymore, even though he was still looking at me too closely and standing too near. But I didn't care about any of that because, for a reason I couldn't begin to wrap my head around, Jess was touching me.

Just like with Mr. Briant, the touching seemed to yank out some of the wiring in my head, leaving me unable to function. I couldn't move or react. I couldn't even form a thought. There was no fight, I just let him.

Jess pulled my hand down from my mouth and wrapped his fingers around the side of my neck. He let his thumb rest against the side of my jaw. It was an intimate sort of touch and not friendly at all. Leaning down, he stooped to be closer to my face and catch my gaze. Somehow, I came back to myself just enough to try to push him away, but he was insistent. The way Jess held on told me he wasn't letting go until he was ready to. That was scary and exciting enough to make me too weak to do much of anything. His face was a breath away, with those two-tone eyes and soft, full lips. He was my friend but he wasn't acting like it. The Jess I knew and the Jess I was faced with were two different pieces of a puzzle I couldn't see or even begin to fit together.

I kept pushing, uselessly, drawing in rough intakes of air. He easily held me still, looking sad in a way I didn't pretend to understand.

I shoved uselessly and cursed him. He was too big to move, too determined to leave. Then, he was hugging me to his chest, holding me there by the back of my neck and my lower back as I ground my teeth together and fought old, strong feelings of being far out of my depth, of not knowing what was happening to me or why, just that I was a helpless fool.

I felt his lips pressing against my hair.

"Not like this," he was saying. "*I didn't want it like this*. Jesus... I'm sorry. I'm so sorry."

Hating that he was embracing me, I couldn't let go of him either. He wasn't the only one holding on. My hands were clasped to his sides, a thin shirt the only thing separating me from the firm, warm feel of him. And god, he was big. I never quite realized *how* big until I was gathered up against him like that. It started to flip all the wrong kinds of switches in me—the same ones Kennedy hadn't been able to trip. The size, strength, and determination of him made me weak in every way that mattered.

It didn't make sense. None of it did.

He backed me to the wall and pinned me there against it with his much larger body, showing me as clear as could be that there was no more running. He touched the side of my face, hooking his hand around my ear. He brushed my hair back with his fingertips, and then they stayed there, tangled in the long strands, as he bent lower and kissed me softly on the mouth.

It would have been less shocking if he'd punched me in the teeth.

Chapter 21

Quicksand

I made a soft, bruised groan of hurt, fear, and shame. Dumbstruck, I watched him, *felt* him put his lips on mine and refuse to pull away until he knew I really, truly felt them there.

Those pretty, bowed-shaped lips I'd admired earlier brushed against mine a few times, slow and steady, and he was fucking *kissing* me. He breathed out a shaky exhale, almost broke contact, then kissed me harder before I pushed him off of me entirely.

Like a cornered rabbit faced with a bear, I looked for escape I knew I'd never get. For the life of me, I couldn't figure out why he was hurting me the way he was.

"You're making fun of me," I realized.

It came out so quietly, it was almost too low to hear. It felt like the words tried to slip back down my throat so they wouldn't be true. But his response was to chase me, backing me to the wall again, like he had to get closer to hear. He leaned in with a hand braced against the wall beside my head and his other by my side. I tilted my chin up instinctively, not out of choice. He kissed me again when I exhaled, and it was deeper that time. His mouth turned at an angle to push inside and open me up.

I gasped as he got inside of me and grabbed hold of him. His tongue slipped into my mouth and I came apart, grabbing the back of his head, getting hard. He licked my tongue, sucking on it, moaning like he loved it. He had one hand wrapped behind my neck and the other rested in the curve of my lower back. The one on my back rubbed in a firm drag downward to cup my ass. He squeezed, hard, and I groaned, breathing heavily through my nose as he kept using my mouth.

When we broke apart, it was only because he pulled back. By then, I was dizzy and bewildered exactly the same way I used to be with Mr. Briant, like the whole world was trying to make me out to be an idiot. Feeling the ghost of his kisses on my lips, tasting him on my tongue, I realized his hand was holding me by the hip like he had every right to do so.

But Jess was frowning with worry, brushing the tears from my cheeks with the pad of his thumb. He began smoothing my hair back like he couldn't stop touching it. He was looking at me in a way that no one in my whole life ever had. I didn't recognize it, then, as love, but that's what it was.

"I'm not making fun," he whispered, wearing that strange, regretful frown and sounding choked up. "I know you're gay, Tucker, and that you're trying to pass as straight. If you were just having sex with that woman, I figure that has to mean one thing. And I am truly sorry. Let me get you some water."

Opening my door, he nodded to the empty room and said, "Have a seat. Please. I'll be right back."

Obeying him without knowing why, I sat and stared at nothing, my heart pounding away.

True to his word, Jess was back a minute later with two bottles of water. He walked through the door without closing it and crossed to me.

"I don't want to be in here with you," I confessed deliriously, my head swimming. He passed a bottle to me. I drank it down, fast, wishing there was a pill dissolving away inside of it. When I was done, I screwed the cap back on.

The bed shifted as he sat on it beside me, facing me.

"Why, because of *her*?" There was more than a hint of jealousy there.

He thought we'd fucked, not that it mattered that we hadn't. Not after everything else I'd done.

"No, because of me. Everything goes wrong because of me. Our friendship is one of the few good things I have, Jess. And you're *married*! I know I've been... relying on you, more than is proper, and I apologize if this is my fault, if I gave you the wrong idea or anything.

I don't want to screw anything else up."

He was staring down at his hands folded in his lap, his water lying untouched and unopened at his side. After a moment, he slipped the gold band off of the third finger of his left hand and set it between us on the sheet.

We both gazed at it, gleaming there.

"What are you doing?" I asked him. My heart was still beating hard. I didn't like that ring, sitting alone on the bed like that. I wanted to stick it back onto his finger, where it should have been, placing him securely in a world apart from me and the danger that always got swept up in my wake, not somewhere where it was possible to find him kissing me and touching me like he had. The scariest part of all, though, was how very much I'd enjoyed it, even though there were whisperings in the back of my mind that somehow I was hurting *him* by letting him touch me.

"It's a fake," he told me in an embarrassed sort of way, his voice hushed. "I'm not married. Never was."

"*What?* What are you talking about? You can't be serious?" Carefully, I watched his face. "Jess, man, I'm so confused right now...."

After a moment, he sighed and continued. "I've had a crush on you since we first met. During everything with my dad, I needed an out. Music had always been my escape and when I heard your voice, I was hooked, right away. That was my ticket out of hell. It was my hope. I was an instant fan of your work, so I spoke to people who spoke to people to see if I could work with you, but, Tucker... when I *saw you*, and met you, I knew how screwed I was. And, god, you were so nice, so sweet and genuine. There was nothing arrogant in you at all. I could tell you didn't buy into your own hype like so many stars do, and you just cared so much about your craft in a way I've always respected."

Looking embarrassed, he met my gaze for just a second. All I could see was how different he was that he wasn't hiding and I was really looking. I didn't think I'd ever let myself *really* look at him before. He'd always been this solid guy who never seemed to screw things up, but would always press at me to open up when I didn't want to. Maybe that led me to close my eyes to how beautiful he was. But now I saw, beyond surface nonsense, the ache in his blue-green eyes, the way the shape of his lips echoed all of the noise in his head making him second-guess himself, and how he was still there, solid as ever, yet now even more able to press at me and get inside, in deeper ways.

"The ring was so no one would question my orientation or expect me to go after female fans," Jess was explaining. "I figured if everyone thought I was married, it would make sense that I wasn't fucking around. I'm gay, Tucker. I've known since day one that you can't be anything but straight if you want to make a living in this industry, and I wanted to *work*."

He waited for it to sink it.

It didn't really. Not at first.

"I haven't been interested in hooking up with men, either, because there's only one man I'm interested in anyway, and he was... unavailable."

"Me," I guessed. He was sitting close enough to touch and I kept waiting for it to happen, with butterflies knocking around in my stomach.

He smiled quickly, looking embarrassed and adorable.

"Yes," Jess told me. "It took me a while to figure you out, I'll admit. I kept my crush on you secret for a long time. I was so embarrassed by it. But I never suspected... I think mainly it's how you are with Mags that tipped me off. I can tell you really love him. You deserve better, though. A *lot* better. Does he even know? He doesn't, does he? How can someone be your closest friend for most of your life and not know you're gay?"

"I don't know!" I blurted, since I'd been angry about that same damn thing for a long time. Shocked at my outburst, quieter, I said, "I don't know. Selective perception, maybe. He sees what he wants to see."

It was a difficult thing to accept so fast, that Jess had been hot for me, and still was. There he sat, right on my bed, wearing his intentions where I could see every last one of them. It was intimidating, and it was making me really fucking hard.

I thought of him jerking off while thinking about fucking or sucking me. It was exciting as well as dangerous to know he saw me in a sexual way, mostly because of how wrong it seemed.

"The beard was another way to hide," Jess explained. "The shaved head, too. It made me look like someone I'm not. It was necessary. I'm trying to go back to how I normally look, because I want to be honest with you. Actually, I wanted to be honest in Houston, since the tour was over, and I figured that if you decided to fire me, at least it would happen at a good time. But things were so... heavy, there. I kept trying to talk to you about it, but I could tell you were upset, and I couldn't figure out why. Things had seemed fine when we were on the road, but in Houston..." he shook his head. "It reminded me of a bad time in my life. Those scars on your arms and the way you were looking, especially when you thought no one was paying attention—it gave me a really bad feeling, like something bad was going to happen and I had to try and stop it. And when you went camping, you were gone for so long. When we did talk, I could hear how tormented you were, but I didn't know how to help. You shut down, cut us all off. It really scared me."

"Fuck," I sighed. "Look, I'm sorry for worrying you. I wasn't thinking of anyone else's feelings when I took off. It just seemed like the only choice I had. It was wrong not to consider the bigger picture. That was... I don't know. Selfish? I've been worrying about my own damn problems so much, I guess I stopped being able to tell if I was hurting anyone in the process."

So far he hadn't pressed forward again, like he had in the hall. He stayed seated where he was, respectfully. There was something about that that bothered me more than my reservations.

The image of that pen, there and gone, flickered in my mind the way it had on my phone, not that long ago. That along with everything Jess was saying just made me feel like I couldn't begin to protect myself from harm even if I wanted to. There was just too damned much out of my control. Reaching up, I broke the invisible wall between us with my right hand, touching his handsome face and his shaved-smooth jaw. In a way, I just needed to feel he was really there and not just a something I'd imagined. So many of my feelings had been caught up with ghosts and daydreams, he could just as easily have been one of them.

He was really there, though; as real as Ken had been that morning, weeks ago, when I'd wondered at his scars and secrets while my body still ached from the ways he'd used it. But Ken had left, the way everyone left, eventually. Jess hadn't left, though. He'd been a constant. It was refreshing to be faced with a man instead of the idea of one.

"You're kind of gorgeous without the beard," I told him self-consciously. "I wasn't prepared for that."

I'd been letting Mags outshine him. Funny how the glare of idolizing could blind you to what was right in front of you, even better than the dream.

He took hold of my hand and brought it to his lips. They brushed my knuckles for just a moment while he held my gaze with his blue-and-green-colored eyes. Then he uncurled my fingers and kissed my palm. It felt like he was seducing me, and it kept stirring the butterflies in my stomach. Jess had always taken his time with songs, learning them inside and out until he knew them better than anyone else in the band, understanding them on a level others didn't so he could add new layers of sound beneath what the rest of us were doing. That was due to his patience. He was showing me how his diligence and care had been practiced on me, too. *I* was Jess's song, and he'd suddenly decided it was time to start playing the hell out of me.

Drawing closer, he kissed the inside of my wrist, then a little farther up my forearm. His eyes closed with what looked like pleasure.

Our hands linked, he let them drop between us and sat up straight again.

There was a heavy pause. He wasn't looking around the room, but I suspected he wanted to.

"What'd you do with her?"

It wasn't his business even if we had done something. But everything that had happened so far since Kennedy left felt like we'd already crossed a lot of lines. With Mr. Briant, as soon as he'd ever gotten me alone, closed a door and given me a knowing look, that was it. We were in it. That's how it felt with Jess, then. He'd kissed me, touched my ass, and confessed to wanting me. We were in it, too. Speaking a few more truths about how fucked up I was, was nothing to me.

"We didn't do a thing and that's not a lie. She got here, because I'd been... lonely, but... I don't quite know how to say this. I'd like to stop lying so damned much, even to myself. For a little while now,

I've been looking to be with people who were smaller than me, people who'd do exactly what they're told and not say a word about it because it made me feel more in control. But that was just fear talking. I don't want to have to be in control all the time. So, anyhow, she left. I asked her to. She wasn't what I'm looking for."

Jess asked, "So you're looking to give up control?"

"You could say that."

"What else could you say?"

"That I want to get fucked."

My confession had the effect of causing Jess to shift closer until our legs touched. Heat rose under my skin and the flutters in my stomach made me fidgety. Then, he asked, low and soft, "That's your preference?"

He was still holding my hand. His thumb brushed the inside of my wrist in a way that sent hot spirals of want twisting into me.

"Mm-hmm," I hummed, feeling dizzy. He was leaning close again, like he was going to kiss me, so I couldn't glance up to measure the look that might have been in his eyes. The heat and intensity of him were intoxicating. He was making me feel nervous, because I understood what he wanted, but it was different than how I'd been nervous with William, Ken or Jade. With them, there had always been the sense that they were treating me as they'd treat any of their clients with my sort of disposition. It wasn't entirely personal. It was business.

Same thing with Mr. Briant. He'd always called that business, too.

There was nothing about Jess that was business. Though we were band mates, the relationship I'd thought we had vanished into thin air. He was a friend, but at the same time, he wasn't. He'd tried to know me, my secrets, and been after me on a long, slow chase. Now, he was making his move. Everything he did, every little bit of his lust, was just for me. It was *entirely* personal.

Maybe because there was nothing familiar about the situation I was suddenly in, eager anticipation trampled down my self-consciousness. There was no need to win Jess over, or convince him I was nervous, because he already wanted me. He was already convinced. He knew I was scared, but that didn't mean he was leaving, especially given the things I heard myself telling him.

"I have your permission?" he asked with heavy implication.

"You can have any damned thing you want as long as you start touching me."

It was an automatic response, a need to give of myself to someone who wanted to take, and only from me.

When he started to move, I did too. I fell back to lie on the bed as he got on top of me, advancing and acting faster than I thought he would. As soon as my back settled on the bed, his thigh was already slipping between mine, parting my legs, and drawing up to gently nudge my balls. One of his hands was planted on the bed, by the side of my head. The other clasped around my cock through my pants.

He gave a heavy, pleasurable exhale, his eyes closing over. I rocked into the grip of his hand, reaching up to hold him, just to steady myself.

"Do it," I urged, moaning, loving the dangerous freefall of letting him touch me. "Want you to." My hand slipped into a pocket, drew out a condom. "The lube is on the nightstand."

"Why do you want me to?"

"I don't know. I guess I've never...." The words trailed off when he opened my fly, and slipped a hand inside.

My breath caught sharply, feeling his palm against my bare flesh. I whimpered a wordless plea as he fondled me, slowly. As soon as he heard my gasp, his mouth was on mine, kissing away the sound, like he was starving for it. The weaker he made me, the more confident he seemed to become.

I couldn't stop watching him. It was *Jess*. It wasn't a random stranger who was only going along with it because I'd paid them to, and it wasn't rape. Those were my only other sexual experiences. Jess was someone who meant something to me, who had always been attentive and respectful. That was something very, very new.

"I've never been with someone who gave a damn about me," I told him, leaving out the rest.

"*I* give a damn," he replied, looking intent. There was passion in his eyes, his body, and *I'd* done that to him. That was amazing. Even more amazing was his gentleness and caution. "To say the least."

I smiled. "I can tell. I give a damn about you too."

It was hard to tell how much I cared about him, and in what ways. I couldn't make much sense of how I felt, not in that moment. I'd already made myself as vulnerable as I was able, physically. I couldn't give him my heart, too. Not quite yet.

He pulled his hand out of my pants. My dick was so hard from what we were doing and how dirty it was, it made me want to beg him for more. He caressed up my side, under my shirt, pushing it out of the way. Lying down on top of me, Jess straddled me. His fingers found my nipple, twisting it. His dick rocked against mine through our pants and it made me want to rut and fuck myself against him.

Jess warned, "You have to be sure. I've wanted this for so fucking long. Wanted *you*."

"I'm sure," I replied impatiently, without pride or bashfulness. It was all used up.

He sat up. Arms crossed, he yanked the shirt up over his head. His chest was thickly muscled, chiseled with definition.

"Jesus," I breathed. "Okay, now I *really* want you to fuck me."

He laughed and reached for my shirt, too.

"My pleasure," he grinned.

Chapter 22
Truth

From the outside looking in, if the sex between me and Jess seemed to happen really fast, and too soon, that's because it did. One moment I was horrified my friendly, eerily perceptive, formerly straight and married pianist was kissing me. The next I was flat out asking him to fuck me.

Consider my history.

My only experiences with consensual sex involved people who were paid to get in, get it done in an efficient manner, and get the hell out. Taking it slow wasn't in my vocabulary. The thought of sitting there, having a heart-to-heart with Jess about how we were hot for each other without doing anything about it, made me queasy and uncomfortable. I never could have eased into sex gradually that way. Not in a million years. With Mags, our threesomes were painted in shame, and with the prostitutes I'd hired, the novelty and general unease about the whole thing had never gone away. Sex was the biggest, most intimidating obstacle in all of my relationships. It was always better to dive right in rather than sit there thinking or talking about what was going to happen, making the discomfort last longer than it needed to.

Of course, the time I'd spent with Mr. Briant had an effect on me, too. When a man had some leverage on me, and also wanted to get in my pants, I instinctively wanted to cut right to the sex to please them and fix things. Sure, it was wildly different. Mr. Briant seemed to have a thorough professional hold on me. Jess's power was tethered to the fact that he could now take me apart privately or publically should the mood strike. If he got mad at me, for whatever reason, he could tell the media that Tucker Reynolds was fond of whores of all varieties and genders, as long as he was the one taking it up the ass. What a career-ending story that would make. He could even give them Kennedy if he was a real son of a bitch.

That was the cold, beaten-down part of my mind talking. The rest of me — which was so afraid of falling for someone who could make me feel and care and want to give my heart as well as my body — was cowering in the corner of my soul. It would have been better to let Jess hurt me, than ease into something real and likely to break my heart.

But Jess wasn't cruel... was he? My first, shallow thought was to make him happy the way I'd satisfied Mr. Briant. The good news was it went deeper than that with Jess, which became clear to me faster than seemed possible.

He was my *friend*. He'd been my friend, *first*.

That scared the living daylights out of me.

I cared about Jess as a person, a musician, a friend, and a man before we ever set foot in that bedroom. He was one of the good ones. He'd stood up for me, supported me and tried to reach out when he saw I might need help. Even when it came to Mags, Jess was the only one who tried, time and time again, to break that dysfunctional cycle we'd been stuck in. Lots of people could see how corrupted my relationship with Mags had gotten but Jess was the only one with the balls to call it like it was to my face.

There was a real chance Jess was my hero.

He was straddling my thighs, shirtless, with his security-guard-sized body, his dark, soft hair and freshly-shaved, handsome face. I lay there, equally shirtless, and acting on pure instinct. His hand was on my opened fly.

It trembled.

"Hey, are you all right?" I asked him, putting the brakes on hard.

Propping myself up on my elbows, I looked up at him more closely.

I wasn't the only one questioning things. It was possible Jess was even more terrified than I was.

Jess rubbed his head nervously. Then he wiped his hands dry on his pants and chewed on his lip. I'd put him on the spot and it only made it worse.

"Yeah. Yeah," he said breathlessly, trying to laugh it off. It wasn't working.

"What's wrong?"

Our eyes met. It sent a funny tickle wriggling through my belly, because it wasn't a hooker looking back at me and pinning my hips to the bed. It was *Jess* I was about to fuck.

With a heavy sigh and his hands braced on his upper thighs, he glanced away, and said, "Kind of been thinking of how this would go... someday... for a while. It's embarrassing to admit. Like, *really* embarrassing. When you fantasize about someone for so long and then get the chance to actually make it *happen...."*

His chest was rising and falling quickly. I stared as it swelled and contracted, mesmerized by the rhythm. He had plenty of chest hair and it was driving me wild. I wanted to run my fingers through it while I sucked on his tan nipples just to see what it would do to him.

Never had I been with someone who was the slightest bit nervous about sex. *I* was the one who always played that part. But Jess was a lot more scared than I was. It had a calming effect on me, letting me focus on what I wanted, and showing me how experience had taught me a few things while I wasn't paying attention.

What I wanted was simple: to have Jess's warm, thick cock in me, as fast as humanly possible. I wanted to possess it, ride it hard, and have him come inside me.

Pushing down my pants, slipping my legs out from between where he was perched above me, I shucked them off and threw them aside.

His eyes got really big, because I was suddenly completely naked and wrapping my legs around his waist. His surprise was cute as hell.

"Stop thinkin' about it, then. I'm not a fantasy, but I *am* horny, thanks to you. I've always heard the shy act was sexy but never really believed it until now."

I gripped his torso with my thighs. Looking like he was coming apart, Jess leaned down over me. He was breathing hard, and sweaty, warm, beautiful, and wonderfully familiar. He cared about me, treasured me in ways that boggled the mind. Even better, he had no expectations. Every little moment, each touch and kiss was like a gift he'd always thought he'd be denied. Jess groped my body with his eyes, full of gratitude and tender care, before he touched me anywhere. His hand planted by my head and nuzzled my neck.

"Damn, you're sweet, too," I groaned. "Sweet *and* sexy. You're killin' me here, man. Touch me or somethin'. *Please,*" I begged. Need for relief made me shameless.

Hesitantly, Jess stroked my dick, making me shiver. He felt the re-action and it seemed to give him courage. His lips brushed against my neck. The tip of his tongue drew a thin line up to my earlobe where his teeth captured it and tugged oh-so-gently. My cock pulsed pre-come. I thrust against his fingers with a quivering, "*Please.*"

He stroked and stroked and stroked, until I was rocking steadily. The hair of his chest brushed mine as he caught my lips in a kiss, frowning. I held his face in my hands and kissed him as well as I could, luring him in. I wanted his tongue in me the way I wanted his fingers and cock in me, too.

When he stopped stroking and instead rubbed down, rolling my balls, I moaned for what I knew came next. It was loud and throaty. He broke the kiss and stared down at me, watching me sing my pas-sion like it was a show, just for him. Reaching even lower, he caressed over the skin behind my balls, then over my hole.

He paused to get some slick on his hand.

Fuck, but I needed him. Arching on the bed, throwing my head back, I yelled as two of his wet fingers slipped into me, then I clenched around them. The palm of his free hand slid up over my chest, feeling sound vibrate through the flesh.

"Jesus wept," he swore. "Look at you."

It felt better because it was *him*. It had never occurred to me that being aroused emotionally and mentally could make each little touch mean that much more.

He gently, slowly explored my body, and I pushed down on his hand to take more of it, holding him behind the neck for leverage as I tugged my dick.

"Please, Jess. I'm ready for you, come on," I gasped between sharp cries that had him staring at my mouth in dirty ways.

"I'm not in a hurry," he replied. "Kind of enjoying this part, actu-ally."

The fingers up my ass twisted around. He was right there to kiss away my moans. When his hand slid up my neck, up under my chin, I undulated, riding him with small circles of my hips. The first two fingers of his free hand brushed over my lips and slipped into my mouth. I sucked them like I wanted to suck his cock. His fingers were hooked inside me at both ends and I was about to fucking *erupt*.

Almost too late, I realized I didn't want to come just yet. I let go of my dick and grabbed him with both hands instead, growling like an animal around his fingers as I writhed and fought back the orgasm. I reared up, tensing my thighs. The fingers nestled between my lips slid back over my tongue, which wrapped around them like my legs wrapped his narrow waist. I pressed my ass down on his hand, feeling the two fingers bend, prying at my inner walls, the knuckles grinding.

I don't know how long it went on. I could've kept going like that for hours, but very suddenly he pulled free and stopped touching me.

Catching my breath, I heard him rip open the condom wrapper. The bed shifted as he got up and took his pants off, then climbed back on, ready to go.

He astonished me by hooking each of his arms underneath one of my legs, bending them sharply back toward my shoulders and folding me in half. The position pulled me more open than I'd been during any sex I'd been conscious for.

Then he was driving into me, all of him at once, and I gave a rough, raspy yell, with all the air in my lungs. It felt like I was choking on him, he was in so deep.

Shuddering, gasping, I clawed at him, fighting how damn good it was, and he watched me, kissing my face, dragging his lips over my chin, my cheek, and the line of my jaw. There was no pain, no fear or shame. It was all joy, wonder, and gratitude.

At first, he didn't move. Maybe he was making sure he hadn't killed me, because I sure was shouting like he'd tried to.

"You okay?" he asked with a chuckle.

But I couldn't form words. I could hardly breathe.

Slowly, he started to move, just a little at first, then with longer thrusts that had me making desperate sounds. With one squeeze of his fist, I climaxed almost violently, sobbing with my mouth pressed to his shoulder. He rode my ass harder as it tightened around him with my orgasm, hissing, "Fuck. Oh fuck. *Tucker.*"

Without warning or explanation, he stopped completely.

He stopped moving. Every muscle froze in place.

He even stopped breathing.

I didn't know why. Every nerve in my body was firing with after-shocks and I'd begun to hiccup softly as I calmed down, panting, my face streaked with happy tears.

Jess sat up straighter, his body gone perfectly still. One hand reached out to the doorway, palm out.

"Hey. Look, man," he said urgently, and not to me. "It's not—"

That's as much as he got out before being cut off by a primal roar that made my blood run cold.

A voice I knew as well as my own, bellowed, "GET OFF OF HIM!"

Someone violently ripped Jess backwards and off of me, then off of the bed entirely and punched him, as hard as they could, with a closed fist to his left cheekbone.

I heard the impact. It was a meaty, solid, sickening sound.

Another fist caught him in the stomach, doubling him over as soon as he was on his feet.

"No. No, stop. Stop! Stop it! STOP!" I screamed. "Mags, stop!"

Mags was on Jess, who had crumpled to the floor. Successive punches to Jess's head were blocked by Jess's arms. They deflected blows that fell like the rain. The rest of his body was unprotected, though.

Rage-filled, growling roars kept coming from Mags, his face blood red as he went into attack mode like I'd never seen before.

"Mags, stop! Stop it! Stop! For fuck's sake, stop hitting him!"

"Get out of the way," he warned me viciously. "Stay the fuck back!"

I got an arm around Mags' neck and tried to drag him off of Jess, who was curled up in a fetal position, both arms wrapped around his head to shield it.

Mags' legs kicked but I was desperate and managed to pull him a foot or two back. He tried to wriggle loose but was probably too concerned about not hurting me to actually fight back like he could have. I got in front of him and shoved with both hands as he sprung to his feet.

"What the *fuck*, man?!" I wheezed. "Jess, you okay? Jess?!"

"I'll kill you," Mags sneered, staring past me at Jess, who was on the floor, moaning with pain. "I'll fucking *kill you* for touching him. Gonna snap off every one of those piano-playin' fingers and your dick, too, you sick son of a bitch."

"Are you crazy?! Are you fucking out of your *mind*?"

Mags just ignored me.

I got between the two of them. Jess staggered to his feet and Mags tried to surge past me, his arm cocked back and his teeth bared like an angry dog at the end of a tight leash.

"Stay down, you sick motherfucker," he snarled at Jess. "I'm gonna fuckin' take you apart."

"What is wrong with you?!" I slammed my hands against Mags' chest.

He still wasn't listening and pulled me away from Jess, not ever letting his gaze drift. Jess just stood there, fuming but silent. Blood ran from beside his eye where Mags' ring had caught and torn the skin open. Jess was clutching his side.

"This is none of your goddamned business!" I protested. "I wanted him to! He wasn't hurting me, you fucking idiot!"

"Got him making excuses for you, huh?" Mags said to Jess, looking unhinged and still ignoring me. "It was the biggest mistake of your *life* when you touched him."

I grabbed his face, yanked it toward me to make him stop looking at Jess. "Magnusson Palmer, you do not get to beat on my lovers like a fuckin' psychopath, you hear me?"

"Stop making excuses for him!" Mags demanded, screaming the words in my face, his voice breaking with the strain. He really did look at me then, though. His gaze drifted down my naked body, then up to my face. He touched it lovingly and bit back a sob. "It's not your fault, okay? You're confused. He brainwashed you."

"No, he really didn't."

It wasn't getting through. He either didn't or couldn't hear me. All he understood was that I was trying to protect someone who had just been sodomizing me while I screamed and cried.

He pressed a kiss to my forehead, breathing roughly, then bolted for Jess a second later when he figured my guard was down.

I grabbed him under the arms and yanked as he tried to lunge for Jess and tear him apart.

It became clear to me, then, how out of control the situation was.

"Fuck. *Fuck!*" I yelled, furious and frustrated. "Mags, get out," I demanded, yanking with all of my waning strength. "Get out of my damn house!"

"NO!" he roared. "No way, Tucker! I'm not leaving your side, and I'm not leaving you with him!"

"I love him!" Jess shouted, his voice cutting through and quieting Mags, fast. "And I'm not going anywhere!"

"Fuck this, I'm getting my gun," Mags snarled.

"What?! No! *Mags, no!*"

But it was too late; he was already out the door, going for the weapon I knew he had stashed around there somewhere.

I slammed the bedroom door shut behind him, locked it, and then, with Jess's help, wedged a chair under the handle.

It was stupid as hell. Jess and I were naked. Mags had lost his mind. I couldn't stop him from doing whatever it was he thought he needed to do and there was no doubt in my mind he would murder Jess if given the chance.

"We need to get away from the door," Jess was telling me, guiding me away. "He could still try to shoot through there. It's not safe. Get in the bathroom. We need help. We need the police."

"Mags, don't do this!" I shouted through the door, not knowing if he could hear. I let Jess move me away, toward the bathroom and another layer of protection. "Hide the fucking gun! You hear me? Hide the gun, Mags! I'm calling the cops!"

Lowering my voice as Jess closed another door between us and Mags, I said, "I hate this. Getting the cops involved... It's messy enough without exposing shit to the public!"

"I know."

There was no choice, though. We were out of options. Mags wasn't listening to me and Jess was in danger. Protecting him was more important than my reputation.

I held my head in my hands.

"Shit. Shit!" I shouted, knowing how screwed I was and stomping with rage.

Chapter 23

Consequences

The police showed up about five minutes later, after I put in a call for help.

It was an uncomfortable situation to have to explain, though it all boiled down to a domestic dispute. No one mentioned the gun. I reported that two of my friends had gotten in an argument and we needed the police to mediate in order to get the situation under control.

When the police asked me and Jess if we'd consider Mags to be the primary aggressor, I insisted that Mags was just trying to protect me in a situation he didn't understand. The injuries to Jess pointed to Mags being at fault, which seemed to make the cops want to arrest Mags, but I tried to talk them down. I just wanted Mags out of there, not to be thrown in jail and have to testify about what he saw when he walked into my bedroom. And what Jess told the police when he was questioned, separately from me while he was being tended to by the paramedics, must have also convinced them not to make an arrest.

Jess and I had each put on a pair of pants. Jess was sitting on the back of the ambulance, answering questions while the paramedics bandaged his head.

Mags was across the driveway, arms folded and talking to another officer. Divide and conquer seemed to be the strategy for getting us to spill the whole story. When the cops first showed up, I gave them a general idea of what had happened. Next, they then went to Mags and Jess to get their take on it. As long as no one was being led away in handcuffs, giving the press an even juicier bit of gossip to run with, that was enough for me.

Meanwhile, I was inside, hanging out in alcoves of the entryway and putting in calls to my manager and publicist once flashes started going off in the shrubbery around the property. They told me to stay out of view, so I did, but it left me unable to mediate the way I wanted.

The paramedic was finishing with Jess as the officer came to talk to me again.

"Just a few more questions, Mr. Reynolds," she said.

"Yeah. Of course," I agreed distractedly as Jess came striding up the front steps toward me. Though I began walking out to meet him, he stopped me and blocked the view from the yard with his broad back.

"Stay in there," Jess said, grabbing a sweatshirt off a hook by the door and passing it to me. "Put this on. Cover your head with the hood so they don't get shots through the windows or something."

"Why are you still here? You should go to the hospital and let them make sure you're okay," I argued, fearing broken bones or internal injury. Jess walked the perimeter of the room, closing curtains, one by one. I pulled the sweatshirt on, tugged up the hood.

"I'm fine," he said waving off the concern and coming to my side.

"So, Mr. Grayville and Mr. Palmer have both been living here, correct?" the officer asked, consulting her notepad.

"Yeah," I nodded. "Just for a few weeks. Before that, we'd been on tour and I just got back from a trip, today."

"Mr. Grayville appears to be the only one to have received injuries, but Mr. Grayville says he isn't interested in pressing charges against Mr. Palmer."

"That's right," Jess nodded. I sighed, frustrated with the whole thing.

"Now," the officer said, flipping a page, "Mr. Palmer contends that he witnessed Mr. Grayville sexually assaulting you, Mr. Reynolds, when he entered the room."

"That's not true. There was no sexual assault, he just walked in on something consensual that he didn't understand," I said heatedly. I was panicked about how bad this could go if things started to slide out of control, so I had to do whatever I could to keep everyone else out of handcuffs. "Look, I'm fine. What's not fine is him losing his temper with Jess. Thank you for all of your help, officer." I wanted the cops and the paparazzi to go, and my peace and quiet back. How the hell I'd gone so fast from silence in the woods to press and cops scattered on the lawn was beyond me. "I really appreciate it. I think I'm going to ask Mr. Palmer to stay somewhere else for a while. That should solve the problem. If y'all could just stick around until he's gone, I'd feel a lot better."

She agreed and left to have a word with the other officer.

"I need to talk to Mags a moment," I told Jess. "Go back in the kitchen or out with the police for a sec, okay?"

With a nod, he went, choosing to wander out onto the lawn and sneer at the snooping photographers. Mags approached the door with a uniformed chaperone waiting nearby.

Tucking my body beside the doorway, I gestured with my head for him to come closer.

"I'm not comfortable leaving you with him," Mags said. The anger was gone, and that made it harder, because it left him looking only sad and worried.

There was too much to say that was long overdue to be aired. I felt it rising like the tide inside me, ready to pour out and wash away everything he thought he knew.

"Mags, you've been doing this, trying to be my protector, since fuckin' high school." I was desperate to get through to him for once. "I'm a *man*. I need you to let me take care of myself now. You're holding on to me so tightly, I can't fucking breathe. You have to let go, Mags. I will always be your friend, but I can't be there every minute of the day to keep you going or let you shield me from the world, either. It's hurting both of us, can't you feel that? Maybe with space, you could find someone to care about in a real way, instead of using these women like you do to fill a void. You deserve so much better than that, and so do they.

"And you know what? *I like guys*, okay?" was my pathetic, exhausted confession after years of pretending otherwise. "I'm gay and I'm not a virgin. Not even close. Not by years. This wasn't my first time with this kind of sex. You can't save me from it. I've been gay for as long as I've been alive, but I've hated myself for it and I knew you'd hate me, too, so I didn't tell you. But I can't— no, I *won't* hate myself for it anymore! I won't!"

"Keep your voice down!" Mags snapped, looking over his shoulder at the police and the press, not too far beyond. "They'll hear you!"

"You're still not listening to me. I don't care if they know, Mags! Let the world find out I'm queer. *Let them.* It's made me miserable for too long. Fucking *years.* Nothing could be worse than what I've already been through. Jess is not the bad guy, Mags. He's probably the only one who's seen me for who I really am, and cared about me anyway. Jess isn't going to hurt me. I'm sorry you had to find out this way, I really am, but there's nothing I can do about it now."

He held me with an anxious, intense gaze. Jaw clenched and rubbing his arm, he chewed on that a moment. Still blocking me with his body, trying to keep me quiet and out of sight, he said quietly, "No. I know what this is. You're just protecting him!" He was angry again. "It sounded like it hurt. *I know you,* partner. Better than anyone. I even know how you sound. And *that?*" He jabbed a finger at the stairs, leading to my bedroom, and trembled slightly as the rage came back. "That sounded like it *hurt.*"

I blushed a little in admitting another hard truth. "Fine, Mags. Okay. Yeah, it hurt a little. *I wanted it to.*"

He rubbed his mouth, more unsettled by the moment.

"You want to know what I've been hiding? Hmm?" I unbuckled my watch, pushed off my many bracelets and leather ties, all of which had been gathered on my left wrist. Letting them tumble to the floor, I ripped off the bandage and showed him the shallow, horizontal slice, scabbed over now. The other scars were right next to it, a whole network of them. *"I'm tired of hating myself!"* I screamed at him. "Fucking believe me! Listen to me! I have lived through hell and I need you to hear me when I say I need it to stop! PLEASE!"

There was movement at the door. The officer was holding Jess back with a hand to his chest while Jess tried to push past her and get inside, to us.

"Let me go! Let me go to him!" Jess yelled. "Tucker!"

I hurried past Mags to Jess, holding my hand over my wrist to hide it. The officer let Jess through after seeing me coming to him. Jess pulled me behind the door, where no one outside could see us, and hugged me to him as I fell apart.

"Get out, Mags! Go!" Jess scowled.

Mags looked at us, how we were holding each other, how upset I was, and nodded. He walked to the door, without a word, and left.

From just past the doorway, I heard Mags call back, "Love you, kid. You know I do."

I was a wreck. When Jess let me go after a few precious moments, he went to close up the house so I didn't have to. I sat curled up on the floor with my back to the wall. I held my head, wringing out the pain, unable to breathe while Jess calmly got rid of the cops.

He locked the front door, then led me upstairs. As we walked, he caressed my back and arm to soothe me.

Feeling hollow and thin, I let him undress me and turn on the water in the shower. He waited there, silent and steady, as I washed off. I could see his silhouette through the fogged-over glass, watching out for me, his gaze politely focused on his feet. There was so much thankfulness in me to just have him there like that, present and ready without asking questions or pressuring for answers.

He must have heard what I'd said to Mags. I knew he'd seen. It was time to acknowledge the scabs and scars.

"It's a long story, okay? And not one I can tell tonight. Maybe soon. That's the best I can promise," I told him. "But I'm not..." I took a breath, tried again. "I'm not going to try to kill myself. I promise."

"It happened while you were camping, didn't it?"

"Yeah," I nodded. "Toward the end, after I started to feel more like myself again. Funny."

"Not funny," Jess argued. I could hear how upset he was.

"No, not funny. Look, I'm not stupid. I know I need help. I've got the time, the money, the... willingness. I've even got some real support for the first time ever, thanks to you. So, I'll get the help. It's time. I'm ready."

"Good." He took a deep breath, sighed. "Tucker, what do you... what can I do to help? What do you need from me?"

"A drink'd be nice, to start. It's been a long night."

I reached for a towel, gave him an honest, humble grin. He must have seen I was all right, because he said, "All right then. One drink, coming up. Be right back. Holler if you need me. I know you can."

"Ass," I sighed, with a chuckle that lightened my heart.

After I'd dried off my body and my hair was merely damp instead of dripping, he wandered back in holding a mug of something hot.

"Coffee," he offered. "Decaf. Should be cool enough to drink."

"You're incredible," I smiled, taking the mug in both hands. It was wonderfully warm and smelled fantastic. The towel wrapped my waist. He was looking at me in a new kind of way, as someone who had seen me, felt me, and heard me coming apart in a few different ways. "Thank you for being so patient. Things have been a mess. But time away from it all really did help make things clearer. Despite my wrist and what it might imply. And now... I don't know." I turned toward him, liking the feel of him there, a sturdy presence to lean on, if I needed to. "I have a pretty big reason to try to get better. And I really am so goddamned sorry about all of that with Mags. I hated to see you hurt, and him causing it, just because of a stupid misunderstanding."

"Don't be sorry. He loves you, that's all. I can respect that. It's not your fault. I am relieved you're willing to talk a little about all of this now. It's not weakness to accept help, you know. It shows you have strength, and are making progress. That you're at a place where you're open to it is a really good thing."

Gazing up at his handsome face, and all of the emotion it conveyed, I saw the white bandage which held together the cut by his eye. He'd have bruises all over his body the next day.

"You don't owe me anything if you want to take off or go have some peace," I offered.

"Why would I want to take off?" he asked.

I set the mug down on the bathroom counter, thinking of those flowers, the champagne and the photo of the pen. He stepped up close and wound an arm around the small of my back. His fingers brushed my skin there, making a shiver race right through me. His other hand was laid upon my chest, holding there like he was feeling for my heartbeat. It was a strange, amazing moment, but I couldn't meet his eyes.

"It'd probably be better for you to be away from me. I'm afraid of putting you in harm's way, and I'm not just talking about Mags. There's something else that's been going on, but... I need to think about the best way to start talking about it. I will, though. You deserve the whole truth. I just don't feel like I'm good for you, as much as I want to be with you. It's not about what I want. It's about what's best for your wellbeing."

"How about you let me worry about my wellbeing? If there's some other threat you're under, Tucker, the last thing I want to do is leave you alone."

"It's not your job to protect me. You didn't sign up for that."

"That's not the sole reason why I want to stay."

"What are the other reasons?"

"Hmm," he said thoughtfully, pulling my hips against his, tilting my chin up with a bent finger. He leaned in and kissed me gently. "There *are* some benefits to being in your company, you know."

"Why, 'cause I'm a slut?"

He laughed. "Yeah, I never knew that about you before."

"Me either."

He laughed again. "That's not what I was talking about, but yeah, I'm a fan of your energy and volume, among other things, some of which it wouldn't be polite to mention."

My face went so red; I could feel the heat coming off of it, blood pounding under the skin. Jess smirked down at me, watching the blush spread. Caressing down my chest, over a stiffened nipple, down my abs, he offered, "Let me make you dinner. We'll relax, have a quiet night. How's that sound?"

"You cook?"

"I do," he said. "Very well, I'm told."

"Okay then. But, um, Jess?"

"Yeah?"

"I have no goddamned idea how to do this with someone I'm not paying to stick around. Just being honest."

"Love when you're honest," he admitted. "It's not complicated. Just dinner. Maybe some wine. We can sit on the couch or go get some sleep. There doesn't have to be a goal. I'd be sticking around even if you were celibate." Maybe he was having trouble reading my admittedly confusing signals, because he added, "Are you letting me hang around just for sex?"

"No. No, I want you here because you're my friend, and I trust you in ways I've never trusted anyone, ever. The, uh... the sex is new."

"It was pretty damn good though, wasn't it?" he asked and bit his lip. It was fucking adorable.

"Are you kidding?" I chuckled, "It was so good it makes me nervous!"

Throwing his head back, he laughed wildly and gave my ass a playful squeeze.

"Why?"

"Well, once you figure out what a kinky, sex-starved person I am, what are you gonna think of me? I'll lose your respect forever."

"Ooh, I like the sound of that," he said, watching me maintain that impressive blush, kneading my ass like he owned it. "Kinky how, exactly? Give me details."

"You want more details after catching me with a transgender prostitute? Really?"

"I do, because I can tell you like me asking," he chuckled, tugging at the end of the towel to try and unwind it.

"Oh, no you don't," I protested, holding it closed, blushing somehow more since I knew, then, that he could feel my stiffened dick poking him. "I was promised dinner."

"And luckily, *I'm* not on the clock, so you're stuck with me all night, and all tomorrow too. This could go on for *days*. Weeks even. We might need to get some more security in this place, though."

"Ya think?" I sighed, scooting past him in search of clean clothes. He spanked my ass through the tightly-clutched towel as I went.

Chapter 24
Done Running

After having some supper and sitting around with wine to sip, we decided it was time to retire. But once I'd brushed my teeth and we'd walked into my bedroom together, all I could see was Mags throwing punches and Jess groaning in pain. It made my chest feel tight, and way too anxious to think about relaxing in there.

"This isn't gonna work," I murmured, feeling Jess's eyes on me. How could I get undressed and lay with him in there when just a couple hours ago, it had gone so wrong so fast? "This whole damn room makes me nervous now. Maybe you should go sleep in your room, and I'll take one of the other guest rooms instead."

"Or you could come share my bed," Jess offered. "A little change of scenery, and I could watch out for you if you're still feeling unsettled."

"Oh, I don't want to impose or assume—"

"It's *your* house," Jess grinned.

A little self-conscious and unsure, I asked, "You really want to sleep with me?"

He walked up to me and slipped a hand around my waist. "You do know who you're talking to, right? Or was that whole thing earlier just a daydream I had? 'Cause that's completely possible, too."

"Yeah, okay," I surrendered. "If you don't mind."

He laughed a little and took my hand. Leading me from the room and down the hall, he gave me a sideways look and shook his head. When we reached his door, he pushed it open and turned on a light, saying, "I can't believe I get to be with you like this, sharing a bed, holding your hand. Don't wake me up too early tomorrow in case this is all just a dream, okay?"

Jess began to set things like his watch and wallet down by one side of the bed. I figured it to be part of his bedtime routine. When he pulled his shirt over his head automatically, my breath caught a little. I could tell he was just used to doing it, sleeping shirtless, I guessed, and that it wasn't part of some seduction plan. Funny how something so small and real could serve to wake you right up.

"Oh," he said, noticing my bashful reaction. He held the shirt in his hand. "Should I leave it on?"

My gaze was fixed right on the bed and I couldn't raise it, but my breathing got rougher. His room was a lot smaller than mine, so when he came around to me, to check if I was all right, it only took a few steps. It was cozy in there, dark, warm, and felt like the world couldn't get in to hurt us even if it tried.

"Tucker..." he started, sounding worried.

I didn't want to talk about it. In fact, I didn't want to say a single thing, so I reached for his jeans and began to work open the fly, trying to hurry. His lips pressed against my hair at the top of my head, his breath warm as he sighed. His hand was on my waist again, and he pulled at my shirt, too. I let him take it off of me, then pushed out of my pants without looking up once.

Jess followed me right down to the bed and I couldn't remember the last time I'd breathed so hard or wanted so much. I just needed to have him again, to feel him in me and be back there when, for just a moment, all that had mattered was letting him take me apart.

We almost kissed as he folded back my legs and pressed down against me, our lips barely brushing as I fought for air. He smelled so damned good and the way he looked at me so closely, like he could see all of the truth behind my lies, made me spread and pull him in.

I frowned when I felt his dick pushing to get inside. There was so much ache in my heart just from having to have him. I palmed his ass and pulled him in. Jess sank right back into me. With a wild, desperate cry, I shuddered and took him in, gasping.

He was kissing along my jaw, down the side of my neck, but I just wanted to keep feeling him there, filling me up. There wasn't any ache at all, but I was so damned scared of everything waiting outside that room, the only thing holding me together was him.

Jess caressed up both of my arms, guiding them above my head, then wove our fingers together and kissed me deeply. That's when I started crying. He kept trying to look into my eyes, and I felt a few of his tears fall onto me, too. He just kept whispering, "I'm sorry. I'm so sorry."

But none of it was his fault and he couldn't fix it either.

Finally, I looked up at him; let him see as much as he wanted to. It felt so safe, and I'd been nothing but a shell for so long, it was pure bliss to feel so full and seen. The care in the way he kissed me made me want to believe things could get better. With his warm, silky lips dragging over my skin, his fingers folded in mine and holding me down, I felt him tug back out in a slow pull. Quivering and trying to thrust against him, I let out a hard moan.

He was watching me, not letting me get close enough to kiss as he thrust back in. Mouth fallen open around my cry, I pressed down onto his cock to take it. He glanced lower, saw how soaking wet my cock was, and reached for it. I whimpered in anticipation, knowing how close I was already, but as soon as his big, warm hand wrapped my dick, I couldn't fucking shut up. He rode my ass, slowly stroked my dick, and I came all over him.

With a curse and a grimace, Jess started to thrust faster as I clenched up tightly around him with my orgasm. One of my hands was free, so I grabbed hold behind his head, scratching through the short strands.

"Gotta slow down," he groaned while pounding my ass.

"Don't you fucking dare," I warned. He laughed a little, breathing hard. His brow furrowed as he bottomed out, then held there, coming with a gasp. I clenched my ass and he dragged a hand through the come on my stomach, rubbing through it. Kissing the side of my neck, he caressed over the scars covering the inside of my forearm and quit looking at me.

I watched the door, waiting.

Touching those scars so gently, he said, "Please don't leave."

I just wrapped myself around him and held on. He did the same, covering me up and gathering me against him like he wanted to protect me from anything, but knew he never could.

The frantic call came near dawn the next morning. Jess was fast asleep next to me in bed when my cell started ringing. At first I assumed it was Mags, checking up on me. Caller ID told me it was the label, though, so I had to take it, no matter how tired and comfortable I was in that bed. For the first time in my life, I'd slept beside someone who cared about me, who I'd had spectacular sex with, and who gave me something to fight for — even if it meant fighting my best friend — and already life was retaliating. The thought of that would squelch my joy if I let it, so I didn't. The call was just about business. It had to be. It didn't have to mean anything.

The ringing roused Jess, who rubbed the sleep from his eyes and frowned adorably at the phone in my hand, murmuring, "Who is it? It's so early...."

Shaking my head, I answered before the call was directed to voicemail.

"Yeah, Tucker here."

It was a woman I didn't know and had never spoken to before. She sounded shaken up. She was a secretary or assistant to someone else — she said the name too quickly for me to catch it — and was passing along the message that my presence was needed immediately at an emergency meeting.

Right away, I knew it was about the previous night and the police presence at my house. We'd seen the paparazzi on the edges of the property. Surely, they'd gotten some shots, and had made some assumptions about what was going on. It occurred to me, as I agreed to hurry on over to the meeting and jotted down an address on a scrap of paper, that I'd told the police consensual sex had taken place, involving myself and another man. I'd also been shouting to Mags about being gay. If that piece of news had gotten out to the press, I was doomed. My career could be over in an instant. Sure, I'd told Mags I didn't care, but to actually have to witness my world crumble would be a nightmare.

What the hell had I done?

I hung up and couldn't look at Jess.

"What's wrong?" he asked, concerned about my shift in mood. It made me want to kiss him all the way back down to the pillows.

"I'm sure it's nothing," I lied. "They want to see me, right away."

"About what? The new album?" Some of the drowsiness lifted from him as the seconds passed by. Realization lit his face. "Shit, this is about last night, isn't it?"

"I don't know," was all I could say. "But I've gotta get my ass over there. Do some damage control."

"I'm coming with you," Jess insisted. "This is my fault." He sat up, threw back the sheet.

"No, it's not, and it's better if I do this by myself," I told him. "If it's you and me they're worried about, showing up with you at my side won't help any. They just want to talk to me, so I'll go. I'll come right back after and fill you in. We'll have a late breakfast and figure out what comes next."

"I can't let you do this on your own," Jess worried. "That's not fair to you. You didn't ask for this. You didn't know that tight-assed fucker was going to barrel in here, swinging fists and—"

"Hey," I said softly. "You know how Mags gets, the heat of the moment and all. He thought he was doing the right thing and trying to protect me. Everyone just needs to let things settle. I'll handle the label."

I watched Jess put on his boots, then find his pants, and remove the boots in order to put on the pants. It just proved he was too tired to deal with executives. I'd had enough practice at getting by on little sleep, so I knew I'd do just fine. The cold finger of fear did trail down my spine, but that was mostly from knowing there was more truth to face, and hadn't I been craving that anyway?

Frowning with worry, Jess began asking what my favorite breakfast foods were so he could plan a menu. I just walked over to him and drew him down for a kiss. Those eyes of his—green on the inside, blue on the outside—seemed to yearn to protect me. It gave me enough courage to try to face what was waiting, whatever it was.

"Maybe I could drive with you in the car," Jess wondered.

"I'll be fine. And hey, if the wrath of the industry comes crashing down around my ears, what say you and me head on up to Washington and leave it all behind for a little while?"

That made him smile, my heart was glad to see. "I think I like the sound of that," he admitted.

"It'll give me something to look forward to." I smiled back. His arms wound around me. Then his mouth was on mine again, warm and welcome. It was so easy, being with him. It stole my breath away and made me see possibilities I never knew were there.

I called for a car service to take me to the meeting. After giving the driver the address and, dressed as nicely as my clear conscience would allow, I mentally prepared my defense without knowing what the charges would be. Juice was the only thing I'd had to eat or drink. The thought of coffee on an empty stomach made me fear jitters I didn't need or want, and I hadn't had time for food. As the car sped away from my house, I soon realized the driver wasn't headed to the center of Nashville, where the label's offices were located, but toward the outskirts. That was strange but I figured with the early hour and the circumstances, I would soon be sitting in the living room of one of the head honchos where it would be less likely I'd run into more paparazzi. If they were trying to get ahead of the tabloids as the twenty-four-hour news cycle churned through social media, it made sense.

We soon pulled up to an estate with a long, curved drive leading up to a dramatic entryway.

The driver let me out and promised to wait around. There were no other cars in sight, or any sign of movement or wakefulness in the estate itself. That was a little strange, but possibly a good sign. If there wasn't a crowd of executives waiting to let me have it, that was fine with me.

I walked up to the door and rang the bell.

It took a minute for someone to arrive and answer the door. It swung open and with what appeared to be a servant on the other side. It was an older woman dressed in a crisp black dress.

"Mr. Reynolds?"

"Yep, that's me," I answered.

Inside the entryway, a large man was waiting, working security if I read his plain black suit, earpiece, and stiff-backed stance correctly. The woman nodded and gestured for me to enter. "Very good, sir.

You're expected. Up the stairs and the first door on the right."

"Thanks, ma'am," I smiled tensely. The security guard didn't look at me or blink as I passed by.

The place was silent as a tomb, with no other signs of life. The lights were out, the curtains drawn. My footsteps echoed as I made my way over the marble floors to the curving staircase leading up-ward. A short climb and a few steps down the hall had me facing a door that was cracked open slightly. Light shone from inside.

My nerves started to get the best of me as I pushed the door open wider.

"Hello?" I called.

There was no response at first. I stepped into the room, which was large. The curtains on the far wall had been parted to let in the bril-liant morning light. It blinded me after moving through the darkness of the rest of the house.

Then, a few things happened at once. I realized a huge video screen was displaying images, which I slowly began to make out as my eyes adjusted. I also saw a man sitting a few feet away and, as soon as he began to speak, realized who it was.

"Close the door and lock it," he said. "It sure has been a long time since we've seen each other."

Nathan Briant looked exactly as he always had. He rose to his feet and began to walk toward me. I froze, the reality of the situation sinking in.

To be faced with that man again wiped everything else away. No words would come out. Not a single muscle in my body would be moved, like the drugs had already kicked in. Jess, Mags, the car out-side — everything seemed so far away, like they were part of another world entirely.

My gaze never left him as he walked slowly closer. He reached past me, closed and then locked the door behind me since I'd failed to do so.

Strangely, as the initial surprise passed, resignation settled upon me instead. If I'd been searching so hard for the truth, well then here I had it. All of those notes and gifts had been a prelude to this. A debt needed to be paid. He'd probably been waiting for me to return from my camping trip. It was time. The worry I'd had about explaining things to Jess and Mags was nothing compared to what I'd need to do before I could ever set foot outside that building again. Once again, nothing else in my life mattered except making Mr. Briant happy. At least the simplicity of that was something I could accept. Numbness was my barrier of self-preservation. It was also my only means of defense.

My gaze was drawn to the screen which clearly showed images for my benefit only. It was a slideshow of all of the pictures Mr. Briant had ever taken of me. Vaguely, back in the shadowy corners of my memory, I recalled the sound of the shutter closing, the flash of the bulb through my blindfolds, or not, as my poses were recorded. He'd warned me of this, maybe not in so many words, but he'd warned me all the same.

I'd been so full of Jess, felt so damned safe, but that was something I needed to forget about and push away. All it would do was weaken my ability to feel nothing.

There was no instinct to run as I stared at a younger version of myself on hands and knees, naked, on top of a desk with that silver pen stuffed up my ass, my cock undeniably stiff and held tightly in Mr. Briant's hand. The image changed and I was on the bed in my old apartment, my legs pulled open widely and held in straps as a cock I knew must belong to Mr. Briant was buried completely in me. My erection, bound in rope, jutted up into the air, thick and red. The slides switched again and a man in a suit, whom I didn't recognize and whose face was out of the frame, was in mid-thrust, fucking me from behind as I was draped limply over a desk, my eyes blindfolded and mouth gagged. The identities of the other people were concealed by the way the images were cropped, but almost all of the photos showed my face in some form or other. There was no question it was me in those pictures.

It was blackmail.

I felt weighted to the floor. That spot where I stood was exactly where I belonged. There was no escaping it.

He was right next to me, facing me. From the corner of my eye, I could see the brightness of his white, toothy smile.

"Let's have a little chat, son. But first, you know what to do. It's just you and me here. Take off those clothes so we can get started."

Chapter 25
End of It All

I didn't want to take my clothes off. There was once a time when I wouldn't have thought twice about following his orders, but things had changed. *I'd* changed. Experience informed my queasy dread of taking the next step.

But if I didn't comply, other people would be hurt. Jess, Mags, and everyone who depended on me for their livelihood would be affected should any of those photos find their way out of that room.

Without any better option, I reached for my belt buckle with unsteady hands.

"I bet you're a little surprised to see me," Mr. Briant chuckled. He inhaled deeply through his nose to catch my scent. He was barely inches away, his voiced hushed. It was making every single one of my hairs stand on end.

My fly undone, I shrugged off my jacket and reached for my shirt buttons next. While I worked them through the button holes, Mr. Briant pushed my pants down for me, along with my boxers, leaving them to bunch at mid-thigh. The shaking in my hands spread outward to the rest of my body. It became harder to work those small buttons, especially when he palmed my ass with one hand and my balls with his other. The fingers of one hand pried into my crease and the others pulled at the skin of my sac.

As expected as it was, and as many times as it had happened before, it still didn't feel natural. I hated the feel of him touching me like that, but there was nothing I could do.

"Unfortunately, I'm not here to make a deal with you, son. This isn't about you *owing* me. This is about you stepping out of line and forgetting your *place*. Now, I have some friends who know *you* and know *me* and they decided I was the best one to motivate you into getting back where you need to be. So, it makes me sad to say that there won't be any pills today to make you sweetly oblivious to how very much what I'm about to do to you is going to hurt. You'll be wide awake. I need you to pay *attention*."

Quaking violently, I pulled the shirt open and off, letting it fall to the floor. Inside, I was screaming in protest. Small, scared grunts and groans were all that wanted to come out of my mouth. More details about the room caught my eye. There were shackles bolted to the floor. Handcuffs hung from a chain leading down from the ceiling, fed through a pulley and attached to the wall. A long table was carefully laid out with a variety of metal instruments of torture which I immediately glanced away from.

The hand pulling uncomfortably at my balls shifted, gathering them up, yanking upward, then twisting sharply enough to bring me up onto my toes. A groan of pain slipped past my lips. Mr. Briant said, "Now, put your hands behind your head and lace those fingers together. You don't move a muscle otherwise. See those red lights up in the corners of the room? Sure you do. Those are taking your picture right now, making sure you don't decide that this is the time to start thinking for yourself."

He stopped twisting my balls and eased up, rubbing them instead. With his other hand, he reached into a pocket and drew out something I recognized instantly. His left hand flattened over my lower abdomen, bracing it as if he expected me to try to escape what he was about to do. His right held up that shiny silver pen with my name engraved on it.

I made a terrible pleading sound. That very pen had violated my body, over and over again. All of those memories came back, warning me about just how bad this was going to get. The fear was still there, but it had changed just like I had. The fear had grown smarter, with many layers. It knew the whys and the hows and the meaning of it all.

There was a bang from far away, but it didn't resonate. It couldn't pierce that dungeon, where I was locked inside with the devil himself, dressed as the man who had always easily brought me to my weakest place, just by being himself and smiling that polished, patronizing grin. I'd sold myself to that. I'd reaped my rewards, and they'd been plentiful. Mr. Briant had done everything he promised. That was the bitch of it. It had been a transaction as much as anything I'd arranged with those prostitutes. He had made me famous, and rich, and gave me a way to do what I'd been put on earth to do. All that was asked in return was secrecy. All I'd had to do was keep my private life private.

But I hadn't. Letting Jess in had doomed me. It was the first domino, slapping against Mags, who slapped against the police, who knocked over the press, and on and on it went. The pieces had all been scattered, and all that was left was this sadistic man the masochist in me couldn't defend myself against.

Though he intended to remind me of it, the funny thing was, I *did* know my place. Ever since his first lesson, I had known it. I'd been living there, just waiting for him to visit me again.

"You know what this is for, don't you?" Mr. Briant asked.

There was more banging, and voices yelling, but it was in another world. Mr. Briant lowered the hand holding the pen to my ass and slipped a long finger into my crease. It probed at me, right where I knew it would. The feel of his touch made me want to piss myself, cry, or break apart into a million little pieces. In reality, all I did was stay quiet and let it happen.

"It's to remind you of who *owns* you," he told me in that sing-song tone as he pressed his finger into my body. "*This* is what I own. Paid good money for it, so I intend to use it and do some mighty unpleasant things to it. I can do anything I like to this little pink hole, because it's *mine*."

"Please don't do this," I managed. It was humiliating to hear how small and weak my voice was.

The finger pushed in deeply, then pulled out and was replaced with the pen. The cool metal slid in easily, like I knew it would.

"Oh, that's not so bad, is it? That's nothing compared to what you've got *coming*, son. I'm not here to make you feel nice today. I'm here to punish, and *oh* how creative I can be when given free rein. You might not be too happy to hear that they've given me *days* with you this time. See those chains? You won't be leaving this room for a long, long time. No time to sleep, either. I've got some things here you won't like at all to wake you up if needed, and all sorts of uncomfortable tubes to feed inside your body to keep you from having to use the bathroom. How's that sound? Bet that helps you enjoy how nice this feels, huh?" The pen twisted and he took hold of my cock, which wasn't hard at all, squeezing it until I made a hurt whimper.

"We know there was a *lover's quarrel* at your residence last night. We know you told the police how you were having such a happy time gettin' buggered by your friend Jess Grayville." He *tsk*ed. "That was a bad thing to do, son."

The pen was held deeply within me, another awful promise. He pulled, twisted and squeezed the head of my dick. My knees almost gave and a hurt shout was ripped from my lungs. My fingers clawed at the back of my head. My whole body trembled as that little pen felt so huge, actually and symbolically, and the shame was like a white-hot knife slicing me apart. Why the hell couldn't I just tell him to stop? Why was there nothing in me able to fight back? I ground my teeth together and told myself to hit the fucker, to do *something*.

When nothing happened, no matter how much I wanted to stand up for myself, I just didn't, and the self-hate only made it easier to let him keep going, because I deserved to feel as low as he always brought me.

He started to laugh as my tears began to tumble down. My mind was prepared to lash out, but my body wouldn't disobey him. There was a disconnect inside me somewhere, like he'd found some magic off switch in his probing.

He stopped twisting the pen. Instead, he gave the end a firm *push*.

"No," I begged, too late. He pushed until the whole thing was well inside me and it was pure fear that helped me find my voice. "No! Take it out! Please take it out!"

Heavy footsteps pounded behind me, back behind the locked door, insignificant and low. The torment in my bruised dick, held in the vise of his fist, and the less physically severe but mental torture of that pen now lodged in my body, was much louder. The idea of it being there, perfectly smooth and bullet-shaped, and with no way to pull it back out, started to fray my shaky hold on control. That pen was the bullet I'd wanted to inflict on myself over the course of six years, and there was no way to avoid it now.

Somehow, the shame got even bigger, and sharper, carving me up.

Then I realized I didn't want to avoid that bullet. I wanted it to kill me. I wanted Mr. Briant to go too far for once and just end this for good. It was all too much. It would have been better, perhaps, if he had choked me to death like I'd always been so afraid he would. At least it wouldn't hurt anymore. There would be no more confusion, no shame, just nothing. Nothing would have been so much better.

Even when the door swung in with an ear-splitting bang, I didn't understand or much care. All I wanted was to be allowed to die and let it all be over. The presence of other people who weren't Mr. Briant just made me wish they'd leave.

I tried to block them out. Reality stopped making sense.

I was in *agony*! All of the days I knew Mr. Briant would keep me there, torturing me endlessly, spun outward on a path to hell that just went down, down, down, and I was *screaming*.

A tire iron connected with the back of Mr. Briant's head, just as he started to turn away. It made a heavy, thick sound that was deeply disturbing. He let go of me then.

I almost dropped to the floor to make sure he was okay. I would have, if I hadn't been paralyzed by my disorientation and continued need to obey his will.

The blow seemed to knock him out cold. Mr. Briant had fallen in a heap, a life-sized puppet whose strings had been cut. Redness oozed from his skull, through his perfectly styled hair.

Though some of my pain had eased, it didn't make any difference, because the shame just kept carving me into little, bloody pieces. I waited for the tire iron to bash my skull next, ready to get down on my knees in surrender to the sweet peace of death and let it wipe it all away. At the same time, part of my fractured thoughts fixated on the bullet I'd already taken — the pen. I was screaming over and over, "Get it out! Take it out!" There was no way to tolerate the way the pen felt, jabbing at me from inside like a finger of accusation, still marking me as Mr. Briant's bottom boy, his eager, guilty whore, even though the man himself had gotten disconnected, just like my thoughts.

A familiar voice was letting out primal growls and shouts, a layer on top of my yelling. It was another echo, but one of the previous night and much more easy to recollect. It triggered me to look, even though I was standing there, naked and crying, hands behind my head, frozen there by my abuser's commands.

What I saw was my best friend.

It was Mags.

He was wild.

If he'd been furious with Jess, he'd crossed some bad line with Mr. Briant. In his eyes was certainty. There was nothing keeping him in check.

Images from the past came through. I saw him punching the bully all the way to the ground. I saw him hitting the man in the alley with his guitar, the pieces raining to the ground. I saw him beating Jess, not intending to stop, not *able* to stop.

The bloody tire iron was gripped in Mag's right hand. His eyes were too big, too empty.

"He hurt you," Mags snarled, spit flying from his lips like he'd gone rabid. "He's gonna die."

Mags was going to beat Mr. Briant with that tire iron until someone pulled him away, even if all that was left of Mr. Briant was pulverized bits of flesh.

I knew Mr. Briant was my only way out. I needed to let him finish what we'd started, and kill me. It was time. I couldn't wait for it anymore, pretending to exist when part of me was always with him in a meeting, learning my lessons. It had to end.

I had to stop Mags from killing Mr. Briant so he could finish it and kill me first.

However, the pen inside me kept me rooted, afraid to move, to make real what was going on. As much as I needed to save Mr. Briant, I needed even more to not feel that pen shifting inside of me, burrowing deeper. I needed it *out*.

But that slideshow was still playing. I was up there, taking the pen, taking my lessons, taking cock. I didn't want Mags looking. Those images were sacred. Even *I* hadn't been allowed to know what they'd contained.

Mags was looking at the screen. He looked, too, at the chains and shackles, at the instruments of torture, laid out so neatly. The room was filled with fuel for Mag's fire. He was the loaded gun I'd been too afraid to use, the guitar pick that wouldn't carve deeply enough, now razor sharp.

Knowing that broke the spell, just a little, just enough.

Mags was the most dangerous thing there to anyone else, but he was still my best friend. He could do what I had failed at over and over.

"Mags, I need..." I could barely see him through the tears. "It *hurts* and I-I can't... make it stop, make it all end. Please, make it stop, Mags," I begged in a tear-choked, thin voice. My hands were still behind my head, but my legs trembled and threatened to give out on me. "Can you... can you, *please just kill me?*"

Just like that, Mags' focus shifted to me instead of Mr. Briant. I saw the way his face paled and for the first time it felt like Mags could really see me.

The tire iron lowered, then, and I was the only thing he was looking at.

Suddenly, a cop burst into the room with his gun drawn. After surveying the scene, he rushed over to Mags.

"Drop the weapon. *Drop it, now, Mags,*" the officer commanded. He looked familiar, but in a way that only heightened the wrongness of it all. His brown skin and warm eyes, the broad span of his shoulders....

"*No,*" I begged as the tire iron clattered to the ground. The officer went to check Mr. Briant's pulse and breathing.

There were sirens. There was no telling how long I'd been hearing them. They seemed to creep up slowly until they were everywhere, inside your head, rattling your bones.

"No!" It was getting away from me, my one chance, and my panic climbed.

There were shouts and movement from below, beyond the busted-open door, but getting closer.

"Mags, *please.*" Finally, he acted, coming over and guiding my hands down from behind my head. My chance was slipping away so fast, it was probably already gone, so I cried harder. If he'd had a gun, I would have taken it and put it in my mouth.

But he didn't. All he had were my hands, held in his.

"You're okay, cowboy," he told me, holding my gaze with such strength. "I've got you now."

I tried to shake him off.

"It's *not*. It's *not* okay." The pen. The damned pen. It made me want to tear off my skin.

That's when the tidal wave of police washed over us.

My knees started to give out. Mags caught me and tried to hold me up, but couldn't since I was still fighting him, so he eased me down to the ground. The world grew fuzzy at the edges as the shock took over. Pushing his hands off, I kept yelling, "*No!*" over and over again.

Mags was crying. That was the main thing I noticed, not the flood of law enforcement trying to bring order to chaos, but the tears running down his face. Maybe I was already dying. Maybe the pen *was* a bullet.

Chapter 26

Possessed

"Help me! Help me with him! He needs help!" Mags was calling, trying to cover me a little. My pants were still down and my chest was bare. Then more people, wearing uniforms—police uniforms—were surrounding us, barking things like, "Hands in the air!" or swearing with wide eyes and open mouths, "Jesus Christ, what the hell happened in here?"

"Please, just help him! Please! He needs help and I don't know what that son of a bitch did to him!" Mags begged, sniffling as he raised his hands.

The sound of Mr. Briant's voice drew my fractured attention and I saw him, face down on the floor, in handcuffs. I didn't catch specific words but it didn't matter. Hearing him again was enough to be deeply upsetting. My yelling grew in strength and volume.

"Tucker, are you okay? Hey! Tucker, can you see me?" The cop who'd come in with Mags asked me. "The ambulance should be here momentarily. They're just a minute away. Don't move, all right? Just lie still until they get here."

He'd come out of nowhere, swooping in like he had wings. Like he was an angel.

Angel...

"Angel?" I murmured.

"Yeah," said my old grade school friend turned football hero, Angel Rivera. He'd always had a habit of that, catching me unawares. Before, it was singing in the schoolyard. Now he'd caught me at what all of that singing had led to. "Mags called me. We go to the same gym, been catching up. He asked me to come check up on you as a favor.

Call you tell me if you're in pain? Are you hurt?"

He sounded so normal. He wasn't upset at all, and was in total control. We were on opposite ends of the spectrum. He still had it all figured out, and I had nothing.

They were leaning in close, looking at me, touching me, and it was too much. I was naked, terrified, and frantic. I pushed them away, as hard as I could. The pen shifted, jabbing at me, and I winced.

"It hurts," I gasped, still pushing them off, trying to kick or pull my arms from their grip, but it only made them hold me tighter. "It hurts!"

"Where? Tucker, where does it hurt?"

The pen. The stupid fucking pen. If I told them, they'd want to see. They'd want to *look*.

"*No*," I groaned, unable to cover myself with the way they were pinning me. Realizing how helpless I was, even to make them stop looking, I begin trembling violently, like the room's temperature had just plummeted forty degrees. I didn't want the touching. I didn't want them to see.

"Tucker, lie still!" Angel commanded. "We're just trying to help and you need to lie still!"

"Where the hell is that damn ambulance?!" Mags screamed at the officers who were trying to figure out what exactly they'd walked into. "Shut off that vile shit on the screen and can't we get him out of this evil fuckin' place, for Christ's sake?!"

Things blurred for a little while. People were shining lights in my eyes and checking for visible injury, poking and pressing while other people held me still. I wouldn't tell them where it hurt. I didn't want them looking. It became harder to fight them as the exhaustion took its toll.

For a while, it was all black.

When I came to, I was covered in a blanket, strapped tightly to a gurney and being wheeled out into the sunlight. There were people everywhere. I glimpsed a few suited men being led away in handcuffs. One of them was the man who'd been standing at the front door.

Somewhere nearby, Mags was saying, "Can I go with him? I need to go with him to the hospital."

"*No*," I argued. "Leave me alone!"

"Take it easy, Mr. Reynolds," a female paramedic told me as they moved me up to the rear of the ambulance. "We're just going to get you checked out."

Jess ran over before they could lift me into the ambulance.

"Wait! Wait one second!" Jess was yelling. He came running from the place where all of the police seemed to be gathered. I fought the straps, grunting and panicking about being trapped — trapped with the pen. Skidding to a stop next to me, Jess took hold of my hand, squeezing it gently to get my attention.

When I kept moaning, "No," Jess said sharply, "Hey, you're not alone, Tucker. You're getting help."

Something in his tone made me mentally shift gears and really understand that he was there.

"Jess? Jess, please," I begged. "Please, they don't know!"

He looked up and down my body with a desperate expression, as I writhed and started to cry again. There was something evil inside me and no one knew.

"Don't know what?" Jess asked, holding my gaze, leaning in closer so that he filled my vision rather than the strangers or chaos. "What don't they know?"

I shook my head, feeling the weight of it pressing down on me, the truth and the horror. Part of me wanted to never have to admit to it, ever. The rest of me would have gladly jumped in front of a bus just to stop thinking about it there, inside me. But Jess was someone I'd realized I could talk to. Out of anyone, it was him I could tell. I squeezed his hand and pleaded desperately. "I don't want to say it," I sobbed. "*I just want it out of me.*"

Jess felt very still, his gaze locked onto mine. It was easy to let his steadiness affect me, pinning down my thoughts a little, because I did trust him. "What are you talking about?" Jess asked, listening close, ignoring the madness around us. His direct attention helped me to let it all fall away, just enough.

"I want it out!" I cried. I was losing it; I could feel myself losing it. To anyone else it was only a pen, but to me it was a connection to Mr. Briant. I had signed my life away with it and now it was deep inside me. That pen was everything I'd let him do to me and everything that had ever been wrong.

"What do you want out?"

"The... the pen. The metal pen. *They need to take it out. Please just get them to fucking take it out!* I don't want it anymore. I can feel it and it hurts. *I don't want it in me anymore.* Tell him to take it back. *I don't want it. It's not worth it! I can't do this anymore. They can take all of it back. All of it. The contract, the money, I don't fucking care. They can take me too as long as it stops now. Just make it stop, please? Please, Jess? Please help me make it stop?*"

Jess seemed to pale. "Where is it, Tucker? Where's the pen?"

I couldn't tell him. I wouldn't. I tried to turn my face away, but he pulled me back. All I could do was cry. He kissed my forehead, smoothed my hair.

"It means he owns me. He stuck it in me," I whispered while he stayed right there, a breath away. "He pushed it too far."

"Oh my god," Jess moaned.

Then, Jess sat up straight and set his jaw, his eyes burning. "Excuse me!" he called loudly to the paramedic nearby, waiting. Jess explained, "He's got an object—a pen, lodged inside of him. Someone raped him with it. That's why he's panicking like this. It needs to be removed."

Hearing him say it out loud made me pull at the straps again, trying to get away, to shut it out. When Jess looked down at me, I saw his tears, heard him start to get upset.

"Okay," the paramedic said in a cool, composed voice. "No problem. Mr. Reynolds, we will take care of that, all right? It will be removed. You're going to be just fine. Let's just get you to the hospital first, okay?"

Jess rubbed my arm, trying to soothe.

"O-okay," I replied shakily, my breath hitching from all the crying.

"The best thing you can do," she told me, "to help us get you there quickly and safely is just try to remain calm and lie still, okay?"

"Okay." I took a deeper breath and blew it out. I looked up at Jess again. "You're here. Why? It's too dangerous. It—"

"Hey, it's all right. We've got you. I'm fine. I was downstairs, keeping an eye on the guard at the door. Officer Rivera—he disarmed the guy but said he needed to find you, and I needed to find you too, but Mags ran off before either of us could stop him. I should have been there for you, Tucker. I wasn't there for you and I'm so sorry. I'm here now though."

"Just don't leave, please," I begged Jess. The pen was driving me out of my mind, but that wasn't all. Jess being there caused tightness in my chest. It was a bad place we were in and I didn't want Jess anywhere near it. That was instinct, primal. Thinking of how Mr. Briant was there, somewhere, nearby, *near Jess*, made my pulse race.

Being tied down to the gurney, unable to do anything to protect myself or Jess, caused something to snap inside my mind. Or maybe I had finally lost my mind. I couldn't keep the pain inside, like I'd always done, because Jess was in danger now, too. So, I fought them, and the damned straps holding me down. I needed to move, to get free, and get between Jess and Mr. Briant.

I was shouting, bucking inside the restraints, trying to twist free. Paramedics were suddenly surrounding me, holding me down, giving me oxygen and making it impossible for me to warn Jess about the danger he was in.

"Tucker, just let them take care of you, okay?" Jess pleaded emotionally.

There were people everywhere, and so many faces I didn't recognize. I couldn't see Mr. Briant anymore, which meant he could be anywhere.

They lifted me into the ambulance. Being enclosed like that helped me to stop fighting back as much, especially when Jess spoke up from by my side.

"Can I please come with him?" Jess asked frantically. "Help keep him calm? Please? He's my... I love him and can I please...."

"Yes, okay, get in," the paramedic relented. Jess climbed in, took a seat and held my hand.

"Stay here, okay? Please stay?" I begged Jess.

"I'm staying. I'm right here with you," Jess promised. "Not going anywhere, all right? Just breathe. You're safe. Help is here. Just a short trip to the hospital, okay? They'll get it out."

My heart rate and breathing began to normalize once I realized nothing too awful was likely to happen. I managed to pull the oxygen mask off, despite the frown and murmur of protest from the paramedic.

One of the back doors of the ambulance was still opened, and I thought I saw the flashing of camera bulbs instead of just the lights from the emergency vehicles. I was probably just imagining it.

Looking worried out of his mind, Jess leaned down and kissed me gently on the lips. His hand smoothed back my hair from my forehead.

"I'm right here." he assured me. "I'm with you. You're not alone."

"Okay." I held his hand as tightly as I could. The feel of his kiss lingered on my lips, as brazen and life-altering as anything else that had happened that day.

Chapter 27

Aftershock

"Told you I didn't want to leave you with that guy," Mags was saying. At first I thought he was referring to Mr. Briant, then realized he was grumbling about Jess again. My head was still in a fog. Very little was making sense.

After we'd gotten to the hospital, they'd wheeled me away from Jess and everyone else. Alone, in an area behind a curtain, I'd confessed to the doctor and nurses what was wrong. I told them I'd been sexually abused, and the man responsible had let things go a little too far this time, so to speak.

They did an ultrasound and physical exam to ensure the pen hadn't done internal damage. When my panic climbed, they gave me oxygen and had a nurse hold my hand while they removed the goddamned pen with some forceps.

It was sealed in an evidence bag and given to the police, waiting nearby.

A few hours passed. Slowly, I came back to myself a little. Just lying there for so long without something tangible to fight or fear gave me time to get my scrambled thoughts and rattled emotions in some order. I'd been admitted for observation due mainly to the shock. I was in a private room but about to be discharged from the hospital at my own insistence.

It didn't matter, though. I was stuck there until they figured out what to do about all of the paparazzi waiting outside. After the photos taken at my property, with all of the police activity surrounding the fight between Mags and Jess, and now that members of my band had been spotted in the hospital, the press was in a frenzy. I'd overheard

Mags tell Jess that there had been photographers following my ambulance. Who knew if they'd found out about the sexual details yet or not? It was only a matter of time.

The only thing to do was keep my head down, maybe put on a pair of sunglasses and a hooded sweatshirt, and hurry to a car before any usable photographs could be taken. Then it'd just be gossip, not news, and I could go somewhere to hide.

I kind of didn't want to do that, though. I didn't care about their pictures, or their motives. All that mattered was what had really happened. The need to die had passed again. For six years, I'd been under Mr. Briant's control while pretending I wasn't. I'd been pretending to be straight and healthy while I wasn't. Those lies would have kept me in chains for days in that place with Mr. Briant. I might never have gotten out. He may have just slowly taken me apart until there was nothing left to release. Only the truth, as frightening as it was, would keep me out of that dungeon, metaphorically or otherwise.

Mags was still talking away. Angel Rivera was there, too, watching over us. They'd explained some more about how Mags had been killing time at the gym since returning to Nashville, and had run into Angel there. Ever since, they'd been exercising together. Now we knew how Mags had been wasting time between hook ups. As much as I appreciated what Angel had done by believing Mags enough to follow his hunch and come along to check out my 'meeting', it was unsettling to have one of the cool kids from high school standing there, staring at me when I was at my lowest. "I came to check on you," Mags was saying, "'cause Lord knows Jess had all damn night to do unspeakable things to you, but Jess said you'd just gone."

Mags and Jess were managing to be fairly close together without elbowing, strangling, or tackling each other. That was the only thing holding me together. The rest was pretty disgusting and hard to face, but seeing the two people who meant the most to me get along after there had been such violence gave me a little hope that maybe things could be all right, eventually.

Jess was glancing around at everyone on the whole damn floor, like there had to be some textbook bad guy with a handlebar mustache, dressed in a black cape, sneaking around and trying to get me. Maybe he hadn't learned yet that the real bad guys tended to look just like everybody else. Arms folded and pulling in on himself more and more, Jess seemed ill at ease with everything and everyone who wasn't one of the four of us. Jess had seemed to vet Angel because Mags had called him in, specifically. But Jess was sticking close to me, and I kept him there, looping a hand through his arm. The contact helped hold the lingering panic back.

Mags had calmed quite a lot. He was still a little keyed up, and he was still sniffling and wiping at his nose with the remnants of tears, but it was a huge improvement to how he'd been. I was glad, because his panic only fed mine and made me want him to stay away. There was enough screwed up inside of me without trying to fix what was screwed up in him, too.

I knew, without a doubt, that Mags could have been a murderer. He had it in him. Jess was only going on hearsay but Mags had *been there*. He'd seen Mr. Briant crushing my dick in one hand and shoving the damn pen up my ass with the other. He'd heard me screaming, hurting in ways he'd imagined Jess had been hurting me, but with Mr. Briant it had been the real thing. Not only that, the images of me getting raped had been flashing on the video screen, and the torture chamber setting, only compounded the issue. I imagined my mental state at the time and how I'd asked him to kill me hadn't helped at all either. Everything Mags had mistakenly blamed Jess for was absolutely true about Nathan Briant. Mags' fury had been justified, and I was grateful he'd been saved from it.

There was enough to try to recover from without having to worry about Mags facing murder charges, a lifetime in jail or the death penalty, all because of me.

Mags' actual reaction to witnessing, first hand, the way Nathan Briant had always treated me was hard to live with. The ways Mags had gotten violent, right away, only showed me how very differently my reactions to that man had always been. Mags would never have allowed Mr. Briant to victimize him, and if Mags had been there with me on that first day, at that very first meeting, maybe none of this would have happened.

Part of me wasn't able to forgive him for that, even though Mags had done nothing wrong.

Shifting a little closer, as if he didn't completely trust Jess's nearness to my side, Mags rubbed his arm, sniffled and plowed on, "But where could you have gone? It didn't make sense, them calling you so early to meet so soon. It was weird. And why just you, you know? If they were worried about last night, they would have wanted to see all three of us. We were all involved. No part of it was only on you. Hell, none of it was on you! It was a fight between Jess and me. You were just a bystander! So, why the fuck would they only want to see you in an emergency meeting first thing in the morning? I wanted to be ready for anything, so I called Angel right off. I figured he could tell the label guys that it wasn't going to be a problem, legally, and the whole situation was so weird, it seemed a good call to bring some backup. I'd just seen him last night anyway, at Gold's on Second Street. I knew he was around but not on duty yet, and been meaning to see you anyway. When I pestered Jess to show me the address they'd given you, I knew it seemed off. They should've had you go to the offices, if anything, not the outskirts of town.

"So, we raced over to the address in my car, and met Angel there. The driver in the car you called was just pulling away as we pulled up. But you weren't in the car, and you still weren't answering your phone! Why would the car leave without you, you know? It was fucking suspicious. It hadn't been long enough for the meeting to be over already anyhow." Mags was talking so rapidly, the words overlapped and blended together. He wiped at his nose with the back of his arm, then put a hand on the back of my shoulder, shooting mean looks at anyone else that gazed too long in my direction. I didn't really want to be touched, but knew his intentions were good.

"While I was driving, Jess called the label. As we were pulling up to that fucker's address Jess said the label claimed to have *no record* of any meeting and I *freaked*. I mean, Jess freaked too, but you know me, cowboy," he laughed at that, his voice catching slightly. "I called the cops. Not just Angel, I called *all* the damn cops. I couldn't figure out why they'd want to get you alone like that. I imagined some scary shit, like an overexcited fan turned stalker trying to kidnap you or something, but *nothing* as bad as that. He... he was *raping you.*" Mags made a face of disgust and horror. "That sick mother*fucker.* I *saw* what he had in that room. He fuckin' had chains and shackles rigged and that vile stuff on the TV? What the *fuck*, man? Just thank god. Thank god we got there before he could hurt you any more than he did, you know?"

"Mags," I called out softly. "Hey, Mags."

He stopped ranting and glanced over at me. He looked so scared and his nose was runny. His face was pale with shock. There was a strange sense of the floor falling away, as I saw him not as the star he'd become, with horny fans, a big ol' ego and co-dependency issues. He was just that poor little boy, kickin' ass and punching bullies all the way to the floor, because he knew how it felt to be picked on, too. But he was so much more than that. He was my hero in that alley, after our late gig, swinging his favorite guitar at the head of a crazy guy with a knife. He was the best friend I'd ever had, and damned if he wasn't loyal as hell, even if a resentful part of me wanted to lay some blame at his feet for my suffering.

He wasn't at fault for my poor choices, just as I wasn't at fault for his. We were our own men.

"What? You hurt? You need a nurse or a doctor? Fuck, you're really hurtin' and here I am rambling on...."

"Nah, I just wanted to say thank you," I said quietly, not able to hold his gaze long, or speak with much confidence. "If I haven't said it enough, I'm saying it now. Thank you for being there, and for caring."

The moment breathed, then he just nodded once and seemed to dismiss the gratitude, like he didn't need it. As long as I was by his side, safe, he had everything he needed. It made me feel guilty for holding him at fault in any way, and especially for not wanting him by my side.

Jess was frazzled in a different, quieter way than Mags, though to the same level. He was shaken up, waiting for everyone else to go so he could look at me closer, ask me his questions about what had happened and get some real answers to set his mind at ease. Unlike Mags, though, Jess was keeping it all inside. I liked that I sensed he wanted to chase everyone off, though. Jess was the only one who I felt could really understand how screwed up I was feeling about it all.

Looking ready to step up and chase off anyone he needed to, Jess didn't say much but seemed rooted to the spot. His left hand overlaid my fingers curled around his bicep, brushing them gently.

He'd heard from Mags and the police about the official account of what had happened, though I hadn't given them many details about what Mr. Briant had said and done in the moments leading up to their discovery of us. They didn't need them for the charges to stick, and I wasn't ready to talk about everything just yet.

He'd been there for some of the doctor's exams of me, too, but he didn't have anything like the whole story. When Mags and Angel had gone upstairs to get me, Jess had been forced to stay downstairs, making sure Mr. Briant's hired guard stayed down. Then, when the rest of the police showed up, they'd disarmed Jess and taken him outside for questioning instead of letting him run upstairs to find me like he was aching to do.

Unlike Mags, who was scared of what he could have done *and* what he saw, Jess was afraid of what did happen and what it could have led to. Lord knows where we'd be if he hadn't trusted Mags with information about where I was. And if they hadn't called Angel in for backup, it could have been much, much worse for all of us. Jess and Mags could have been overpowered by Mr. Briant's security, and imprisoned for a lesson or two right alongside me. There were a whole lot of ifs and could-have-beens hanging in the air. They were making our skin crawl, the air around us infected with a general sense of the creeps.

As big as he was, Jess seemed smaller then. The evil of the world was crowding in on him, and shrinking him down. He would have thrown himself between me and harm's way, though. I could feel it.

I tugged on his arm a little, to let him know I was looking. He gave me a faint, brave smile and drew himself upright. Setting his jaw again, he kept scanning the area for threats.

"It's okay," I told Jess. "I think it'll all be okay."

Mags mistrustfully watched our linked arms from the corner of his eye. A doctor came over with papers for my discharge to be signed and didn't bat an eye about the sight of me holding on to Jess. It was a gentle, delayed realization that hit me.

The big, triumphant moments had already passed. They'd happened. The world hadn't ended. Jess had kissed me in public in the back of that ambulance. We'd told the cops we'd been intimate. We were in sight of many different people, holding on to each other, and it was okay.

Sure, there were photographers outside who'd be beside themselves with joy to snap a shot of me and Jess they could use as proof that we were gay. But... so what?

After all I'd been through, did I really care if my label disapproved? Did it matter what anyone thought? Jess cared for me. So did Mags. I wouldn't be alive without them. The different forms of love they each offered were all I needed.

It felt like the burden of having to pretend to be the persona of Tucker Reynolds, saintly straight singer, had been lifted from me. The fake, contaminated identity I had taken on ever since I met Mr. Briant could be shed easily. All I had to do was keep holding on to Jess and follow my heart. I'd finally found my path. It would lead me away from all of the trouble, the darkness and pain. It might cost me my singing career, but it was a price I was willing to pay if it earned me a genuine, happier existence.

Jess was watching me again. He gave my fingers a gentle squeeze and asked, "You ready for this?"

"Yeah," I replied, getting to my feet. "Let's get out of here."

All I had to do was put one foot in front of the other. We fought our way forward, carving a path through the throng to the car. Mags led the way, happy to be the blade parting the masses so we could follow. Jess stayed right behind me, holding my hand. I never let go of him for a second. Nothing could have caused me to. As long as we were connected, it was like part of me was still back there in bed with him. Morning had barely risen and we were happily hiding away from the world, together. That was my daydream. In reality, a member of security held the rear passenger door open for us. Mags jumped inside, waving for us to follow. Jess used his body to block the people pushing to get closer and motioned for me to go ahead and get inside.

All of those cameras and onlookers were swarming us, but I hesitated. Jess gave me a quizzical look.

I remembered what Mr. Briant had said, that I'd forgotten my place. Had I? Or had I just found a better one in the meantime. Already, just by standing by me, Jess had given me more peace than I'd ever expected to find again.

What Jess and I had found together was important, and he was the one helping the most to get me through, so I pulled him down a little with a hand wrapped behind the nape of his neck and let my lips touch his in a gentle kiss. When we broke apart, I said only, "Trust me."

Then, we got in the car. The door slammed shut as a storm of flashes threatened to blind us. A storm of voices crashed against each other while people shouted for our attention. The driver ensured we were settled and took off.

It was that easy. I had done it—without permission, disregarding the entire way I'd learned to exist.

Mags looked uncomfortable. He shot me a few confused looks before giving up and keeping to himself. Jess gave me a crooked smile, though his eyes remained haunted. "You kissed me in front of them," he said.

"I know I should've asked you first," I started to apologize.

"It doesn't matter," he said, shaking his head. "What you went through today—"

"Jess," I interrupted. "That man's been fuckin' with me in ways you couldn't believe for six damn years. I don't care about this morning. All I care about is tonight, and tomorrow, and every day after that. I know I owe you truths."

"No, you don't—"

"I do," I insisted. "I'd like you to stick around a while, but for that to be possible, I've gotta let you know me. The *real* me. I need some time, first, to work stuff out. I know it was selfish to kiss you in front of them."

"Hell, I kissed you first," he said with an even bigger grin.

"And I'm damn glad you did," I replied, kissing him again, just because I could.

Chapter 28

Recovery

"Talk to me about what's on your mind," my therapist suggested.

"Well, work is," I told him. Sitting on the couch in Jess's cabin up in Washington, way up in the mountains on the edge of the West Coast, I leaned forward toward my computer screen and folded my hands. My therapist, Dr. Hank Cross, with whom I'd spent the majority of the past month, gazed back at me through the video chat window. "Part of me wants to get going on the new album, but everyone keeps telling me there's no rush. The media firestorm is still out there, so I know it's better to let things die down and not stress myself out. And who we make the album with, who's going to produce it and release it..." I shook my head. "All up in the air. I've been writing, though. It's good. Cathartic."

"Have you been in contact with Mags?"

"Not for a few days. It's still weird when we talk on the phone. I can hear it in his voice, how he's accepted that it really happened — all of those things he saw in the pictures. He's not as angry with himself as he was at first, but I always feel like he's trying to apologize for things that weren't his fault."

"Think about what you just said there."

I did, and it knocked me silent for a moment.

"Yeah, okay," I relented. It upset me a little. I grabbed a tissue, dried my eyes and took a deep breath. "Wow, okay. Yeah. See? I know this stuff. It still sneaks up on me sometimes. It wasn't his job to save me. It's my job to save myself."

"Good," the doctor said encouragingly. "Your memories aren't acting as a trigger for you any longer?"

"No, it hasn't been bad like that since I was camping. Mainly, I think about things after I talk to you, now. I'll go on a walk with Jess and that helps a lot. But I'm not the only one who's enjoying the break. We've all needed it, I think. Still committed to each other and the band, but balance is key."

"One of the things you mentioned a few days ago was the photographs that have been posted online," Hank said, looking down at his notes. "But you changed topics quickly. Let's try to go back to that."

I ran my hand over the back of my head, over my hair, dropping my gaze from the screen. "Well, they're... they're everywhere. The photos. Or so I'm told. I don't go online to look, but I've heard whisperings through my lawyers, my agent, my manager—the way they talk about it is like it's this grave situation. I can tell they're scared. It's way beyond their ability to control it now. Magazines, entertainment news, and all sorts of websites have latched on to the story and ran with it. People try to get in touch with me every day, but I ignore most of it. I was told I should make a statement, explain how a kiss doesn't mean anything, talk about how in some cultures a kiss between men is merely a sign of respect, not a condemnation of someone as being terminally homosexual."

"Is that how you see it? Being terminally homosexual?"

"No, I'm projecting, I guess," I sighed. "I haven't made a statement."

"That's good. I think the statement can wait. It's my opinion that it's best for you to continue with our sessions for a few more weeks and focus on healing before moving forward publicly."

I'd checked myself into a mental health facility in Nashville almost immediately after being released from the hospital following my encounter with Nathan Briant. I'd agreed to undergo intensive therapy for the abuse I'd endured and everything tied to it, specifically my suicide attempts.

It was a quiet, introspective month, during which I received therapy eight hours a day, five days a week. It was strange and difficult to look inward constantly in order to understand how I was feeling, and why. They taught me that most of my self-perceived emotional problems during my career had not been my fault. Nathan Briant had made me psychologically dependent on him, similarly to how Mags had always been so dependent on me. All of this time, I'd been trying to get Mags to see how strong he was, if only to get him to try to stand on his own two feet, and I could have been saying the same things to myself. I wasn't weak, I was just conditioned to accept negative, abusive things in my life and believe I deserved them. The more I saw how Briant's rhetoric had shaped the way I saw myself, the more I understood how the learned behaviors I'd been subjected to could be undone, and consciously overruled, with time, patience, and a lot of hard work. Luckily, work was something I wasn't afraid of.

Once I was feeling more content with myself and stable, they'd released me after I agreed to continue sessions remotely with Dr. Cross.

"Okay," I nodded, feeling kind of relieved to get permission to put it off a little longer. "Honestly, though, I haven't been trying to hide that I like to hold Jess's hand when we're outside together. I'll loop my arm through his as we walk, or kiss him now and then. We never really go anywhere where there's a ton of people, but still."

"That seems like progress," Dr. Cross smiled. "No anxiety from that?"

"Nope. I think I'd feel more anxious if I was trying to consciously ignore Jess or how I feel about him."

My thoughts skipped around. There had been a buffer of space around Jess and I ever since I'd moved from one hospital to another. My lawyers had been handling the label. There were so many go-betweens relaying news to Jess, since I wasn't taking many calls, my days had felt very surreal for a while.

Jess had been my focus in a lot of ways. He'd been the one there through it all, at my request. Mags visited occasionally at the facility in Nashville, but we kept our talks strictly to safe topics. Now he was staying at his own place and I was giving myself permission to let his calls go to voicemail more often than not. One of my tools for progress was to set boundaries and stick to them, especially with Mags. It was important for both of us. He still wasn't comfortable with the idea of me and Jess being together, but he tolerated it for the sake of our friendship, and what I was going through.

"And how do you feel about Jess?" Dr. Cross asked gently.

I bowed my head a little, hiding a smile. The smile faded as one thing led to another in my mind. "There's been this fog around me. I don't like talking about things with anyone but you. I haven't explained things to Jess. You know how he goes off for a while when I start a session with you, to give me privacy, but... Just being here with him, it's got a better energy than my home in Nashville. I was only there one night, before I admitted myself, but I kept seeing cops in the hall, or hearing Mags yell in the bedroom, beating Jess on the floor. And if the phone rang, I felt like it was Mr. Briant trying to get at me again. That's why I let Jess take the calls. Helps lessen the nightmares."

"You're kind of circling around it, Tucker. Try to put it into words for me, how you're responding to Jess."

"I'd been scared of him on tour, and right afterward. Because of his questions, you see, and how he seemed to see through the lies I'd wrapped myself in for my own protection. He kept trying to find out the stuff I least wanted him to know—wanted *anyone* to know. But now," I sighed, gazing out the window at the tree line beyond the edge of the property. He was out there, somewhere, walking. "He's down in it with me. Those photos of us kissing, the public assuming our sexual orientations... it's changing his life as much as mine.

"He's stopped asking for specifics or details. He respects my process, but he still cares." I looked up at Dr. Cross, trying to explain as best I could. "Every time he looks at me, I can feel that he cares about me, the way no one else ever has. He gets it, how you can want a person but still know you might not ever get to have them. It makes me feel comfortable with him. I'm not scared of him anymore."

"So, it's mainly comfort you're feeling?"

I laughed softly, feeling guilty. Thinking maybe I should admit to that, I said, "This part's hard for me."

"What aspect?"

"Talking about Jess." "Jess or *sex* with Jess?"

Something eased in me, hearing him say it first. I blew out a breath and made myself relax my shoulders. Dr. Cross gave me a moment, seeing me work through my reactions by practicing some of the stress management techniques he'd given me. "You're right," I confessed. "No, you're right. It's still separate in my head, that I... I might be falling in love with him. That's in a whole other category than the way I feel about my sex life, with him or anyone else. The emotions are their own challenge but the physical stuff... that's harder."

I thought about that brief moment I'd shared with Jess in my home in Nashville, before Mags walked in on us and then after the cops had left and we'd been alone again. I recalled how it had actually felt to have sex with Jess, instead of how I remembered it, or the things I projected onto it.

"He was sweet with me. Respectful. It just meant so much more, to both of us. It wasn't anything like I'd experienced with the, uh, prostitutes. Or Mr. Briant."

"It sounds to me like you're still giving him power," Dr. Cross observed. "That's the second time you've called him that."

"Fuck, you're right. Nathan. Not Mr. Briant. Force of habit."

"But I want you to recognize those habits instead of giving in to them. This is just part of the process of rewiring those instincts, okay?"

"Okay," I nodded.

Nathan Briant was being treated for a fractured skull, thanks to Mags' tire iron, while being held in protective custody. There had been plenty of evidence at the scene of the crime to condemn him. The video; stills from the slideshow; the motherfucking pen retrieved from the hospital with his fingerprints, my DNA *and* my damn name on it; the shackles, instruments of torture and fetish gear found in the room with us; and the camera feed recording our brief conversation before the police arrived — it wrapped the case up in a big, neat bow. That bastard was fucking *screwed*.

When the authorities began to tie him back to contacts within the label, since he'd implied their involvement himself, it had become a game of lawyers and detectives. I stayed the hell out.

"Before you become sexually active again with Jess," Dr. Cross told me. "It's important that you get to a place where you can have an honest conversation with him, and lay it all out there. Even the toughest stuff. That's key if you want to have a healthy relationship with him."

"Yeah, because I really..." I laughed, self-consciously. "I really want to be with him. It's been kind of killing me to sleep in the same house as him, every night, and not go there. But I haven't because I want to go about it the right way. I need this to work, or at least give it the best chance I can to work. I really..." That L word was right there, but it was so big, so rare, I hesitated to touch it more than I had to. I didn't want to frighten it away. "He's really special, and he's really... he's so good to me."

Choked up, I wiped my eyes and grabbed a tissue to dry them, but smiled for the doctor's benefit, to show him I was okay.

"I don't want to lose him, or scare him off," I admitted.

"You can't control him, but he can't control you either, remember. He's been patient this long, hasn't he? That seems to indicate he's willing to hang in there a little longer."

"I hope you're right," I murmured, gazing out that window, watching the trees and counting the minutes until I'd see Jess again.

Chapter 29
Traumatized

I loved Jess's cabin instantly. On a cliff, overlooking the ocean on one side and dense wilderness on the other, our bungalow took the heat off of us when I most needed it. No one could get to me there if I didn't want them to. It was like being camping again, where it had been so peaceful, only with all the comforts of modern conveniences, such as the chats with my therapist.

There were other benefits, too. Rather than sleeping on the hard ground in a sleeping bag, there was a feather-topped mattress, a roaring fireplace, and a sizable man at my side to keep me warm. Instead of eating only fish and canned food, there was a gourmet kitchen in which Jess created all sorts of decadent meals. Most importantly of all, at night Jess provided the light and care needed for me to keep the darkness out.

Outside, birds swooped down the cliff side, dancing in the wind, slicing through the spray as the saltwater threw itself against the rocks on the beach below. The trees crowded around our hideaway, sheltering us from everyone but the sea.

We didn't always talk. Jess was good about sometimes letting silence or our music speak instead. There was a lot to overcome, and a lot to get used to.

Some days I sat for hours on the porch, mesmerized by the constant waves tumbling over the rocks, not wanting to be touched or bothered, and he understood.

In the interest of setting boundaries, I only spoke to Mags on the phone once a week. We talked about everything but Jess and what had happened. It helped make things feel more normal than they were. At least I still had him, in some limited, safer form. The weaning had started. Mags knew it. I was letting him go.

I'd waited until I felt less resistant to talking about things out loud before daring to think about having my conversation with Jess. It had been two months since he'd found me in a panic, strapped to a gurney, surrounded by police and paramedics, with Nathan Briant bleeding and being taken away on his own gurney. Two months of recovery, with years more of it on the horizon.

Jess deserved to know what he was committing to, by being with me.

"One thing I can't figure out," I started, looking at my hands instead of him. "Is why you're bothering to wait so long for me, and put up with all of this trouble?"

We were each holding a mug of hot cocoa, sitting on rocking chairs on the cabin's porch. The porch was well covered and the cabin sheltered us from the worst of the icy wind and rain, but we were wrapped up in thick blankets, boots, and hats to stay warm. All of those layers worked wonderfully at helping me feel nestled safely inside. The words came a lot easier than they might have otherwise. The harmony of the tireless ocean, stirred up by the showers, underscored each word and breath. Jess was by my side, the coziness of the cabin was at my back, and the view made me feel comfortably small, in the grand scheme of things.

He sighed and seemed to resign himself to something. Watching him struggle with it, I realized Jess had his own secrets he'd been keeping.

"I'm used to waiting. And hoping," he murmured. There was a look on his face, furrowing his brow, worrying at his mouth, like he was upset but trying not to show it, to shoulder his way through it. "I never told you why I stopped being a studio musician. I mean, part of it was wanting to work with you, or someone like you, but that wasn't the first reason I went for it, and left this place."

God, but it got worse. He struggled in his seat, hands beginning to tremble, anger in the tightness of his mouth and the fire in his eyes, even as they took a shine that spoke of pain. Setting down my mug on the table between us, I reached out, set my hand on his arm.

"Please tell me," I said, worrying about him.

Something had taught him, along the way, how to bury things deep. It sent a chill down my spine, wondering about what he'd gone through, imagining all kinds of awful things.

Sniffling, wiping a hand roughly over his face, he shook his head, cleared his throat.

"Please, Jess."

"I mentioned, about my dad," he started, hunched forward a little like he was ready to spring out of that chair and walk away if things got too hard.

"You said he was young, that it was his birthday."

Jess nodded, "Yeah, he would have been fifty." An angry tear slid down his face and he wiped it away.

"Ah, fuck, Jess," I groaned. "I wish you'd said something. If I'd have known what you were going through—"

"No, I... I had to walk away from it. Keep it separate. He, um, was in the army. Captain Brett Grayville. Served in Iraq, the Gulf War. He got caught in some cross-fire. There was an explosion. He lost some men. Dad lost his left arm above the elbow, and about half of his left foot. Up until then, I'd lived with my mom, but he needed someone with him, so I was right there. Moved in with him to help get him through recovery and rehab. I won't get into the whole mess, but he just was hurting on the inside so much more than on the outside. They called it PTSD but it was so much bigger than a simple diagnosis. He just was always on edge, never opened up about what was really wrong. For years, I tried. We'd been so close, but then... he was gone. He was there, but he wasn't my dad anymore. Not like I remembered him. I kept hoping, eventually, it would get better, that he'd be himself again."

My chest tightened up, afraid of what Jess would say next, but I had to know. I could tell by that look in his eyes that he'd been living with these secrets for at least as long as I'd had mine, that they'd worn him down and drained some of his ability to hope. It broke my heart, wishing I could turn the clock back and find ways to be there for him, too, the ways he'd tried to be there for me. Wanting to do whatever I could, even if it was just listen and try to understand, I whispered, "What happened?"

"His car veered off a windy road on the side of the mountain.

It was raining a little, so they said slick road conditions could have caused it. But I'm the only one who'd seen the look in his eyes that day, before he went out. There was nothing there. They were hollow. Resigned. That was right before I left here for good, to go on the road. I missed him too much. I kept expecting to see him come through the door or call me up. Having a new stage name, lots to keep me busy and think about... it helped."

He turned to look at me, took my hand in his and weaved our fingers together. With a sad smile, he said, "That's why I'm patient, I guess. Part of me will always be waiting for him. And part of me will always be waiting for you, too. I just *have to believe* it gets better, you know?"

"I'm so damn sorry, Jess," I told him, understanding him more than I ever had. "What you must have been going through. And *him*, too. I love that you were so loyal to him. Knowing how you are, I can tell you did everything you could and then some."

"He was so brave," Jess said passionately. "I think he just cared too much. About taking care of me, about serving his country, safe-guarding his brothers in combat, and then taking the blame for not being able to save everyone he'd wanted to. Some days I just wished so hard I could lift some of the weight from his shoulders to ease his burden. I'd have done anything, but there was nothing."

He stopped, seemed to gather himself, then turned to look at me, squarely, holding my gaze. "What can I do to ease your burden, Tucker? There has to be something. I feel like being here with you isn't enough anymore. Please say I can do more. I just... I need to un-derstand what you're going through, too. You can trust me. I swear you can."

I could see it, how he'd sat with his dad, trying to pull the pain out through the air, with all of his love. The pain didn't belong to him, though, and it wouldn't be moved. Pain stayed where it grew.

"Well, I'd like to try to talk to you about some things we've been avoiding, if that's okay. Ease into it a little. No pressure, just talk."

"Yeah, I can do that. Absolutely. I mean, if you're feeling ready...."

"I think I am."

All I could do was hope what I had to say wouldn't change how he looked at me, and it wouldn't push him out of reach. Feeling scared to go through with it but knowing there was no going back, I took my hand back, picked up my mug and took a drink. The ceramic was soothingly warm against my palm. I sat back in my seat, trying to relax. He did the same, settling into a similar pose so that he wasn't staring right at me anymore.

Before I began, I reminded myself that if it came down to it, I had to be ready to let him go, too. It had to be his decision to stay.

"You have many serious relationships?" I asked Jess.

"A few," he admitted. "But none for a few years, now. Not since I moved out of Washington for the most part and joined up with you."

"We are pretty joined, aren't we?" I grinned.

"That we are," he agreed with a smile of his own.

Curious, I murmured, "What's your type?"

He gave me a knowing look, then an up-and-down glance, measuring me, telling me without telling me. "Oh, I'm sure you could guess."

"Humor me. Please," I asked gently.

"How about, if I answer, then so do you," he challenged. "Fair is fair."

I swirled my drink, taking a sip. It warmed my throat, then my belly. I huddled down lower in my coat and blanket, thinking of people I would have rather forgotten. It was as good a way to get into it as any. Small steps were best. "Yeah, okay. It's a deal. You go first."

"The men I've been with have all been younger than me, and physically smaller than me."

"How old are you?"

"Thirty-four," he answered, head bowed, giving me a sidelong glance. "You're twenty-seven."

Jess didn't need to tell me that he had a nearly foot of height and plenty of muscle mass on me, either.

"Anything else?" I pressed.

"I'm a top."

"Exclusively?"

The conversation and the attentive, heavy tone in his voice were making my dick hard. I just hoped he couldn't tell.

"So far, yeah. That okay with you, cowboy?"

I smiled, chuckling nervously, blushing again. "I'll make do," was my answer.

"Your turn," he prompted, sipping his cocoa.

I knew I'd tried his seemingly fathomless patience with my months of silence. There was a lot of explanation he deserved, and regarding much more than my type. It was because the last thing he'd ever do was ask me outright about Nathan Briant that I needed to give him answers.

It was the effect the answers might have, though, that made me hesitate. Mine was an ugly story. Maybe I'd lose him before I'd gotten the chance to really have him. Maybe that spooky, rare feeling in my heart for Jess would be unrequited, and Nathan Briant wouldn't be the only one left to haunt my dreams.

It was like I could feel Jess going, before I said a single word.

It was selfish, though, to deny Jess facts just to increase the chance he might stay to love me back.

"I just don't want to lose you," I confessed, tearing up and hanging my head. "You might not want me anymore after I tell you this."

Jess reached out and grasped my knee, frowning at me. "Hey. Don't presume," he scolded. "Give me a chance to prove myself to not be an asshole." I thought of all of those magazines with his face plastered on them, next to mine, marking him publicly as a gay man, and felt bad again for dragging him down with me.

"I was confused about myself for a long time," I said. "I'd always had a thing for Mags, but I knew it would never happen. Those feelings were safe and impossible, and they got me through my early teens. After that, well, my singing career started to happen. That was my focus. My everything. I had to pretend to be who the public wanted to see, instead of myself."

"I hope you see how that hurt you," Jess told me. "I know from experience how hard it is to be gay, openly, while trying to be a success professionally. There's so much stigma there. But you've got no reason to lie about yourself, Tucker. The real you is incredible."

"There was no place for a gay country singer," I countered. "They would've laughed me out of the room. Besides, I was too damn shy. Taking on a persona allowed me to get on stage and be braver than I felt. It was a trap, though. I was lying to everyone—Mags, my manager, my family, and myself. The more I lied, the harder it was to stop. When I got the chance to get signed... that's when it all changed. I met Nathan Briant when I was twenty-one. He cut through all the lies, then gave me new ones to tell. He was my first."

There was a moment of silence in which Jess said nothing and I just waited for him to react. "Your first," he echoed, carefully controlling the tone of his voice.

"You're angry," I observed.

He took a deep breath, staring out at the grey, weeping world beyond the safety of the porch.

"I wish, so often, I'd gone into that room with Mags, or *instead of* Mags. I've wanted to hurt that fucker. Thinking of him, hurting you—"

"I'm damn glad you weren't there," I told Jess, letting him hear how much I meant it. "It would have killed me if you'd seen that, seen *me* like that."

"I love you, Tucker," he said urgently. "I love you at your worst, your best, your strongest, and your weakest. Protecting you is all that matters, especially from sick people like Briant."

"You would have been way too late for that. When I met him, during our very first meeting, he explained how if I wanted a future, I had to know my place, and my place was keeping him happy. We were alone in his offices, with the secretary right outside the door. He was intimidating as hell, and the only thing I knew for sure was I had to make a good impression. So, he had me blow him, held me down to take it, choked me a little and treated me rough. It scared me half to death. You have to understand, Jess, I'd never even *kissed* a boy, let alone...."

When I couldn't finish the sentence, he said, "No one stopped him, did they?"

"No one knew," I tried to tell him. "I felt like he only did it because he could tell there was something wrong with me, that since I liked guys, he thought it was an opening. I'd never done anything sexual like that before. It was all so much more than I could handle. But it got me in the door with the label, probably because he could tell I was easily manipulated. At our next face-to-face meeting, he'd just gotten me and Mags signed, and said I owed him for it, much more than before."

Jess had a hard look on his face, but he wouldn't tear his gaze from me. He was still holding my knee, but looked like he wasn't sure whether he should let me see how furious he really was or not.

"He told me to take my clothes off and drugged my drink. I saw him do it. He said it'd help me relax, so I drank the damned shit. Then... bad things happened. But I fuckin'... I *enjoyed* them. The horror and *guilt* of that? That kept me quiet. Mr.— Nathan didn't have to do a damned thing. He... touched me... had me get on my hands and knees on his desk, naked, while he sat in his chair behind me, wearing his suit and looking important, looking like someone who could make things happen. Then he started to stick his fingers in me. And he stuck..." I swallowed hard. It was funny, how the words came easier the more of them I said. "You know the pen they took as evidence that morning? It was our ritual. Before he really started, every time, he did... that... with the pen. It had my name engraved on it, and it's the one I used to sign the contract. That morning, when you, Mags, and Angel found me, he did it again. But, right before Mags busted in, Nathan pushed it too far. It got stuck. That's why I was so fuckin' frantic on the gurney. I hated it. I hated feeling it in me so much. He always told me it meant I belonged to him."

"It's no wonder you were so upset," Jess murmured, shaking his head. "That was a way he tried to control you. Get inside your head."

"Damn right he did," I agreed quietly. "It went on. He took pictures. Some of them were playing in that room in Nashville. In all of the pictures, he made sure it looked like I was enjoying myself, or that you could see my face. They were more trophies. More ways to put me in my place. Make me fall in line. Another part of the ritual was that he'd force me to climax, make me think I wanted it, and was enjoying everything, even if I wasn't consenting to any of it. Then, the drugs would really kick in, and I'd get sleepy. That first time, after I passed out in his office, I woke up in my apartment with no clue as to how I'd gotten there. My ass was so swollen and raw, I couldn't move. I don't know what he'd stuck in me or how long he'd... had sex with me. Obviously he'd done a lot, but I couldn't remember a damn thing."

"He raped you, during a meeting," Jess said. He searched my face, clenching his jaw.

"It didn't seem as... cut and dried as that. That's why it screwed me up so bad. It felt like I'd enjoyed most of it. I always knew, from that first moment when he told me to get on my knees, that I had the option of walking out. He told me to lock the door, but he didn't force me to. He told me to get undressed—he didn't hold me down and forcibly strip me. Sure, he'd remind me that if I left, or if I disobeyed him in even the slightest way, he'd tear up the contract and make calls to make sure I never worked in Nashville again. But that's what made me feel like such a whore. I was selling myself to him in exchange for my career. I never used the word rape, even in my own head."

"He made you believe you deserved it. All of it."

"Yeah, he did. It worked."

Jess was still so angry. I could feel it. How to explain to him, though, as he sat there, that he was trying to save me from something that had already happened?

Chapter 30
Conditioned

Jess asked, "Do you understand, now, that he raped you?"

"Yeah. I do."

"Good. Keep going. Is it helping at all, to talk about this stuff?"

"I think so. I've never tried to put it all into words like this, all at once. Even with Dr. Cross, it was a process."

"Well, maybe this is good progress then," he held my hand, gave it a squeeze. "You said you'd just woken up at your apartment?"

"Yeah, and, on my body, there were... marks. He used this fetish gear on me while I was passed out—things that pinched or were stuck inside." I shook my head. "I never felt the hurt while he used them on me. While I was awake, he'd make me think I was getting off on it all. But I guess he only really got going once I couldn't fight back. He was usually there when I woke up, and then it hurt. It'd be in agony, but he'd still be telling me how surprised he was that I'd enjoyed myself so much. Then it was all about the healing process. And if I even considered telling someone why I was so sore and bruised... he gave me reasons to stay quiet. There'd be a new truck outside, registered in my name and paid for, or more money in my accounts.

"Things snowballed. He kept showing up at my place or telling me to come in for more 'meetings'. Our encounters kept happening for a little while. Then... he left. There was no warning. Maybe someone had started to suspect. Maybe he just found a better opportunity, but he was transferred overseas. I was... in a bad place. Wanted to kill myself, but wasn't brave enough to really try. I'd sit there, with my gun, and set the barrel in my mouth. That's as far as I'd get. I kept waiting for him, and what I felt wasn't really dread. That was what made me hate myself the most."

"You were so damn young and impressionable, Tucker. Of course all of his shit turned your head around, made it hard to see it all clearly. He was a fucking predator. How long did this go on for?"

"About a year, with a month or so of recovery time between visits."

"How many times, specifically?"

I couldn't say it at first. It wouldn't come. "The simple questions are the toughest, okay?" I warned Jess. "What does it matter? It was too many. One would have been too many."

"You've been speaking with your therapist about this?"

"Yeah."

"You know, with my dad, there were one or two events that haunted him most. Something happened a week before the attack that crippled him, and then there was the attack itself. Those were the two things he always thought about. He never talked about them, no matter what I tried. Wouldn't open up, even to the professionals. And I think that's why he drove off that fucking road. You have to let go of the bad stuff, Tucker. Or else it festers."

"I get that. I do." I rubbed a hand over my mouth and went somewhere else for a moment, in my memory. "Eight."

"Eight times," Jess echoed. I could feel his eyes on me, but I couldn't look up at him. Now he knew I had eight times when I could have walked away or asked for help, but I never did. No matter how deep the shame and pain ran, I didn't walk away from the only person who seemed to want me. My face felt hot and Jess's hand was cool where he slid his palm along my jaw and gently tilted my head up and back so that I had to look at him. When I did, the only thing I saw in his eyes was what looked like worry and concern for me. His voice sounded a little rough when he said, "Thank you for telling me, Tucker."

"You're welcome." Breathing easier, I could feel it, how that number was outside of me, now, not just sitting inside, damning me, mocking me and weighing me down. It was good to put it out there, and try to let it go. The urge to apologize again was very strong. There was a voice in my head telling me if I kept trying to show Jess how sorry I was for all the bad things I did and the good I didn't, maybe it would help me keep him and he'd understand how much I didn't want those eight times. "You're right, it does help just to say it. I've always told myself it was just a few times. But eight's more than a few. It's a hard thing to face. And the worst thing..." I knew I needed to tell Jess about it. There would be no going forward unless Jess knew everything I most wanted to hide from him. "Dr. Cross knows all about it. The worst thing was the last time. There were rituals, things that would happen each time, in the same sequence. I relied on those, to get through. The last time, he didn't follow the rituals and the effect it had on me...."

Ever patient, and so damn strong, Jess coaxed me to look up at him again by setting his hand on my arm and saying, "Hey, I'm here to listen if you want to tell. Nothing you say is going to scare me, Tucker. Okay? I'm in this with you."

The world around us had been drained of color, but that day was still vibrant and too bright to ignore.

It came alive in my mind, like a button had been pushed, triggering memories.

I was back there.

'Come over to the desk, son,' Mr. Briant said. Sliding his chair back, he gestured to the spot directly in front of him, between him and the desk itself.

"His office was always empty of any furniture other than his desk, his chair, and the wet bar behind him. That day, there were other chairs. That was my first clue something was off."

I walked to the place he wanted me. He grabbed hold of my hips to move me around so I was facing the desk instead of him. His hands were on me, right away, squeezing my ass through the jeans.

"There was an order to it all. And he was screwing it up. It made me upset and I forgot myself. He was supposed to tell me to take my clothes off, first, right away. He wasn't supposed to touch me until after I was naked. But I stood there with him seated behind me, groping my ass, breathing a little heavy, and I didn't know what to do, or what was happening.

"'Open your pants,' he said. And it was a relief, not scary. Him changing things was a lot scarier. So I hurried to get my buckle undone while he kept touching my ass. I undid the fly, pulled down the zipper, hoping that would be good enough to get him back on track."

'Hands off. Put 'em on the desk. Lean forward.'

"He pulled the jeans and boxers down instead of making me do it. That was wrong, too. And he didn't even pull them all the way off, just down past my knees. I didn't like it, that I was still wearing them. How could I predict what would happen next if he was changing the rules on me? The rules helped me wrap my head around it, as scary as it always was, and got me through. It made it feel safer. Without them, it was just as bad as the first time. Hell, it was *worse*."

Two hands palmed my cheeks, spreading them. A single finger brushed lightly over my hole, tickling.

'Good. That's good. That's real nice,' he said, still more breathless than I'd ever heard him. 'Lean all the way forward, son, 'til your face is resting against the wood.'

"He told me to bend sharply at the waist, so I was lying against the desktop with him behind me. He'd always been so calm, you know? Eerily so. He didn't sound calm then."

Briant's hands spread me roughly, his fingertips digging in near my rim. I hated being pulled open like that without knowing the pill would knock me out soon. He kept tickling my hole with one finger, then suddenly thrust a single finger through to the last knuckle. A hard shiver raced through me and I let out a hard grunt.

"He fingered me, doing all of the things he knew got to me most. Things like knowing he was looking at me, or him touching me gently always got me hard. It all started to add up to something really bad. I needed it to not be different. I wanted it to be like it had always been. I couldn't get through it otherwise."

The finger pulled out and he used his fingers to spread my rim. Then, something soft and wet touched me there. I felt a warm breath against the skin, then his tongue pressing through, filling me up.

'I thought you liked me sleepy, sir?' I asked, daring to question him. 'You haven't given me the pill. Can I please...' my voice broke as he kept licking, circling his tongue around and thrusting it farther. 'Can I please have the pill?'

"So, after he started using his tongue instead of the finger —"

Jess growled a little, turning his face away momentarily.

" —I asked him, flat out, for the pill. I begged him for it. I fuckin' *begged* him."

"You didn't want to be awake, and feel it all," Jess observed.

"Exactly. He removed his tongue. Right away, something cool and hard was pressed into me, with two of his fingers. I hated it. It was uncomfortable and awful, feeling it in there. It was bigger than the pen, but I didn't know what it was. Still don't.

"Then he pulled my pants back up. He grabbed hold of my dick and pumped it a little as if to make me aware that it was getting stiff, before he pressed it down to my leg and closed my pants back up."

'Fasten that belt. Go sit down in that chair.' He pointed to it. It was in his line of sight and turned a little toward the other chairs, so whoever was in them would be able to see me as well. 'You need a lesson in minding your place, boy, and staying quiet when you're expected to, but if you stay silent as the grave as long as our guests are here, that will please me.'

'Yes, sir. Is this my lesson?'

'No, this is a test. If you pass it, I'll go easy on you during your lesson, you hear me?'

"It was a test. I was told to sit in a chair, where the whole room could see me, and he warned me to keep my mouth shut, or else he'd have to remind me of my place."

"That's why it was different?"

I tried not to think about how trapped and hopeless I'd felt sitting there, waiting for anything to happen, knowing whatever it was, I couldn't stop it. "In a way. These men filed in, all wearing suits, all looking like top-level executives. Briant went to shake hands with them, completely composed and professional, no sign of what he'd just done. They kind of nodded to me, but no one cared enough to shake with me, too. They were there for him."

Jess started to figure it out and shook his head in amazement, cursing softly.

"About an hour later, they left. I barely heard what they'd been talking about, but the gist seemed to be they needed Briant to fulfill some obligations. They seemed satisfied when they left the room. I didn't move to follow, but stayed there, waiting for him. I was fucking *waiting for him*, Jess."

But Jess knew I'd gotten so conditioned by then, it never would have occurred to me to walk out and save myself. For so long, I'd wondered, privately, why my survival instincts had never seemed to kick in as strongly as they should have, but Jess saw the mental hold that man had gotten over me. Though I'd been beating myself up over it for six years, Jess forgave me that quickly. Or maybe there was nothing there to forgive at all. Maybe I was just surviving the only way I'd known how.

"What did he do to you?" Jess asked, like he didn't want to know but *had* to know.

The door closed. Briant locked it himself. I was standing by my chair and not moving more than I had to. The dull sort of ache and humiliation of having that thing up my ass was making me crazy. It was almost impossible to stay calm. That thing inside me was all I could think of.

He walked up to me and gave my cock a squeeze through my pants. I'd gone soft but that changed as soon as he started to touch me there.

"He didn't even ask me to," I admitted, my voice quiet with guilt. "I started to undress on my own."

I opened my pants first, to feel him touching my cock, skin on skin. And he did. He stroked me while I took the shirt off, and only stopped when I bent to remove my shoes and socks, then the pants and boxers. When I straightened up, naked, I was relieved to feel him touching me like he always had.

"Go ahead," Jess prompted when I fell silent.

"I'm so damn ashamed, Jess. He didn't even...." Choking on the words, I shook my head, trying not to cry anymore. I ran my hands over my face, leaning forward in my seat. Jess's warm hand wrapped behind my neck, slipping under my hair where his thumb moved in a small back-and-forth arc over my skin. It helped me feel connected to him. I wasn't alone with the memory, like usual. "He didn't force me. I knew he'd hurt me, physically, psychologically, every time I'd seen him, but I was so relieved to have him touching me like he'd always done, I wanted more. I didn't want him to stop being nice like that. And I've been working through it. I really have tried. I see it was conditioning, survival instincts, but still...."

After a quick glance up at his face, I saw he was smiling down at me. His hand kept working my shaft, getting me harder. That thing was still in me and I wanted to ask him to take it out, but felt like that probably wouldn't make him happy.

'That's better, isn't it? Makes me happy when you're nice and quiet, son,

and just do as you're told,' he said with his sing-song voice. His right hand wrapped around the head of my cock and squeezed painfully until I whimpered, curling forward a little, my knees feeling weak.

'Stand up straight, boy. Just a little pain, is all.' I tried to straighten up, but it was so damned hard to. I was shuddering and grunting since he didn't ease up. It never would have occurred to me to say stop. When the pain climbed to a peak, I whimpered sharply and he finally let go. It took effort to leave my hands at my sides and not cover myself. I tried to just stand there, but he was looking right at my hard-on, slightly wilted now.

'Can you feel that gift I gave you, tucked in your bottom? Would you like me to take that out or would you rather enjoy it a little longer?'

'W-whatever y-you'd like, sir.'

'Do you like the way it feels in there, son?'

'No, sir.'

He slapped my dick, right to left, then left to right. Shocked, I groaned and forced my arms to stay at my sides, to let him do it.

'I think you do need that lesson, don't you? About what your place is?'

'Yes, sir. Thank you.'

"He kept testing me. Inflicting pain to my... genitals... while he talked about whatever he'd stuck inside me, asking if I liked it, then asking if I wanted my lesson. I said I did.

"He went back to his chair behind the desk and opened his pants. I went to kneel at his feet without waiting to be asked."

I stared at his uncut cock. I liked the way it looked and my ass clenched up instinctively. There was no hiding a damned thing. I was naked and hard for him.

My hair had been tied back since I arrived, but he played with the loose ends hanging over my left shoulder. He gathered them up and let them slide through his hand like he was thinking of pulling on them instead. Then, he took hold of my head with both hands and held me in place as he shifted forward.

'Clasp your hands tightly behind your back, now,' he told me. He reached down to wrap a hand around his cock and bring it closer to my mouth. As usual, I opened wide for him. The hand behind my head pulled me closer and like some love-starved whore I closed my mouth around him and made these moaning sounds I knew he liked to hear. It was all about him and making him happy. As long as he was enjoying himself, I had hope that he wouldn't hurt

me anymore. By that time I was getting better at knowing how to use my mouth and tongue, so I did everything I could to make it good for him.

'Deep breath, now, son,' he warned. Opening my mouth a little wider, I sucked in as much air as I could before he jerked my head forward. His cock filled my throat, all the way past my tonsils, and cut off my air. I gagged and choked on him, but that was just reflex. Instinct made me tense up and want to struggle, so I dug my fingernails into the palm of my hand in order to steady myself and let him do what he wanted. I knew better than to actually fight him. It never did any good. My eyes filled with tears that I blinked away.

'That's it,' he said with a content smile. He used both hands again to keep my head still while my body shook.

When he relaxed his grip and pulled back to only fill my mouth, I fought to fill my lungs as fast as I could.

'I like this view of you, son, and seeing just how very much you're enjoying doing that. No hiding anything from me this way.' He let his dick slide free of my mouth. 'Take a look at yourself. Go on. It's okay.'

I didn't want to face what I could already feel, but knew I had to follow orders. Sitting back on my heels, I looked down at my dick. It was completely hard, red, and wet.

'See how stiff that is?' he asked. 'That's how we know, isn't it? This is your place – sucking cock and trying your best to please.'

'Yes, sir.'

"Tucker?" Jess's voice yanked me out of the memory. It was so easy to get lost there, looking at all of the ways I could have done things differently. Jess had a look on his face like he'd been calling my name for a while with no answer. He was kneeling at my feet and his hand cupped my jaw. After meeting his gaze for only a second, I squeezed my eyes closed. He wiped my tears away and drew me into a hug. My breath hitched. I held on tight. "It's okay," he whispered. "It's okay."

"I'm sorry."

"Don't you dare." He pulled back just enough to kiss me. Then I rested my forehead against his shoulder as more of the memory played in my head.

Chapter 31

Raw Honesty

I swallowed Briant's load of come. He pulled out, let me go and sat back. 'On your feet, now. That's a boy. So...' I stood between his spread legs. He wrapped my cock in his hand, and started to pump it, his fingers sliding in my pre-come. 'Ladies' choice. How do you want this to go?'

He pulled the pill from inside his jacket pocket. As soon as I saw what he had, I opened my mouth and stuck out my tongue. He set the pill there. I dry-swallowed it and started to feel calmer right away.

He was still waiting for me to keep doing what he wanted, so I stepped back. He stood up, coming forward each time I moved back. He stopped stroking me but kept groping at my dick and balls while I moved to lie back on top of his desk. I drew up my legs, holding my ankles as he took something from inside a drawer.

'Time to take back my gift! You hold onto those ankles, now, and don't move an inch. I don't think you're going to enjoy this part very much, but the more you move, the more it'll hurt. I'll make sure of it.'

He gripped whatever it was in his hand as my heart started to pound. That was as much as I saw before tilting my head back to look at the ceiling instead. Sometimes it was better not to know. There was pressure against my hole – lots of it – as he fed something hard and cold up my ass. I tried to swallow down a scream, then felt even more pressure inside, enough to make me cry out roughly in pain.

'That's a boy,' he said soothingly. The more desperately I yelled, the calmer he became. 'Feel that? That's just for you. I know how much you enjoy me playing with this little pink hole, and we both know how wrong it is that you enjoy it as much as you do, so that pain you feel right now is good. It's cleansing. See son, perverts like you need to be punished now and then,

so you don't forget what you are and what your place is.'

I could feel him digging around in there and, as the seconds ticked by, it only hurt worse. The seconds turned to minutes as he seemed to deliberately draw it out longer. That thing in me pushed and pulled, grinding against me from inside. Shaking and sweating, I had to grip my ankles even harder to keep still. Very slowly, he pulled out whatever object he'd put in me before his guests had arrived. It took much longer than I hoped it would, to get it out. When it was only halfway out, my hole stretched wide around it, he left it there and watched me shudder, begging him, breathlessly, 'Please... please...'

Even when it was over, I kept shaking and my ass was throbbing. A few tears slipped down the sides of my face.

He pumped my dick to get it stiff again. 'Oh, I enjoyed that,' he said, 'and I could tell you did, too. It's good to hurt sometimes, isn't it? Bottom boys like you just love to get stuffed full and taken for a happy ride, and hey! That ache you feel in your bottom? That's just the start of the fun for you today, son.' He let go of my dick, swollen red again. 'See that? See how eager you are for more?'

'Yes, sir. Thank you.'

'You're very welcome,' he grinned as I stared at how hard I was, questioning instincts that told me I hadn't wanted the pain. 'Gotta grease this hole, huh?' He laughed and gave my rim a hard pinch that made me wince. He set the lube down by my side. 'Oh! But first... can't forget, can we?' He pulled the pen from a baggie. I started breathing harder when I saw it. The silver gleamed in his hand and my cock twitched. I wanted it. The pen meant things were back to normal. He slipped the pen up my ass and twisted it around. It didn't hurt at all. I moaned a little and he brushed the head of my cock with his fingers. 'I know how you like that. That's our special pact, isn't it? That's just for you.'

'Thank you, sir.' I calmed down. Things were right again.

The pen was put away. Two fingers, wet with lube, pushed into me as he swallowed down my cock.

I let go of Jess, sat back and ran my hand over my head. "I blew him. He was still rough about it, but I was used to it by then. He made me look at how hard I was, so I'd know my place was sucking cock and trying to please. Then he asked me what I wanted. I let him give me the pill, then got on his desk. He pulled that thing out of me, probably with forceps, and it hurt a lot. He fucked me with the damned pen to try to calm me down, getting back to the rules I needed him to follow, then started to prep me for sex while he sucked me off."

When I was about to come, he pulled off, his fingers triggering my gland and stuffing me full. I kept my legs folded back so my ass was pulled wide open for him. He jacked me hard and shook my cock to spray the jets of come over my stomach, chest, and all the way up to my neck. I was panting, soaring, moaning.

'More,' I begged. 'Fuck me, sir, please.'

Gripping my dick, he stood up straight and had a dark, dangerous look in his eyes. His pants hung open, and I stared at his rigid cock. I pulled my legs even more widely apart and back. Stepping forward, he tapped my hole with the end of his dick. Moaning, the drugs finally clawing at my brain and dragging me down, I felt how I wanted it, how I was already trying to push down onto him.

He moved around the desk holding leather restraints. Straps were tied to the legs of the desk, then came up to wrap my ankles, keeping me in place as my muscles gave out. Even before the drugs knocked me out, I was bound, spread and begging for his cock. I made a sleepy, greedy whimper, and watched him step up between my legs, angling his cock down. It pressed at my hole.

"Did it matter that it started out as rape if it didn't end that way?" I asked Jess. "That's the question I've carried for five years. I wanted it that last time, even though I knew, as soon as I was asleep, he'd start to torture me. I begged him to do it. I was so frustrated that I fell asleep just as he was about to have sex with me. I wanted to remember it! I needed to! But that was the last time."

"He knew it was coming, that he was leaving," Jess told me. "He was trying to scare you into keeping quiet about what he'd been doing to you. That's why it went that way."

"Looking back on it? Yeah. Absolutely. Even after he moved overseas, he'd still send me reminders all the time, just to let me know he still had power over me. After the tour—hell, on the last night of the tour—he sent me flowers with a card. When I arranged for a hooker to come to a different hotel than the one we'd all been staying in, for a date with me while the rest of you went out to dinner, he sent champagne and a card telling me to enjoy myself. *He knew.* He knew I'd hired someone to fuck me. Somehow, he did. He kept track of me, very closely. That's why I went camping, to get away from his spies, or however he was watching. And as soon as I came back from camping, he sent me a picture of that fucking pen on Snapchat. So, when I found myself in that office with him again, at first I was *relieved*. At least I didn't have to anticipate it anymore, and things could make sense again. Right away, I felt myself becoming that pathetic victim, hoping he'd hurt me some more, just so that I could please him and I wouldn't have to be so scared of what might happen if he got angry.

"After Nathan had left, I paid for my partners. It was easier and it was pretty damned similar to my arrangement with him. A deal was made, money exchanged, someone got fucked and kept quiet about it. You, uh, you're the first one I've been with, where the feelings were mutual. That truth is real damn embarrassing. So, to answer your original question, I don't know what my type is, Jess. I really don't. I'm just trying not to be so afraid and ashamed of myself all the time. I don't want to hurt anymore. I'm trying to make healthier choices."

Jess looked like he wanted to find that tire iron and beat the bastard with it until he was just a smear of red on the ground. He was finally starting to understand Mags' wildness. Maybe that was good. Maybe it would bring him closer to Mags. I needed that to happen, for my own peace of mind.

"I like that you want me," I told Jess, while he still tried to find words to respond with. "I like that you care, and you worry. I like that you're a good, respectful person. And I like that you're patient, because you'll need to be, to be with me. I'm sorry."

"Stop apologizing," Jess said, choking up, standing and pulling me up as well. He gathered me in his arms and pulled his blanket around both of us. With a hand clasped to the back of my head, he held me to his chest. "Don't be sorry for surviving impossible, dangerous situations. Don't *ever* be sorry. None of that should have happened to you, but I will do whatever I have to so I can help you get through this."

"I haven't scared you off?"

"You couldn't if you wanted to, cowboy," Jess whispered. "I'm here. We've got this."

"Thank you." Something loosened in me. I could breathe easier, stand straighter.

"Mags doesn't know, does he?"

"He just knows what he saw in that room. The rest of it?" I shook my head.

"What happened in that room before Mags interrupted, Tucker? What did Briant threaten you with?"

I sighed, holding on to Jess, glad he couldn't see my face. "He wanted to punish me for the way I'd been acting. Said the folks in charge had ordered it, to scare me out of coming out of the closet. There were shackles, all sorts of sharp, scary things there that he planned to use on me. He meant to keep me there for days. He said he had ways to keep me awake, even if I passed out. And it was so terrifying, Jess. I couldn't move or speak. I just felt so trapped. Thank god y'all found me. When Mags burst in, it hadn't gone far. He hadn't... raped me, yet. But he'd... you know. Had me take my pants down. Touched me while he threatened. All part of the ritual."

"And the pen."

"Yeah."

Jess held on tighter, wrapping his arms around me. It was nice and warm, our little cocoon. I felt his breaths, heard his soft groan. The rain pattered all around us. "Could have been really fucking bad, huh? If we hadn't gotten there... if Angel hadn't come... if Mags *knew....*"

"Why do you think I've been so damn quiet and gone to therapy every single day for so long? So many bad possibilities. When I realized what Briant had planned for me, and how much worse it was going to be than anything I'd gone through with him before, I wanted to die. I was hoping he'd kill me, and...." I exhaled, wondering if I was going to really say it. "When Mags hit Briant and knocked him out, I was upset that I wasn't going to get to die, that I'd still have to live with all of this. You wanted the ugly truth? Well, there it is. I flat out asked Mags to kill me. But I need you to know, Jess, I'm seeing things more clearly than I ever have, and I'm not afraid of the hard work it's going to take to keep working through this. Fuck it, I am proud of how far I've come and everything I've earned. Healing, and you, along with Mags and everyone who's stuck by me—that's what's worth the most. Not the money or the fame. I'm trying to love myself the ways I need to, in order to be a decent partner for you. But I'm still scared sometimes, of a lot of things."

I looked into his blue-green eyes, seeing me, trying to take it all in, and felt so rewarded, just to witness him *trying*. That alone was a miracle, even before you counted the anguish in the twist of his lips, or the tears in his eyes. All of those little signs that he cared were priceless. He was so beautiful, then, trusting me enough to let me into his heart. It just made me resolve to take care of him too, in any and every way possible.

"I'll do whatever it takes to keep you safe, Tucker. I swear it. Even if that means protecting you from yourself. Thank you for trusting me. I know how hard it must have been to get all of that out. You've been carrying this alone for too long," Jess said, filled with ache. There was some desperation in his voice, like it was vitally important I hear him and not slip away anymore. I thought of how many times he must have tried to get his dad to talk about the horrors haunting him, memories of war and loss. There were just some things that needed to stay buried. They'd shred your sanity if you tried to cough them up. "This is why you were so tense after the tour. This is why you went camping and didn't want to come back. This is why you have those scars on your arms. This is the reason for everything."

"Yeah." I loved the feel of him, holding me. He was so many things I needed, it made me want to be everything he needed, too. In his pretty eyes I could see glimmers of his good spirit, fighting so hard to do the right thing. "Would it scare you if I told you that I think maybe I love you?"

He shifted his hold on me to take my face in his hands. "That's the only thing that doesn't scare me," he sighed, then kissed me hard. "Do you have any idea how long I've wanted to hear you say those words? I love you too."

Chapter 32

Pleasure and Patience

The cabin was cozy and rustic. The walls, the ceiling, the floors and the furniture were all built of walnut and cherry, hand hewn and lovingly crafted. Being in there gave me such a sense of warmth and comfort. The outside came in. It was the opposite of sterile and intimidating, and had nothing in common with the settings of my most traumatic experiences. That place was ideal for healing and recovery.

With a fire crackling in the hearth and nature singing her song just beyond the windowpanes, Jess took me to bed.

There was hesitancy in every gesture he made and worry in his beautiful green-blue eyes. I sat on the edge of the foot of the bed and gazed up at him with a smile. It was so good to be the one who wasn't nervous for once. Jess's attitude, his respect for me, it shifted the balance just like that cabin did. That place was good for me, and so was he. He was everything I never had but always wanted. Being in that bedroom with him, up in the mountains, with the world already aware of how we cared for one another—it was a whole new kind of existence I couldn't wait to explore. Each way Jess made me feel protected and at ease just made me crave more. I couldn't get enough. Every moment I spent with him was a single step away from my past. Gradually, I was leaving behind the person I thought I had to be and becoming a new man.

Sure, there was a lot of pressure. Two months had passed since we'd had sex, and that time had been filled with many things that made me want to question every instinct, wondering whether I was being true to myself or letting the conditioning take over. But Jess was terrified of hurting me if we touched. He was a humble man,

247

who knew how he felt and what he wanted. When he looked at me, I suspected he saw things between us. Layers of history lingered. They were keeping us apart.

I couldn't have that.

Maybe the world knowing was part of the cause of his anxiety, too. But he didn't have to perform for them. It wasn't a show. There was no stage. It was just us, being together. The world wasn't invited in.

"I want this," I said to him, watching him watch me, knowing there was too much going on in his head for his body to act. "I miss you."

That was as plain as I could make it. I just needed him, even if it meant going slow and figuring it all out as we went along.

"I haven't gone anywhere," he replied, but his frustration with himself crept in. His gaze dropped to the floor.

Since I had always been naturally eager to dive right into sex to ease my own awkwardness and doubt, I'd been working against that. Jess and I hadn't crossed that line, no matter how much we wanted to. But it was enough. No more waiting. Even if I was a little scared, it was time. I needed him too much.

Leaning forward, I clasped the side of his leg and drew him closer, pulling until his legs straddled mine. Feet planted on the floor, I sat while he stood and my hands caressed up the outsides of his thighs, wrapped in tight jeans. All of that wood around us made me feel like I'd never left the campground. It gave me peace. Nature was kind. Society and its games were what was cruel.

"Be with me," I asked. Reaching for his hands, taking his in mine, our fingers slid, one alongside the other, fitting together perfectly. I wanted to feel him against me, and tugged at his arms, trying to draw him down to lay on top of me.

He resisted at first, then came with a sigh and a frown. Pressing me back to the bed, he laid his body on me, covered me, another layer of warmth and comfort in that tranquil place — one that knew me, inside and out. Jess smelled like aftershave and wood smoke. He looked at me like he truly saw and cherished me. When I looked at him, feeling him touching me, I saw the man who'd been by my side, long before I understood his true value. Jess had been hiding in plain sight. Now, the blindfold was gone, and I was seeing clearly. This was love, and his soaked in through my skin. I heard it in his breaths, saw it in his anguish, and caught the perfume of it in his perspiration and heat. Jess took over every one of my senses.

"What if I can't stop touching you once I start? What if I scare you? You know how much I want you," he warned. My hands moved in a smooth slide down Jess's strong back to his narrow waist, then lower to palm his ass. Gripping him, I thrust up against him, letting him feel how hard he'd made me. His hand wrapped my jaw, his fingers pushed back into my long hair, loose against the bed.

"I trust you," I promised. "I want to feel you inside me. I need to have you so deep, all I'll ever feel is you."

His lips dragged briefly against the skin of my upper cheekbone, beside my ear. He exhaled heavily and whispered a question, "Is it okay if I take my time with you? I'm not in a rush and since we were interrupted before, I kind of want to make it last."

I laughed out loud. I couldn't help it. His palm dragged down the side of my body and caused butterflies to knock around inside me, especially when his fingers slipped under my shirt and found bare skin. My answer was a low moan. I thrust again, harder, sharper. He pressed down on me with his hips, pinning me to the bed, trapping my cock beside his and I shivered. My eyes slipped shut. My lips parted as my breathing grew heavier.

"I want all of you, Tucker," Jess said. "Every part."

"Then *take*," I urged, wanting, needing.

"Gotta warn you, though," Jess said with a hint of mischief in his voice. "I can be patient in bed, too. Gonna keep you hard, draw it out, have you begging for it."

"I'm already beggin'," I said on a groan. He just smiled and kissed me quiet.

"And I've been fantasizing about you. Things I've always wanted to do... how I want to suck you so slow and feel your thighs quiver when you come...."

"Jesus, Jess," I panted. He pushed all of my buttons. Knowing he'd thought about me and was dying to do this, was *my* fantasy come to life. I'd always been the dreamer, the one harboring secret desires. Being on the receiving end was so much better.

"Gonna take such good care of you. Just promise you'll tell me if I step out of line or do something wrong."

"I promise."

"I mean it."

"I know."

"Move on up the bed, so your head's on the pillows."

He shifted off of me so I could do as he asked. Desire changed him back into that man who'd made love fiercely and gratefully back in my home. His eyes were dark, his focus all on me. It was like when he was playing piano, how much he concentrated on his work. But *I'd* become his work. The doubt and shame, which had always been there, faded back. What had I done to deserve someone like him, who made me so happy? It sent a thrill shooting down the center of my body. I was so hard, I was kind of embarrassed by it. There was no denying how much Jess turned me on.

We were both still dressed, but my feet were bare. When he started to open my shirt buttons, I realized he wanted to undress me. But, knowing myself better than I had before, thanks to therapy and experience, I shyly confessed, "I don't wanna be the only one undressed, okay?"

I said it as soon as I remembered the way it felt to be displayed for Mr. Briant. Jess stopped, the meaning coming through, and I saw his anger flare briefly, not *at* me but *for* me.

"Fuck, I'm—" he said with regret, intending to apologize.

"Don't. These are the instincts I'm still learning to recognize and talk about. Part of the process. Just let me see you, too. It'll help. That's all."

He nodded, and began to work his buttons first.

Soon, he had his shirt off, and his hands went to his buckle next.

"Oh hell," I moaned, my heartbeat speeding up to see Jess, half-naked, muscular and bigger than me, there in that bedroom with a head full of intentions. Some of my typical nervousness kicked in.

His buckle opened. Standing by the bed, Jess pushed his jeans down his legs, freeing his big, thick, heavy cock. My breath caught. I realized I liked seeing how much I was turning him on. It gave me confidence and eased the nerves.

I sat up before he had the chance to come back at me. He looked confused as I crawled over to him on my hands and knees. Reaching out, I wrapped my hand around his thick cock, guiding him closer, so he was right up against the side of the bed. Then I opened wide and took him into my mouth. My lips slid down past the head of his prick and I savored his taste, sucking gently. My long, wavy hair did its job by falling over my right shoulder, partially hiding my face from his view. Sometimes I needed the little bit of privacy my hair gave me. Jess made a low groan, let his head fall back on his shoulders and palmed the back of my head, his fingers weaving through my hair. Sucking harder, feeling him out with my tongue, I took more of his shaft into my mouth. It filled it up and I moaned, curling my tongue around his shape, swallowing saliva mixed with the tang of his pre-come as my mouth watered and my hand worked his shaft.

He eased me off, and I let him. Jess dried my lips and chin with a caress of his fingers and said, "Lie down. I need to see you. And I don't intend to come until I have *all* of you."

His words did wonders for my libido, and made me want to do whatever he said just to keep him so hard. He settled on the edge of the bed while I lay down again. So slow it was torture, he went back to opening my shirt buttons, peeling the fabric back to expose my chest a little at a time. When I got impatient, feeling his gaze skimming up and down my body like fingers, I reached out to stroke his gorgeous cock, so stiff it begged to be touched. The silken skin slid so smooth through my grasp, and the touch made him tremble slightly. But he didn't let me get away with that. He just guided my hand off of him and finished with the shirt. I sat up to let him pull it from me.

In lying back, he arranged my hands above my head, on the pillow, fingers curled and relaxed. His touch skimmed downward, wrists to elbows to the underside of my arms, down to my bared chest. His thumbnail flicked my nipple and made me arch into the touch but he kept going, caressing down over my navel to my belt. The fabric of my jeans was strained with the size of my hard-on, and I think he slowed down intentionally again in getting me freed, just to watch me lie there as he'd set me, wanting him as much as I did, and unable to hide it.

By the time he was pulling my fly open and inching my pants down, I was breathing hard. Once the jeans were down past my hip, he gradually slid them down my legs. His hands brushed my skin as he took the jeans off, setting them aside with my shirt. He caressed upward from my ankles to my thighs. I wanted him to touch my cock so badly. My legs had been lying straight, held together, but when his palm brushed up the underside of my dick though the cotton of my briefs, I couldn't help but spread for him, letting my thighs fall open and rocking against the contact with his hand.

I always knew he was skilled with his hands, but I had no idea what it would be like to be played by them. The tempo of his caresses made me weak. He didn't make me feel like a famous singer or a media sensation but just a man who was loved and wanted.

The damp spot on my briefs made me self-conscious, but he'd been drawing it out so long, making it so good, I couldn't help it. Caressing up my shaft again, his thumb folded over my tip, rubbing in small circles through the pre-come-soaked cotton. I moaned and shuddered but he just kept rubbing, making me wetter, making me ache.

"Jess," I begged. My hips canted, tilting into his touch.

"Easy, cowboy," he hushed, rubbing over and around to trigger the nerves under my ridge, and I could've come just like that. I was right on the edge. He'd taken me apart to that extent already. "Is it okay if I take these off?" he asked, his fingers hooking in the elastic band of my briefs.

"Please," I moaned, shameless. He smiled and watched me writhe. I knew then his patience would be the death of me, but what a way to go.

Jess took just as much pleasure in removing the briefs. Once they were off and set with the rest of my clothes, I felt my face get hot when he just sat there, watching my cock twitch. He shifted on the bed, moving between my legs and I spread wider for him eagerly. His gaze was all over me, but focusing alternately between my expression and my cock. Taking hold of my legs, he bent them slightly so my feet were braced on the bed, my thighs fallen widely open. After he'd finished positioning me again, he settled there. His breath warmed my exposed skin. Dragging open-mouthed kisses over the insides of my thighs, he folded my balls up in a hand, massaging carefully. I wanted him inside me as much as I wanted to come. I needed it, I realized, and flushed redder.

It was so different from any sex I'd ever had. There was so much tenderness in every touch and glance he gave me, it held me in the moment with him. Nothing else mattered but enjoying Jess and giving myself to him. I wanted to make him happy, because of how much I loved him. There was nothing I needed in return, but to sense him giving me his love in exchange made every single second feel so damned important. I wanted to stay there with him, forever.

"Jess," I cried with ache.

"What do you need?" he asked, pushing my legs back a little farther, his lips brushing over my sac, then up my shaft. "You wanna come?"

"No. Lube," I managed, not able to be more specific than that, just hoping he took the hint.

His gaze was on my face then. I felt it, and chanced a glance to confirm it. Jess's eyes were dark with lust, utterly focused on me and how completely he intended to claim me.

"Lube for what?" he coaxed. He took a slow lick with the tip of his tongue up of the underside my cock, then suckled briefly on the head. That feeling took me apart, unraveling my control in a way that was the opposite of threatening or worrisome, but only like finally figuring out how to relax after being tense for ten long years.

"Finger me."

Lord, my face was hot. I threw my head back as he reached for the bottle, which was nearby, on the other side of the bed. I heard him get some slick on his hand. The bottle snapped shut, and I waited. When he didn't touch me quickly enough, I pulled my legs up and showed him my ass. A fingertip rubbed over my knot, teasing it and I thrust helplessly, reflexively. My arms tensed, the need was so huge to touch myself and get off, but he was just watching me, teasing my hole with his finger. I bit off a rough cry and that's when he pushed inside me, sliding the finger through the clenched ring. One knuckle, then two pushed inside, and I shuddered, hard. A low grunt shifted into a moan as I pushed my ass down onto him. I was so close way sooner than I wanted to be. My balls drew up and I whimpered. It was paradise to lay there and let him play me. Nothing else mattered.

Jess was damn good at what he was doing and he knew how fast

I was about to tip over, but that wasn't in his plan. Instead, he trailed kisses up the inside of my thigh and worked the finger in and out, pumping it with long, slow strokes. It kept me in that luxurious place, savoring the build-up and anticipation of climax without quite getting close enough to reach it. That was new too, having someone ease me away from the edge instead of hurrying me there. I glanced down and saw him watching my body pull his finger inside.

There was a cute, crooked grin on his face, his lower lip bitten in concentration as his pretty eyes held my gaze for a moment before focusing again on his work.

"Breathe until it eases," he told me softly. His lips moved over the inside of my hipbone, making the spot tingle. Shifting upward while his finger worked, in and out, twisting around, feeling me out, he climbed my body, kissing my waist, my ribs, my nipple, my throat. Then we were face to face. I was desperate, quaking, and unable to be still or shut up. His mouth hovered above mine and he acted, pressing a second finger in, and making me shout as he sought, then found, my gland.

We kissed and it was rough, I bit and chased his lips, moving on his hand, humping air. "Ride it," he urged. "You're so beautiful, Tucker. Love you like this."

"Jess," I begged, keening and trembling. He eased up and let me catch my breath. While I panted, sweat dripping down my body, he spread those fingers apart and held my jaw as he kissed me, fucking my mouth with his tongue like I needed him to do with his cock. Desperate to touch him, too, my hands left the pillow where they'd rested and tangled themselves in his hair.

I broke the kiss to find some air and he lowered his head to my nipple, sucking at it, then tugging with his teeth. He scraped them over the side of my ribs, too, then down over my hipbone, and then even further down to go over the upper inside of my thigh. He pulled his fingers out, rubbed up through my crease, over my hole, then fed three inside. The ache made me moan and that's when he lowered his mouth on me, using the small pain to push my orgasm back farther. But to have the wet, hot softness of his tongue, lips, and the insides of his cheeks hugging me tightly made me buck. I scratched over his scalp and pushed down on his fingers. He took me all the way down his throat and hummed. The sound vibrated into my body. He swallowed and I tipped over the edge.

"Ahh, fuck," I groaned as I came, strung tight as a bow. His fingers were in me to the last knuckle and my cock was lodged in his throat. I yelled and kept coming, shuddering and helplessly pushing into him as he pushed into me. He sucked me through it, taking long pulls of my cock, swallowing everything he wrung from me. I quivered and clenched. It took a long time for it to fade back and away, and he very reluctantly let me go, letting me slide from his lips only when I was soft again.

Purged and panting, I met his gaze and murmured only, "Let me turn over."

"You sure?"

"Yeah."

He pulled out and I rolled, getting up on my hands and knees, with Jess kneeling between my legs. He pressed up close, his wet, thick, hard cock riding the crack of my ass as he draped himself over me and kissed me from over my shoulder.

"Come on," I said impatiently, wanting to have him. He nipped my earlobe and I shivered. Shifting slightly, he got his dick lined up with me, holding there a moment to gauge my reactions again. But I only sighed and hummed. It felt right. I tipped my ass up for him, bracing myself with my arms and he pushed. The hurt of him breaching me was only a spice to the pleasure. Jess palmed my pelvis to steady me and worked his way deeper. I quaked and panted, quivering around him in pulses, clenching now and then around his thickness burrowing farther into me. It was different than with Ken, or those memories that seemed like dreams, or even that first time with Jess. Because we both knew it wasn't just sex, or a one-time thing. It had meaning and implied a future filled with possibilities.

Jess owned me. He had no intention of leaving or letting go once he was there, inside me. Briant had always told me I belonged to him, but I never really felt like I belonged anywhere until I was joined with Jess that day. The need with which he took me, intended to keep me and take me over and over again, added bittersweet depth to the moment. It wasn't just sex. It was a beginning.

The meaning behind it made me a little bashful. That feeling only deepened when I realized how much attention Jess was paying to how I felt, sounded, and reacted to each little thing.

Pulling me by the hip back onto him and simultaneously thrusting forward, he was soon fully seated. Overwhelmed by how full of him I was, the ache and the joy, the relief and the completeness of how vulnerable I was, I was briefly lost to it all. Thrumming around him while he caressed my sides and along my spine, I tried to grab hold of time and slow it down. This wasn't something to rush or take for granted. I'd waited twenty seven years to feel so complete. Jess kissed along my neck and the shell of my ear. Tingling, I caught my breath and was restless.

There was so much release of fear and worry; it left an anguished sort of calm behind. There was so much to mourn and regret, but at least my path had brought me to such a wonderful man as Jess. Gratitude choked me up a bit.

Listening to the small, helpless noises I was making — small whimpers, sighs, and groans — he gave me time and attempted to hold me still. God, but I was full of him, in every way — heart, mind, and body. I tilted my head to the side to offer my neck, loving the feel of his mouth there, and the sound of his murmured words: "Love you, Tuck. Love you."

I reached back to touch him, unable to speak. He heard my breath catch on tears and just kissed me more.

By the time he started to move, I was ready to urge him on. It started with shallow movements, with me pushing back and pulling forward counter to his thrusts, but I needed more and his passion began to overtake his seemingly endless restraint. Soon his hips were slapping against my cheeks and he was driving his cock into me, hard.

"Oh... god... *damn* it," I moaned. "Don't you dare fuckin' stop."

He straightened and quickened his pace, taking me hard and deep. I hollered loud enough to fill the cabin, my rasping, guttural cries shivering the wood.

He knew how to fuck and his massive cock dragged over my gland every time. I rode him while I could, then just let him pound into me and cried it all out with my voice. Jess came with a growl and unloaded deep inside my body, holding there, flush to my ass, until he was drained. I throbbed and felt like I'd always be able to feel him, like he'd gone so far, he'd become part of me.

He withdrew, and the friction made me moan again.

"Lie down. Rest a bit," he told me. I did, but glanced back, exhausted, with a single raised eyebrow.

He just gave me a crooked little smile, eyes shining with happiness, and lay down beside me. I drew his arm around my body and cuddled in close, letting him spoon up behind me.

"Love you, Jess," I murmured.

The bed was comfortable and my body tired, so sleep pulled at me. I only dozed, though. Jess's right hand rested on the curve of my ass, his thumb moving in a gentle arc, back and forth. He felt so good next to me, I'd never felt so sated and calmed.

Time slipped by. His caresses roamed outward more and more. He combed his fingers through my hair, brushing it back from my face. He traced my spine and the clench of my ass when his touch ventured low. Coming up between my legs to the junction of my thighs, pivoting his wrist, his fingers pressed inward, parting my cheeks. With a shaky exhale, I felt my hips tilt in invitation just as his middle finger was fed into me.

Whimpering softly, shuddering gently, I turned my mouth toward the bed and buried my moan there. It was so good; I was willing to beg to keep him from stopping. Then his lips were trailing over my jaw and I reached behind my head to get a handful of his hair, clawing at it while his finger twisted and probed.

"What do you need?" he asked me when I made a broken sort of sobbing sigh.

"Don't stop. Tell me you want me."

"I want you, Tucker. I'm gonna take you again, now. Gonna take you as often as you'll let me, I want you so much."

He turned me onto my side, pressed up close and entered me again with a determined push that just made me want to spread and yield. Holding my leg up and open with a hand, he moved in an easy, lazy rhythm, and never stopped kissing me.

"God, I need this," I sighed. "Need *you*. You feel like home."

Moaning happily, he fisted my cock and squeezed. "So do you. How's it feel?"

"Too damn good," I groaned.
"Perfect," he smiled, nipping at my ear.

Chapter 33

Face the Music

Some of dawn's light broke through the tree cover, made it past the porch and filtered through the cabin's windows. Standing in the kitchen, wrapped in a blanket, I caressed the warm ceramic of my half-full coffee mug and lingered in the shadows. It was so nice and quiet there. Looking out on everything, I used the stillness to get a better read on myself. Whenever I looked inward, strange things rose to the surface. Waking up after having sex in what felt like the first time in forever, even weirder things were creeping out of the corners of my mind. I knew it had been lovemaking rather than fucking, but I couldn't completely escape the struggle to process it all in a healthy way.

That's why I stood there, in shadows, bundled up. I figured it might help me avoid the guilt that was trying to seek me out. Logic didn't always outsmart instinct.

The bathroom door opened. Jess walked out into the hall. Right away, he started to turn and head back to the bedroom. Then he caught a glimpse of me in the kitchen and stopped short. He looked surprised to see me up and about, his eyebrows rising as he ran a hand over his sleep-mussed brown hair and changed direction.

Shuffling my way with a huge yawn, he was most certainly still half asleep. It made me grin.

"You're out of bed," he commented, sounding only a little disappointed.

"Are you sure?" I teased.

He glanced back over his shoulder, through the opened bedroom door and at the empty bed. Then he murmured, "Yep," and came up behind me, drawing me and my blanket into his arms. They crossed over my chest, holding me tightly to him. "Mmm," he hummed in a happy, lazy way.

"You're out of bed, too." I peeked up at him and tried to contain my smile.

"Not for long. I have some very important unfinished business to attend to there."

Everything he said had a cute, drowsy slur to it. He cuddled me in even farther, tucking his chin over my head and rubbing my arms through the blanket. He even spread his feet wider in order to straddle mine. I'd never been so enveloped, and it made me laugh. "You know, the only way you're gonna get us any closer than this is if you shift this blanket and your pants out of the way and just get inside me already."

"Mmm, that's my important business," he smiled, his voice a low rumble I could feel through his chest against my back. "Love how warm you are." The backs of his fingers caressed over an exposed patch of bare skin beside my left nipple and at the edge of the blanket. His hand dipped underneath to palm over my heart, stroking a little back and forth there.

"Nah, you're all personal." It felt so good to be held like that. There was so much affection in it. It was so new.

"Well, I consider taking care of you to be my primary job now, Mr. Reynolds. How are you doing?" It had been a few hours since we'd made love—our first daring, and successful, attempt at it in the cabin. I felt even more joined with him already, like we'd risen to a higher level where nothing bad could touch us, or so I wanted to believe.

"Just fine. I'm not really sore at all. You did quite a thorough job at preparing me, so that's all to your credit, handsome."

"And how about here?" He caressed more deliberately over my heart, then patiently waited for my response. My eyes prickled a bit, just from loving him so much.

Drawing into his embrace, I said, "Never better, thanks to you. You're so damn good to me, Jess."

Sounding like he wanted to reassure me, he said, "I know we have to do this at your pace, so just let me know what you need, all right? I'm right here with you. I'll take care of you."

It was like he could sense my mood, but I couldn't quite believe he was that skilled at reading me already.

The memories were what had gotten me out of bed and seeking coffee. Remembering all of the awful details I'd shared with Jess about what I'd done with Briant, part of me couldn't totally accept that Jess was fine with it all. There was still so much shame. It was the sharp thorn, tearing a hole in the fantasy I was living.

Bowing my head, closing my eyes, I frowned and shivered despite the heat of the blanket and his embrace. That gentle caressing over my heart felt like a dream I'd wake from soon, not real at all. People like me didn't deserve such devotion. Not when I'd crawled up onto that man's desk so many times and stayed there while he scarred me, without putting up any fight at all.

"What are you thinking?" he murmured when I stayed quiet, letting the sadness pull me down.

It wouldn't come. It stuck in my throat.

He turned me around, held my face in his hands and looked into my eyes even though I tried not to let him. Whatever he saw made him frown, too, his sleepy levity vanishing. My tears came out before the words did, and they weren't quiet or soft, but hard and ugly sobs. They weren't for me. They were for how I wanted so badly to spare Jess my troubles, and knew I couldn't.

"Hey, I've got you," he told me, hugging me to him. I sighed and laid my face against his chest. "I've got you, all right?"

At first, I held my breath rather than let the tears flow.

When I finally exhaled, the words came in a thick rush, along with my hitching gasps. "I keep wanting to apologize to you. I'm so fucked up. Nothing is as easy as it should be, but *you've been so patient.*" The words were filled with anger and frustration, all of it shot right back into me, trying to carve away my happiness.

He smoothed my hair, saying with force and conviction, "Tucker, I will always be patient with you. I will always wait for you and hold your hand as we figure out which path we belong on. Believe that. Please? I know how much pain you're in. *I can see it.* You don't have to be strong with me. You don't have to *prove* anything. I love you, just the way you are. Of course this isn't going to be easy for you. I know you've been hurting, just like I know sex is scary for you. I'm just glad you trust me enough to be honest about it now."

I wrestled out of the hug, out of the damned blanket, and hooked my arms behind his neck. Skin on skin, I grabbed hold of him, burying my face in his neck. He easily lifted me right off the ground and just held on. I wished that I could melt right into him, where I'd always be safe. I let go of trying and he still held me, as broken and pieced-together as I was. But his carefulness and awareness of my jagged edges helped me stop being so afraid of causing him harm.

"Come lay with me a while," he asked in a whisper.

"Thank you," I managed, getting my tears all over him as I gave a shaky sigh.

He set me down, wrapped me back up and I held his hand as he guided me back to bed. We lay there together for what felt like hours. I let him see me, flaws and all, while I just counted my blessings.

There would never be enough 'thank you's for him.

We couldn't stay hidden away in our love-nest in the wild forever, as much as I would have liked to. The more I healed and moved past the complicated emotions stirred up due to Nathan Briant as well as my public coming out, the more I realized the next thing to do was face everyone I'd been hiding from. With Jess at my side, loving me through the rougher moments, I knew I could do it. Sure, there'd be hate and intolerance to face, but if there was a chance to be myself and make music that mattered to everyone who'd ever felt the way I had, it had to be seized.

But how to do it?

The more I changed, the more my circumstances changed with me. I dreaded the machine of society which had tried to chew me up. I couldn't see going to an office in a nice suit to face cameras or standing in a crowd of reporters yelling questions and commentary. There was always the possibility of doing a written statement, but I was a musician. The printed word did nothing for me.

A few months into my seclusion in the woods of Washington with Jess, I decided on a course of action.

He went with me. We walked out into the forest, and stopped

when we reached a stream. After readying a camera, set to record video, on a tripod in front of where I sat on a fallen log, with Jess beside me and the water running behind me, I said my piece.

"Howdy, y'all. I'm Tucker Reynolds. You may have heard rumors about why I was seen with this man next to me." I gave Jess a small, sideways glance and a grin. He smiled back and bowed his head slightly, deferring to me. "Maybe you saw photos with big splashy headlines across them. The truth isn't that extraordinary. Gray North is a valued member of my band, and he's also a dear friend of mine. I've been going through some rough times but Gray holding my hand in public or kissing me outside a hospital is the best of it, not the worst. I hope you can see it that way, too."

Then I reached forward and shut off the camera. Jess helped me post the video to my website. It soon went viral. Some people complained that I wasn't direct enough, that I should've just said I was gay, but I'd always hated labels — in every sense of the word — and I wasn't going to stick any on myself if I could help it.

Some people said I was going to hell. Little did they know I'd been there already and had been lucky enough to find my way out again.

Some cheered and voiced their support. It was the usual mixed bag, and it was much easier to face than I'd thought. It was just a little video, after all. Not even a minute long.

My label dropped me a few days later, citing breach of contract. After all of the questions about when they could expect some new tracks, it was Maribel Lane that ended my run with them. Since it had begun it as well, I thought it a perfect circle, finally, blessedly closed. My lawyer told me they had documents proving I'd booked time at a local recording studio with Jess. I had indeed done that, but the dates had yet to roll around. They claimed there was a previously agreed upon recording schedule that allowed a specific amount of time between albums. I'd attempted, they said, to prematurely record a new album without their go-ahead. They could have sued me for millions, but instead they were dissolving the contract entirely. It was all bullshit, an excuse to dump me for being gay and admitting to it, without me being able to claim publicly that that's why they really dumped me. Their involvement with Nathan Briant was partially to blame, but that had been the case from the start. All any of them wanted was for me to go away quietly, hoping the legal storm would somehow pass them by.

They didn't pursue the lawsuit because they hoped I'd take the hint and leave without any more of a public spectacle.

It was done quietly, without fuss. After I'd gotten the news confirmed over my mobile, I hung up and let it sink in. I could almost feel that whole part of my life detaching and drifting away. It felt good to let it go. Sitting out on the cabin's porch, with Jess playing piano in the house behind me, it was a beautiful moment. The circle had turned. I felt complete.

Wandering back into the cabin a little less tied down than I'd been, a little less *owned*, I lay on the couch by Jess and listened to his song. A small fire heated the room, the popping of the wood underscoring Jess's notes. My booted feet were kicked up over one armrest. My head was propped on the other. Jess found his way through melodies, trying things out. The tune became mournful, and I felt the notes connect to some of the lyrics I'd scrawled in my notebook, way back when.

Softly, tentatively, almost as if I didn't trust my voice, which had carried over arenas filled with thousands of screaming fans, I began to sing.

Eyes closed, I brought up those feelings of thinking I wasn't good enough from way down in the core of my being. They were too tangled to sort. It was good and evil, inseparable, but mostly it was a struggle. A few tears slid over my cheeks, adding heartache to the words. They sounded torn from my chest, a beating, bleeding heart, offered up for judgment. The piano played along, kept going. When my lyrics grew angry, passionate, the music was too. He banged on the keys. The notes tumbled together, building to frenzy. When I drew out the pain, he slowed his tempo and wove a cloak of rich, layered melody to lift my voice up.

Then the hope built underneath. It tumbled through the anger, broke free and ran loose, taking over.

I finished, holding one last note as long as I could, until it faded away. The piano was silent. Jess had come close, and was crouched beside the couch, holding my hand in both of his. His soft lips pressed to my temple, feeling like forgiveness.

"That was beautiful," he whispered.

"Just got word," I told him. "We've been cut loose."

He dried my tears with gentle swipes of his fingers. First he sagged; then he brightened. "That's great news," he managed. A smile transformed his face and he kissed me. "You're rid of them. I'm so happy for you, Tucker."

I studied him for a second, trying to reason out the emotions I'd just seen him fighting. Was I hurting him again? I wasn't sure. "You're not scared?"

"Scared?" he was still smiling. His lips were so hot and silky smooth, I couldn't get enough of them, so I looped an arm behind him to keep him near. His arms wound around me, too. "Of what? We've got the music, the concept, the *talent*...."

He nipped at my chin and I chuckled.

"Times are changing," Jess said. "If we have the music, the fans will come to hear it whether there's a label in the middle or not. And who needs money? If I've got you and this place, I'm happy."

"I'm happy too." My fingers trailed back through his soft, brown hair. "So, you're not disappointed? My star may be falling. I didn't want to take y'all down with me."

"Tough luck, partner," he teased, nipping my jaw again. "I've got you now. I'm not letting go." The scrape of his teeth and drag of his lips were really distracting. It made me groan in a way that seemed to give him ideas.

"Mm, partner. I like the sound of that," I confessed.

"Me too," he growled, gorgeous and all mine. "You're not falling. You're just landing in my arms."

"You fuckin' romantic," I grinned. He just rolled on top of me and kissed my breath away.

When it became obvious that I wasn't going to be returning to Tennessee, Mags came out to visit us and brought Jovie with him. It wasn't a permanent solution, but nothing was in those days. It was all about figuring things out as we went along.

The look on Mags' face said it all for me, when I opened to door to find him standing there, guitar case in hand and strawberry blonde, angelic Jovie squinting out at the sun filtered through the trees. They were both beaming, but Mags seemed as different as I felt. There was a sort of surrender in the way he nodded to Jess and shook his hand.

"You didn't think you could hide from us forever, did ya?" Mags said with a wink.

All I could do was laugh. "Man, I've been hidin' at least as long as forever. It's good to see you." I let him pull me into a hug and clapped him on the back. Something eased in him and he gave my cheek a tender pat as he stepped back to let me greet Jovie.

"Hey darlin'," I said to her, kissing her cheek. "You know what you're gettin' into here, don't ya?"

"Hell yes," she teased. "Heard there's been a dangerous overload of testosterone, or somethin' like that. Ain't that right, Mags?"

"Oh, yes ma'am," he said, tipping his hat. "I always say, things go so much easier when there's a lovely lady to keep us boys in line." .

"That's not exactly what I meant," I cut in. Facing Jovie, holding her gaze, I told her, "We've got a lot of eyes on us right now. Lots of *opinions* going around. If it's known you're in with us—"

"Sweetie, you know what they say about opinions," she replied with supreme politeness, laying her dainty hand on my arm and guiding me back into the house with her. "Everyone's got one. And you can't *buy* this sort of press."

"Did she just make an asshole joke?" Mags asked, his mouth hanging open.

Jess was laughing so hard, he doubled over. I just shook my head.

Jovie, still holding my arm, *tsk*ed, cocked her head to the side and said to Mags with the sweetest sort of condescension, "Oh, bless your heart."

A couple of months passed in a blur of activity and new paths to carve. We all figured it out as we went along. Jovie worked her ass off nailing the melodies and working guitar along with Mags. She balanced him out and kept him on track. Her soulful, feminine voice added yearning and the sweet ache we needed, blending well with my gruff, masculine lead. Jess was mainly on keys but did step in to play violin now and then.

Their joint efforts allowed me to focus on my job, which was translating words on paper into impactful music. Before each studio session, I'd meditate or get Jess involved in my quest to tune in to old emotions. Having him hold me, letting him love me in ways I never dreamed I could be loved gave me perspective on the past. With Jess's help, I could distance myself enough to know the way forward.

I sang about William, Ken, and Jade by name. They were hope crashed right up against regret. My fascination with those facades, and the true human beings they were underneath the superficial, carried onto Maribel Lane. It was my tribute to everyone who felt, for one reason or another, that they had to hide behind masks, false name, or lies to get by. It was also my way of asking everyone I could to stop hiding and own their own truths, whatever they may be. The album was about release of all sorts—sexual, temporary, practical, psychological, and spiritual. It was my dearest wish that we could all start to let go of the fear and break through to a freer place.

I sang about Nathan Briant as well, but in more roundabout ways. Specifics like his name and the particular nature of our interactions stayed out of the songs. The themes he carried into the songs were those of releasing toxic people from your life, and recognizing when you were worth more and deserved better than you sometimes had.

Jess was diligent about keeping on top of the lawyers and getting regular updates on the criminal trial. That was farther than I cared to go. Nathan Briant couldn't hurt me anymore, and that's all that mattered. Every day, I reminded myself that there was no more cause for the dread of more encounters, that endless winding up, waiting for him. I shelved him with the rest of my history, locked him up and threw away the key. Sometimes, he'd whisper through that locked door, but then I'd just go to Jess, and he would understand. He'd seen so much darkness with his father, I knew mine would never overwhelm him. He was so much stronger than that.

Jovie always had a difficult time getting through the song about Leigh because of what she knew about the truth behind it, and possibly because of things she saw in me when we worked on it together. But she might have brought her own history to it too, personalizing the pain. It was easy to imagine. Jovie was a pretty, talented young woman. Perhaps there had been men looking to take advantage of that, claiming it was in her best interest, when it was only in theirs. She would listen to my verse and the chorus, then get choked up by the time her part came around. It took us a few days to lay down that track, but when it was through, it swelled my heart to hear Jovie's torturous empathy come out perfectly in each and every note. Leigh's ironic presence and sweetness in that lion's den built of pain and shame became Jovie's. She owned the role like the pro that she was.

One Wednesday, in a car driven by John, my bodyguard, on a winding road on the coast of Washington, Jess and I headed home after a long day at the recording studio. It was almost time to return to Nashville and pursue a few offers from competing producers. That was good. We were ready.

If I had learned anything since using what humble talent I had to form a successful career, it was that real success could only be found by drawing from within. It didn't come on the backs of others.

I watched Jess Grayville, sitting to my left, holding my hand like it belonged to him, as we wove our way through the woods, climbing up higher and higher, propelled by greater forces. Though I was blatantly staring, and he could tell, he humored me for quite a while before giving me a slight, knowing grin.

Holding his hand tighter, filling what I had to say with all of the power of what I felt, I told him, "I just wanted to say... your patience is my greatest blessing. Thank you for that. You waited for me, stood by me, watched out for me, and loved me through a damn rough time. Lord, I hope someday I can pay you back for it all."

He kissed my cheek and let go of my hand only to bring his arm around me, gathering me closer to his side. The trust, honesty, and mutual commitment we had together were my saving grace. It was the light in the dark.

"I love you," I told him. "So much. You're my hero."

"Well, hell," he smiled prettily. "I was about to say the same thing about you. Quite a man, you are, Tucker Reynolds. I'm so damn proud of you."

Happiness so big my chest ached from it, eyes prickling with tears for it, soul singing with praise of it, I asked, "Where do you think this road leads?" It spun on and on, looping around, shooting straight, passing through patches of murky shadow and glorious sunlight.

He followed my gaze, thought it over, and answered, "Don't much care as long as I'm next to you."

I kissed him then. John, the bodyguard, blushed. I laughed to see it and still the road led on.

Author's Notes

Tucker Reynolds first came into existence in my novel, Whatever the Cost. The book begins with Tucker's point of view as he awaits the arrival of William, a prostitute hired for the evening. Tucker is nervous. William is beautifully, mysteriously irresistible. During his time with William, Tucker fights a small internal battle over how much he wants to do and how far he's willing to go. Once their sexual transaction is complete, the narrative follows William out the door and back to his life, already in progress. Tucker reappears later in the story twice — once for another appointment with William, and again as his music plays on the radio in the background of a scene.

It became clear to me, long before my beloved publisher and editor suggested Tucker get his own story, that there was still a lot left to tell about Tucker. He was the flip-side of the coin when it came to The Company, a powerful, far-reaching organization dealing in prostitution and serving some of the world's wealthiest clientele. William was The Company's pawn, trapped in a ten-year contract as a sex worker, and Tucker was just one of The Company's clients... wasn't he?

The question of whether The Company was behind Nathan Briant's schemes and perversions is not definitively answered in the context of this book. Yet, the idea of the darker side of the "casting couch" phenomenon — trading sex for a career boost — doesn't seem to me to be so very different from prostitution. On one hand, we have the buying and selling of bodies for the sake of pleasure. On the other, we have someone in power pressuring a young, impressionable person to engage in sex while convincing them somewhere along the way that it will be beneficial to their career. Either way it's a transaction in which a person's value is measured in flesh. The psychological consequences of being victimized in this way, of trusting exactly the wrong person at exactly the wrong time, can only be magnified in the case of a young, deeply-closeted gay man like Tucker.

My goal in writing this story was to show how even those who seem to have it all can be secretly fighting a tragically losing battle. Money, influence, glamour, and success have no worth when they're attained through suffering, a loss of innocence, the ability to trust, or even at the cost of a healthy sense of one's self-worth. Tucker's interactions with Nathan Briant affected every single aspect of his life, yet for years he managed to cover it all up and keep the pain to himself. Even the people closest to Tucker couldn't see what he was going through. But there were cries for help; there were signs. Thankfully, Tucker had Jess's concern and kindness to help him bridge the gap between solitary suffering and the path to healing. I hope it can be an example that looking a little closer, opening our hearts a little wider and letting those we care about know we love them might be the small miracle that saves a life.

This was not an easy story to write, or to rewrite. I do not, nor have I ever, lived in the South. I am not a gay, male country singer. This was my first time writing in first person point of view, so it was a massive learning experience as I discovered how to let Tucker tell his story in his own words. Heartfelt thanks need to be expressed to my wonderful editor, Rylan Hunter, for kicking my ass and getting me to do the hard work needed to make Tucker's voice really sing. Thank you also to Dany, for her priceless guidance and encouragement, to Leyanne for her moral support and valuable insight, and to my family for being such a source of joy, love and stability whenever I'm doing a great job at driving myself crazy.

—Lynn Kelling, 2015

About the Author

Website: lynnkelling.com

Lynn Kelling began writing in order to tell stories that weren't afraid of the dark, didn't hold anything back and always strived to be memorable, forging lasting attachments between character and reader. Her inspiration comes from taking a closer look at behaviors and ideas lurking at the fringes of life — basically anything that people may hesitate to speak of in mixed company, but everyone wonders about anyway. Her work is driven by the taboo in order to expose the humanity within it. Lynn is an artist, designer and lover of any form of creative self-expression that comes from a place of honesty and emotion, whether it's body art or opera. She has had multiple novels published, has written over fifty works of erotic fiction of varying lengths, and always has several novels in progress.

Works by Lynn Kelling:

Deliver Us series:
Deliver Us (Book 1)
From Temptation (Book 2)
Forgive Us (Book 3)

Twin Ties series:
My Brother's Lover (Book 1)
Twin Affairs (Book 2)

Other Works:
Whatever the Cost
Bound by Lies
Arctic Absolution
Song of the Lonesome Cowboy

Cursed Blessings (short story)

About the Publisher

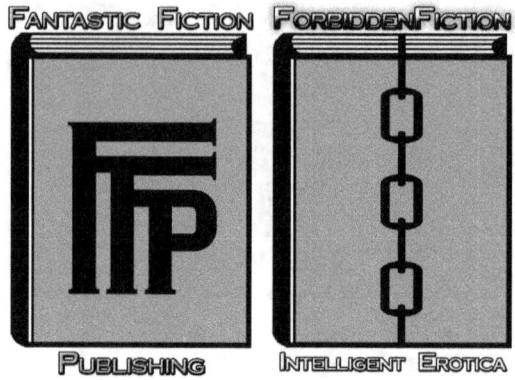

ForbiddenFiction.com is a publisher devoted to writing that breaks the boundaries of original erotic fiction. Our stories combine intense sexuality with quality writing. Stories at ForbiddenFiction.com not only arouse readers through sensations, but also engage them emotionally and mentally through storytelling as well-crafted as the sex is hot.

ForbiddenFiction.com is also designed to be a social reading environment. You'll have fun even if just reading the latest post each day, yet you will have the chance for so much more. Readers and authors can be part of ongoing discussions of specific works and individual authors as well as more general topics.

Sign up for a FREE Membership today at ForbiddenFiction.com

www.ingramcontent.com/pod-product-compliance
Lightning Source LLC
Chambersburg PA
CBHW051534260626
47170CB00003B/934